Tales Of The Wind

By

Stuart Rushworth

_*_

*This
book is
dedicated
To:
Natalie
and
Matilda
And
Annette
And
Paul
My
Mother
And
Father
and
Pippa
and
Milner
and
all
The
writers
I have
known
then last
but most of all to
Dr David Anwwn Jones
who when I knocked
upon the door of words
found himself answering it.*

Mr Woollybreathers
And The Boy
From Grymethrin.

Chapter 1.
A Speech To The Masters.

No crime of any sort had occurred in the village of Grymethrin for over one hundred years, the last being the theft of a horse, apparently by travellers, for which no one was found responsible. No magic was in any way involved and I can say that no magician had lived in Grymethrin until Woollybreathers himself had turned up, though he was commonly regarded as being no such thing. He was known as a strange fellow who lived in a tree, something that was not considered magical at all.

My own particulars in those days were plain enough, my being the boy Mullen Ogginley whom all knew who required manure in the village of Grymethrin, since my father sold and delivered barrels that were filled to their brims with it. It had been supposed quite naturally that I should be collecting and selling manure myself one day and except for a strange turn of fate I would certainly have done so. Instead as things turned out I was flung, as it were, into an entirely different profession. For while the apprentice to the swill-man was busy mixing swill and while the apprentices to the smiths were concerned with fuelling the furnaces, I, by my calling, had nothing more to do than tend my master's books, my master being Woollybreathers himself and the books being concerned with works of magic.

"Shame on you, Mullen Ogginley! My mother had said one Sunday long after the present business. "And to think that I brought you into this world so you might serve no better purpose than to perch with that mad old owl doing absolutely nothing!"

My mother, being as complete and as honest a person as I had ever known, had expected a better course for me than what I had got. Seeking to sway me towards the sweat and the iron she had inquired of the second smith to see if he would take me. The second smith had therefore agreed to attend my 'Speech to the Masters' in the Common Barn where I should, in the time-honoured tradition, present my better qualities to any who might listen. Unfortunately when the day arrived the second smith received a face full of boils, while equally unfortunate was the wheelwright, who found he could not stop yawning. Neither could the fletcher attend on account of his thumb growing to twice its length. The candle-maker set fire to his own beard and while the traps-man trapped his own foot. When I arrived at the barn, which had many benches arranged in it, I found that only an exceptionally tall and hairy gentleman was present at the very back, though he, by my reckoning, was fast asleep.

At the commencement of my address I noticed that the old man did not wake as I expected. Instead he wrapped a large black cloak more fully about himself. He appeared not to listen to anything I was saying and thus I was sure that I would have another full year of uncertainty before I would have a chance to present my qualities again. Without a master I should be a master of manure, as uncountable Ogginleys had declared themselves before.

In the middle of my speech the notched candle that measured the time had melted hardly at all but even so I had lost my way and in my meanderings I was talking thus:

"And it might please you to know, esteemed sirs and madams," I said, "that I am able on many occasions to find things which others have lost. Indeed if a button is misplaced in our house then I can on such occasions soon reacquire it. Next I should mention my whistling at birds, for I have many times had long and pleasant whistling at birds, so much so that I could have continued all day."

At this my mother nudged me in the back for she had noticed the tall gentleman had stood up and revealed himself to be even taller than I had expected. Not only was he stood up nearly to the lowest beams but he was also clapping fiercely and approving of what I had said.

Then as that towering figure removed himself from his place I saw his large pale grey eyes watch me like clouds in autumn and while his giant face seemed as gnarled and as nobbled as a tree. Then as he passed through the spring sunshine that was aslant through doorway he showed his great bulbous door-knocker nose and his overhanging forehead like a lintel and his chin like a doorstop but which had a black beard that had been plaited and tarred to tails just as sailors have them.

4

Woollybreathers was the most imposing figure I had ever seen, though he carried neither a sword nor an axe nor a whip. It was instead his enormous size and strength that caused me alarm and also for his choosing to live in Claddon Forest, which is a much maligned place requiring much courage. Although Grymethrin folk were apart from the wider world we were not hermits ourselves. We were brook and stream and river-people and we gathered ourselves together more often than standing apart. We were brave too, though in the pursuit of domestic aims. That day my mother, being no size at all, showed her resolve before the giant from the moment she was forced to reckon with him.

"Mr Woollybreathers!" my mother said angrily, "what use can you put my son to when you have none yourself?"

Woollybreather's shoulders sank in a most pitiful way at this sudden onslaught.

"Madam," he sighed but with a voice that carried a lumbering depth, "I am merely a solver of puzzles -,"

"- A puzzle you certainly are, Mr Woollybreathers," retorted my mother, "for I have no recollection of you solving anything – indeed when Mr Greenlow lost his dog last year there was no sign of you looking for it!"

Woollybreathers stretched his huge arms out as if in surrender.

"But I am always here," Woollybreathers said meekly, before seeming to write with one finger in the air, "and the word 'investigator' is written clearly on my door for all who wish to read it."

This did not placate my mother who folded her arms in defiance.

"Unholy enchantments, I hear is what you do, Mr Woollybreathers!" she said loudly.

Woollybreathers raised a hand in protest.

"I use magic only if nothing else will do," he said painfully.

"So you admit to your heathen ways!" my mother said loudly, at which Woolybreathers gazed up to the rafters.

"I am not on trial here, dear lady," he said, "I am merely in need of a librarian," and he sighed, "I have mislaid a book."

Then he came to gaze down upon us.

"An apprentice librarian, for all its minor duties, is a respected position," he said softly.

My mother raised her nose.

"I know very well what a librarian is!" she replied sternly.

"Most excellent,"Woollybreathers said before standing straighter and then he began to pace back and forth while adding upon his fingers.

"I shall pay your house two silver shillings per week and one shilling extra if he refuses board and lodging," he said.

Then Woollybreathers closed one eye and rolled the other, as if calculating further.

"Then there is the matter of food, since my associate, Mr Grobbings, eats one quarter of the stew, so there would be a need for more vegetables – save for Sundays when an apprentice should dine with his family of course," he said kindly, "it being the Sabbath."

Then Mr Woollybreathers continued to pace and pronounce.

"The dust and laundry lady, Mrs Minnow, who brings dairy will occasionally eat cheese, should there be any -," then he listed other eats and drinks that I do not readily recall now.

My mother seemed most changed at the mention of silver shillings, since there was no apprentice paid anything more than threepence a week in Grymethrin in those days. Her attitude seemed suddenly altered as she thrust a green apprentice's cap into my hands. The cap that had once been my paternal great grandfather's. He was, I should say, the last Ogginley to have been formally trained for a short time in anything out of the manure.

"My dear Mr Woollybreathers," my mother said whilst pushing me behind her. "He shall certainly be the one, for though he cannot read so well he would know one book from another."

Mr Woollybreathers cast me a doubtful look and Mother responded immediately.

"But he can learn such things as were required," mother said.

Then Woollybreathers, who seemed to have other reservations, came to voice one of them.

"Tell me, good lady," he said, "has your son by chance ever found himself lost?

"He has not known anywhere to get lost in," my mother said.

"Excellent!" said Mr Woollybreathers before readying another question.

"And has he ever attracted unusual beasts?" he asked next.

"Well he has attracted flies," my mother said knowingly, "but every Ogginley has attracted those."

"Very promising indeed," said Woollybreathers with a smile. "And finally does he have a propensity to somnambulate?"

Then seeing my mother's blank expression he twirled his finger about.

"That is, does he walk in his sleep?"

"He does not," said my mother proudly.

Woollybreathers clasped his hands together.

"That should be the most important thing, given that I live in a tree."

Then having me fetched out from behind my mother's apron I was fully presented to Mr Woollybreathers who gave me a stern look.

"Mullen Ogginley you shall come to my house tomorrow morning early bearing a sack of vegetables to add to our stew. Do you know where Claddon Forest thickens after Troll's Fen?

I nodded earnestly.

"I do Sir," I said with some nervousness.

Woolybreathers raised a mighty forefinger.

"There you will see a line of stakes that mark a path that will lead you where the trees tangle overmuch. Follow the path down and you shall find my house, where you shall be required to learn a great deal on your first day," and then he stepped closer. "There is much to do."

At this my mother patted down my jacket and was busying about my hair that was to be cut very short later.

"He shall be there, just as you say, Mr Woollybreathers, brave as brave is, I can guarantee it," Mother said.

Mr Woollybreathers then smiled and bowed and then strode away towards the doorway. The spring sunshine there was shut out by his giant frame and then with a sudden brightening he was through it. Then I heard the man's playful whistling that caused birds both near and far to repeat it merrily, and then he was gone.

Chapter 2.

The House in Claddon Forest.

The next morning at first light found me walking westward along the north bank of the river Methrin. I was carrying a sack containing rotten vegetables that my mother had declared unfit for her own consumption but which she thought were likely a fair meal for others. Nor was the green apprentice's cap on my head for instead another cap made from sacking was there, something that would no doubt amuse the other apprentices on the first Sunday when I would walk home.

After a quarter of a mile I passed the water meadows where many frogs were calling in the cool air. The woods began there also and thickened until all semblance of ordinary life seemed absent in their thick shade and where moss was thick about walls and the fallen branches. Then a mile beyond where my fellow villagers ventured the trees grew taller where an old stone bridge that once served orchards was ivy-clad and entangled. Then a good walk later I reached Troll's Fen, which in ages past was said to have been home to a rather large one. Around the mud and the reeds some stakes had been set along a path that led me to a descending ferny bank and a ravine where the summer leaves above were so dense that it was like night had recovered me. The staked path continued down and along in the increasing dark until there was a tree with a great girth and height that had a spiralling wooden stair curled about it. At the foot of the stair a picket sign was painted finely in black and it read:

Mordrius T. Woollybreathers.
Investigator of Unusual Crimes.

Then knowing no other course I climbed the stair around and around and I found at the top a large construction like a shed. There was there also a sturdy door beside a rope and a bell and so I pulled thrice on it.

As I waited for a reply to my bell-ringing I came to think that my choice of career might not be appropriate for me. The forest was so thick that thieves had at times made their hideouts in it. Then also I remembered the tales of my grandfathers who said that Claddon had been known for darker and unnatural things. I had received no adequate explanation of what these were, but knew that those who spread these rumours were most often allied to the thieves themselves, with the result that they were allowed to hide out for as long as they liked.

Then while I was considering these perils that large door was drawn inwards and a very tall golden-haired young man with crystal blue eyes and a wonderful smile was there to attend me. He wore green boots, green trousers, a green shirt, a green jacket and a green scarf and, for me at least, he was the best dressed person I had ever seen.

Stepping back at his sudden appearance I stood up straight and spoke loudly and clearly.

"My name is -." I tried to say.

The golden man joyfully came forward and plucked the sack of vegetables from my shoulder like it weighed but a pennyweight and then with his other arm he picked me up also and carried me inside and kicked the door shut. He then set off up a further spiralling enclosed stair in a bounding fashion and after kicking open another tall door at the top he deposited me in a wooden chamber. That room, which was of some size, had a thatched roof through which a chimney departed from a small pot stove. In the middle of the floor was a stout desk while leaning forward across it and considering me was Woollybreathers himself. He waved away my companion who went back the way he had come swinging the bag of rotten vegetables as he went. The door slammed shut. Then taking stock of my surroundings I saw the right hand wall there were some double doors that were closed, while to my left side the wall had racks containing many scrolled and unscrolled maps.

When Woollybreathers and I were alone I felt his presence deepen as if he had serious things to present to me.

"Master Ogginley I am seeking a book that Mr Grobbings, whom you have met, has not been able to find for me."

I looked about me then with much distrust of my surroundings until finally I replied to him.

"If you have looked so thoroughly" I said politely, "then perhaps it is no longer here."

Woollybreathers sighed and rose and began to pace about the room just as he had paced the day before.

"Books of a certain kind can hide most expertly," he said.

Then stepping towards those double doors he turned their brass handles and pulled them open. What came into view were the boughs of the great trees dappled with sunlight. Between them were many rope and plank bridges and while above these in hidden places there were lamps that shone. Then above these where the light could trace them I saw the many thousands of books balanced together. They were large and black-bound and not one had words upon its spine as if it was disposed not to communicate anything.

Woolybreathers seemed altogether uninterested in the scene but while I stared out.

Wollybreathers then turned and explained a matter that was most pressing and important to him.

"Long ago there was a sorcerer here," he said softly, "very much more powerful than any that live now. In the wars of ancient times he was defeated and with his final spell his books took flight and were scattered to the skies. But once in every thousand years," then Woollybreathers strolled about, "there is a flocking season, here in this place," he said, "and a great deal can be learned by it."

Then having me follow him to his desk he unfurled a map of boughs and branches whereby the unusual bridges were shown to traverse a great part of the forest.

"It is the reason why I came here," he said, "to await this time and to acquire one single book, The Book of Sneezes, which would bring many advantages in my work."

"The Book of Sneezes?" I said, as if I had misheard.

"Indeed," said Woollybreathers, "a most unusual work, quite beyond what people could write these days."

"I am sure," I said whilst thinking. "How many sorts of sneezes are there?" I asked.

"Oh, an incalculable number," said he, as he rolled the map and handed it to me.

"I shall accompany you tonight after an early supper, this being the last night, for the books shall take flight tomorrow at dawn. Then neither you nor I shall live to see them again."

I was inclined not to believe anything Woollybreathers had said, not least because there were many sensible people in the village who would counsel me against it. Indeed it was these people that had reported seeing Woollybreathers singing into the wind or a wearing a bucket on his head.

"You wish that I find one book amongst all those that are there," I said, as I turned towards the door again.

Woollybreathers raised a hand.

"Quite so, but not before you have rested for the whole of the day and learned to read," he said.

Then ignoring my objections he led me out through those double doors to a balcony overlooking that leafy library and where there was another stair immediately to our left that went down through the foliage.

"This staircase will take you a good way down into the roots, where Mrs Minnow is installed and where Mr Grobbings has a purpose for you."

I went along to set off down but then I paused.

"I am here for the sake of one book?" I asked.

Woollybreathers glanced about without interest.

"You are apprenticed as a librarian, Master Ogginley, which includes attending to books."

He then raised a forefinger.

"But among them are many unruly and dangerous books. We would be wise to avoid those and instead locate the one we seek."

I came to look out across the boughs of books.

"They do not look very dangerous to me," I said.

"It is hard to tell," said Woollybreathers with a tone of warning, "it is hard to tell the good from the bad when they are sleeping."

Then finding this made no sense at all I left him there and set off down the steps that I found went all the way down into the cold earth. Deeper still went the steps into a cold place that had candle-glasses hung on chains beneath black-stone arches and a cobbled floor. I had come to a cellarage where it seemed all the glooms of the world had made their home and where even those bright tall candles had few rights within it.

Then like I had no rights too, I wandered and came to feel that in the barm the previous day I had made the gravest error even by opening my mouth.

Chapter 3.
Mrs Minnow.

I cannot say that I was a believer in magical events when I was installed at home. My mother, whose interest in money exceeded all other matters, plied me with her own ambitions regardless of what I might want for myself. My father, whose knowledge of manure quite surpassed the knowledge that anyone else had on the subject, ensured that none but he was permitted to visit farms and stables with his shovel. Indeed by his calling he maintained that to succeed at anything we must have the fullest knowledge first. To this end I entered that dreary cellarage with a view to learn, for against my first impression I saw that this was also a library of sorts, for in the darkened alcoves and other confines there were many books there. These books were altogether different from the supposedly flighty ones that were described as asleep above me. These were heavier bothersome books with brass clasps and while the shelves were given strange symbols that might not have been words at all.

During my wanderings in that second library I came upon a chamber with a wide bright hearth where a stove had a cooking-pot ticking with heat and while to its right and many shelves of plates and dishes and pans I saw my mother's sack of rotten vegetables set on a strong oak table that had six chairs drawn to it. Some of the vegetables had been spilled onto a chopping board over which some candle-glasses hung and spread their light. There also and busy with halving and quartering and chopping was a lady wearing a thick brown dress, a brown apron and brown woollen shawl. She was short and mouselike with brown tidied hair and sharp brown eyes in a small face that gave her a keen but careful demeanour. Her reaction to my arrival was at first scornful, for she frowned, then having made some judgement regarding me she ignored me altogether.

"Mrs Minnow," I said whilst noticing that many more dark books, like dark sentinels were about us in the alcoves to my left and right.

She watched be sharply.

"Another one," she said with a sharp little voice.

"Another what?" I asked her.

At this she set her small knife aside and brushed down her brown apron with her hands.

"Another apprentice looking for that silly book."

Then she raised a forefinger to caution me.

"Three months that flock of books has been there and twelve apprentices have searched for it including yourself," she said as a complaint. "Twelve fools looking to suit Woollybreathers and his fairy prince."

Then she frowned again.

"Thank heavens those wizened old books will be flown away tomorrow."

Then she placed her hands on her hips.

"So what great magical parents would you have?" she asked mockingly.

I cleared my throat.

"My family provides nutritious supplies for people's plants," I explained.

"A gardener!" she scoffed. "Some use you will be!"

Feeling much aggrieved I stood up straighter.

"I am most uncommonly good at finding things," I said.

Mrs Minnow came to watch me with narrow eyes.

"You are not magical at all."

"Nor is anyone really," I replied.

Mrs Minnow glanced above her in an exasperated way.

"Then how will you account for those books tonight when they are all flying around like bats?"

I ignored her description of the books as being rather silly and then I glanced about.

"I should not expect them to fly," I said, "because they cannot," I said. "But I can find a book as easily as find anything," I said. "My name is Mullen Ogginley and I can find anything you have lost," I said boldly.

Mrs Minnow seemed most impressed with my challenge and wiped her hands on her apron again.

"It is a strange business indeed with those books, even if you do not yet understand them. You should be told well and true that

15

those other young men and women stood where you are now and boasted just as much. But each and every one was bid farewell by old Woollybreathers in the morning."

Then seeing that I was unmoved she sighed.

"Very well," she said. "Then you will know where my mother's recipe for Hurrow Soup went."

At this I closed my eyes, as it was common for me to do in my parents' house, and I turned about thrice - that being ten heartbeats. Then I whispered the missing article to myself with my eyes still closed. Then my arm went out as straight as a rod, so that when I opened my eyes I stepped in the direction I felt I should go. Then following that way exactly I came to an alcove to my right side and grasped a particularly weighty book and drew it from its crooked shelf. Then returning to Mrs Minnow I set that book down upon the table with much ceremony whilst looking her straight in the eye.

"It is saved in there," I said.

Mrs Minnow, being a suspicious type, approached the book cautiously and opened that books heavy cover to find a sheet of old vellum.

"The Right and Favoured Recipe for Hurrow Soup," she read, before picking the sheet from the page and rolling it in her hands.

"Why I remember now, that I put it there some years back."

I took up the book and returned it to its gloomy place.

"Are these your books?" I asked her so as to ease her surprise, for I should say that in this one skill my parents were never surprised by me, having found innumerable things in the past."

Mrs Minnow shook her head.

"No, they are the old fool's, Woollybreathers' own books, brought here from The Mountain School by his own witchery."

"The Mountain School," I said.

"That would be a place just as strange as here," she pointed out.

Then at that moment I heard many echoes chatter about us and soon Mr Grobbings was come to my side and without warning he picked me up. I could do nothing, of course, but allow myself to be taken and while Mrs Minnow had some final thing to say as I was carried off.

"You might even be the one to succeed at this," she said in a wondering way.

Mr Grobbings rushed along out of that chamber and then he turned right. Then dashing through junctions we were a few tunnels further when we arrived at a curtain that he drew across before he set me down. In a small chamber a little bed was there and beside this a hearth where a small log fire was ember lit. Shelves about had more books, for it seemed we should not be able to visit anywhere without them. Then also a modest desk and a chair was fast against the foot of the bed to my right side and above it three candle-glasses were hung by chains to light the place where Mr Grobbings invited me to sit.

Chapter Four.
The Lesson of Mr Grobbings.

Mr Grobbings had, without doubt, a demeanour entirely opposite to my ambitious mother. Whereas my mother saw no scheme better than to acquire money, Mr Grobbings, being from somewhere altogether different, saw my immediate education as his highest duty. He stepped about and picked books from the shelves and opened them as if presenting meals, whilst I in my oblivion could read not a word in them. There were in some cases illustrations of little scenes in which someone appeared to be conversing with another but I could glean nothing from them.

Then when I thought that it would waste Mr Grobbings' time to persevere with this he then removed from his pocket a neatly folded green cloth that was embroidered with green patterns and on unwrapping it he revealed a small green bell with a thick green ribbon that was tied in a loop. Then holding the bell still and after smiling broadly, which was not unusual, he gave the bell a single twist. A beautiful note rang out across the room, but also I should say range through me. My body trembled with the sound, yet after the note had faded in that room inside me I should say that note played on. Then as it rang it continued not as music but as a voice, a voice that I should say remains the gentlest voice I have ever heard.

Before I could remark upon the voice consider Mr Grobbings presented his next book to me and that voice spoke what must have been the words upon the page.

"In the practice of gardening we should be most concerned with soil and light, for these are the two masters under which green things can feed and grow. Even when some plants have dominion over the shades they yet have need of light's blessing, and even when they have roots that hardly bury themselves deep they must rely on the soil for its many treasures, including water that attends it as a loyal servant."

Thereafter, and after a loud scream, I knew the book to be a book of gardening. Indeed as I leapt up and madly perused the shelves I came to know by that voice's direction that the entire collection of titles in my room was concerned with plants.

Therefore there seemed no doubt that Woollybreathers and Mr Grobbings had acted with kindness towards me, so that I would feel a sense of home.

I chased about as I say, opening books and then closing them until finally I smiled at Mr Grobbings very nearly as joyfully as he smiled at me.

"Mr Grobbings," I said, "you have given me so precious a gift," I said with tears running. "It is a miracle I can scarcely believe, for I can learn, Mr Grobbings - more than I ever believed - more than my heart ever hope I could!"

Tears escaped with more force then as I made such a search of books and delighted in any scrap of information no matter how banal. I read with such haste, as if I might lose the gift altogether, but that voice persisted. After much reading of gardening I understood I had been lit up by magic, by the thing I had denied most or was afraid to admit it.

Then Mr Grobbings had me leave my room and follow him beside the crooked shelves of the other places. By this we left behind the subject of gardening and entered upon what I would say was a library of crime.

One book had a title on an inner leaf that read:
"*Theives Of Sleep.*"

Strangely when I saw the language was very different from English I found it made no difference, for that silver voice spoke regardless.

"There will in some cases I have described be thieves that will not rightly steal a dream but instead swap a better sleeper's dreams for their own. These are not thieves as such but instead they are those that would rid themselves of say a repeating dream of singing boots. Theirs is the predicament of being chased by these dreams and they would have magicians remove them. Given the poor state of magic it is not surprising that those dreams are these days merely exchanged for the dreams of those that have happier ones. To restore the sufferer of any discarded dream and give them good health is however very easy, since they must be presented with some real singing boots, for in this way the dream to loses its grip on the impossible."

The odd course of this topic had me scratching my head and I had much the same experience with other volumes that included accounts of people stealing heads of hair from others and other such peculiar offences.

I was finding my sudden transformation into a reader both alarming and exciting. I glanced at Mr Grobbings many times to see if he appeared changed, but I saw him dressed in his brilliant greens whilst smiling as wonderfully as anyone could. Then entering another tunnel in my exploration I saw a candle-glass raised aloft to a great height and I found it was Woollybreathers who was there and who addressed me abruptly.

"Fully prepared for tonight, Ogginley," was his observation, to which I replied like a drunken youth.

"I know such things that would amaze the wisest of the greatest city!" I said with wonder and pride.

Then stretching my arms out wide I said more.

"This change in me would bring kings to my side!" I said.

Woolybreathers made a glance upward.

"You are a librarian who can read; I see nothing unusual in that," he said.

This rather plain thought caused me to face him awkwardly.

"But I could not read a word before before I learned," I whispered, still in my amazement.

"Neither can anybody," he said whilst leading me on.

He took me to a book-shelved tunnel like any other but where there was an iron door at the end.

"These cellars are the remains of the castle of Coldus Pewnes, the sorcerer I spoke of. Ten years ago I came to these parts to make my claim to read his lost library that would land here for a mere three months. I was most careful in my reading, very careful indeed."

Then he sighed.

"But when the library arrived The Book of Sneezes became known to me. It is rare, it is useful. It would allow me to investigate more fully those cases that aim I solve. It is a book that is important to me, though complicated at one and the same time."

Woollybreathers then bowed a little and lowered his voice.

"You are the last of a line of apprentices, hired on the very night, so that everything depends on you."

Outside of the doors some mossy steps ascended to the forest floor above us. We climbed into the beautiful light of that sunlit day that sent beams down to the ferns through the lingering mist. The forest was silent and while high above in the leaf masses I could see those books tight like river mussels in the enormous branches.

Woollybreathers and I listened to the birds singing and we both, I am sure, had some faint need to whistle back. The air of the summer forest delighted me, as did the noble trees, and I felt at last that I had somewhat freed to think directly and clearly.

"If those books can fly," I whispered, "then why should I need a map?"

Woollybreathers stretched and sighed.

"It is a map of the branches and also the paths of the forest where we can safely tread. There are many worse things in Cladden than books."

After this I was bade to return with him to the cellarage where he closed the door. He then gave me a brief tour of places I had earlier seen and then we met Mrs Minnow again, whose stewpot was bubbling and all my mother's sickly vegetables had gone into it.

Woollybreathers waved me to stay while he set off to who knows where.

"You and I shall meet here for supper, Ogginley, a while before dark," he said, though his mind seemed already to be concerned with other things.

"I will have us equipped," he called back. "Then we shall then go up to where I showed you the boughs and the bridges. We shall walk amongst the books and find our quarry amongst them."

I was left there, seated at that table with Mrs Minnow beside the stove watching me occasionally with no enthusiasm while she washed knives and ladles in a bucket.

"I can read," I said with astonishment like I was announcing that I could fly.

"I should hope so," Mrs Minnow said, who also could see nothing unusual in an apprentice librarian doing such a thing.

I set my elbows on the table and slumped and had my chin on my palms.

"It is so hard to accept that any of this is happening," I explained to her.

"That is because you have not cleaned and tidied and shown the old fool the ways through the forest for these past two years."

I raised my head at this.

"Claddon is old, isn't it?" I said.

"Older than castles that tumble down and books that fly away," she said as she set washed ladles aside. "It should be the woodland folks' duty to never go deep within it."

Then she cast me a glance.

"But I was the girl that did, and now I am the woman that knows so much that even magicians would consult with me," she added.

"And Mr Grobbings?" I said, "is he from within the trees?"

"That gentleman teaches Silence at The Mountain School, or so others say, for he does not speak for himself."

I laughed.

"How can anyone teach silence?" I asked her.

Mrs Minnow turned and aimed a ladle at me.

"That is exactly what I asked him but he would not tell me."

I then gave her a puzzled look.

"Where is that place?" I asked, remembering that it had been mentioned before.

"It is where all magical books are finally taken, or so I have heard," she said, "all knowledge of a strange sort must eventually go there."

I turned more fully towards her.

"And does my master really solve crimes?"

"He has been away many times and has come back more tired than ever. Sometimes he is covered in frosts, at other times he has returned with the sea scent about him. There is no telling where he goes, but for each journey there are many books missing from here, from that library of dark doings."

She clanked those ladles away after drying them quickly with a towel.

"I would not follow him no matter what he paid or promised," she said before she laid a heavy stare upon me.

"Just be thankful you are only a librarian."

Chapter 5.

The Midnight Forest.

For the whole of that day I read books, though they were books of magical crimes. The books presented situations that I could scarcely believe, but since I myself had learned to read in one day I could not entirely discredit them. Mrs Minnow passed by, who was dusting the shelves, and at around the middle of the afternoon we shared a pot of tea and I remembered many peculiar accounts from the books. Then towards the end of our rest there was a chance to address again the matter of Woollybreathers.

"Where did Mr Woollybreathers come from?" I asked her with great intensity.

"How should I know?" was her response. "I only hear things," she said, then noticed that I meant to here any information whatsoever.

"Well, there was a seller of pears and apples on the high road above where our chimneys are smoking and from that road there is a clear view over the miles of forest. It was there that Mr Peckles, who is a kindly man that makes wines, came upon him with a view to buying fruit for his concerns. Mr Peckles heard from that fellow that Woollybreathers is from The Mountain School himself, though he has long retired from it."

"I see," I said. "And Mr Grobbings has some connection to there too?" I asked her.

Mrs Minnow gave a look of exasperation.

"There is no knowing about him owing to the fact that he never speaks," she said.

"Though you said when we met, Mrs Minnow, that he is a fairy prince."

"That is only what Mr Woollybreathers said of that gentleman when I was first employed here, that he is from a family that is high up in the hidden world - nears to say that Mr Grobbings has no equal in these parts," Mrs Minnow said.

Our conversation took many turns after that and was interrupted by the needs of the stove upon which the great stewpot was bubbling. I spent the rest of that afternoon reading much the same material as had attracted me for the whole of that morning.

The subject of robbery or even murder by magical advantage was quite enthralling and thrilling, particularly regarding how such acts could be prevented. I read for too long, I would say, and well beyond my understanding.

Then given that I was required to enter the nighttime I returned to my room and lay down and finally slept. When I stirred I heard the clanging of ladles and the movement of chairs from afar and when I went to investigate I found I had slept too long - entirely though dinner, if there even was one. When I went along the tunnels towards the activity I found preparations were underway that my master had spoken of, for it was a suppertime of an early sort.

First of all I was greeted by the scent of the delicious stew, which Woollybreathers (who was much too tall for the table) and Mr Grobbings and Mrs Minnow were already enjoying. I found a domed lid was covering a bowl at my place and when I seated myself and chose a large spoon I found the meal was extraordinarily delicious. Just as I had learned to read it seemed next I should learn to taste. Never before had I enjoyed such a meal, and soon after I had finished then Mrs Minnow came alongside with a serving jug and offered me some more.

Besides the stew, which my mother would surely have been ashamed to taste, there was a light wine that I could not identify but yet I enjoyed nonetheless. The whole occasion suited me very well and when I was sated I gazed at the others who had left their places and were fetching lamps on shoulder-straps from hidden places. I saw Woollybreathers bring down one of his big coats from a high hook and while Mr Grobbings donned a beautiful green outer cloak and a scarf. Even Mrs Minnow found a coat, a little brown one with knitted gloves peeping from the pockets. On seeing these preparations I fetched my map of the forest paths from my chamber.

When I returned I was given thick coat too and a shoulder bag that the scrolled map fitted neatly into. My own lamp was one that had a wrist-strap, perhaps to read the map by, but it also shone very bright when I chanced to raise it.

Being ready I joined the rest and we climbed the stair that eventually reached that balcony and from where our search must begin.

I had arrived in, my apprentice's hat, if that is what it was, and finally the scrolled map that I too care with. I arrived back in the tunnels to find the others marching passed me and so I hurried after.

"We shall all of us go," Wollybreathers said with his calm assurance. "Mrs Minnow is the only one of us that properly knows the forest, and Mr Grobbings is the only one of us that knows the hidden world within it."

"As for myself," he said, "I have some knowledge of the books, while you, Ogginley, must find the one that matters. You have the map. Where ever you go, we shall follow."

This unexpected news made me a lonesome figure on the first bridge. The sunbeams that had patched the forest floor below us had been replaced by an inky darkness and while a night breeze chanced its way.

The high masses of the foliage was revealed to me again by the light of our lamps but when I stared out I saw that the books had been pressed together were now gone. Not a book could be seen anywhere.

As we proceeded the timber and rope bridge swayed but those golden lamps did not, for they floated without chains or strings, as if this was another among so many. All about there the leaves were like garlands of green and high above I saw books too, in ones and twos, fluttering like giant moths.

Where the bridge ended another three began, there being two both to right and to the left and while there was a rope and plank staircase that descended.

At this place Woollybreathers had us stop.

"There is no further we can go together, since we cannot be quiet enough."

Then Woollbreathers indicated that he and I should head left and while Mrs Minnow and Mr Grobbings should go down to the forest floor.

"Whoever needs the others should whistle thrice and they shall reply with the same," he said and then he raised a hand.

"Be aware that there is more than ourselves in this forest tonight."

Then Mr Grobbings and Mrs Minnow left us and set off down that stair and Woollybreathers and I took the leftward bridge where my arm had pointed, this being the method, you will remember, by which I can find anything. It was a strange and mysterious passage under the lamps that gave so strange a light. Then at a place where we both heard the sound of footfalls we stopped.

"That will be Mr Grobbings below us," I whispered.

"That is a two-headed troll named Hordrake," Woollybreathers said softly back. "He is too heavy I think to climb but he will use his slingshot and bring us down if we chance upon that book. He is a slow one, but has four excellent eyes for us."

I looked down and around but I could see nothing but darkness. Then seeing nothing I came to reply to Woollbreathers with great suspicion.

"There are no such things as trolls," I said.

"Unfortunately they would not agree with you," said Woollybreathers who motioned that we go further.

I closed my eyes and waited and then my arm flung out and pointed away to our right, where another bridge began. The bridges then led us over streams where the smell of garlic seemed to plume and thicken in the the air. Then when I was stood listening to the water I heard a voice that was very much lighter than it.

"An old man searching for what he cannot have," said the light and chancing voice.

Wollybreathers shook his head and pushed me forward.

"Do not listen," said he. "There is no good sense will come to you from there."

As I went on I thought I heard that voice sing a little song though from an altogether different place. Then when we took

27

more bridges I saw we were aimed where darkness was fuller where there were few lamps.

"My influence is weak here," said Woollybreathers who hoisted his lamp to shine it forth. "Our book has flown out of the way of the safer ones, and in amongst the wild ones," he said with a cautionary tone.

There was then the sound of that heavy tread far below us, which I took to be the progress of Hordrake.

At this Woollybreathers had me turn and listen and then look behind us.

"They seek it too; Hordrake the troll and the water pixie, whose name is Peppakaleptra. They dwell in the forest, though in a hidden part. The library of Coldus Pewnes has come as a great treasure to them, just as it has for me."

After this unusual speech Woollybreathers ventured forward along the bridge into that darker place and while Hordrake and no doubt Peppakaleptra followed us as surely.

Then while our two lamps were shining about there came a tremendous sound of flapping and a giant black book came to settle lightly on the bridge before us. Two clawed legs appeared from the covers gave it purchase on the wooden slats and while two taloned hands emerged from the masses of pages to either side. A strange stillness came then, as if, most unusually, the book was watching us.

Woollybreathers had me hide behind him.

"This, Master Ogginley, is one of Coldus Pewnes' diaries, a most difficult volume to negotiate with."

"Negotiate with?" I whispered.

"Indeed," said Woollybreathers, whose enormous size would seem enough for him to negotiate with anyone.

"Coldus," said Woollybreathers loudly but wearily to the great black book, "how long have I looked forward to meeting so revered a practitioner of the craft."

"*To whom do I speak?*" asked the book, which to my eyes resembled in a part a giant crow.

"Merely an investigator of local riddles," said my master. "I am Mordrius Woollybreathers of The Mountain School, come to these parts specifically to study your library - for the sake of my own humble purposes, which could never amount to anything that you accomplished in the great ages."

"*The Mountain School?*" snarled the book.

Woollybreathers bowed.

"An academy of some modest repute," said my master, "built north of here in the invisible peaks."

"*That house that fool Maldahabbra built?*" said the book with derision.

"The very same," said Woollybreathers, "though he was worn away many centuries ago. We learn from what little is left, this being our sorry state."

"*And that?*" asked the book, which aimed a single talon at me.

"The son of a manure stockist from a nearby village," said Woollybreathers helpfully.

"*Manure?*" hissed the book.

"The very best that can be purchased," said Woollybreathers, "so I am given to understand."

That book, being such a fierce thing, caused me to look above me and where, if my lamp was not deceiving me, its light revealed a great flock of ferocious books perched above us.

"My friend from the manure," said Woollybreathers, "seeks safe passage, for he has no skill with spells, save for his being able to read underwords."

"Underwords?" I repeated.

Woollybreathers leant over.

"The words spoken by most people, even learned one, but which amount to nothing."

I nodded at both Woollybreathers and the book, feeling somewhat unimpressed with my reading now.

Then after another pause that book prickled with its many sharp points.

"*The manure-boy can continue on his way,*" it said with a cruel tone, "*but you Woollybreathers of The Mountain School may not.*"

At this Woollybreathers gave my apprentices' cap a quick pat.

"Very good indeed, Ogginley," said he. "Like all others before you, you are not a senior and you are able to walk where I cannot."

Then he crouched down and spoke more softly.

"Mr Grobbings and Mrs Minnow are far below us and following through the ferns. When you have located the book you must find your way down and then whistle three times and then our friends will reply and then find you."

"And what if Hordrake finds me?" I asked.

Woollybreathers made a little frown that did not impress me.

"Or Peppakaleptra?" I asked.

He frowned again.

After this I looked behind me at the way we had come and then reluctantly I stepped forward with my map and my lamp. The black diary flew upward and settled upon a bough in the beam of Woollybreathers' lamp as if keeping watch. Then after I had passed beyond both of them I looked above me to see what books were there, but I saw only the countless leaves. Then looking behind me to see what Woollybreathers and that strange book made of me I saw neither comfort nor malice, since Woollybreathers and the diary were gone.

Chapter 6.

A Fall of Words.

It is true to say that when I knew I was alone in that greater dark I found no comfort in magic nor the lack of it. Had I not amounted to very little in Grymethrin, save for whatever manure had in store, I would have taken anything to make progress in life. At the same time I felt unprepared and unskilled in magic also. My sudden ability to read, which I had considered magical if anything could be, was merely a proficiency with 'underwords,' meaning that I might only be suited to read in my village after all, where most could read to one extent or another. Then there was the matter of what I was doing here. I was required to find a book that each of the former apprentices had failed to succeed with. If each time Hordrake or Peppakaleptra had stolen it away then why had they given it back? Then if the book had some power of escape then why was another apprentice seeking it?

I could find no answer, nor did I expect one. I believed, as I followed the many bridges through the leafy heights, that I would find nothing here, especially amongst book that could fly, its being an inconvenience beyond all others.

I reached a place where many bridges met and where my lamp shone about in its meagre way. I listened with an intention to hear the slightest sound but I could hear nothing. Nor could I see anything unusual, for the oaks and beeches that were grown together in that place, presented an immense variety of twigs and branches and boughs so that I would have considered it impossible to find anything in it.

Then while I was stood and leant upon one of the posts of the bridge the full moon shone its silvery beams from above and I saw my surroundings lit by them. Though this I felt suddenly freed from the forest in a most unusual way, for it was as if I was home again and watching from my tiny bedroom window towards the moonshine on the river. I felt raised up like I should go home, and in fact I felt that I would most likely set off there and then! I turned about with all the confidence in the world, but when I turned I saw that in the moon's pattered light upon that bridge's wide anchorage behind me there was a tiny black book laid fully open before me. It was so tiny a thing, like a book that might be concealed in a pocket, and though it had an air of the commonplace about it I yet knew it was a book from the same collection that I had met thus far. The pages had a silvery aura, as if it shared some quality with the moonlight, and while the pattern that was inked finely there was golden and elaborate. Then when I stepped closer I saw the pattern untangle and shimmer and when I was stood over the book I saw the golden lines moving, so that I suddenly could not help myself and I picked the book up.

Almost at once I felt a comfort that I can barely describe and as I stared at the golden patterns tangling and untangling that it became to my poor distracted mind the very picture of my bedroom at home. Then like it should be the thing itself I heard the river flowing just as I remembered it and felt the cold air from the water touch my fingers. Then when I was entranced and smiling a great shower began that caused me to step back.

They were not raindrops that fell but instead golden words that pattered about me and each word was the same before it glimmered and was gone. The word was 'Home.'

Then from the book a strange peppery cloud appeared that seemed to be wrapping about my head and without warning I sneezed, louder than I had ever sneezed before. The sneeze nearly lifted me off my feet and when I was steady again I found the bridge had vanished. My bedroom, which had been a fabrication in ink, was now as real as it have ever been.

I was standing in my bedroom in my parents house, where that same moonlight lit the higher quarter of my bed. Beside the bedhead the tiny thick-paned window was open a small way and the sound of the river was chancing and churning. Then also, as if it could be nothing else, the smell of the manure barrels thickened and reeked like there was a barrel inserted up each of my nostrils. Then after my sneeze I heard the door to my parents' bedroom below me open and close and then there was the sound of my mother's footsteps beating up the stairs to my attic.

"Whoever is there shall find me with a poker and a bucket to lop off your head - you cursed invader!" my mother cried out and who was always good at threats. Since I was prepared with the excuse that I had walked home I was ready for her when that door opened and my mother walked in. Behind her stood my father reeking of manure and staring with great intensity. The two of them, framed in the doorway, caused me to leap and laugh and sing out.

"Mother! Father! It is I, Mullen! I am all up with living in a tree and I have come home to you!"

My joy was short-lived however, for instead of replying they saw nothing and heard nothing, for my presence had not affected them.

I waved my arms excitedly but no avail. Then deciding that I would engage with them differently I went to pick up a scarf that was draped over a spindly chair's back but when I reached my hand simply passed through it. Nor could I attract their attention with my handkerchief that I drew from my sleeve. Nothing I could do made any impression on my parents, who toured the room with great suspicion and twice walked straight through me. Then when they were done they closed the door behind them and the room returned to the bliss of the night as when I had appeared in it. I cringed and stared at the book and then flicked through its pages, though they were all the tangled language as when I had seen it first of all.

"Return me to whence I came," I said loudly. "Return me to Claddon Forest and to the moment when I left!" I said angrily.

Then as I watched a page the pattern of golden ink was changing once again. Then from above me that golden rain fell and the beautiful words were shining and about my room and they read: Return.

Almost at once the room was gone and I was landed back on the bridge and that perfect silence and the moonlight was the same as before.

Then, and as I had been instructed by my master, I searched for a stair that would take me down to where Mr Grobbings and Mrs Minnow would answer me. I found a bridge that was a stairwell of ropes and planks that curved down about a stout elm, and with each turn of my descent I stopped and listened but I could hear no footstep or see any lamplight below me. Then when I was at last returned to the thick fernery of the forest floor I felt my heart calm to the slightest beat and my breath fall without sound upon the dark. Therefore I knew the danger of my place, for this was that hidden world around me.

Chapter 7.

The Two Loyalties.

In that place there were only the faint moonbeams to show the shapes of where I was. Many oaks grew enormously and grandly and while the beeches were more shaded still. My lamplight touched across them and showed nothing of any note, just as if nothing lay in wait for me. Thus I used my own great sense for finding and I closed my eyes and my arm swung out to my right, so that Mrs Minnow should be that way. Then stepping across the crackling of oak litter and beech mast I was soon passing between the huge trunks and avoiding the deep crevices between them.

I cannot say how long I had walked, for I was all in wonder at the benighted trees. The heavy growth of summer had altered to a lightness and while those flowers that bloom for the sake of moths brought scents that encircled me. I was some time moving as silent as I could when I heard that song-like voice again just as I had heard it before.

"Poor child of manure and false hopes come to the magician to find his better self," said the voice.

"I cannot listen to you," I said as I pressed on. "It is not my place to take heed of what you say."

"Whyever not," said the voice, "when I bring aid and relief to you, carrying so strange a thing."

I looked behind but my lamp showed nothing but the glade.

"You are Peppakaleptra, come to steal the book," I said before I turned and continued. Then walking more briskly I came to find the moonlight brighten and then out of it stepped a girl of such an unusual sort that I stepped back and drew my arms up against her.

The girl was tall and slender and her skin was of a pale blue shade. Her eyes were blue also, but as they caught the light they flickered like the night river water. Also she wore silver swathes as someone who might mimic the scales of a fish, and while her fingers were long with rings of river pearls on them. Her hair was many spikes of white, as when the river falls, and besides these she carried a lamp that shone brighter and more silvery than my own.

35

On approaching me she aimed one slender forefinger and then her chancing voice weaved through the air again.

"You are the last of many that found the book," she said, "but they did not succeed with it."

Then she looked up to watch the branches shimmer from the light she was carrying.

"It returns here every thousand years, as do the others."

I had by this time retreated but some broad roots encombered me and caused me nearly to stumble.

"Indeed," I said hurriedly, "I have been told the books return to where they were written," I said, whilst hoping to see some gap in the trees by which to make my escape from there.

Peppakaleptra smiled, a smile that had me listen to her every word.

"I should know that because I was there, five thousand years ago," she said, "when the castle was tall and the magician learned such things as a man should never know. It was my right to watch him from the river Methrin, which is both the beginning and end of me. But then he wrote," and her eyes came to gaze upon my pocket, "*that* book, but he used my song, he stole it for his magical words. He made strange use of me."

On hearing this I looked away but she caused me to look at her again.

"The words in that book fall like water, the blessed rain that I am made of."

At this I hung my head.

"I am sorry to hear this," I said. "I am sorry to hear that you were so wronged."

"By Pewnes," she sighed.

I looked about me.

"My Master, Mr Woollybreathers seeks it?" I asked her.

She seemed altogether very sad then, for a greyness like winter showers filled her countenance.

"He would visit bad men to find their crimes out. He would sneak upon their dark places and bring justice down upon them."

I frowned at this.

"But that would be good," I said.

36

Her face became as delicate as due then as she stared at nothing in particular.

"So Pewnes said, all those years ago. To find his enemies before they found him. To use the rain and the lakes and the rivers to carry him abroad," she said.

Then her eyes that changed to something like ice met mine again.

"But it drove him mad," she whispered before she looked above us. "And all those darker books he wrote - outnumber the good," and she pointed at my pocket again, "because of that one."

It appeared that I had inadvertently learned something so peculiar that I knew it not be false. Whatever Peppakaleptra was she was not a liar, and I had come to understand her as I had long understood the river Methrin itself. My heart was made clear, for I should give the book to Peppakaleptra, so as to protect my master from the misery of it.

I reached into my pocket to fetch out the book but just at that instant the undergrowth about me was split apart by something that shot through it at great speed. Flinging myself back I tripped over the roots and I lay flat, but just as what appeared to be a large rock shot by and broke the low hanging branch of that tree above me. Peppakaleptra vanished, the moonlight seeming to open once again. Then rolling over onto my side I peered at the forest and saw a great lamp was being carried through it. A figure swept apart the trees boughs like they were bushes and I saw that lamplight catch the side of one giant face and then another. Then above the noise of the heavy footsteps and the creaking of the trees there came a voice that thundered about me.

"Come to me! Come to me, little man!" boomed the giant.

Then what must have been the other head called out nervously.

"If you don't mind, if it isn't too much trouble," said the second.

"It does not matter if he minds or not," screamed the first head.

"Well it does to me," said the second.

37

By this time I had covered my lamp with my cloak and I was lying amongst the ferns and hidden in the dark. When a gigantic stone shoe beat down upon the earth beside me and I did all I could not to cry out and instead I scrambled over the roots and then around that oak tree until I was hidden behind it.

From my place I heard the monster lumbering until some distance from me and in a clearing where the moonlight shone down and that lamp was bright I had a clear view of it.

The ogre was as tall as the great barn in my village yet its gait was stooped, for a breastplate was made of stone also and weighed heavy on it. Its legs strode beneath a cow hide skirt and were thick and bare and were scarred from the untold number of briars the creature had stepped through. More scarred than were the creature's great thick hands and arms that had the marks of the trees' lashes upon them. Then stooped as I say was the ogre while one head studied all below with bright red eyes within a terrifying face that had the anger of thousands of years upon it. Seeing its awful power

I was about to make my escape when I was staid by the sight of a second face that was quite beautiful. That second head looked upon the forest in so sensitive a way that I felt sad that the beautiful head should have the company of the other. However I believe my hesitation was my undoing that I had waited so long, and before I could react that giant lamp shone directly at me.

Without hesitation that monster bounded and its footfalls were shaking the ground. Then unveiling my lamp I ran but I could find no clear way through the undergrowth. Then that great hand came down to bar my way in one direction and then another. Then that hand like a clawed cage came down to trap me and that darker voice breathed its dread words.

"Got you! I have you full and final - my little man!"

I whimpered as that enormous hand dug deep into the earth and grasped the rootage and ferns and me also and then carried me aloft.

It was my pitiful fate then to find myself a prisoner of the beast while it made for some place across the forest at great speed.

Its huge stone shoes pounded and the tree branches scratched about that imprisoning hand buy did nothing that could release me.

Chapter 8.
The Domain of Hordrake.

When the ogre had carried me some distance it slowed and then I heard a slab of stone being drawn across. Then swaying widely my captor descended into what might be a pit, for I saw between the thick fingers a circle of bright lamps of the same kind that the monster carried that lit root and rock. Above me I heard the slab slid back to its place and after this I heard the creature sit down heavily, perhaps upon a boulder. Then like I was no more than a mouse would be to you or I, I was dropped into a wooden cage that was willow branches woven together. At one place there was a gap, not large enough for me to wriggle through but large enough for me to look out, and by this I saw the monster's two heads and the two pairs of eyes considering me.

That beautiful face then watched me with increasing sadness before speaking.

"It was my idea to have you brought here," said the beautiful youth.

At this the angry face sniffed loudly and closed its red eyes in a frown, just as if it reluctantly served the other.

The youth continued.

"You see I, or rather we," and the youth looked sadder still, "are a double-ogre; one that has two natures: one that is fine and one that is rough."

The youth then smiled.

"For three months now, for as long as this magical library has been here, I have been reading the good books and while he has been reading the bad ones."

I nodded and leant against the willow bars, for it seemed, as with Peppakaleptra, I should be hearing an unusual account of things.

The youth sighed.

"For my own sake I would like your book, the one you found, the one you possess, to travel to a place to be on my own, since the book can carry my spirit alone, to where ever I wish."

I nodded, since from my own experience of the book I understood this.

"I would go to The Mountain School," said the youth, "and wander its halls and listen to the magical music and read any books that were left open. I would be able at last to walk in the daylight, which ogres ordinarily cannot do. I would walk in the sunshine, among the summer flowers. I would never been seen for what I am. I would stay in the free air forever and never wish myself back. I would remain as a joy that few knew was there. I would learn and better myself the rest of my long life," the youth said.

Then just when I was about to answer that other head spoke loudly.

"Where is ye from?" the angry head asked.

"Oh," I replied, "not far."

"Not far," repeated the angry head. "And why did ye come here?" it asked next.

I paused, because it was the question I had also asked myself.

"My parents live amongst manure," I said.

"Sounds wonderful," the angry head said, which seemed genuinely cheered at the thought of it.

"Except there is of course the smell," I explained.

"Hmm…," said the angry head with relish until it nearly smiled.

I looked hopelessly about.

"You see I wanted something better for myself," I said.

"Than manure?" the angry head said as if I had made the wrong choice.

Then with such reassuring thoughts as manure and the smell of it the angry head closed its eyes to sleep and in time youth remained and the two of us were talking.

"I do feel," I said from my willow cage, "that I would certainly give you the book. It would be away from Woollybreathers, my master, for Peppakaleptra says it would be harmful for him."

The beautiful youth nodded.

"The hidden world is not always safe for men, whose lives cannot put right error, given they are so very short."

After this I saw the youth make that giant body stand up and the stooping figure came close to where my cage was. He opened the cage and then very gently he lifted me out. Then that great slab above was pushed across so that the moonlight was shown on the boughs of the trees above. Up the ogre went carrying me and I was set down among the ferns again.

I reached into my pocket and I drew out the book and then I held it out. The enormous finger and thumb took that tiny book so lightly and like the book had found its purpose its pages flapped so that it lifted into the air. Then down it came to land like some extraordinary butterfly on the ogre's palm.

As I watched then I saw the many golden words came raining down and the word that was so briefly written was the word 'free.'

That beautiful face calmed and then it sneezed with such a power that I was blown over by it. The noise of the sneeze resounded about the forest. Then after the sneeze I saw the youth was asleep, as soundly as if all the dreams of hope had come to him. Then in his stead that other head woke and seeing that I was free he sighed long and hard.

"Manure!" he snorted.

"I shall endeavour to bring you some," I said.

Then, as is my gift, I closed my eyes and my arm was flung out, this time to my right, and so I set off and waving back as I went. The loud thumps of the ogre's stone shoes were soon sounding lesser and lesser until it was only I that I heard. Meanwhile the forest had changed, bringing back its greater character now that the hidden world was gone.

I found Woollybreathers' treehouse after much walking and also the night had changed. The dawn was close, though no sunlight was visible. When I came finally wearily to that room high above Woollybreathers' desk I saw that door had remained was open to the treetops just as we had left it. Then nearing that doorway, and where the first light of the day was searching I saw he was there.

Woollybreathers' enormous frame was still, just as if he had not heard me, though I knew he had.

"I am afraid to tell," I began, "that I have some unfortunate news," I said, "that my efforts were not enough."

"Indeed," said Woollybreathers with a saddened voice.

At this we both looked out, and where the first gleams of the sun was causing those magical lamps and bridges to vanish. Then like that great flock of black books came whirring in their urgent flight and made the branches of the trees sway and the leaves flutter. Then a thousand years of waiting began again, for the books were gone.

Very slowly Woollybreathers led me indoors and he closed those doors so that the view of the forest was removed.

My master's tread was slow and his great face seemed lost in thought.

"We cannot have all we would like, Ogginley," said Woollybreathers, who to my mind had accepted his loss after some torment.

He pointed to a second chair facing the desk that I had not noticed was there. Then afterwards a slice of cake and a spoon was on a plate before me that I had also missed. He offered me a cup of apple juice in a tall glass, which I could not remember him pouring and in time we ate cake and drank each other's health.

When I felt that our hearts were easier between us I had some things to say regarding the night had had just passed.

"The Book of Sneezes has gone with the good side of Hordrake so he can get some peace," I told him. "And also Peppakaleptra told me the book would only tempt you, just as it did Coldus Pewnes."

Woollybreathers' great head nodded.

"It has ended as I thought it would," he said.

Then Woollybreathers leant back in his great oaken chair.

"Desire is a treacherous thing, Master Ogginley, since most crime is inspired by it?" he said. "I taught this most emphatically to my students for many years, implored them to avoid the thing that would serve them least."

I sat back.

"But how did I even find the book at all?" I asked him.

"It found you," he said, "because it knew you would do good. Those before would have brought it to me, given me the same life that Pewnes had. His was a bitter heritage."

Then after a pause I spoke again.

"Then what is The Mountain School?" I asked.

Woollybreathers nearly smiled, a most strange outpouring for him.

"A most unusually high place with great fires that should be seen to be believed" he said, "and it is there, Master Ogginley of Grymethrin, where you must go."

"Me?" I said with some surprise.

"Indeed," said Woollybreathers with very little interest, "to learn things a little better."

I laughed in a mocking way.

"I could not possibly travel one hundred miles to the north. My mother gave me strict instructions to return on each sabbath."

"Yes, yes," said Woollybreathers, "there is that. It is a long way. But worry now, Mr Grobbings will throw you."

I was objecting to this ludicrous idea when Woollybreathers interrupted me.

"And his brother will throw you back," he said.

Chapter 9.
Afterword.

I cannot go into more things than I have told you, at least not yet. I have at least begun my tale and given you the shape of it. My journey to The Mountain School must be another story.

I can tell you however that I returned on The Sabbath after my first week and delivered to my mother two silver shillings, which she was very pleased with. She did not approve of Woollybreathers, in fact she never would, but approved of my earnings and in return she sent me the following Monday with a sack of vegetables that were more rotten than the last ones.

Mrs Minnow was found to teach at The Mountain School herself, her being extraordinarily good at drawing maps and finding her way around. However in her modesty she was not willing to boast of this. Even for her family in that settlement beside the forest there was no knowledge of her other life, though that is of course how the hidden world is.

Mr Grobbings cannot be delineated further, for I would never hear him speak or learn any more about him. He remains the happiest person I have ever met, and by far the strongest.

Finally I can say that my master, Mr Woollybreathers, continued his secret investigations and did not confide in me. However, against what I expected he would require me to help with many of them. Those situations required me to be his librarian, which I was, and his fool on occasion, because I remain rather lost as to what to do with him.

Then generally I can say that I am better in my career as a librarian than I otherwise would have been. Books have become the main concern in my life and I shall write, as well as read, a few more of them before I am finished.

The Uncommon Sleeper.

Chapter 1.

The Memory of Farva Mop.

Farva Mop awoke and took deep breaths of light instead of air, as all starry people do, but when she opened her eyes she found the stars were grey and sour tasting.

Next she saw the boat on which she lay was a starry boat and was a crooked one with planks that were shaken apart, and that it had battered old lanterns that shone grey and while a cabin-roof was set lopsided at the stern where a crooked chimney was sprouting from it.

Farva Mop got to her feet and tried to remember. The fact is that Farva Mop found she could remember only her name and her forgetfulness appalled her, though she could remember a few things.

She could remember that altogether there were The Ten Thousand Heavens and that starry boats could travel up and down between them. She remembered that the highest stars were the colours of flowers and that everything was beautiful there. She remembered that the deeper your boat went then the more miserable and colourless the stars became. Then houses as they fell, heaven by heaven down, were not ever as cheerful as the heaven where they had started off in. She remembered that the masts of boats must eventually become blunt, so that boats too must become wrecks and sink into the deep.

Then finding herself to be more confusing and enigmatic than anything else she came to gaze out at where her boat was moored.

Above and beyond her rose an enormous white marble building that had been carved from a single block. Four statues of giants were shown leant out from it as if hauling on ropes and while above them was the edge of an overhanging roof shaped like a row of stars. The giant statues seemed to stare down at her with great sad eyes, whilst lighting them in places were hundreds of dimly lit windows that seemed cold and secret.

Then she came to see how much grey dust there was pluming about her and that the comfortable place where she had slept was a great heap of dust. Her clothes were thick with dust and her skin that was pale lilac in colour had dust caked upon it and while her hair that was dark purple was matted with dust. Dust was heaped about the buckets and deck-brooms and while a mirror at the base of the mast that should show her standing proud and ordering the boat to here and there was encrusted with dust. When she wiped the surface there her face was shown so grey that it looked sad, and while her dark purple eyes had a loneliness nearly as deep as the giants had.

Then suddenly, and from somewhere near, there was a voice.

"Gji dl lagzee vul?" a boy was repeating.

Then another voice came.

"Sy tzikarr!" a younger girl cried out.

Then seeing she was not alone Farva Mop peered to her left and to a boat was mooring alongside hers.

The boat was pure white with silver lamps and a wonderful mast that rose high and was white also. At the prow the two children stood and the boy had black hair and brown eyes that at once seemed rather odd, being a little too close together. The girl meanwhile was quite pretty in her way with her blonde hair, but had a rather sullen face.

Then both of the children children stopped and turned when an important-looking man dressed in a white cloak and white shirt and white trousers and white slippers came striding along the deck towards them.

"Maradsha! Koliana! Ht? Ht kcee crarr?" he asked in a wide language, which is one that is much more complicated than we would know, by which I mean many things can be said at one and the same time.

The gentleman was shorter than perhaps he liked to be and while his eyes were rather beady like the boy's were. His brown beard made him seem very stern but altogether he appeared comical, much like the boy did.

"Tlaflb?" he asked in his wide language. "Leflinulfi-nompi-wellezi?" he asked after while scratching at his head.

Then next the children's mother arrived in a white dress and cloak that was laced with silver. She was tall and graceful and her eyes were a bright turquoise that seemed to glint like jewels. On arriving she touched her husband aside.

"Ta-lafabel?" she asked Farva Mop.

Then: "No-a-too-r-shar?"

Then: "*Who are you?*"

At this Farva Mop stood up straight, which brought grey dust puffing out.

"I'm Farva Mop," said Farva Mop.

Then pulling a very odd face Farva Mop coughed out a curl of grey shadow that spun between them.

At this the lady frowned and leant forward upon the silver rail of her boat. Then seeming very much concerned she climbed nimbly from one boat to the other.

"Are you unwell?" she asked.

Farva Mop looked glumly about.

"I do not remember if I am well or not," said Farva Mop matter of factly and with a heaving sigh.

The lady then peered about at the boat's sweep of dust and its dim grey lanterns.

"Have your parents also been bathing in dust and shadow-poisoning themselves?" she asked.

Farva Mop made a concentrated face before shaking her head, which caused her to cough again whereby another curl of shadow presented itself between them.

"I cannot remember having any parents," Farva Mop explained, "I cannot remember anything."

The lady again studied the dust about them and then many other things.

"Well you are certainly someone," the lady said with a sideward glance, "to own a boat is no small a thing." she said, "if this - is your boat."

49

Farva Mop could find no answer to this.

"I don't know that either," said Farva Mop with greater disappointment.

Then the lady looked back to where her baffled family were watching her before taking Farva Mop in hand.

"My name is Carua Unessia and this is my husband, Ogwal, who knows no narrow words, and there is my son, Maradsha who speaks widely also and my daughter is Koliana who is the same."

Then she narrowed her eyes.

"I will search your boat for maps," she said, "and if I do not find maps then I might find books. If I do not find books," then she shrugged her shoulders, "then we might not know where to send you."

At this the lady removed a fine silver pencil lamp from a pocket.

"You wait here," she said.

Carua turned with her lamp and set off beside the cabin roof, after which there was the sound of her opening a door and taking a flight of creaky steps down.

After a time Farva Mop was required to smile at Mr Unessia and the children Maradsha and Koliana and to stroll about until Carua returned. She decided she was very pleased to be aided by the family but at the same time she was not sure that anyone could properly help her. She hoped there would be something below decks to explain her, for starry boats might collect lots of things. However when the lady returned she explained that she had found nothing.

"This is certainly your boat," Carua said, whilst patting a lot of dust that had collected on her too. "Everything has been built exactly for you. Also there is no one here but you," she said, "for the dust has only my footprints in it? Yet also this means also that you have long been sleeping in it and not once walking about," and at this she seemed even more confused.

"Also there is a dinner table that is set for one," she said, "and the bath-barrel in the hold is just your size."

Then the lady came to shine her lamp upon the dust itself and she stooped and took a pinch of it.

"And it is an ancient dust you have, of a most uncommon kind. Indeed it is hard to believe that even in a thousand lives you could have collected even a few grains of it."

Then the lady gave out a sigh of her own.

"It is as if you had been asleep for ever and ever."

Farva Mop came to stare at Carua.

"No," said Farva Mop, "I cannot have been asleep for ever and ever," she said in nearly a whisper, "I would be very old myself," she pointed out.

Carua and she and made for a odd pair standing on the ancient deck until the lady came to appreciate that nothing might explain this girl and her appearance and that for now and perhaps forever there might be no answer to it.

"Well," Carua finally said, "there is no point you floating anywhere since there is no other house or world for a thousand stars, for this place is rather a lonely one," she said.

Then they both came to look upon the house where the windows flickered with candlelight and no sign of the occupants showed anywhere.

"It is called The House of Naws," Carua said, "and in spite of what you might think it is not really as scary as it seems," she said, "though not altogether friendly either."

Then from the gloomy skies about them there appeared more boats, glittering and floating and coming to moor at the quay just like theirs had.

At this Carua led Farva Mop back towards the cabin roof and had Farva Mop sit down on a bench there.

"You must wait until someone sees to you, Farva Mop," she instructed. "You are a stranger, which is most unusual for this house, and a decision must be made about whether you can stay here."

Then above them they saw the bright white flashes of more boats arriving, their tall shining masts dimming and while their white lamps turned rather grey so as to be in keeping with the gloominess. Meanwhile Farva Mop saw many tall bronze mooring-posts light up, for they had crown-lamps perched on their tops, and these shone down as many guests prepared themselves and disembarked.

Soon there were many figures passing wearing fine clothes and hats and while hurrying to their boats were porter-boys hauling trolleys that became loaded with cases and bags. The scene was soon hectic as a great parade of finely clothed guests to hurried along.

Carua and her husband and Maradsha and Koliana were disembarking now and were greeted by more porter-boys who searched their deck for bags and boxes. The porter boys drew their wheeled carts along and while perfumed fans fluttered about as if to sweeten the light of this dull heaven.

Then when the Unessias themselves were passing Farva Mop saw Carua look back.

"There is someone who will come along in time and who is required to consider you," she said; "be patient Farva Mop and he will come. Be just as honest with him as you have been with me and I am sure things will settle for the best."

Farva Mop watched them go, Carua and Ogwal and their children strolling with ease and grace as the porter-boys followed them pulling trolleys of luggage. The Unessias joined the throng and not long after the procession of grandeur and importance was dwindling as the last of the guests passed by, with the children watching her briefly as if she was monstrous thing.

Then after the crowd was gone she left her place and went to the prow and she leant out to see where all of them had gone to.

The last of those families were turning left at the corner of the building, where beyond it a wide white marble square extended for a great distance. After the square's limits there were those miserable stars again, for as with all starry buildings the house was floating.

To her left and towards the other end of the quay were finally some tall black railings before a forested garden of a sort, where black and leafless trees had further lamps to illuminate them. Then from all places then a great loneliness seemed to come down to her, just as if there be no hope whatsoever for her.

She felt the chill now and feeling that she should leave and not cause any more fuss she turned and addressed the mast and spoke into the mirror in a steady and serious manner so as to be perfectly understood.

"I wish to go home now," she said loudly, but saw the mast did not light up.

"Take me home - and right now!" she said more strictly.

She was some time engaged with the mast and finally pleading with it in the most awful way, and finally she began to guess at places but not one of them caused the charm to work, just as if it was her doom to remain here.

Then away to her left, when she came to hear it, there was the sound of someone knocking hard upon the mooring-posts one by one. And peering out where the crown-lamps seemed darkening one by one she could see a severe-looking man dressed in brown and carrying a long pole of some sort. Then after some time more and when he was closer she found that he was glaring at her.

Chapter 2.
The Scrutiny of Mr Flast.

The man in brown had raggled greying brown hair and a thick brown messy beard and was dressed in heavy brown cloaks with straps bound across them. A long pole gave out a green light at its tip that made a dazzling shine when he aimed it.

Sooner than she liked the man was close upon her and his deep frown and hooked nose made him the very picture of unpleasantness.

"Snardi-gravdi-fen-di-zark!" the man snarled

Then seeing her retreat to her bench he spoke more loudly still.

"Foolish child - dim your lamps!" he shouted.

At this Farva Mop hurried about and covered each lamp with her hands so that the crystal dimmed. Then at the end of her chasing around there seemed only that crown-lamp above them that could properly cast a light. Then the man's disapproval seemed to increase when he shone his green light upon her crooked boat.

"What a shadow you have brought us, as full a crock of dark as was ever sent out, Be gone - be gone!" he said whilst waving his hand and wincing. "Going is better than staying for a busy life!"

Then when he understood that she was not in fact leaving his face made all manner of angry expressions.

"I am Nazum Flast," he said in a low manner. "Those that come to disturb this house must get by me, and by this I give them every chance to be gone - for I have powers to expel them should I wish to use them."

Then he made that pole glow brighter as if it might turn to fire.

Yet in spite of his threats and gesticulations Farva Mop remained seated on her bench and Mr Flast was forced to deal more roughly with her.

"You shall go forthwith, ragged villain," he said angrily, "and I shall see thee not ever again, "or your horrible little boat," he added.

Farva Mop felt a sudden pang of despair.

"But I have only just arrived," she said pitifully.

Mr Flast shook his head.

"Tramps and unthankful drifters," he said with menace. "Lone-lamps and trouble-feeders," he growled. "Meddlers and home-stealers," he said with a face that now carried a considerable warning.

Farva Mop sighed.

"But Mr Flast, I am nothing at all like that," said Farva Mop while giving him one of her own stern looks, "and if I could remember who I was I would certainly be leaving, just as I told Carua Unessia, who would have reason to tell you if she was here," Farva Mop explained firmly, "for I have no memory of my boat or where it has been, or anywhere I should be going for that matter."

At the mention of Carua's name Mr Flast seemed to have been forced to pause. He watched her with some new consideration that slowly spread across his face.

"You are a strange one," said Mr Flast said before glancing at her aslant "Likes as not you have some purposes whether you make them plain or not."

Then that pole was withdrawn and it was swung against the mooring-post before him and that crown-lamp went dim and nearly out. Then Mr Flast, with his mean face returning, showed more of his difficult tendencies.

"Well do what you must. Go to the door or else leave here!" he said fiercely.

Then Mr Flast turned and he wandered along and while a curtain of darkening seemed to follow, for the crown-lamps dimmed one by oneand while the faces of the giants high above her were shown only in window-light.

A time later when no crown-lamps at all were lit the deck grew rapidly colder and bitter tasting, there being only the starlight to attend her. Then being fully persuaded now she decided to 'go to the door' as Mr Flast had directed.

She left her boat and after descending her little mooring-ramp she walked to her right along the white marble quay in the direction that all others had recently taken, but with a great weight of uncertainty now bearing down upon her.

What a place she had come to with her forgetful heart was her only thought! And what a mournful sky was set above, which seemed spiteful too, as if no welcome of any sort might be found here.

The House of Naws.

After walking along the quay and passing moored boats of great quality and reach, she came to that place at the end of the building where she must turn left.

Before the building's enormous front facade some grand white marble steps rose and where two large globe-lamps were hung on chains above them. Some ramps rose also to open black-wood hatches where luggage in great quantities might be hoisted up.

Then strolling some distance from the foot of the steps was a small group of ladies dressed in in silver and white robes who had their white hoods drawn up against the dreariness of the sky. Between them danced an infant, layered in white silks, who threw sparkling grains upon the paves. The globe lamps that shone to the front square could light no more than a quarter of it, whilst in the middle distance, and like a silence of a further sort, stood a wide marble bandstand that seemed marooned there. Then beyond there, where the square extended to its limit, was Mr Flask who could be seen dimming the crown lamps one by one.

The ladies laughed at the child's antics but while Farva Mop felt resigned to turn and to climb the steps. Listening sometimes to their jumbling language, when she chanced to hear it, it was a slow and despondent climb she had.

At the top of the steps was a pair of tall strong black-wood doors with black-iron bolts riven through them. The door to the left was open a good way and while the other had a black-wood sign with bright white thick-ink words marked on it. After many wide-languages some words were written narrowly and they read:

The House of Naws (diminished).
The Five Hundred And Second Heaven
Above The Cold.
Being The Home Of
Miss Aricel, Ranidia, Ellense Naws

Descendant
Of
Seri-len
She Who Was
Sculptor To The Ancient King Aro Kem Semique
In Another Place

It was an odd thing to read, for it made her think of books that might be too serious to read, while the doors themselves had a very determined character, as if she would be wise to simply turn away from them. However just then the ladies behind and below her were returning form their strolling as if the miserable starlight had exhausted them. Then things being being so for Farva Mop also she pressed hard upon the heavy black-wood door, which allowed for a larger gap. Then leaning into her stride she very carefully she stepped inside.

First of all there was a crooked black-wood floor that made wincing creaks when she stepped upon it, and though she tried her best there was apparently nowhere to step that did not creak and so she remained where she was. She was stood in a finely carved black-wood panelled hall where four jagged-leaved bronze chandeliers had been winched above. In these the grey flames of many lop-sided grey candles were wavering whilst caught in their light and directly ahead was a wide black-wood staircase that went darkly up. Through open doors to her left and to her right were long cloakrooms where the trolleys were now hung on chains and while black-iron cages with luggage pressed hard into them could be raised to floors above.

Ahead of her to the left of the stairs there was a retreat of some sort with a black-wood counter set before it. The counter had a black-iron candlestick to the left side in which more candles were burning grey. Then in some secluded place behind there was a tall winged cabinet in which hundreds of keys were hanging.

Before these all stood a tall, darkly-dressed and cheerless man. He was stooped and had propped a cheek upon one elbow as he wrote some tiny detail with a black-iron needle-pen in a huge black book.

Continuing her approach the floor whined and creaked while also the lower black-wood panels in the walls to either side were open and they had brooms and trap-pans that seemed eager to spring out. The many candles in the chandeliers above seemed to aim their that heady grey light while the unyielding scent of polish came from all places as if the light was thick with it.

Further and further she crept but while the tall man, against what she might expect, appeared not to notice her. His smooth greased blackened hair was like a ball of black wax set never to move, while his mouth tightened now and then at the most careful marks in ink that he was painstakingly making. There was a deep reserve in the man's face and no movement either in his eyes, which were darkest grey but with a pale expanse of the page reflected in them.

All of the man's attention was directed at the book and while the needle-pen scratched or else dipped for ink in a black-iron pot that was a hand's width away. On the bridge of the man's nose rested a fine apparatus of petal-lenses to aid him and as Farva Mop drew near she saw those lenses change until his solemn eyes were magnified as still as lamps.

Then the man took a long and steady breath.

"Ran-tradce-sqar?" he said softly.

Farva Mop expected the man to look at her but he did not.

Farva Mop waited but the man but he continued marking the page as he liked and it was some time before he spoke again.

"Parents...*late*?" he asked.

Farva Mop watched the needle-pen scratch.

"I am not with any parents. I have my own boat," Farva Mop said, then saw the needle-pen had stopped.

The man's dark grey eyes moved and the petal-lenses swung away.

"Children are not permitted... rooommms," he said slowly.

Then there was a pause and Farva Mop waited.

The huffing and the puffing of the brushes and trap-pans seemed louder but these made no impression on this man who had returned to his writing.

Farva Mop looked away and saw that a darkened room away to the left of the counter was a room for music, though many of the instruments were covered with grey sheets, which only added to the silence there.

"Why not?" Farva Mop asked when she saw the man was not likely to notice her again.

"Why...not?" asked the man seemingly of himself.

Then when she least expected the man took a deep breath and gave her a most thorough reply.

"Because, as I can happily inform you, we are not a school, we are not a playhouse, we are not a house of fun, we are a guest house and we have not invited................you. "

He then returned determinedly to his work.

She watched him write while the alcoves were now quite heaving with noise but she ignored them.

"How do you know that?" she asked.

The man stopped writing and his grey eyes moved to study her but then flicked to watch the ladies who were returning from their stroll.

In an instant the man seemed utterly transformed. He smiled agreeably and nodded happily while the ladies waved and greeted him in their mysterious languages. Then when all seemed happily settled the man fixed his gaze upon Farva Mop, and the smile vanished.

"Because we only invite historians," and his eye-brows were raised in mock surprise, "unless you are an historian."

Farva Mop watched him uncaringly now.

"I might be," she said absently.

At this the man stood straighter and raised his nose in a rather superior way.

"Then you will be able to identify," he said, "the oldest object in this room," and then he waited.

Farva Mop felt very put out by this, since she could not possibly know.

She felt ready to return to her boat, since she felt the defeat of the man's challenge overtaking her.

Farva Mop turned.

"Well I cannot know exactly," she said, "but I would say it is those doors," she said, but was saddened to see the man was delighted.

"Wrong," he said tunefully and with great pride.

He then leant forward to whisper.

"It is in fact The Book of Guests itself" and he tapped his pen lightly on the thick pale grey page of that enormous book that had large black-iron clasps about it.

The man's thin hands gripped the counter's outer edge.

"It is older than the greater part of the house itself."

However suddenly, and like it might explode at him, the book shook and slammed! Its violence put out the candles and caused the man to leap back. The terrible noise of the book echoed in other places too.

Then the echoing was replaced by gentle laughter.

The first of those ladies was stepping eagerly across the creaking floor towards them.

"Not quite the oldest thing, Mr Grinsnick," she said softly before patting some of the dust from the sleeve of Farva Mop's grey dress.

Then she examined the fabric even more closely.

Then minding that she was not overheard by the other ladies across the hall she came close and whispered to Farva Mop.

"Sweet heavens child, where did you get this?"

The lady's fingers then counted stitches in a particular place while her face became very wooden and strict. Then both of them saw the sleeve sparkle with so bright and pure a light as if anyone about might see it.

This caused Farva Mop and the lady to stare at each other.

The lady was of a middle-some age though a great pride shone brilliantly through it. Her silvering hair was tied tightly up, where it had once flowed down, and where a silver spiralled hair clip was the final trace of it.

Then as if they were in peril she led Farva Mop along so that the end of the counter partly hid them.

"There is such a spell upon this," she whispered before looking towards the ladies who were making their way to the stairs.

Then she stood before Farva Mop as if to cover her.

Then next Farva Mop was drawn past the counter and into the corner beside the music room door was beside them.

The man behind the desk who was somewhat recovered now encouraged the candles that had gone out to restore their flames.

"If we might rest the light, Mr. Grinsnick," the lady said before turning back to Farva Mop.

"Come with me, my dear," she said sweetly.

In the panelled wall that was quite narrow there was a hole for a key and then drawing a large bunch of bronze keys from her pocket a lock was sprung and a door was opened and then Farva Mop was led quickly through it. At the last Farva Mop glanced back and saw the little brushes and the pans had escaped and were sweeping away the dust that her clothes had scattered and then swiftly that panel door was shut firmly against all else.

"Come!" the lady said Farva Mop was made to follow her at a pace.

Farva Mop was drawn along where many grey lanterns were lit on hooks above them. Then fetching a lantern down from a hook the lady set off again and as the floorboards creaked at their every step.

Then at another place the lady unhooked a better lamp and gave its place to the other and then when she was ready she glanced strictly down at Farva Mop. Yet oddly for Farva Mop it was just as if, for a moment, the eyes of Carua were there, for the lady's eyes were a beautiful turquoise.

Chapter 3.

Miss Naws.

"Such a busy day!" exclaimed the lady who drew Farva Mop along the passage within the walls. On they hurried until Farva Mop found the lady had again stepped squarely in front of her as if to hide her. Then from ahead of them and hurrying too came a young housemaid dressed in a black with a white apron and a black lace hood.

"Mrs Lasanti!" the maid called out, who was a little out of breath. Then she lowered her hood to show her earnest face.

Mrs Lasanti, as Farva Mop now knew her, replied to the girl in a friendly way.

"Inkle, my dear, whatever is the matter now?"

"The morning-maids asked me-" and Inkle took a deep breath, "- asked me to tell you that Mr Boam's bath has exploded."

Mrs Lasanti waved a hand.

"Then go to the kitchens and tell Mr Flast to take up an old laundry-barrel," Mrs Lasanti calmly instructed.

"A laundry-barrel!" replied Inkle, who appeared shocked at this.

"Yes," Mrs Lasanti insisted, "tell Mr Boam it is a special treat and it is how we used to bathe in the old days."

The maid stared at Mrs Lasanti for a moment and then she turned and ran.

Then after Inkle had gone Mrs Lasanti took Farva Mop's hand and they set off more briskly so that Farva Mop was skipping to catch up with her.

Next they walked out through another panel door and into a wider but rather dimly lit corridor and at the corridor's end they came to a narrow black-wood door with a dull brass plaque that read:

Miss A.R.E. Naws.

At this door Mrs Lasanti paused and then knocked thrice and quickly and then opened the door a short way and looked in. Then after a glance back Farva Mop was invited forward.

Then quite unexpectedly Farva Mop saw that Mrs Lasanti had not herself entered and that the door was abruptly closed behind her.

Turning there, Farva Mop then found she was alone.

The black-wood panelled room room was empty except for some black-wood items that seemed lost in it. A hanging brass lamp amongst others that were battered had remained lit but they were chained rather low in a room that was a simple one. Two black-silk draped black-wood armchairs were set right and left of a short-legged black-wood biscuit-table that was set longways towards her. There were tall black-wood windows too, though tightly shuttered, just as a doorway to the right side had a thick black curtain drawn partly across it.

Farva Mop crept along and after watching the curtained door for a moment she came to the chair that was before it and there she sat down and waited.

Then as she came to look she noticed that all the while the chair opposite was occupied.

A figure of extraordinary age was seated in a swathed manner as if the chair was not simply a fashioned thing but that instead the old lady had grown out of it.

A pair of strong dark eyes peered out to watch Farva Mop, just as now and then the old lady took quick double-breaths - one and then immediately another.

Then as Farva Mop watched, and as if the chair itself was opening up, the lady pointed a thin and trembling finger at her.

"Knock the dust from yourself; I should like to *see* you," she said.

Farva Mop stood up and raised her arms to show the lady that she wore no better thing than her ragged grey dress. Then she patted at the silk which caused more dust to come puffing out. The dust that was rising made her cough while the old lady maintained her firm gaze before beckoning Farva Mop to retake her seat, then she in her turn rested carefully back as if she was thinking.

The lady was wearing a lacy black shawl that wrapped her completely except for some tresses of her hair, that was silvery white and were drawn away by unseen fastenings. Around and around her too turned a silence thick as sleep and the cautionary scents of ointments and medical powders. The lady was so extraordinarily old that her face had returned to a child's face - as sometimes happens. Her bottom lip protruded and while her eyes were quite hidden by her downward gaze, as if she was dozing.

"Sometimes," the lady said suddenly, "guests come who are not historians," and the lady breathed twice in her forced way, "though often," she continued, "there is nothing to be said of them."

Then the lady pinched two fingers upon her bottom lip.

"Then sometimes -" but all at once the lady seemed distracted by something above her and her voice became louder.

"What shall we expect of things!" the lady shouted, "shall they work or not!"

Farva Mop said nothing in her alarm, as if the old lady had somehow forgotten her.

Then from above them both both, where the crisscrossed black-wood beams were deeply shadowed, there descended a dented silver kettle and a teapot on fine chains and also a tray carrying cups, saucers and spoons and other things. The kettle boiled and poured while making many sniffs and sneezes. Then after many particulars were done the kettle withdrew to its place above them.

"Thank you," the old lady said.

Then there was a final sound from the hidden kettle, rather like a sigh.

The lady offered Farva Mop a faint smile that was soon gone.

"I am Alicia Naws," and she breathed hard and twice, "and this is my house," she said.

Then next, seeing the lady waiting, Farva Mop elected also to introduce herself.

"My name is Farva Mop, and as far as I know I only have a boat," she said.

The lady took a sip of tea.

Farva Mop took a sip of tea also.

Some moments passed.

"This house is very old," the lady began again before setting her tea-cup down, "and has been falling for a very long time."

Miss Naws stared and then her eyes seemed to harden.

"This is why" Miss Naws said, and she took her breaths, "we prefer historians."

Then Miss Naws leant forward.

"Historians make so little noise," Miss Naws said, "historians cause so little trouble and amongst these stars," she said, "and for half a heaven down," she said, "and with historians, nothing at all has happened."

Then she gave such a stare that Farva Mop felt nearly imprisoned by it.

Farva Mop smiled at Miss Naws.

Miss Naws smiled at Farva Mop and then that smile vanished.

"This house," and her voice was like a growl, "hangs by a single thread and we have tried to repair things - that were so finely made," and then she breathed, "but we do not know how."

Miss Naws then rested and seemed composed and still.

"But now there is you, in your ancient clothes," Miss Naws said, "for Vansa Lasanti knows also when something is wrong."

Farva Mop blinked at Miss Naws.

Miss Naws raised her hand to silence any reply, and then she sipped her tea and afterwards set her teacup down and then stirred it with a crooked spoon.

For a time Miss Naws was unmoving as if turning some matter over in her mind.

Then when Farva Mop least expected Miss Naws spoke again.

"Ancient things must fall," she said, "into The Cold," and she pointed the spoon down with a violent action while her eyes darkened. "Nothing survives my dear. Nothing comes back. Don't you see?"

Miss Naws then breathed a slow breath that came to words eventually.

"It would shatter the histories, if ancient things came rising up and floating back," she whispered, "when history is nicely settled as it is."

Miss Naws then rested back into her chair with a weary elegance.

"Let us not think of haunted dresses," she whispered, before breathing twice again. "We already have so much to be concerned with."

Miss Naws then seemed unsure of herself until instant by instant it seemed to Farva Mop that the lady was drawn to think of something else and was withdrawn fully into her chair.

Then in time Farva Mop surveyed the room again, though there were no cabinets or shelves or other things to consider. And long after the onset of silence she heard Mrs Lasanti renter, though Miss Naws did not acknowledge her.

Mrs Lasanti had brought a cumbersome black-hooded cloak-coat with long sleeves and many belts and buttons and she motioned to Farva Mop to leave the chair and stand correctly and straight. Then once she was stood facing her then Mrs Lasanti proceeded to wrap the great coat around her.

"All I can do is to cover you up" Mrs Lasanti said. "We cannot have you so precious and walking about. There is no place where the light from your dress might not betray you. Even under in this coat there is still a risk - your clothes carry such a spell!"

Farva Mop glanced about.

"Perhaps I could leave my clothes here," she said.

"No," Mrs Lasanti said quickly, "you must keep them with you, and any other impossible things you might have. You should take them back to where you found them, that is what I would do."

Farva Mop found the great coat weighed down upon her and while Mrs Lasanti had Farva Mop raise her chin as the coat was belted and buttoned up to her.

"So what shall we call you?" Mrs Lasanti asked.

"I am Farva Mop," answered Farva Mop.

"And where did you come from, Farva Mop?" Mrs Lasanti asked next.

"I do not remember anything like that," said Farva Mop truthfully.

"Then how did you come by such old clothes?" Mrs Lasanti asked next.

"I do not remember that either," Farva Mop said, "but I should think that mine is a wild wreck," Farva Mop said rather knowledgeably, "a wild wreck that must have snatched me up."

Then Farva Mop described how dusty and shaken her boat was and she described the clothes that were all her size.

Then Mrs Lasanti stopped heaving the coat about and gave Farva Mop a serious look.

"A wild wreck that moors at a quay, when they never do?" Mrs Lasanti commented. "A wild wreck carrying clothes that fit you perfectly in every way. A wild wreck with clothes that are older than all of the stars - that is another impossible thing is it not?"

Farva Mop sighed, for she could find no reply to what had been said.

Then Mrs Lasanti began on the final buttoning.

"Do you remember nothing at all?"

Farva Mop shook her head until Mrs Lasanti shook hers.

"Then maybe thishouse is where you will finally remember." Mrs Lasanti said softly, who was straightening the collar and the large black hood.

"But if you should remember," she whispered, "you must tell no-one and nobody and go quietly in your boat and take these ancient things to where they rightly sleep. They are sleeping things you have found, Farva Mop. They are sleeping things and they are full of dreams, and these dreams," and she came close to Farva Mop, "are too much for us."

Chapter 4.

When all seemed ready then Mrs Lasanti led Farva Mop through the curtained doorway. Above them were many lanterns on little hooks that lit the way, which was was both narrow and a straight one. They were walking in the walls again, only now there were stairs and soon Farva Mop was following up and down them.

Then at a place Mrs Lasanti stopped, as if she was listening to the house.

"There are some empty rooms and a secret way to get to them," Mrs Lasanti whispered, "but we must walk very quietly in the walls of the house."

Then Mrs Lasanti set off again.

Their journey became a long one until at a place where three panel-ways met there shone a brilliant beam of light through a keyhole that made a spot of light on the opposing panelled wall. So pure was the scent that came from there that Farva Mop put her hand through the beam and while Mrs Lasanti watched her do it.

"Why yes, of course, we should visit Seri-Len," said Mrs Lasanti, but which caused Farva Mop to wonder at the name.

"Seri-Len built the house," Farva Mop said, "thousands of heavens ago."

"Yes," Mrs Lasanti said calmly. "Seri-Len is long passed away from us."

Then before Farva Mop could puzzle more over this Mrs Lasanti unlocked that door and led Farva Mop into a white marble room that was silent and brilliantly lit. The floor and the walls of the room were smooth white marble, while above them were dazzling white crystal lamps arranged like the branches of a great tree. There was a tall arched arched window too that was unshuttered and that gave a view to the rear of the house where that forest had long ago withered.

Beneath the chandelier was a block of white marble, and it was to this that Mrs Lasanti stepped and where Farva Mop followed.

"It was carved when she was very young," Mrs Lasanti whispered, "when she was at her mirror."

On the far side of the marble there was a young girl leant out, although the eyes were sightless and the ears unhearing. Yet the statue to Farva Mop's mind copied exactly how a living girl might be, for the hair was fastened lightly with strings of bells, whilst hung about her neck was a midnight-lamp and a holder for crescent-shaped magical chisels.

Farva Mop took the statue's glance so keenly that she looked away and towards the window, where her own reflection was as motionless as the girl's, so that both were shown together there.

Then Mrs Lasanti exited the room with Farva Mop staring back and the door was closed and that pure white light was reduced again.

After there the corridor turned right and then right again and went along for such a way that it seemed it might never end. No junctions met them and no other doors were visible and it was as if they should walk at a depth back to the very front of the house. Then they reached a space that was nearly too small for the two of them, where black-wood timbers and white marble met. Beside them a wide white marble pillar had a black-iron lift shaft fitted into it. The shaft smelled of soap, just as up through the shaft from somewhere below there came the sounds of laundry-pans boiling and emptying.

Mrs Lasanti reached into the shaft and grabbed a black-iron chain and gave it twelve tugs and as Farva Mop watched there came down from above a giant black-iron bucket with a gate in the front of it.

Then Mrs Lasanti ushered Farva Mop forward towards the bucket as if she was meant to climb into it.

"This is your only way," Mrs Lasanti said who then pointed upwards. "Your room is on the seventh floor," she said, "and your room number is three hundred and twenty two."

Then she brought out her ring of keys.

"You must raise your hood and hide yourself as best you can, which is really not unusual here," she said.

Farva Mop raised the hood of her great coat and it came fully over her head so that she had to fold it back.

Meanwhile Mrs Lasanti found the keys she was looking for.

"Do you see these eight lamp-keys here?" Mrs Lasanti said and she pointed to some keys that were heavier than the others and had lamps for heads.

"These are the master-keys for each of the eight floors and they will open locks on that floor no matter how they are made."

She removed one key and handed it to Farva Mop.

"This is the master key for the seventh floor and mind you go to room number three hundred and twenty two – that is three hundred and twenty two - and to no other."

Then she made Farva Mop grasp the key hard so that it made an increasing grey light.

"A lamp-key and will not forsake you in any darkness," she said.

Then Mrs Lasanti smiled.

"You will find that the wardrobe in your bedroom will soon contain a change of clothes and a message from me. Only when you are entirely changed can Mr Grinsnick receive you and mark you in his book as he does all others. Then he can give you your proper key. Do you understand this?"

Farva Mop nodded.

Then Mrs Lasanti held the bucket as Farva Mop climbed into it, after which Mrs Lasanti and Farva Mop came to stare at each other.

"I will explain to the other guests that you are in the care of my daughter," Mrs Lasanti said, "whose name is Carua Unessia. She will look after you."

Then Mrs Lasanti gave instructions for getting the bucket to move from floor to floor.

"Pull on the rope to tell it the height to go; seven pulls to the seventh – remember that. If you should have trouble then give the rope twelve pulls and that will be the sign for the bucket to come to you like it is the very beginning."

Then Farva Mop looked above her and saw only darkness.

"Seven pulls for the seventh floor," Mrs Lasanti reminded her.

Then Farva Mop gave the rope a sharp pull and the bucket suddenly started upwards.

Almost at once there came Mrs Lasanti's voice calling after her

"And that takes you to the first floor," Mrs Lasanti called up, "and your rooms have windows – aren't you lucky!"

Then for Farva Mop the noise of the bucket in the key-light's shine became thunderous and all sound of Mrs Lasanti was gone.

The bucket ascended slowly and the clamour from the laundry became distant. It was dim and enclosing in the marble shaft and then at the first floor the bucket stopped.

She found herself level with a keyhole that shone a dull light, and so leaning forward she put her eye to it. Through the keyhole she could see a wide black-wood panelled corridor and a crooked black-wood floor and a ceiling with black-wood beams. At intervals on either side she saw grand double-doorways each with a bronze lamp to illuminate it - though few of the lamps were lit. No one walked there, against what she expected, while the many lamps that still shone sent a dull grey light.

Next she tugged on the chain twice and in time she reached the third floor where an identical grey-lit black-wood corridor was presented to her. Then after this she tugged on the chain more times and up she went.

It was strange to be in a bucket, she thought; it was strange to be here at all. Then while she pondered this she knew that the tugs on the rope had added together and the bucket had risen to the eighth floor where the bucket could take her no higher.

There was no keyhole there or a panel door or hatch or anything. Instead the open panel had many black-iron bars sent across it. From the dimness there came the scent of burned out lamps and flows of dust and there was a place halfway along where a dim shine at the head of some stairs gave sound and sight, though not a sound came, just as if the eighth floor disused or else entirely abandoned.

Then thinking that she should not linger here she tugged on the bucket's chain twelve times as Mrs Lasanti had advised and then after a pause she pulled on that chain seven times and the bucket descended. Down she went until a keyhole came close again and she peered through it. Then seeing that all was still she put the lamp-key into the lock and the lock released. Then pushing hard on that panel it opened and she opened the gate in the bucket and she climbed out.

The seventh floor corridor was cold and she walked stiffly in that heavy coat that slid along the floor behind her. Those floorboards had their music to play, though no one peered out from doorways to notice it.

Then after a rather long, and as she thought, boring walk she came to a black-wood staircase going down that had ponderous bell-lamps illuminating the rails. There was also the stair rising that she had seen from the floor above though more black-iron bars had formed a cage so that no one could ascend there. Some grey-lamps shone upward too, to places that were grey with dust and where no guest, welcome or otherwise, might follow it.

After the stairs and to the left side was a set of double doors numbered *322*.

The bronze lamp that hung above gave barely enough light to see by and instead she used her key-lamp to locate the lock. Then before she could turn it a commotion began away to her left and from the way she had come. A wide sliding panel had opened and revealed a cage-lift and from it Mr Flast's green light shone. Also there was Inkle and the two of them were rolling a large laundry barrel along. Down the corridor that barrel came, so that Farva Mop hurriedly unlocked the leftward door of her rooms and after pushing the door open she stepped eagerly inside.

The rooms began with a great shadowy study lit by a black-iron chandelier with only one candle in it. Besides the chandelier a small hearth was unlit, having but a few long-coals. The single candle's flame showed the study had two tall and arched black-wood windows that in turn gave a view of that dreary sky. The windows had long black curtains that could be hauled together by black-iron chains and while the window-frames themselves had an assortment of inner panes with long levers to open them.

To the right wall of the study a black-wood writing-desk with uncomfortable looking benches commanded the room. Across from these were empty shelves with no other use than to surround a doorway to a huge bedroom that had a single-candled chandelier again and an eight-poster bed with dour black curtains drawn about it. There was a black-wood wardrobe too, thus completing a room that was entirely black.

Then back across the study she went to an opposing door that led to dressing-rooms to either side of a passage. After these were smaller poorly lit rooms with single black-wood beds. Then finally there were two bathrooms, one with a window and another without, and where every last last thing was grey in both of them.

Returning to the study she came to the right hand arched window and climbed into its deep sill. There was a half-window there, where people can throw out ash and cinders, and it was large enough by far for Farva Mop to put her head out and to stare out and down.

The heaven showed its great propensity for gloominess but while beneath the house a spiralling mist had silent lightning leaping silently across it. For just as Miss Naws had said the house had come to its time to fall. For better or worse, as was the course of things, the house was fall to a heaven that was even bleaker.

Farva Mop shivered and drew back and she climbed down from the sill and gazed plainly at the window where her reflection stared mournfully back.

All was still and silent about the rooms that were many times too large. She struggled again with her thoughts but no memories came and while the house to its every corner seemed filled with memories. She felt herself lost in such vaults of time and while the candle above watches her with no more concern than the stars did. Then more than anything else she wanted to leave here.

Chapter 5.

How strange it was to be nowhere, Farva Mop thought. How strange it was to have no clear memory of things, which was twice as much nowhere a person might think.

She had been searching that huge tinkling black-wood wardrobe and at the back was another laundry-shaft, like the one she had so recently travelled in. In the bucket she found a bundle of clothes with a large label attached to it that read:

For your needs.

For all other matters

tell Inkle, she will

find me.

Soon she was dressed in baggy black balloon-trousers, black slippers, black spiral knee-socks and a black long-sleeved apron-coat that had deep front-pockets. Every garment was black and it was perhaps Mrs Lasanti's intention that she should join with the black carpentry of the building, should be something of a shadow if she walked here or there, and with the hood drawn over her face should be a trouble to nobody.

The gloomy bedroom was cased with black-wood and had thick black beams above while those unsettled black floorboards creaked below her. The eight poster bed was set with its footboard towards the door while to the bed's left side as she looked a round table had a wheel of different sized candles for three powers of dim grey light. A black-wood window had black curtains, much as she expected, while under the bed she found wheeled chamber-pots filled with vanishing-powders. Finally and around the bed's curtain tops hung unstopped bottles of a thick scent that made the bedroom seem even older.

In the larger of the two bathrooms she found a cupboard filled with bath-powders, face-buckets, mirrors, bath-lamps, combs, soaps and giant hair-brushes. Then when all matters seemed known to her she allowed herself a glittering bath. Afterwards when she was ready and dressed up in black and with the black silk hood drawn full over her head, she unlocked the door, dropped the lamp-key into her deepest pocket and ventured out into the seventh floor corridor where there was no one.

She came to the stairs where the upward half was caged and forbidding, then descended beside them to the sixth floor where she expected someone would join her but no one did. With some relief at being unobserved she set off down the creaking stairs, skipping and hopping and at each landing she found there was no other guest, no porter-boys, indeed not anyone at all. When she finally reached the bottom of the stairs she found a stair-hall that had a giant door to either end. The door to her left had a black-wood sign hung above it with many wide languages written in white ink until there at the bottom the sign finally read:

The

Sunning

Room

Then finding that door locked she walked the other way where she was met with a sign that read:

The

Shading

Rooms

From beyond these doors came the muffled sound of people and hearing the sound suddenly increase she took hold of the black-iron handle, pushed the door open and was overtaken by sound.

Here, at last, was a part of the house that was busy!

The door had opened into a white pillared hall that was as wide as the house itself. Bolted halfway up many hundreds of white marble pillars were tread-ways for journeys between sidelong balconies, while descending from these were spiralling black-iron staircases. The staircases' supports made frameworks for black-iron casement rooms in which many grey lamps were shining. Besides the chamber's great size there was also, like an impossible wall of its own, a dense and swelling crowd of arguing guests whose voices shrieked louder and louder. Then like a powerful wave of shoving and crushing that crowd suddenly forced Farva Mop back against the door through which she had come. Fearing she might be trapped Farva Mop lowered her hood and wriggled between the arms and elbows, yet however she forced her way the crowd recovered its every advantage. There was no gap that did not close before Farva Mop could reach it. Those about her that were poised to sip tea or taste pastries did neither, for the cups and plates were dropped or scattered about. The crowd's first and resolute interest was to read one of a nearly uncountable number of books that were piled on tables or stored in the casement rooms on black-wood shelves or else on the balconies above her.

Men without books became enraged and their desperate eyes cast ferocious glances over the shoulders of those that were reading, while ladies in ornate dresses prepared to wrestle each other for the sake of catching sight of a single word. All ears strained to gain advantage from any word read aloud while all mouths relayed those words from one to another in a thousand screaming languages.

At the same time and with no apparent hurry there stepped waitresses carrying trays of tea services over their heads and who deposited them on tables where earlier teacups had been discarded. Those that could manage to find a book forced themselves out of the reach of others while above them raged riotous disputes on the high balconies.

In the room's centre the crowd's crush seemed even worse, where books were argued over or snatched. Then from within those places some volume would be waved about and then guests would huddle together like sudden flocks of attending noses.

All the while Farva Mop pressed on, while the mix of wide languages was tangling and while those grasping hands were like a forest she could not find her way out of. Above her fine and luxurious hats were all nodding in the battle to read while others then screamed what had read for the benefit of others in those languages that, as I have said, folded and doubled to say many things at once.

Then above them all and sounding from the high rafters came the strike of a great black-iron cup and kettle clock that measured the time with cups and kettles and that tolled upon the crowd below. Such was the size of that clock that when it struck it blocked out the noise of the voices of below. However, many times at the strike she had been swept back into the vast room's centre where she could rarely move even a little. Then finally, and after a terrible effort lasting a terribly long time, she reached the top of a black-wood staircase and nearly tumbled down it.

At her first chance she stood up straight and saw the crowd was not following her, and so brushing off crumbs and wiping her face of cold tea she took those stairs down as her only retreat.

Only after a good descent did those voices recede and as some rattling sounds announced that she was in that entrance hall again. The trap-pans, brooms and brushes shook and edged forward from their places, whilst beyond them that great open door showed the unhappy banquet square and the grey stars. To her right there was the counter again with its black candles lit and while beside them was Mr Grinsnick, with his needle-pen who was was attending to his book.

Mr Grinsnick remained writing while Farva Mop stepped closer until all of a sudden she threw back the hood and gave him the most extraordinary smile.

Mr Grinsnick remained unresponsive, his face remaining grave and unmoved, for it seemed that for Mr Grinsnick there was no smile available.

Then after a lengthy stillness his left hand uncurled its long thin fingers at the edge of the counter and then were still.

"The.............. key," Mr Grinsnick said.

Farva Mop dug down into one of her deep front pockets and drew out the lamp-key and reached up and placed it in that open hand that then withdrew. Then another key was slid forward to where Farva Mop caught it. Then when Farva Mop had pocketed the proper key, which was dimmer and smaller, there was the sound of Mr Grinsnick sighing as he added some tiny addition in to a page.

"Farva.........Mop," he said dismissively, "a guest of unknown purpose. Destination...unknown."

Then as Farva Mop watched she saw Mr Grinsnick's dark grey eyes briefly glance at her.

"WelcomeIhopeyourstaywillbeverypleasant," he said as one droning word.

He was next quiet for such a long time that Farva Mop understood that he had finished.

She was utterly convinced now that there was very little kindness here and so she turned from the counter and seeing the open doorway she marched along and stepped through it.

All of the crown-lamps had been dimmed now by Mr Flast and the quayside with the dimmed boat-lamps was nearly dark. Her new small key-lamp was her only guide and she walked a great distance past many fine boats before she found her own. The deck was still dust-laden but now had many more slipper-prints across it. Then when she reached the door to the cabin-steps she found someone had barred it. A black-iron cage-work had been expanded across the frame and had been secured with barrel-locks. Then hanging from these was a grey label that had been tied with black twine and the label read:

For the sake

Of so many

Things

Please

Be patient

Until you

Remember.

Mrs Lasanti.

Nothing could free her now, she thought, and besides which she could remember no place where she might go. Then like a call to her heart a lonesome bell sounded from within the house. The bell sounded thrice and then stopped. Then looking again at the cabin doorway, which was simply impassable, she knew it would be better to occupy her rooms in the house and be a guest there.

She marched back into the entrance hall and made no remark to to Mr Grinsnick, who in his turn made no attempt to talk to her. When she was halfway up the entrance hall staircase she paused and listened and found to her relief that there was no sound of that crowd at the top of it.

Slowly she climbed while shining her key-lamp and found that the great hall of The Shading Rooms was deserted.

In the highest rafters the cup and kettle clock moved its black-iron wheels. The clock's chained lamps were now the only light, for all middle parts of the room were now in darkness. The walkways and balconies offered no light either and instead some faint gleams came from the far end towards the stair-hall doors where there was candlelight remaining. The hall was so immense, even half-lit, and while her key-lamp shone across the books' old titles that were too widely written to be read by her.

The creaking black-wood floor was strewn with biscuits and cakes and broken cups and saucers, such being the speed of that crowd's exit.

Then to the left of the stair-hall doors, which were were tight shut, she saw there was a maid busying about the final alcove there.

The maid was a thin chalky girl dressed in the usual laces of black and was carrying bunches of stopped candles. The girl put the candles out with a sharp wave of her hand before snatching more from their sticks and holders. Soon she was hurrying across to the alcove on the right side.

When Farva Mop was close upon the maid then she seemed most annoyed, for she turned and pointed a long thin forefinger at Farva Mop.

"*Moshna ler-tooooshhhhha!*" the girl said, who was no doubt complaining at being delayed in her work.

Farva Mop did as she was asked and moved on but very soon she turned back.

It seemed that not a stitch of the girl's trailing dress returned any light while her black hair too, being cast into wild trails, gave her face a most wayward look.

Then the maid rolled her severe black eyes to watch her.

"*Ler-tooooshhhhhh!*" the girl said on seeing that Farva Mop was still watching her.

Then feeling suddenly impelled to say something of herself Farva Mop gazed about her.

"I don't -" said Farva Mop helplessly, "I mean," she said, "I don't know anything."

The girl stared back in an impatient manner.

"*I don't know anything either,*" the girl said in a creaky voice before throwing some of her collection of candles up but which then rather oddly did not fall back down.

Above them both those candles were stuck to the ceiling downside up and their flames relit and then focused like little eyes watching them.

Next the girl wrinkled up her paper-white face and bared some sharp little teeth and aimed a thin finger at Farva Mop.

"*You're strange.*"

"I suppose so," replied Farva Mop and noticed the girl had returned to her slender ways and she threw the last of the candles that hit the ceiling with loud thumps.

It was now that Farva Mop had the strangest need to say something and her mouth opened and the words tumbled out:

"I just need someone to tell me what I should do," she said.

The girl, who seemed distracted by the light above replied narrowly.

"*I cannot tell you what you should do, I am supposed to be a ghost.*"

At this Farva Mop cried out and stumbled back; for she understood now that everything had been so completely wrong. The girl was dead, or at least she was 'supposed' to be so.

Then next Farva Mop stared at the floor; a floor that creaked for everyone but this girl and who, Farva Mop decided, was most likely a ghost.

From the ceiling the trails of smoke twirled oddly downward instead of up and they passed through the ghost's slender figure like silk in water.

"Yes, I see," said Farva Mop hurriedly.

The ghost turned a fathomless eye.

"*So?*" asked the ghost creakily, "*Why don't you run?*"

Farva Mop suddenly felt more unhappy than ever and she slowly drew a chair from the leftward alcove behind her and after setting it before the stair hall doors sn seated herself and stared.

"I do not know why," she said wearily "I do not mind you being a ghost," she said, "just so long as you tell me what I should do."

Then the last candles above them brightened so that their eerie light shone down.

Then the ghost complete in her own private darkness stepped into it.

"The book says you are F-arva M-op," the ghost said, *"but knows nothing of why you are here or where you are going,"* then the ghost pointed slowly at Farva Mop, *"and neither do you."*

Farva Mop stared back at the ghost, who it seemed could out-stare anybody, and then the ghost spoke again.

"My name is Esferini," the ghost said in her creaking way, *"I have a second name but I cannot remember it."*

Farva Mop then avoided the ghost's gaze, which was rather entrancing, and made to speak while looking away.

"Then why is it you are here, Esferini?" Farva Mop asked and then looked up at the high ceiling with its lit candles stuck around in all ways.

The ghost then glared at Farva Mop with her black eyes.

"Because I am to haunt here," said the ghost, *"and knew I was a ghost for all this time hiding in the smallest rooms,"* the ghost's dead eyes met Farva Mop's again, *"as all the ghosts must do."*

Esferini's eyes were next fixed on Farva Mop's and then slowly and menacingly Esferini approached Farva Mop, so that she immediately rose from the chair and was pressed back against the rightward door. Yet all the while she felt drawn by the ghost's black eyes as moment by moment she stared into them.

"But now there is you with your haunted clothes and your strange ways," said Eferini as Farva Mop watched those eyes and saw a single tear appear in one of them, *"just like a mirror,"* said Esferini as the tear ran, *"and that's when I knew that I was still alive."*

Farva Mop continued to watch the girl and then blinked - and the floor was suddenly noisy with bouncing and rolling candles.

Behind her was the leftward stair-hall door that had swung open and Carua was there with a lamp, and who was motioning for Farva Mop to come. Then when Farva Mop approached then Carua took a handkerchief from her sleeve and wiped a tear from one of Farva Mop's eyes.

"It is not for us in the dark, Farva Mop, as I think Mr Flast tells everyone," Carua whispered, and then reaching out she took Farva Mop's hand.

Then from The Shading Rooms they went stepping and creaking and across the star-hall to The Sunning Room where those strong tall doors were opened inwards. There was a second enormous black-wood chamber where a great fire blazed in a hearth in the facing wall. To either side of that hearth a tall arched window reflected a brilliant display of rows of white-silk covered tables where hundreds of guests were sitting down to dinner.

Chapter 6

Esferini.

Farva Mop was led along, but it was a dreamy walk she had, and was confused again by the wide-languages that were unbearable about her.

The table that Carua led her to had silver trees for decoration and was the furthest table to the left of the fire, being end-on to the tall window there. The window gave a full view of that unhappy garden that Farva Mop had seen before in the room below.

She was guided along but her gaze was cast downward for fear of meeting the withering stares of those other guests. Then when she noticed that they were all too busy talking and wrenching books from each other to notice her then Farva Mop came to survey the room.

The Sunning Room appeared to be much like The Shading Rooms except that white marble was everywhere. There were no casement bookshelves or balconies to clutter it. The room had just as many white marble pillars, but near their tops there were chain-wheels for thick dusty tapestries that in some odd way could divide that great room into smaller ones. The pillars, she now realised, contained the laundry shafts, for it was a start in her better understanding of the house.

That magnificent room had brought the guests together in comfort but not in peace, for Farva Mop heard the wide-languages churning and smashing, where words of unfortunate kinds were made by forcing them rather unspeakably together.

When Farva Mop and Carua reached their table then Carua drew out a chair for Farva Mop, which meant that her back should be turned to the giant grey rug before the fire. From her vantage point also she might glance to her right and through the window, though there was little to look at.

When she came see those who would be her companions she found Carua was seated opposite her and then her husband Ogwal, who was to the left. Then across the corner of the table from

Ogwal was a man with a most severe face and then to his right there someone who might be his wife, who seemed altogether more cheerful. Those two seemed not to notice her, since her glances were not returned, and while they most often looked towards the vacant seat beside Farva Mop, as if that was the seat that mattered.

The severe-faced man had a most proud expression, made angrier by his red hair, bronze eyes and red beard. Farva Mop noticed also his red cloak had a row of bronze smoking-pipes and pencils clipped across it. Every so often that man agreed firmly with Mr Unessia as if their conversation, though in a wide-language, should be louder than all others. However it seemed also that the same man was also annoyed with listening, as if he judged Mr Unessia to know nothing.

The two beards, they being the black and the red, seemed unlikely to notice Farva Mop but the red beard's wife was becoming friendlier, talking to Carua about a great number of things. The lady had happy eyes that were a brilliant green while her hair was cinder orange and was cut short which made her face very rounded and cheery.

Behind those strangers and at a small table to themselves sat the boy Maradsha and the girl Koliana. The young Unessias had received a plate of colourful little foods that amused and delighted them.

The seat to the left of Farva Mop remained unoccupied until after some time Mrs Lasanti arrived and seated herself and who smiled at Farva Mop whereupon Farva Mop (who was too exhausted for smiling) nodded back.

Mrs Lasanti persuaded Farva Mop to shed her cloak on account of the heat and after this Mrs Lasanti addressed the others.

"May I present Miss Farva Mop," said Mrs Lasanti who was directing Farva Mop towards the fierce red-haired man and his wife.

Mrs Lasanti touched at Farva Mop's sleeve..

"Miss Mop, these are Mr and Mrs Kurigna," she said. "Miss Mop, like myself, was delayed."

Then Mrs Lasanti waved a hand at a waitress who was some way off, which indicated that their party was ready to dine.

"Miss Mop is in the care of my daughter, Carua," said Mrs Lasanti continued, "since Miss Mop is neither a student nor a master of History."

Mr Kurigna's bronze eyes seemed immediately to lose interest in Farva Mop – to the extent that, for him at least, she no longer existed. He turned back to Mr Unessia and the two beards were soon talking again.

However Mrs Kurigna was not so dismissive, for she smiled at Farva Mop, though she had some matter to discuss with Mrs Lasanti that was rather historical.

When Farva Mop came to glance away from the table she found that the waiters and waitresses looked exhausted too. They had arrived like an army to serve those dreadful guests who had chosen to entirely ignore them.

When a trolley reached their table the waitress seemed nearly to be falling asleep as she served a night-soup to each of them. After the soup, which was tightening and warming, there was a choice of fruit-stews with many spices and after these there were heavy nut-rolls filled with fire-jams and after this, shell-cakes filled with smoke sugars. Finally a smaller trolley brought many tea services, from which the waitress served a selection of teas.

"I am so thankful of your kitchens, Mrs Lasanti," said Mr Kurigna, who was leaning back into his creaking black-wood chair and detaching one of his smoking-pipes. "You must send me some food; my college has angry cooks who make angry dinners."

Mrs Lasanti smiled.

"Mr Kurigna," Mrs Lasanti said, "do not make your cooks more angry than they need to be, better anger than hunger."

Mrs Kurigna in her turn then shrugged her shoulders.

"I am quite happy to eat there," Mrs Kurigna said with a smile that dimpled her cheek. "My own students eat warm food – because mine eat first, while my husband's students," and she stifled a yawn, "are still listening."

The insult was batted away by Mr Kurigna with a wave of his hand whilst puffing on a smoking-pipe that had a spell of a kind, for no leaves burned there. Instead it was a perfume that emerged that often refreshing.

There followed, in spite of the perfumes, a dreary discussion on the history of various foods, with Mr Kurigna naming some book now and then as proof of something other and then Mrs Kurigna proving the reverse.

The table became dense with history and while Farva Mop could think of nothing but leaving the table and escaping to her rooms.

She stared out through the window where the tables were partly reflected. Thereafter she could make out the sinister black branches of the trees.

Then next she turned and squinted up at the rolled and chained tapestries that were above her. Then she turned a little and watched the guests screaming and babbling.

Then away from the noise she heard a narrow language and Farva Mop turned back.

"You must tell us what treasures delayed you, Miss Mop," said Mrs Kurigna in her cheery way, "there are so many here if you can learn how to see them."

Mrs Lasanti also gave some encouragement and smiled.

"Yes, my dear; tell us about Mr Grinsnick and his book, we shall all listen."

Farva Mop thought long and hard about the book but remembered that she had not been tall enough to see it.

Farva Mop looked back at Mrs Lasanti who was smiling and next at Carua who seemed calm and peaceful.

"I," said Farva Mop, "I never got to see it properly," she said. "I did not know there would be dinner; I did not know where I should be."

Farva Mop then found herself dreamy again and looking blankly about, "which is why I asked the girl."

"They are so helpful here," Mrs Kurigna interrupted and who looked towards the others at the table. "My husband has visited here so often while I have not. I hope to visit many more times I am sure," she said.

Then Mrs Kurigna's happy gaze settled upon Farva Mop again.

"Who was it that helped you, Miss Mop?"

Farva Mop looked at Mrs Kurigna helplessly.

"Esferini," Farva Mop said in a rather sorrowful way.

Then suddenly the whole room fell silent and not a whisper was uttered. Then when Farva Mop looked she saw the silence was accompanied by the stares of the guests and while necks were craned to hear to whatever Farva Mop said next.

Then in the reflection in the window Farva Mop saw Mrs Lasanti carefully put her teacup down to its saucer where it tinkled loudly there. All about, since now Farva Mop could hear them, were the soft knockings of the buckets within the pillars but apart from these no other sound was noticeable.

Farva Mop swallowed hard but remained looking down at her empty plate and was reluctant to look elsewhere.

Then Mrs Lasanti picked up her teaspoon and stirred her tea then struck her teacup in a ringing way.

"We have a Nella who is a clearing maid," Mrs Lasanti said rather loudly, "it will be she who Miss Mop asked the way of. Nella is such a fancy sometimes and excited by the past – as anyone would expect to be amongst such learned people," and then gently Mrs Lasanti set the teaspoon down.

Then slowly and from all places the noisy languages began again until very soon great volleys of them filled the room until it seemed nearly to shake it.

Mr Kurigna tapped at his smoking-pipe.

"It is never wise to allow imagination its full course, Mrs Lasanti," Mr Kurigna said through a swirl of perfumed smoke. "Inform your Nella that nothing comes or goes without a boat and that nothing deceives a fine lamp. This is what she was taught at school and that will be her way to knowledge."

Mrs Lasanti smiled.

"Then we shall see how she grows, Mr Kurigna, with all of our good teachings."

"Well," said Mrs Kurigna, who spoke next and who turned to look at the tables behind her where huddles of guests were shouting and grasping at books.

"I was never told there was a mystery," Mrs Kurigna said lightly. "Perhaps I can solve it," she said.

Mrs Lasanti glanced past her.

"Perhaps you can," Mrs Lasanti said, "though I suggest we retire to a room below; I have never been one to shout."

"Yes indeed," said Mr Kurigna, "I agree to that."

Mr Unessia leant towards Carua to hear the proposal in a wider language and then he and Carua spoke to Maradsha and Koliana, who rose from their seats.

Mrs Lasanti led her party along towards the doors of The Sunning Room where the firelight was diminished and the room was very much cooler. There Farva Mop saw Mrs Lasanti give some brief instructions to a maid and then Mrs Lasanti and the rest of them passed through into the stair-hall where Mrs Lasanti waited for her party to gather.

Behind and beneath the wide curving staircase she opened a panel-door and after taking a pencil-lamp from a pocket she descended a narrow black-wood staircase and waved for the others to follow.

The staircase had grey-lanterns hung regularly where they went down and while the creaks of the steps caused all to listen to them.

Farva Mop was glad to leave The Sunning Room. If The Sunning Room had been less noisy then she might have enjoyed it. As she descended then Mrs Lasanti admitted that The Sunning Room was not so suitable.

"The Sunning Room will always be a maze," Mrs Lasanti said, "for you noticed, didn't you, Mrs Kurigna, that the tapestries are unusually set. Mazes were common to the house in the time of an ancient custodian who enjoyed celebrations with feasts and games. He also enlarged the windows to take light from the brighter stars and it was a room for sunning. As you might guess such light was not for everyone and another room was reserved for shading. In these times The Sunning Room receives a poor light and the cook says the fireplace is too small, even though it is the largest here. As for the tapestries for all other parts, which had been mazes too, they are stored in some panel-cupboards or we no longer have them, whichever-the-which."

The group descended in silence for a long time and the staircase passed through a junction with one of the panel-ways, which Farva Mop had expected they should be taking. Instead the staircase descended until Farva Mop heard again the sound of the laundry pans boiling.

Below there the black-wood stair was replaced with steps that were hard white marble instead. The stairwell walls were changed too and became overlapping white marble slabs that were piled without anything to secure them. When Farva Mop heard Mrs Lasanti's voice next it was split to half-echo by the many surfaces.

"We are now in the stacks of marble upon which the building rests, below which there is the master-slab upon which all things rest," she said.

"Above us are the cellars and above them and side by side is the laundry and the kitchen. To cellar's far side there is the building's other quay that is a private quay for those that tend here. To the rear of the house, as you might know, are the private rooms of Miss Naws and in the grounds behind is The Maid's Garden, which you saw from The Sunning Room, and which is only for them."

They then descended passed junctions where much narrower passages began like narrow slots.

"There are other ways," Mrs Kurigna said who paused to examine a passage that was no better than to allow one of them There was lamplight there but at a distance but with no indication of where those passages went.

"There are many ways here, Mrs Kurigna, "Mrs Lasanti said, "but we have no uses for them; we must guess at their uses when the house was first built. We are all Historians now, are we not, Mr Kurigna."

Mr Kurigna made no reply, perhaps because they were all so keen on descending carefully and keeping their feet.

At last Mrs Lasanti opened a black-wood door which creaked in a very familiar way after which they were led into a black-wood room that had grey-lamps just like the others.

Yet the room had one feature that quite set it apart, for the floor was thick crystal glass that gave a view of the stars that were ranged below the house. Through this glass floor could seen the great spiralling storm to its fullest extent and also the silent lightning that seemed scrawled across it.

In that room the Kurignas strolled and admired the soft grey armchairs and the ornate tea-tables and while above them were hung fine scented crystal lamps, though they gave a grey light.

The closeness of the storm brought many speeches from Mrs Kurigna about storing the most precious things in the smallest cupboards to protect them when the house fell. Then, as if to show rather than tell, she stepped around the room commenting on the shelves of fine teapots and other delicate items for the benefit of the others, but who by this time were all sat down.

Farva Mop leant over and looked down beside her armchair. Through her silhouette was shown the lightning moving jagged upon the dark, while all the while Mrs Kurigna took her seat she informed them that their chairs were stuffed with Rappa-Narra Petals that were a tonic against the dark.

Then Mrs Lasanti placed tiny silver drinking glasses on the tables beside each of them and brought many crystal barrels of biscuits. She brought out wines for those that were grown and Yoya Juices for those that were not and by and by she came to settle and speak to them.

"This is the Silent Room," Mrs Lasanti said with a near whisper, for they could all hear her clearly. "It is Miss Naw's own contribution to the house – though these days she is too ill to visit it. She allows anyone to rest here who is done with talking and wishes to be quiet – though, as you can see," and she smiled at all of them, "there is only ourselves."

Mrs Lasanti waved at the children to choose from the biscuits. After which the subject of history arose yet again and to Farva Mop's ears Mr Kurigna droned on about curtain-sashes and barrel-stoppers and door-hinges. His details went on and on, with

Mrs Kurigna adding more and more and meanwhile Farva Mop dozed in her chair with her Yoya juice, which was a heavy drink.

Then Mrs Kurigna remembered the matter from The Sunning Room above and inquired once again of Mrs Lasanti, whereupon her husband warned them all of the dangers of loose subjects. But in spite of this Mrs Kurigna asked again and so, with Carua translating a softer version for her children, Mrs Lasanti looked for words in the colours of her wine and began to speak.

"There is no one left who can explain this house, except historians," Mrs Lasanti said and who was collecting her thoughts in the midst of little pauses. "Books that were written are lost and, of course, the great book is a book of guests and not other sorts of things.

"We know that first of all there was Seri-Len who lived in a warmer place, Four Thousand Heavens Above The Cold. She built this house, which was a famous house and which was in turn left to its maids and its book-master who were also long-lived. But long life could do nothing to preserve the house itself, which like all others is doomed to ruin."

All who listened settled back.

"For many custodians after Ser-Len the house was a peaceful house and the book made sure it was so. Every guest performed some good here and earned themselves some proper happiness. But sometimes there came 'strange ones,' whom no one could decide about. Yet it was assumed that they performed some strange good for their strange kind and so no ill was said of them. If the strange ones withdrew from all others then it was supposed that it was simply their way, which must have been happiness for them."

Farva Mop watched Mrs Lasanti speak and it was entrancing to listen, as if Mrs Lasanti was casting some strange spell herself.

"When the first great custodian, named Glolaf, managed the house, and it became The House of Glolaf when he was appointed, he adored the strange ones and gave the eighth and topmost floor to them and their secret interests. Long did he try to guess their unusual purposes, as if he might somehow profit from them. His were the parties of the tapestry mazes and Glolaf himself was perhaps a dazzled man, charmed by those stranger guests but who were always too much for him.

"The time of Glolaf ended and the times of mystery had ended too. The whole of the house became filled with lamps and on the topmost floor the lamps shone twice as bright as all the others. The hundreds of custodians after Glolaf had some need to bring order to the half-ruin so that it might fall gracefully. It became a time of the brighter door-lamps and the larger Sunning Room fire, though the fall of a house could not be postponed by any of these arrangements. When Miss Naws was a child she saw the eighth floor lamps, which were twice as bright as all the others, so as to keep the strange ones in their beds. The house became quieter in the darker heavens and Miss Naws remembers the last concert in the great square, though she says it was a dreary suppertime spent in thick clothes.

"The greatness of the house was gone and in this heaven, which seeks only the past, she let it be a service to historians, which the stars encourage here. Then when there were strange ones, and sometimes there were, then Miss Naws would speak to them herself and would make it clear what she was about.

"Then half a heaven ago, which for me is a long time now, a guest heard a life-boat's bell amongst the stars below and the lamp-man's boat was sent to it.

"In the lifeboat was a child, named Esferini Anriassa Serain, who said she had come from a great ship that was struggling in the deep. Therefore all boats that were of a strong kind were sent to find that ship – but all returned to say it must have sunk into The Cold, five hundred heavens below us, and no one was saved but this one child.

"For nine days and nine nights the girl cried and cried and no one could comfort her and in the middle of those nights she would walk that topmost corridor in her sleep as if to study her lot.

"Then a man a man and his wife who loved this house, and who were parents themselves, stood watch at the stairwell and to carry lead her back. But on the ninth night when they saw her sleeping her sleep's walk, they guarded her from the drop at the head of the stairs as Esferini came walking in awkward strides.

Then at the moment she should be guided back, she suddenly disappeared."

Mr Kurigna removed one of his smoking-pipes and sighed and when it was ribboned with smoky perfumes then Mrs Lasanti continued.

"And for long afterwards the troubles of the eighth floor grew steadily worse, for guests claimed they had heard animals of unknown kinds, long after suppertime, when they were awakened from sleep. Then worse things sounded in the dark until the eighth floor windows were boarded up and all means to enter it were entirely removed.

"No one sleeps there now, though Miss Naws maintains this is a peaceful house and no one should think it sad."

Mrs Lasanti put her glass on the little table-top and saw Maradsha and Koliana were fast asleep, whilst Farva Mop was awake yet and was watching and listening.

Mrs Kurigna scratched her head and smiled.

"It is an attracting tale, Mrs Lasanti - except that vanishing powders are most likely, would you not not say?"

"None were found or likely used Mrs Kurigna," Mrs Lasanti said, "the eighth floor corridor, unusual in all ways, has a finely woven ornate carpet and no holes were found in it."

"Then surely we should doubt the couple who saw the girl," said Mrs Kurigna tunefully.

Mrs Lasanti shook her head.

"The lady has long passed away from us, I am saddened to say," Mrs Lasanti said, "but her husband is Mr Flast, a trusted man of the lamps and quays and he would never disparage this house. His only daughter is Inkle, my personal maid, and who says he avoids the subject of Esferini and never speaks of it."

Mrs Kurigna seemed most perturbed.

"But we must doubt them again, Mrs Lasanti," Mrs Kurigna insisted, "we must assume there was some box or cupboard the girl could hide in."

"There were, and there still are, many old things on the eighth floor, Mrs Kurigna, many being mysteries in themselves, but they were were searched. The passages behind the walls were searched to their ends but no one was found there."

Mrs Kurigna then seemed weary of the subject.

"As for those sounds the guests heard, there are many sounds in this house, the floorboards themselves need the slightest excuse," she said.

Mrs Lasanti nodded.

"You are right, of course, Mrs Kurigna; the house has a voice of its own. I too cannot say what was heard. It was Miss Naws who ordered the eighth floor closed, but more to close the fear of it; she has never suggested the cause."

Mr Kurigna took the smoking-pipe from his mouth.

"The girl is the cause," Mr Kurigna said sharply. "She simply sneaked through the tiredness of a man and his wife who were grieving with her. The girl then most likely hid away on a guest's boat and travelled far away. As for the noises," and he tapped his smoking-pipe on a tea-table's surface, "even this in the narrows of the night must seem suspicious too."

Then he leant back and made an unpleasant face, for he seemed to dislike that smoking-pipe and chose another.

He then he glanced at Carua.

"Perhaps your brilliant daughter, Mrs Lasanti, has something to say of this?"

Carua smiled at Mr Kurigna but said nothing.

Mr Kurigna then glanced about.

"And Mr Lasanti?" he asked.

Mrs Lasanti smiled.

"Mr Lasanti sends messengers with news of his studies of the heaven below, where as you know this house shall appear in the most sudden of ways."

She waved a hand.

"Below us is a heaven of map-makers and boat-makers, who I am sure have equipped him with better stories than ours," she said.

Mrs Lasanti paused.

"As you know he is a shy man who in this heaven became an historian of sweeping-brushes. That is the subject he keeps to and does not waver from."

There followed a conversation that became more and more detailed, for it was concerning descriptions of old buckets and wash basins.

Throughout these Farva Mop drifted for she was very tired. Her thoughts were full of bleary pictures of her boat full of clothes, of Miss Naws calling down the kettle from the ceiling and then of her closely watching her. Then later, having thought too deeply, Farva Mop was woken by Mrs Lasanti who had come close

Mrs Lasanti whispered

"Time you were off to bed."

Carua meanwhile took the hands of Koliana and Maradsha and then the whole party set off up the white marble steps through the stacks and where their climb was slow and arduous.

When they finally returned to the stair-hall, the lamps in The Sunning Room were dimmed so as to welcome the night.

Then all of them ascended the loudly creaking black-wood stairs. At the second floor Mr and Mrs Kurigna went their way, and on the fifth floor Carua and and her husband and their children went to their rooms.

When Mrs Lasanti and Farva Mop reached the seventh then then Mrs Lasanti inspected the grey-lit corridor that was dim and motionless. Then after Farva Mop lit her key-lamp and unlocked her door then Mrs Lasanti turned about and she bid her goodnight.

In her rooms Farva Mop withdrew to the bedroom where she called the grey candles to light beside her bed. Later, when she was under the covers, she found the sheets and the pillows were icy, until the old grey blankets finally warmed her and there she was turned to sleep.

Chapter 7.

The Search.

At some point in the night Farva Mop was stirred to half-wakefulness by her sliding easily under the blankets and disappearing for a time near the foot of the bed. Next she was squashed uncomfortably at the pillows end. When she yawned and stared uncaringly out she saw the long black curtains at her bedroom window were leaning strikingly to the left. In the shallows of sleep she decided such things could not disturb her any more than the torments she had already suffered.

The next morning she woke to find a large blank sheet of yellow paper resting on her face that had corners attached by lengths of yellow string that were wound about her ears. The paper was so comfortable a fit that at first she was happy to have it there and assumed it was something she had simply collected during her journeys in her bed.

Farva Mop then sat herself up with the paper still attached and then detached it and set the paper down on the grey blankets and then looked about her. The curtains at the window were now slid along and while the candle-table had walked some way from her bedside where also its candles were missing. Whatever the building had been doing it had now stopped. All was quiet and still and so returning to the sheet of paper she had a good look at it, first one side and then the other, but there was nothing written on either. Then all of a sudden a crowd of little golden words arrived at the sheet's edge from the paper's other side and gathered themselves together to form a letter and that letter read:

Farva Mop.
I am a boy
Who is also your navigator.
We arrived here on your boat,
but I have left no trace.
We are investigators
and when the time comes we shall meet.

Begin by looking for plants.
You will be told there cannot be any,
But look anyway.
I am very busy.

After Farva Mop had read this the golden words ran away and when she turned the sheet she found the words were not there either. She left the sheet of paper on the blanket-top and then tried hard to remember if there had been a boy.

After some thought it occurred to her that there must have been someone, for why else was someone writing to her? Then who was he, this navigating boy? she wondered.

Then remembering the evening before she thought of Esferini.

Farva Mop looked about the dimly lit black-wood bedroom but could see no sign of the ghost. Then when she was fully dressed she found the curtains in the study had also gathered to the left side. There there no candles in the study's chandeliers either or in the rooms beyond it, so that she carried her key-lamp around from one place to the next. Then returning to stand beside the little grate in the study she turned her attention to the finding of plants.

She became rather concerned that this heaven was much too dark and that she would not find any.

"Where should I look for plants?" she asked no one in particular.

Then, as if somehow someone had heard her, there came a gentle knocking on her door.

After unlocking she carefully opening the door she peered out.

The light of her key-lamp was met by another, for under the ruinous door-lamp was Inkle carrying a lamp of her own and a pile of fresh black clothes that she had hooked under one arm.

Inkle gave a quick curtsy before speaking in a rather continuous way.

"Mrs Lasanti has told me I can speak to you as plain as I like with you being strange. I don't know if you want people near you, with you being strange. I can be a little strange too sometimes but not strange enough for you I expect. Mrs Lasanti told me to tell you that breakfast is served after the bell, but unless you are four floors lower you will not hear it."

Farva Mop took the pile of clothes from Inkle and saw that Inkle was about to speak again.

"Expect you speak by turning your head inside out, that's what Nella says that Strange One's have to do. You will have to remember though that I cannot turn my face inside out and that turning your face inside out would frighten me quite a lot."

Farva Mop tried to answer but Inkle stepped hurriedly back and then continued with her speech.

"Remember what I said," Inkle said, "if you are going to turn your face inside out then I won't be here very long watching it."

Then Inkle added more.

"Mrs Lasanti told me to tell you that I can carry notes. I can carry things too."

Then Inkle fell silent.

Inkle had large smoke-coloured eyes that were hidden in the shadows of her deep brows. She was quite a tall girl with short thick brown hair that was partly hidden by a black lace hood. Altogether Farva Mop thought Inkle much too pale, but which she decided was understandable from living in such a cold place.

Then if Farva Mop had thought Inkle would leave then Inkle did not. Inkle remained waiting, her lips sucking at her front teeth that jutted out.

Then Inkle spoke again.

"Mrs Lasanti said that you have to say if you have understood."

Farva Mop felt awkward and made a pained face.

"So far there has been only one other person who has made any sense at all," then Farva Mop made a bewildered expression, "and she was dead."

Inkle sucked on her teeth before giving Farva Mop a sidelong glance.

"Mrs Lasanti said I am to tell her if you say strange things but I might not tell her that one."

Feeling that this was a token of respect Farva Mop smiled and moved forward just a little as Inkle moved back.

"I wonder," Farva Mop said, "I wonder if you could fetch me a book on plants."

Inkle watched Farva Mop, as if deciding whether this was strange or not, then, after another curtsy, she left.

Farva Mop leant out to see Inkle stepping noisily along the creaking floorboards to her left. She went that long way towards the end wall from where Farva Mop herself had emerged the previous evening. Into one of those luggage cabins Inkle stepped, then afterwards when the panel door slid closed Inkle was conveyed below.

Some time later when Farva Mop emerged from her rooms in her new black clothes she found that whatever time breakfast had been set then it seemed that she had missed it. When she finally arrived in the stair-hall she found the doors to The Sunning Room were locked. A grey notice with grey string was attached to the handles and after many wide-languages it read:

Tea Served At Eleven Kettles.

Then deciding to seek to find biscuits or cake in The Shading Rooms she found they were just as busy as before.

That same crushing and baffling crowd were crammed into it. Their battering, deafening languages seemed actually to be worse, as if more guests had arrived to shout with them. Reluctantly she went back to her rooms and found nothing at all to do and eventually a gloominess settled on her.

It was then that Inkle returned and who handed her two dusty old books with tea and cake crumbs spattered and scattered on them.

Inkle curtsied and left without speaking and this time descended by way of the noisy stairs, as if she had some duty to perform on the floor below.

Next Farva Mop placed the books on her study's black-wood desk and noted that the first was a book of maps titled:

Better Houses For Blossoms From Heavens Two Thousand Eight Hundred And Fifty Down To Two Thousand Seven Hundred And Forty Nine.

The book gave the full names of houses with gardens of note. These did not include gardens on worlds, since those were

100

considered lesser places. The House of Naws was not mentioned, then she remembered that this house would take on the name of a previous curator. Then in the introduction the book made clear that the map-book was not intended to advise people on where houses were but where houses had been, since people of a rare sort were interested in such things.

Being not a book that was any use then Farva Mop slid it away.

The next book was titled:

Plants at Increasing Depths.

Its introduction was short but helped readers understand how complicated the book was.

The introduction read thus:

*"The highest heavens are abundant with plants that grow in light, while the lowest heavens are abundant with plants that grow in darkness. The plants that require light are called **Aramires** and the plants that require darkness are called **Kurretids**. Between The Thousandth and the Fiftieth Heaven Above The Cold there are no plants at all, for the reason that no plants can grow inside or out in grey-light, it's being too dark or too light for any of them. This has led to The Grey Deep, as these heavens are sometimes called, being of no interest to gardeners."*

Farva Mop came to understand what the secret boy had meant.

She stared towards the window where the stars were certainly as grey as they come.

"No plants can grow here," she said.

Later, when she assumed that it was approaching Eleven Kettles, then she put the books away and prepared herself.

She pressed her ear to one of the double doors and listened. There was no sound of anyone about and so leaving her rooms and locking them she drew her hood over and tiptoed along. She glanced briefly up at the stairwell's cage-work of menacing bars and then she proceeded down the black-wood stairs.

For many floors down the corridors were empty. Then on the landing of the fourth floor she heard footsteps and when she peered around the wide arch of the landing she saw three little maids dressed in black-silks and white lace.

The maids each carried a long green-lit pole much like the one Mr Flast had.

The maids were also unusual for being triplet sisters, since each moved and looked exactly the same.

In all ways they suited the backwood corridor, for the black-wood panels and beams framed them prettily.

Each maid had straight black hair and black button eyes that blinked with something like surprise when they saw Farva Mop.

They were such modest characters, for when she approached the little maids continued with their work as if no one might ever talk to them.

The maids were aiming their poles up at the black-wood ceiling where those green lights shone there. Then when Farva Mop came close the maids smiled together at Farva Mop and Farva Mop smiled back.

"What are you doing?" Farva Mop asked casually.

The first little maid curtsied and stood with the pole at her side and which was nearly three times taller than she was.

Then from the little maid there came such a tiny voice that Farva Mop had to stoop to hear it.

"Looking for cracks," the little maid said minutely, as if she had spoken from her foot.

"I see," replied Farva Mop with interest and then looked above in case she might find a crack for herself. However when she looked back she saw the maids studying her more and more intently while their eyes were opening wider and wider. It was as if, thought Farva Mop, that they thought she was going to turn into something terrible.

The maids' stared with none of them blinking.

"Where are the plants?" Farva Mop asked for something to say.

"Plants don't grow here," the first little maid said in her tiny voice and who then finally blinked, "but a cellar-boy told Nella there is something growing down in one of the cellars, but no one knows if it is a plant."

Then just at that moment all four of them looked towards the landing where a group of ladies rounded the handrail to go downstairs. Each lady was trying to read three books at once by balancing them in unusual ways, whilst clipped in their hair were many pin-lights that shone down on them. The group were reading but also talking and their battering and crashing words were loud and continuous.

On seeing Farva Mop they paused to give her a long unfriendly look, as if Farva Mop herself had upset them. Then all of them were descending again and while their voices reduced with the distance until they could hardly be heard at all.

Farva Mop made a puzzled expression when she turned back to the little maids.

"What do they all do?" Farva Mop asked.

The first little maid watched the stairs and then began on a little speech in an exact fashion.

"Mrs Lasanti says the historians are trying to learn all they can before the house falls. Mrs Lasanti says that is why the historians are talking and reading and writing quicker and quicker. Mrs Lasanti says that if they become wise they and their families can 'solve and go up' to the next heaven in their boats and live in a ruin and they can give up History and learn something else instead."

Then the little maid blinked.

"Mrs Lasanti says that we do not have to run and talk and read like that because we are not educated."

Farva Mop stared back at the landing.

"It must be the fastest history in History," Farva Mop whispered.

The little maid nodded and then all of the little maids formed a line and then the first little maid spoke again.

"Mrs Lasanti says that not all of them do that. Mrs Lasanti says that some of them hide in their rooms and write what they think it all means."

"What it all means?" asked Farva Mop.

103

"What History is," said the little maids all together. "It is what these stars want ," they said, "it is the stars that make them do it."

Farva Mop then became more aware of the silent doors, some of which might have historians hidden behind them.

"Do they ever come out?" Farva Mop asked.

"Inkle feeds them," the little maids said together as one voice.

Then Farva Mop noticed that the three little maids were studying her every detail again."

"Where are the cellars?" Farva Mop asked hurriedly.

Then Farva Mop had to stoop again to hear the voice of the first little maid.

"At the end of the guests' quay , near the garden there are some steps," the little maid said.

Farva Mop then left the little maids to continue with their work. She left them all staring at her before she went creaking down the creaking stairs.

Then rather too soon she was stopped by the increasing noise of a large number of guests who were hurrying up. They came like a rising storm and when they caught sight of her they were suddenly silent and annoyed like those others had been.

Then became a procession of distaste, each bearing a disparaging and unapproving look. The crowd of angry, overdressed and ill-mannered guests passed without saying a single word, which was not like them. They also carried cabin-lamps and key-lamps or pin-lamps, while the books they carried were for that moment of no interest to them.

Then finally there was Mr Kurigna ascending, his red hair and red beard watching her like a fire. He was carrying a lamp also and when he passed her he shot a mean glance.

"Attending to some History today, Miss Mop?"

Farva Mop made a hopeless expression.

"I'm looking for plants," she said.

"Unusual," Mr Kurigna said and then he sniffed before carrying on up the creaking stairs as if following the others.

When she reached the third floor landing there were no more guests but instead there were teams of porter-boys opening the secret cupboards and while maids and waitresses appeared from out of the panel-passages and then disappeared into more of them.

At the second floor landing Farva Mop saw the search continuing but they were waiters and waitresses instead.

Uncountable numbers of panel doors were open, but those that searched took no notice of Farva Mop.

When Farva Mop arrived in the stair-hall it was also apparent that she had missed tea at eleven kettles. There was another notice hung on the The Sunning Room's door handles, which after many languages finally read:

Mid-Meal at Twelve and a Half Kettles.

Thus Farva Mop had no other recourse than to face The Shading Rooms again in hope of finding cakes. Already her head was shaking from the booming conversations she could hear and when she turned the great black-iron handle and pushed the right hand door open then a wave of those terrible languages smashed about her ears.

All of them seemed even more desperate to seek the history of the house, as the little maids had put it. However they now looked most ungainly for they were all of them carrying the heaviest of lamps. There were boat-lamps and bath-lamps and bulbous old bed-lamps and the lamps were swinging and knocking in the guests battle to read.

Then as Farva Mop stepped fully into the hall those conversations stopped.

Not a single guest spoke as she walked the guests parted to let Farva Mop through. All of the guests were frowning at her in the most awful way and it was a silent journey Farva Mop had beside those ill-meaning faces. Then when she had nearly reached the stairs down then the sound of whispers came to speak narrowly and softly, until she heard the voices say "*Strange, strange, strange.*"

When she had at last descended to the entrance hall she found Mr Grinsick's counter had no candles either, and fearing that Mr Grinsnick might have some trouble to give her too, she walked swiftly and noisily through the great doors and left the house altogether.

The crown-lamps were again bright about the quay where newly arrived boats were lit up brightly too, which made them pretty to look at. Her own boat when she passed by it was was shown as the grey-wood derelict that it was. Above her the stars shone meanly down whilst at one and the same time the sadness of her situation came out of her as a number of great sobs.

"I am not - strange!" she cried up to the four giants that were staring down. "I am not –," she said again, and her furious eyes were filled with tears.

Then finally and after a good walk, and at the end of the quay, she looked up at the final giant and wiped those tears away.

"I am not strange, Seri-Len, I am not."

Then with all the hope that she could find she arrived at the quay's end.

To the left and at quay's edge a set of white marble steps followed the quay's wall down. A black-iron rail followed too as if the steps should lead down into the stars themselves.

At the foot of the steps there was a tall white marble bay where barrel-boats and other vessels might unload. Many stout lamps there showed a marble ramp going down with some white marble steps to the right side of it. On descending she took a lamp that had a long chain and the lamp sent swathes of grey light around and about.

At the bottom of the steps she turned through an arch to her right and a entered a grey-lit white marble cellar with shelves and barrels and boxes lining it. The cellar was half the house and as she walked she came to see through arches along the way to her left that another cellar was much the same.

In this left hand cellar and to both sides were alcoves where old pots on shelves where black-wood ladders were set. Then also there were hooked shelves for sacks and others for barrels and jars. The scents of herbs and spices came from everywhere, as did the smell of over-ripe fruits in neglected corners.

As she ventured further then drip-water from the kitchens and laundry above had come down as wide pools where Farva

Mop's lamp's-beam swept across them. Regularly she heard the drumming and rumbling sounds that seemed at times louder then softer.

In those alcoves and about the sacks and pots she began to look for plants, to one side of the cellar and then the other, while the music of the drips played across the near-dark as she made her way. Yet wherever she looked she found no plants at all, and became steadily more convinced that, just as the book had stated, that neither the Aramires nor Kurretids could grow here. Her lamp shone across the wide-languages' extraordinary styles as she climbed ladders to look behind barrels, but found only more barrels were there.

When at last she neared the cellar's end she saw another marble ramp that went up that had steps to its left side. At the top those steps was a great black-wood hatch that had been half slid away She could see steam drifting hither and thither in place above but also she saw a bronze kitchen-lantern placed at the hatch's timbered edge and where sitting beside it, with legs swinging freely back and forth, was a girl who was watching her.

Chapter 8.

Nella and Olris.

The girl wore a long-blue cloak and thick-pocketed blue trousers. Her hair was straight and shoulder-length and was a brighter blue still, whilst the brightest blue was the blue of her eyes, that were as still as crystals.

"I know about Strange Ones," the girl said with a sigh, as if all the sorrows of the worlds were lain upon her. Then she put her hands into her long-cloak's pockets and swung her over-large boots back and forth.

"I am Nella," Nella said in her sorrowful way and gazed dreamily down at Farva Mop.

"I know you are dangerous, but I can defend myself," Nella said. "I have a poem in my pocket and if I read it out it would bring ropes to fasten you. I have a special lamp in my other pocket so that even in darkness I can still escape."

Nella's sorrow seemed only to increase.

"If you try to swallow me I have big boots on," and Nella showed Farva Mop her rather leaden boots that were badly worn at the toes where the wire and black rug-work were separating.

"You would choke on those, you see; I am not so easy to swallow," said Nella.

Farva Mop looked at the boots and then at the sorrowful figure of Nella.

"I have never swallowed anybody," Farva Mop said.

"Which is just what a Strange One would say," Nella replied dreamily. "I just wanted to make sure you knew that I cannot be swallowed; I have never been swallowed, not once," Nella said; "ask anyone."

The two of them watched each other.

"Are you looking for cracks?" Farva Mop asked, thinking this was a reasonable question.

Nella's face became perfectly still with thought.

"Cracks in what?" Nella finally asked.

"Cracks in the house," said Farva Mop.

"No," Nella said, her face seeming uncaring. "The little maids look for cracks; I am looking for wicks."

"Wicks?" asked Farva Mop.

"Wicks; candles," Nella said. "We have run out of wicks."

"Oh," Farva Mop said.

Nella gazed down.

"But it was you that stole them, of course; that is the very least that a Strange One would do," Nella said who then looked beyond Farva Mop as if the matter was settled.

So Farva Mop turned away and raised her cellar-lamp and shone it into the alcoves at the foot of the steps.

"What are you doing?" Nella asked in her saddest way.

"I'm looking for plants," Farva Mop answered.

Then not hearing a reply Farva Mop looked up and saw Nella was gazing down and her eyes were nearly shining with dreaminess.

"There is only one and it should not be here," Nella said, "and there is no telling where it has come from."

Then Nella leant forward until she seemed perilously close to falling and then pointed towards a dark corner below away to Farva Mop's right.

"It is there," Nella said, "though I would not go near it if I were you."

Farva Mop swung her cellar lamp around and it showed that all to her right a lake of drip-water had formed. There was just one little path next to the wall where she could go that led to a corner arch that her lamp-light could not reach.

Then preparing herself Farva Mop made her way along the path and brought the cellar-lamp forward and shone it straight ahead.

There was indeed a sort of a plant that had climbed up some spiralling steps that the corner gave way to. The plant had curling stems but instead of leaves it had large vinegar-coloured bubbles. The bubbles increased in size as Farva Mop stepped closer, then reduced when, in her caution, she stepped back.

Then as Farva Mop stepped closer again the nearest bubble expanded until it slowly burst.

Then a most awful nose-bending and tear-spilling smell rose up that caused Farva Mop to stagger backwards and nearly pass out.

She hurried back along the path, gasping as she went. Then being quite overwhelmed by the smell, and even by the memory of it, Farva Mop returned to the foot of the steps much less inclined to look for plants than when she had set off.

Then Nella with her gaze so perfectly still came to look down upon her.

"It is growing in the marble stacks," said Nella dreamily, "which is why it is no use going down there without Inkle who knows a good corner from a bad one."

For Farva Mop there was nothing else to do than lean against the cellar wall and to lift the cellar lamp about her face to get light and life back into herself. The smell had been so awful that it had stopped her enthusiasm for anything.

Meanwhile Nella had something to say.

"If I was educated I might know the name of it," Nella said, "or whether it is edible or not, or why the guests say it does not exist when it plainly does."

Farva Mop stretched open her eyes a few times after the smell but was still unable to speak. Then, suddenly, and from the arch to that other cellar it was a boy that spoke.

""Nella – why am I hunting for w-wicks?" he asked."Why is my t-time always y-your time?" the voice continued. "Do you know you know how long I s-spend looking for things that you want? And do you know s-something – I am actually a c-cellar-man – oh yes I am."

Then the hidden voice adopted a dreamy voice that was meant to sound like Nella.

"- Oh Olris I had f-forgotten, I am sorry; I will not have you l-looking for wicks ever again!"

Farva Mop took a few careful steps back and sneaked a look through the arch into the left hand cellar where she saw a young man there but who did not at first see her.

The boy was tall and thin and dressed in thick grey bag-clothes, which comprised of a many-hooded cloak that should keep him warm in such a place as this. His trousers were many layered too and his boots were the same as those that Nella wore. More unusual than these was the young man's hair that was green whilst his chin showed tufts of green whiskers growing from it. His skin and his eyes were the palest green too, which for Farva Mop seemed to be the most extraordinary thing of all.

Olris was was looking at shelves and was scratching at his head and then afterwards placed his hands on his hips. Then he raised a green eyebrow and next glanced over at Farva Mop and quite suddenly jumped back, his pale green eyes blinking at her.

"N-Nella, of course you know there is a g-guest down here." Then hearing no reply he frowned at Farva Mop. "One of us - is in the wrong p-place."

Then seeing that Farva Mop was not leaving, Olris casually leant upon a nearby barrel.

"M-maybe - I am in the wrong place," Olris then began to stroll about, "why that is t-true; what am I doing in m-my cellar?"

Then Nella, who had said nothing thus far, made a sad little speech.

"One day, Olris, a Strange One just like this one is going to put you in a big bottle and give you nothing but your own beard to eat. But it is lucky that I have in my pocket a poem which if I read it out would remove you from any bottle so long as you find me some wicks."

"I am – h-happy now!" Olris sang out, who had begun searching the shelves again. "My t-time in a bottle will be short knowing you w-will unbottle me."

At this Nella sighed.

"Olris, you know nothing about Strange Ones."

"Oh yes I d-do," replied Olris who remained busy, "and do you know what: it was y-you that taught me."

"Olris, I speak only the truth," said Nella.

There came a long sigh from that other cellar.

"Nella? I d-do not care."

Next Farva Mop saw Nella gaze sadly down at her from her high place.

"The guests do not have wicks on their boats. There are no wicks in The Shading Rooms or in The Sunning Room. There are no wicks in The Maid's House in the forest and no wicks in the kitchens and even Miss Naws' wicks have been taken from her. All that remains is for Olris and I to find the wicks and we shall be honoured forever by this house and have statues of ourselves placed beside the giants. But we have not found a wick, have we Olris?" said Nella who waited for a reply, though none came.

Then Nella gazed upon Farva Mop in her sorrowful and dreamy manner.

"Unfortunately we have only historians to help us, who know only where the wicks were yesterday."

A groan came from that other cellar.

"Nella? Are you g-going to help me look for wicks or n-not?" Olris cried out.

Nella gazed back down at nothing and no one.

"The hand of the clock has written that it is no longer the time to look for wicks," she said.

Then she studied Farva Mop closely and finally addressed her.

"Inkle and I and Olris and the little maids shall meet you in the stair-hall at Twelve Kettles when we shall all go looking for ghosts," she said.

Then Nella gave an expression of utter sorrow.

"Let us hope they have the time to speak to us and they are not educated."

Then, after this she clambered to her feet in that high place and then Nella was gone.

Chapter 9.

Old Times.

When Farva Mop strolled back through the cellar and towards the guests' quay she was beginning to understand that things might have changed for her. Even under the grey stars she felt an increasing urge to run and to jump.

She had companions at last.

Although was no longer a guest in a regular way, this seemed not so bad a thing. She had fallen down through the ranks into the company of maids and cellar-boys but she did not mind this one bit.

She began to feel happy and more than this she began to feel like she ought to run. She ran along between the cellar puddles and she hurried halfway up the ramp to the marble steps that should return her to her regular life. She set the cellar-lamp back on its hook before climbing the rest of the way and then ascended the rest of the way to boats and the crown-lamps and such things that she knew.

When she arrived in the entrance hall she gave Mr Grinsnick the same stony look he gave her. Then as quick as she could she marched across the creaking floor and up the noisy stairs.

She braced herself for further trouble from those other guests but found when she arrived that they were no longer being unpleasant to her but instead were being unpleasant to each other.

More guests had squeezed into an already packed and busy hall, which made it a wobbling wall of bellies and elbows. Farva Mop was simply appalled at their battles, but when a gap appeared and Farva Mop dived into the throng much the same

Her progress was slow where those mouths babbled in their horrendous way. Dreadful was the desperate turning of pages and the clashing of languages, whilst adding to these were the noises of the many sorts of lamps clashing together. Their brighter light made the noise louder whilst amongst the lamps were the books being snatched then snatched back. It was as if the crowd should turn riotous at any moment and in their anger might tear the books completely apart.

Farva Mop tried to wriggle through them towards the middle of the room whenever the crowd surged towards the alcoves and left the central space for her. But each time that crowd returned and trapped Farva Mop or sent her back.

With her hood drawn over and tied close Farva Mop forced her way but just as strongly the heaving crowd resisted. Those desperate eyes glared at any available page whilst the bellowing screaming mouths tried to pass a sentence or two to some other who should write it down. The biscuits were let go of, the teacups spilled and the cup and kettle clock dispensed the time again and again while Farva Mop rather sent in circles.

On she struggled and pushed and shoved and while the lamps clanged about her and the tea, long cold, was poured over her, and while showers of cake crumbs followed.

That clock had struck three more quarter-kettles when she finally reached the stair-hall's doors. Then back she was sent by more guests arriving through it.

After three more attempts she managed to open and then dive through the leftward of those doors and land unhappily on the floorboards that boomed and creaked.

Dispirited and dishevelled and dripping with tea and coated with cake crumbs she made her way to The Sunning Room doors that were partly open.

The Sunning Room was perfectly quiet but where the tables were ransacked. About the floor broken cups and saucers had been scattered while foods that the cook had so painstakingly prepared had been trodden underfoot. No table-cloth was without inky notes scribbled over it and about the great hearth were piles of scrunched papers that had been thrown there after their owners had rejected them.

Then she saw a single waitress sitting away to the far left corner and at the table Farva Mop knew so well. Mrs Lasanti was seated there too and was nodding and listening while the waitress talked. Then the waitress glanced over and Mrs Lasanti glanced too and then Farva Mop was motioned to come.

114

Farva Mop then made her way between the spillages and spoiled foods and her anger welled up and her face became fearsome as she stamped along. She bore such an expression of defeat that the waitress quickly left.

Mrs Lasanti was seated in her usual place and so Farva Mop took the seat that was opposite her, which was where Mr Unessia had been sitting the evening before. From her place Farva Mop could see tables in the great room being quietly cleared and she came to watch those weary waitresses too who were leaning upon the trolleys they pushed along or else wandering and staggering.

Beside their table the waitress had left a trolley of teapots and also the tablecloth was a clean one and while a fresh cup and saucer was before each of them.

With her usual grace Mrs Lasanti poured tea for Farva Mop and then for herself. Then she passed the remaining plate from the trolley to Farva Mop's place, which was a plain long-scone with a sugar bean on the top.

After this Farva Mop ate in bitter silence.

Mrs Lasanti however smiled and talked, seemingly to herself, about candles and how none could be found.

"All the candles are missing, it seems," Mrs Lasanti said without seeming to care, "even Mr Grinsnick's were not there this morning. Not that Mr Grinsnick cares about candles, he prefers lamps; it is Miss Naws who prefers flames and not crystal to welcome the guests."

She then angled her head.

"I do not care so much, the entrance hall remains dark with either."

Then ignoring Farva Mop's furious face Mrs Lasanti took a silver teaspoon from her pocket.

"The guests are very fond of candles because they turn the flames green and they can talk to each other at a distance and thereby talk to each other all night."

She then fetched a teapot over and stirred it with that silvery spoon , which caused the tea to freshen and to become very hot.

"But with the candles gone those that read and those that write have had a whole night without talking."

Farva Mop gave no reply.

Mrs Lasanti sighed.

"More candles or fewer candles makes no difference to me; I grew up in the heaven above this one where its subject is fine lamp making, so it always seems dark to me."

Farva Mop looked up at this but Mrs Lasanti waved a hand.

"But that was a whole heaven ago and a long story," said Mrs Lasanti, "and not what anyone would want to be hearing about," and then she poured herself some nut and berry tea that had quite a perfume to it.

"Please," said Farva Mop suddenly, "please tell me."

Then after Mrs Lasanti had placed bowls of bright sugars between them both, then she began.

"There was an old house my uncle would visit sometimes," said Mrs Lasanti who then paused, "now my uncle he was the oddest little man, but that is beside the tale."

Mrs Lasanti sipped her tea.

"My uncle told my parents that I was more skillful with the dark than with the light and that I would be better falling with a house than helping our family with 'learning and upping' as they called it."

Then Mrs Lasanti smiled and leant forward.

"You see, it has always been true that falling is so much better than rising if you can learn how to do it."

Then Farva Mop watched Mrs Lasanti look above them to the black-iron chandelier that was without its candles.

"Falling is all about patching and repairing and making do," Mrs Lasanti said.

"Then my uncle said he knew just the right house which had reached its time and was ready to fall. My uncle said also that if I was unhappy or grew tired of it then I must light the emergency-candle he had given me and he would come straight away in his boat and take me home. My uncle told me the house was something of a lonely one, being always, in any heaven, a thousand stars from another house, and that house was this one."

Mrs Lasanti set her teacup down and looked about.

116

"Well I thought it was a haunted old place and I was not keen on it at first. Other young ones had arrived to train before the fall, so as to eventually serve here, and as we knew from our grandparents the heaven below was a heaven for Historians."

She smiled briefly.

"There was Mr Flast, who was just plain Kordiv Flast then, and a boy named Ioz Pordi, who is the head cook now. Lastly there was a boy that the book adored so much and was straight away apprenticed to it – well you can guess who that was."

Then Mrs Lasanti turned and gazed behind her at The Sunning Room where the waiters and waitresses were resetting it.

"Being a maid I stayed in The Maid's Garden and in the house that is hidden there. You would like it I think." Mrs Lasanti said, then she looked towards the window.

"These days I am not a maid and not allowed to visit it, but I know they still go on their midnight journeys, they certainly still do that."

"Midnight journeys?" said Farva Mop who leant forward so quickly that she nearly overturned her teacup and Mrs Lasanti was just in time to save it.

Mrs Lasanti smiled.

"I should have thought you would know all about journeys," Mrs Lasanti said hurriedly, who was setting things right.

Farva Mop looked away to her left and towards the window where there was very little to see.

"I do not remember where I was," Farva Mop said softly whilst studying the view of the forest but where there was no sign of The Maid's House."

Mrs Lasanti sipped some tea and returned to her story.

"First of all the maids have old boats of their own at their garden quay," Mrs Lasanti said, "and they can invite whom they like from the waiters and porters and laundry-boys and kitchen-boys and cellar-boys and the like.

"The Maids' Boats are the oldest of the ancient boats here, older even than Miss Naws' own boat and older by far than any of the guests'.

"As for the midnight journeys," she continued, "well they can only leave when all their work is done, when the last cup is stacked and the last sheet is washed. Then the boats can set off when the kettle-clock strikes 'All Kettles,' which is the beginning of the proper night.

Mrs Lasanti smiled.

"Well of course they all come back from where ever they have been, well mostly," she said, "there are some that find a boat of their own and never come back."

Farva Mop set her elbows on the table-top in a most urgent way.

"I thought they were all trapped here," Farva Mop said who was frowning.

Mrs Lasanti chuckled.

"No one is trapped here," she said, "whatever made you think that?"

"Because," Farva Mop stumbled, "because the waitresses look so miserable."

Mrs Lasanti sat back.

"The waitresses are not miserable they are exhausted, they are never in their beds."

"Oh," Farva Mop said, who understood now. "Then where do they all go?" she asked.

Mrs Lasanti shook her head wearily.

"However should I know. They might be down in the deep or up the highest lights or somewhere in between.

Then Mrs Lasanti then shrugged her shoulders.

"As for our own own adventures, well we would borrow books from The Shading Rooms to find great palaces," she said, "but the buildings had changed their names or else they were by then dark ruins in the deep and were not happy to be visited."

Mrs Lasanti sighed.

"It is how a house ruins faster, when it loses all memory of us."

She raised an eyebrow a little.

"Thankfully our voyages were not always so sad. Most times we would acquire a name of a place from a guest and then off we would go – often upwards, for many guests were returning to the house as my daughter has done."

Mrs Lasanti frowned and then shook her head.

"But the higher heavens never made sense to us, and the lower ones are even darker than this one. They made me think that I should return to my own heaven and to my family and help them solve up at lamps."

Then Mrs Lasanti wrinkled her nose.

"But really I could never do that. There are ten thousand heavens if we have rightly counted them, each one being wider than anyone knows. How could anyone be truly happy if they lived in all of them?"

Then as Farva Mop pondered this she watched Mrs Lasanti gave her teacup a good stir with that same spoon and again the tea became perfumed and hot.

"What is that?" asked Farva Mop.

Mrs Lasanti popped the spoon back into her pocket and gave the pocket a quick pat.

"Something I brought back from a very high place when I was a maid" she said.

Then Mrs Lasanti sat back.

"They say there is many a spoon that is frightened of the mouth," she said, "and it requires a great spoon-maker to balance a spoon so that the food tastes forwards."

Farva Mop burst out laughing.

However Mrs Lasanti remained unmoved and serious until finally she pointed a finger at Farva Mop.

"You see how complicated the highest heaven is; you cannot understand even one small spoon from it."

Farva Mop smiled broadly and then she sat back.

"This house is so unusual," Farva Mop said.

Mrs Lasanti set her fingers together.

"I shall tell you something that is odd. It is odd that Seri-Len should make the giants all white when Seri-Len's skin was not white but black."

Farva Mop made a little face of puzzlement but Mrs Lasanti glanced away.

119

"Just as you should come to puzzle us when your skin is lilac," Mrs Lasanti said.

Then as Farva Mop watched it seemed that Mrs Lasanti was tiring. She fussed around the trolley, straightening saucers until she could no longer smile as much.

"I was just like Nella as a maid," Mrs Lasanti said, "and Miss Naws was a little younger in those times. Mrs Grell, who was The House Lady then, would send poor Mr Grell up and down secret stairs all day to search for me. Mrs Grell said I would never amount to anything because I was such a forest girl or else lost in the stacks. Mrs Grell told Miss Naws that I pulled faces at the historians behind their backs, which is true: I did."

Farva Mop sighed and then her mood changed.

She put her elbows on the tabletop and rested her chin in the palms of her hands.

"You have lived such a long time here, Mrs Lasanti," Farva Mop said as her scowl returned, "with *them*."

Mrs Lasanti laughed.

"Oh dear, they have upset you."

Farva Mop made a pained expression at Mrs Lasanti who in turn ignored it.

"They were never like this when History was slower," she said. "It is the falling of the house, you see, that has hurried them – hurried them to take their last chance – their last chance at solving at History here."

Mrs Lasanti sipped at her tea.

"It used to take them all day to do the smallest thing. You would pass them after breakfast and by supper they had hardly moved. It is why Nella called these rooms 'The Slowing Rooms' and 'The Dying Rooms'.

Then as Mrs Lasanti was returning the teapots to the trolley she caught sight of Inkle at the Sunning Room door.

"There is Inkle who is so very well behaved," Mrs Lasanti said.

Then after this Mrs Lasanti came to her bad mood again.

"As for Nella, I never know where Nella is, I never know if she is doing what she is supposed to be doing. The last news I had was that she was looking for wicks."

"Nella is looking for ghosts," Farva Mop said confidently before looking towards Inkle who was beckoning her to come.

Mrs Lasanti then tidied the cups and saucers away and was shaking her head.

"As if we will ever be short of ghosts."

Chapter 10

Friends of the Dark.

"You will need a cellar-lamp because it will be dark," Inkle told Farva Mop when the two of them met in the stair-hall where that panel door under the stairs was open.

Inkle handed Farva Mop a lamp of the kind that Farva Mop had used in the cellars before.

"The others are searching for ghosts," she said. "They will be ahead of us now," and her grey eyes revealed nothing but a calm assurance.

Then Inkle took out a ring of keys much like Mrs Lasanti had and after they had both descended a few steps then Inkle locked the panel door behind them.

"We will go very deep, but cellar-lamps get brighter in darkness," Inkle said.

Farva Mop then smiled at Inkle.

"What are we going to do if we find a ghost?" Farva Mop asked.

Inkle sucked on her teeth before answering in her direct and honest fashion.

"Nella says that we are going to ask it who you are."

Farva Mop did not feel entirely downhearted by this, because after all she was altogether sure who she was herself.

Then Inkle set off down the creaking panel-stair just as Farva Mop had done the evening before. The kitchens and the laundry passed as noisily and then as before the black-wood stair changed to steps of white marble. The light became sour and the white marble blocks smaller as once again she was led down into the silence of the stacks.

At a place where one of those narrow passages presented itself then Inkle set off along it while her grey lamp unfolded the darkness ahead of her. Then when Farva Mop followed she felt it was a keyhole she had entered and that each of them was some giant key.

Soon they came to a set of steps that went down more steeply than Farva Mop liked. Where the steps ended there was a junction for slot passages to left and right and Inkle went left. The passage went along for a long way and then all of a sudden Inkle stopped.

A slow murmur began that became a rumbling that became a shaking that brought marble dust pouring through the many gaps. Then just as quickly the shaking stopped.

After a period of waiting Inkle glanced back.

"The house will not fall yet," Inkle said in her rather droning way, which caused Farva Mop to wonder what the proper fall would be like. Then Inkle walked on without further comment, with Farva Mop hurrying after her.

When they came to another junction Inkle continued straight ahead until the passage began to widen as a long narrow chamber with white marble slab benches and deep alcoves to either side. There was not much time to consider these because Inkle marched on and the passage narrowed again. Then more of those chambers appeared as the steps took them deeper until Inkle and Farva Mop came to rest in one of them.

Farva Mop sat down and peered about while Inkle said nothing at all.

Then finally Farva Mop spoke softly about anything at all for something to do.

"I wonder how many maids have ever come down here," she whispered.

Inkle's steady grey eyes stared back at Farva Mop's.

"Mr Grinsnick says there have been thousands and thousands of maids."

Then Inkle pointed to one of the deep alcoves.

"No one knows what those were used for. Father says some contain old sandwiches left behind by the ancient ones. Then some historians made lists of the sandwiches they ate, but others say it was not those sandwiches they ate because they did not eat them. Mr Grinsnick says that not every cook has been a good one and Nella says you can always judge a sandwich by how far away it is."

Farva Mop puzzled about this but before she could think of an answer Inkle had set off again and Farva Mop obediently followed her.

This way and that they went until the passage widened and then widened more until a great arch rose in the stacks that were like cliffs, whilst beyond them the surface of an immense and flat marble block extended for a great distance.

Thousands of marble fragments had spilled out widely upon that smooth surface, while on the tops of the cliffs to right and left were the outstretched branches of the black trees that seemed still forever in grey starlight.

Close to the arch many large stray slabs had become tables for cellar-lamps and whilst others had become seats for those she knew.

From left to right the group was made up of the three little maids in a row who seemed excited to be included, then to the right of them was Olris, who appeared less excited, then finally there was Nella who was standing on that table slab with the many tilted cellar lamps shining up at her.

When Inkle and Farva Mop approached then Nella gazed down at them in her dreamy blue way.

"The shaking has left no words in my mouth except the right ones," Nella proclaimed to those that were seated and listening.

"And these are the words I give to you now, which I am happy to be rid of - and I hope you make more sense of them than I did."

Nella then gazed up at the sky.

"We are the beans of a better bean-tree that was a better bean before it," she said dreamily before raising a forefinger, "though to measure what has bean is to see what has been and the tree cannot be what it's been."

Olris scratched his green hair around.

"Nella? I am not sure about the b-beans; you will have to t-teach me History another way, I have barrels and b-barrels of beans."

Nella raised her gaze and looked sorrowfully away.

"Olris, my words are already on the page if you could only read them."

Meanwhile Farva Mop saw the little maids had recognized her, for they stared and blinked their little eyes and pointed.

Nella then folded her arms whilst her blue cloak and blue hair and her blue eyes seemed nearly to shine.

"I could write the word bean on a bean and the word barrel on a barrel," Nella said sadly, "but there are not enough words in all of the heavens to explain either of us."

This caused Olris to put his hands deep into his sack-cloth pockets.

"It is n-not right, Nella," he said with a frown, "you are learning to read f-faster than the rest of us and yet you are the one making the s-slowest sense."

In the meantime Farva Mop noticed that Inkle was looking back towards the arch and she raised a hand at all of them. Then as Inkle stepped carefully back towards the cave then those others came and gathered about her.

Inkle sucked on her teeth before addressing them.

"It could be a ghost," said Inkle, "or it could be the plant; one is easier to find than the other."

Then Inkle made her way into the passage from which she and Farva Mop had emerged and she shone her lamp into the gloom while the others formed a line behind her.

First behind Inkle was Nella and who had fallen into one of her dreams, then next in line were the three little maids and after these was Olris and finally there was Farva Mop.

Olris glanced quickly behind at Farva Mop before shining his cellar lamp forward and then calling out.

"Will I smell anything back here if you f-find that plant?"

There was the sound of the sucking of teeth before Inkle answered.

"You won't not miss any of it," Inkle said calmly before offering some further advice.

"The plant mainly bursts at Father," Inkle said, "it is always bursting at him; it only bursts at people it likes."

Everyone relaxed except Farva Mop.

After this Inkle led them into the passage where after the starlight was gone her cellar-lamp shone brighter.

For a long time then the slot-shaped passageways led this way and that through the stacks. Sometimes Inkle stopped and listened and then after no word came from her then she moved on. Up and down the marble steps they went with Inkle leading the way until they reached one of those alcoved chambers and where Inkle indicated there was a slab seat for each one of them.

Nella and the three little maids sat to one side of the chamber and Olris and Farva Mop sat to the other. Inkle had walked further to Farva Mop's right where the passage had begun to narrow and where Inkle pressed her ear to the stacked white marble wall.

So began a long wait that was prolonged by Inkle shaking her head when anybody spoke.

The silence became fathomless and Farva Mop came to stare at the slot passageways to either end of the chamber where there was only darkness.

Then after what seemed a whole kettle of time there came from the tunnel where Inkle was waiting a pale light.

A ragged grey lamplight stole upon the chamber just as behind it a pale figure of a woman came silently and who was no better than grey light herself.

The ghost's long arms reached out, so as to measure the walls beside it, while the unhappy ghost seemed to pour from one lamp light to the next.

As Farva Mop watched the ghost turned pale her grey eyes towards her so that Farva Mop had to look away. Then the ghost stood a very long time before Olris (whose eyes by this time were larger than the ghost's).

Then the ghost spoke.

"*Widdlidib?*" the ghost whispered.

Farva Mop watched as Olris pressed himself back against the slab wall and if there had been an alcove behind him then he would surely have climbed into it.

Then as Farva watched the ghost drew back and showed its lonely face to all of them and then went on its way and was received by the darkness at the other end of the chamber where its light reduced and then vanished.

"Inkle?" Olris said, who had a most unusual expression on his face, "Widdlidib m-means…what?"

"Yes it does," said Inkle before turning to the others and leaving Olris baffled.

Inkle addressed them all.

"They will answer only two questions; we have one question left."

Olris frowned.

"We have n-not asked the first question yet."

Inkle looked calmly at Olris.

"That is because you did not ask it."

Olris shrugged his shoulders and stared about.

"How was I to know I was supposed to ask a question, the ghost only said "*What*?"

Then Olris glanced at the little maids who seemed as frightened as people possibly could be and then at Nella who had not noticed the ghost.

Olris grumbled to himself and then while he was muttering another ghost came and said widdlidib to Inkle and then Inkle replied with a question and then she the ghost began talking.

Soon Inkle and the ghost were leant against the slab wall and seemed rather cheery as they chatted with one another.

"Not that I ever complain," said the ghost, "you know me, Inkle, I never complain," was a snippet that Farva Mop overheard.

By this time Olris had leaned forward to listen too.

"Why d-do they say widdlidib when they can talk?"

Farva Mop shrugged her shoulders, for she had not expected that the ghosts would be so civilised. Indeed when Inkle and the ghost said goodbye to each other the ghost was laughing.

When the ghost had continued on its way then Inkle sucked on her teeth and thought deeply before turning towards Farva Mop.

"The ghost says you are strange," said Inkle, "but you are not the strangest. They say there is someone else in the house, someone who moves in the passages in the walls."

Farva Mop stared at Inkle and then at the little maids and then at Olris who were all waiting for her to explain this, but Farva Mop found she could not. Then in the smallest way she whispered.

"I do not remember him," she said, "except that he is my navigator."

The silence continued.

Olris and the Little Maids were staring at her until Inkle raised her cellar-lamp.

"We should go back now."

Slowly the little party lined up behind Inkle and they set off again.

No one spoke of what the ghost had said and indeed no one spoke at all. It was an uncomfortable walk for Farva Mop in those dark places and it was some time before the slot-passages became a little brighter and they emerged on some white marble steps whereupon Inkle set off down them.

Then Farva Mop soon detected the smell of biscuits and tea and when the scent was stronger they came upon The Silent Room with its crystal floor and where Mrs Lasanti was dozing in an armchair with many cushions about her.

Inkle woke Mrs Lasanti, who rubbed at her eyes before getting up.

"Inkle, I was wondering whether you had lost your way," Mrs Lasanti said sleepily and who rose from her seat and inspected them.

Inkle made a little curtsy.

"We were talking to ghosts," Inkle said.

Mrs Lasanti waved a hand in front of Nella's face but who seemed not to see it.

"Perhaps they were not very interesting ghosts," Mrs Lasanti said, who was puzzling about Nella, before looking at Olris and the little maids but who returned the uncomfortable of glances.

"Well you four should wait here," Mrs Lasanti said to Olris and Nella and the little maids, "and you can have as many biscuits as you like," which immediately cheered them up.

Mrs Lasanti then turned to Farva Mop and she led her quickly away and back up the marble steps.

"Guests should stay with guests," she whispered, "and not among those that serve," while glancing at Farva Mop's bewildered face.

Then Farva Mop was led back up the steps until they were above the stacks. The little black-wood stair returned and then there was the panel door that Mrs Lsanti unlocked.

"Thankfully there will be dinner soon," said Mrs Lasanti busily.

Then Mrs Lasanti took the cellar-lamp that Farva Mop was carrying.

"And I shall accompany you to dinner and make sure you eat," Mrs Lasanti said.

Farva Mop was then escorted at a pace but at The Sunning Room doors that wwe closed she stopped.

"Nella is a better reader with every book," Mrs Lasanti said, "and will be a story writer soon when the house falls and is finished with History."

Farva Mop shrugged her shoulders.

"Sometimes when I read." said Farva Mop, "the words run about the page," she said.

Mrs Lasanti came to look at her oddly.

"Whyever would the words do that?" she asked.

"I do not know," Farva Mop said.

Then Mrs Lasanti took hold of the handles of the Sunning Room's doors and she pushed and they were met with the sound of the guests shouting and rattling their teacup and wrestling books from each other and reaching from their places and shoving and pushing, which Farva Mop knew only too well.

Chapter 11.

The Returning Heart.

When Farva Mop and Mrs Lasanti arrived in The Sunning Room the tables were crowded with guests and lamps and the guests there talking so much that they did not have an opportunity to put food in their mouths. The noise, as usual, was ear-shaking.

Farva Mop thought that after having spent so long in the stacks that the noise might be easier but instead the noise was worse. The languages pounded upon her ears and forced her to angle her head all ways to escape it. However in spite of her trouble she was tugged along by Mrs Lasanti and towards that same table in the left corner as when Farva Mop had first arrived.

"Miss Mop has been found safe and well," Mrs Lasanti said to Mr and Mrs Kurigna, with only Mrs Kurigna caring overmuch. Mr Unessia was rather quiet, as if Mr Kurigna had bored him, while Carua was as peaceful and as composed as ever.

Farva Mop and Mrs Lasanti sat in their usual places and Mrs Lasanti addressed the others.

"I can report that Mr Grinsnick has received the results of the search. There are no candles in this house."

Mr Kurigna was most annoyed on hearing this news.

"This is most inconvenient," he said. "I had hoped to contact my college, which would have required all the candles in our rooms and more besides. I am unhappy to hear that the house has been entirely emptied of them."

Then Mr Kurigna sent Mrs Lasanti a steely glare.

"Can you explain how this could have happened?"

Mrs Lasanti matched Mr Kurigna's glare with a puzzled expression.

"You may ask, Mr Kurigna, but I cannot tell you, because I do not know," Mrs Lasanti said.

Mrs Kurigna, who seemed eager to calm her husband, nodded towards the windows.

"No doubt the falling house has something to do with it," she said. "The house was shaken last night and also today. I would say the candles have exploded, that is what I think, though I am not at all an expert on fallings and such."

Mrs Lasanti then indicated towards the window.

"Our lamps-man, Mr Flast, and his helpers are fetching extra lamps from the cellars and cupboards and other such places. There shall be light enough I am sure."

Farva Mop turned briefly to watch that great crowd of guests who were making loud gulping and splattering noises as they tried to talk and eat at the same time. In the end she could no longer bear to look at them and instead gazed out of the window at the tangled forest and then at the reflection of their part of the room that was lit by an assortment of table-lamps. High up in the reflection were the dark tapestries that could not be properly seen and while beneath them the black-iron chandelier with its candles removed was there, and making it sway was Esferini who was sleeping.

Chapter 12.

The Many Ways.

Farva Mop's hands fell suddenly by her sides as she watched Esferini swing back and forth, where the ghost's black dress and hair turned to trails of where the lamplight caught her.

Then Farva Mop turned back from the window and instead looked up, but where the last traces of Esferini were vanishing.

When Farva Mop returned her attention to her companions she found everyone else at the table was looking up too.

Mr Kurigna flung his napkin down.

"Whatever is wrong with the girl?" he asked loudly so as to be heard above the screaming conversations of the room.

Then he fixed Farva Mop with a sharp glance.

"You have a most curious ability to lose yourself, Miss Mop," said Mr Kurigna with annoyance.

Then fortunately waiters came and set many jugs and glasses of cooling-waters here and there and while waitresses delivered bowls of brightening soup.

"Miss Mop has been too busy to eat," Mrs Lasanti said to Mrs Kurigna as a means to close the subject, "she is in need of dinner more than you know."

"She has been looking for plants," Mr Kurigna said with a sniff, "when there are none whatsoever."

Mrs Lasanti glanced at Carua.

"I am sure if truth be known it is her memory she is looking for," Mrs Lasanti said. "We hoped the house might help her find it."

Mrs Kurigna leant forward and to her side to look more closely at Farva Mop.

"Her memory, you say." Mrs Kurigna said with sudden concern, "how unfortunate."

Mrs Lasanti continued.

"Miss Mop has breathed in too much shadow," Mrs Lasanti said factually.

132

Mr Kurigna began on his soup.

"Then it seems there is History in the child after all," he said coldly and then turned to raise some matter with Mr Unessia who in his turn welcomed any attention whatsoever.

Mrs Lasasnti and Mrs Kurigna began on their soup too and Mrs Kurigna began on a boring speech about about envelopes of different sizes, which left Farva Mop staring about in a forgetful way, which she was perhaps meant to.

After tasting the soup that was rather too solid for her liking Farva Mop listened instead to the awful noise from the other guests and in time looked idly at those tables where the waiters and waitresses were attending with their serving-trollies.

Then while she looked she saw in places there was Esferini's mist again. It was weaving between the guests and disguising itself as pipe-smoke or as steam from kettles. Then finding that some of the noisy guests noticed her staring she hurriedly turned back and tried harder with her soup.

At their table soup-biscuits were popular and Farva Mop saw Mrs Kurigna choose one but as Mrs Kurigna drew her hand back then Farva Mop saw there was the mist again turning about her sleeve, at which Farva Mop frowned.

"Esferini...," Farva Mop whispered in case the ghost might hear her, but it seemed the ghost did not.

Then next Farva Mop took to hiding behind her soup-spoon and watching the trails of mist before her. Then finally Farva Mop closed her eyes and refused to look at all, which in time caused Mr Kurigna to sigh very loudly and then his stern voice boomed out.

"Do you know, Miss Mop, you really are the -."

Farva Mop cringed and waited for the next word but, very oddly, that next word did not come.

Very carefully Farva opened her eyes and blinked at the table-lamps that lit the foods and then she looked towards Mr Kurigna but found that he and the rest of her party had gone.

Mrs Lasanti was no longer sitting in the seat beside her and even Maradsha and Koliana were no longer at their table of their own.

Then Farva Mop turned and looked out across The Sunning Room towards the crowds of guests but saw they had gone too, yet she knew for certain that the whole babbling lot of them had definitely been there before.

In that perfect silence Farva Mop turned back to examine the table and wondered if by closing her eyes she had fallen asleep. Yet against this assumption was the fact that the soup in her bowl was still steaming.

Then all at once there came a long and gurgling snore which caused Farva Mop to look up and found to her surprise that: there they all were.

Mr and Mrs Kurigna and Mrs Lasanti and Carua and Mr Unessia and the two children were stuck firmly to the ceiling by their shoulders. Their chins rested on their chests and their faces smiled contentedly just as from all of them came the loud snoring.

Then from those other guests a mass snoring began also and became quickly worse. Each new bellowing snore joined another in chorus and became unbearable to listen to.

In the appalling noise Farva Mop cringed and felt she had no other choice than to find Esferini and to have her reverse this.

With a leap she left her place and searched between The Sunning Room's abandoned tables and looking above at the chandeliers even lifting the tablecloth's trims and looking under them.

While the snores twisted their awful notes together she searched but wherever she looked there was no sign of the ghost and so Farva Mop searched further.

She left The Sunning Room for the stair-hall where she saw the doors to The Shading Rooms were open and saw guests stuck fast to the ceiling there also.

A very large lady was holding a teacup aslant that was sending drops down to a puddle of tea on the black-wood floor below, but apart from this and the sound of the cup and kettle clock that ticked, there was no movement of the ghost.

She searched all alcoves but found they contained only spilled books, squashed cakes and smashed cups and saucers. No shadow hid the ghost and she had to accept that Esferini was not hiding there.

Meanwhile the snores in The Shading Rooms and The Sunning Room seemed to rise and join and bellow together.

Escaping from the noise to the stair-hall she went up the black-wood stairs, where guests with lamps were were stuck to the beams above at places as if to light her way. ButEsferini was not amongst them.

Then feeling she must search further she ascended higher and on each landing she came to find the hoisted snorers and no other. One flight of stairs led to another until she reached her own corridor.

All was silent from one end of that corridor to the other except for the softest of snores from the hidden historians who were doubtless fixed to the ceilings in their rooms. in their rooms.

Then turning and surveying all else she came to see the barrel-locks and the chains about the continuing stair to the eighth floor had been detached. For the giant cageworks had been opened.

Chapter 13.
The Secret Past.

There was a silence there that must capture the slightest sound, then while she listened she heard a door close ever so softly. Then raising her key-lamp she rested a hand on the bars of black-iron and a little dust fell. Then taking hold of the black-iron handrail she went carefully up.

At a middle landing she saw the many panel-cupboards were open and contents had been set in lines from the largest to the smallest. Fire-pokers and buckets and perfume-bottles and pencils and lost buttons were arranged so. The stairs were nearly obstructed by these displays and after the turn of the stairs their peculiar arrangements continued until she had climbed the stairs to the very top where the eighth floor corridor was there before her.

Sending the beam of her key-lamp around she saw the expanse of a most beautiful carpet. The carpet was woven to a brilliant blue with embroidered gold stars like it should be a river of them. To both sides of the stairhead the great door-lamps that were dark while all doors in sight were swung inward.

The rooms opposite had become storage place for clocks and their many silver and black-iron faces stared back so sternly as her lamplight flashed crossed them, The taller and heavier standing-clocks were twice as tall as she was and had wide-words carved into them. Then some had words carved narrowly, such as one that read:

The Counting Of Heavens Above The Cold Begun In The Two Thousand Eight Hundred And Ninetieth Heaven Down To Ruin. Set Working By L.D. Savarns, whose family had been custodians for the whole of that age. The house being 'The House of Savarns' in those times.

Here as before the many panel cupboards were open and common items had been removed and set in lines as before. Then passing from that room of clocks to another she came to a room that contained only hat-stands. Again the panel cupboards were open and and the items displayed in the next rooms that were filled with boot-racks. Then after rooms that contained only one type of thing she entered a room containing only chairs she came to sit in one of them and puzzle at everything.

Then while she was sat there with the key-lamp shining ahead she came to examine the patterns of the chair that faced her. Its patterns regular for their type but while some other pattern had seemed have been embroidered over them. Then next she knew the thread was not silk but instead a white starlight until she knew after considering the pattern quite intently that she was being studied in turn by a nearly invisible boy.

The boy was holding a nearly invisible lamp and while nearly invisible ropes were wound about his nearly invisible shoulders. His hair was starlight too, as were his boots that had little starry wings on them.

Then finally there were the boy's eyes, which were tiny stars, and these were now as still as moons as if he had been gathering his thoughts about her.

They watched each other for some time and then the boy's star-like eyes changed nearly to mist as if he was thinking. Then after this he looked away, as if he no longer considered her, and which prompted Farva Mop to speak.

"You were on my boat," Farva Mop said carefully and she saw him nod.

"And you are my navigator," she said next.

He nodded again

Farva Mop then made a face like she was not concerned about him either.

"Unfortunately I do not remember," she said.

Next it was the boy's turn to speak.

His eyes remained blurred, as if he was bored with speaking, though his voice was yet clear and somewhat friendly, but rather impatient.

"I am a sprite. I am a good sprite but I am not a great one," said the sprite.

Farva Mop thought for a moment.

"Then who am I?" she asked.

"You are an investigator," said the sprite rather sharply, "from the most ancient times, and so am I."

Then Farva Mop scratched at her head.

"Then what are we investigating?" she asked.

The sprite's eyes became even more cloudy.

"The answer to that question is not in this room," he said in his annoyed way, "it is in another."

Then the sprite raised that starry lamp that sent beams of starlight all around. Then next after his starry shoes whirred their starry wings and he floated from the chair as lightly as if light itself was carrying him.

He indicated with a wave of his hand that she should follow him.

Farva Mop accepted that she knew nothing about sprites. When she left her seat and followed this one it was because there was absolutely nothing else to do and she wanted to know everything about herself. She wanted to know if she had friends and if she had friends then where they lived. She wanted to know where she herself lived and where her family lived or, if she had been adopted by a family of sprites, then where they lived. She wanted to know what the ancient times were like and whether the heavens were the same or different. She wanted to know what things were definitely hers and what things were definitely somebody else's. She wanted to know how old she was by the reckoning of her own heaven and whether her boat had always been grey or whether it had once been another colour. She wanted to know where home was and how she could go back there.

Farva Mop followed the floating starry lamp along the corridor. After the stairhead they past rooms with their doors wide open that showed the same orderliness as before, they being a room of beds or wash-stands or finely carved mirrors. Then after those doors there were tightly closed doors, as if no one had stored anything in them. Then finally and at the very end at the very end the sprite came to settle amongst the embroidered stars of the carpet and he shone that starry lamp around. Then after this he crouched down low he pressed his starry ear to the floor as if listening and for a long time he was still and he was silent.

"Anyway," Farva Mop said at last, though not knowing whether the sprite was listening or not, "while you have been sneaking around I have been having a terrible time," and she waited to see if he would answer but the sprite did not.

Farva Mop shrugged her shoulders and continued.

"Everything I have done has been wrong," she said, "and everything I have said has been strange."

Then she aimed her key-lamp back towards the stairs but saw only darkness that seemed to thicken.

"And here is the strangest place of all," she said, "for animals of unknown kinds have been heard here."

Then Farva Mop lowered her gaze.

"And then of course there is poor Esferini," said Farva Mop. "Poor Esferini who was lost from a ship, and then of all the houses she might have sought help from it was this one," Farva Mop said despondently, "and was no doubt taken away by the animals and was eaten and there was nothing anyone here could do about it."

When the sprite had listened to the floor for as long as he deemed necessary he then floated over to the panelled wall and pressed his ear to that also. Then only when he had listened for some moments did he return to his place and sat down before Farva Mop.

"We are the only ones awake," the sprite said.

Farva Mop listened and indeed there was only the very distant sound of synchronised snoring from far below as if someone was gently sawing through the house.

Then next she watched the sprite get to his feet and then very lightly he began to pace backwards and forwards while making an important-sounding speech.

"At first like so many others I focussed my attention on the carpet," he said; "carpets have twins and twinned carpets can cast people from one place another, but in this case the carpet is both singular and true. "

He raised a starry finger.

"Yet it was necessary to know this for sure so I removed candles from empty rooms in order to examine it and to attempt to hear noises or voices from another place. However the light of those candles was not enough, and so Esferini fetched all of them."

The boy then pointed upwards and when Farva Mop looked there were thousands upon thousands of unlit candles packed closely together on the ceiling and aimed downward.

Then the boy clicked his fingers and the flames sprang downward as a great blaze of light that caused Farva Mop to cover her eyes.

After she had blinked many times and stared she found the corridor was lit as brightly as it might ever be.

The boy, being nearly invisible, was only faintly shown in the light.

"This was how I was able to disregard the carpet," he said.

Then with another click of his starry fingers the candle flames were put out and the corridor was plunged into dimness again.

Farva Mop rubbed at her eyes.

"So Esferini is helping you – I mean - us," Farva Mop said uncertainly, who felt a little behind the facts.

The sprite floated again and then landed very gently to sit before her.

"It was after leaving the matter of the carpet behind then I knew that we were dealing with Comoglins," he said.

Farva Mop crooked her lip to indicate that she did not know what a comoglin was, but the sprite was already setting himself ready to explain. Thereby there there began one of the oddest explanations of anything she might ever here anywhere.

Chapter 14.

Light and Darkness.

The sprite drew around in the dust on the carpet with a starry forefinger.

"All things must fall," the sprite explained, "boats and houses must become wrecks and ruins, and even the houses of the very wise must one day pass from them and many great treasures are lost," he said. "Houses and gardens of great beauty must sink heaven by heaven down where their windows become dark and their gardens become silent and abandoned. All things must fall," the sprite said, "into The Great Cold where the spelless dark destroys them."

Then turning a little the sprite came to make lines in the dust that was a grey layer on the carpet.

"As most of us know the deeper ruins are homes to monsters, which are most often very bad," the sprite said with a cautious tone, "but there are other creatures, stranger creatures, choosing never to be found, and the rarest of these are the Comoglins."

Then the sprite had drawn in the dust what seemed to be a door-handle, a set of hair-brushes and a rickety chair.

"In the final depths things can change into other things. This is how a door-handle can become a poker and a poker can become a chair," and then he pointed at those he had drawn and she saw how one object was being altered to resemble another.

"But these also must sink and leave no trace," he said, "but there are some objects that survive, because they change into men."

"Into men," Farva Mop said who was startled by this.

"Not men as we would know them," the sprite said, "men as those original objects might have known them, as a walking-stick might remember its owner's tread, or a hat might know its owner's thoughts. They cannot truly be men, for their first duty is to what they started off as. However these things can resemble men enough for the heavens to fasten upon them and to teach them as they do all others. In this way they rise and escape the deep, as men do," he said, "and they must arrive among us."

Farva Mop felt quite unnerved by the thought of comoglins and was relieved when the sprite turned his attention to other things.

"This eighth floor of this house is no longer used," he said, "it hides many secrets from the historians, who care more for what falls from above them that what might arrive from below."

The sprite then shone his starry lamp at some black-wood doors to Farva Mop's left.

The double doors were like all others here, including a great black-iron lamp that had long ago failed to light.

Then the sprite turned back.

"The history of these particular rooms is written in a wide language in The Book of Guests," the sprite said, "and according to that book in these rooms on the night that Esferini arrived in this house there was a guest named Ogral Grolle, an historian of nails and screws, who left in terror shortly after bedtime."

The sprite then rose to his feet and paced about and continued.

"Due to the rescue of Esferini no one remembered Mr Grolle."

Next the sprite indicated that Farva Mop should leave her place and approach those doors that were shut tight against them.

Then the sprite aimed his starry lamp at the black-iron handles and then nodded to Farva Mop, and who took hold of the handles and turned them and with the utmost care she pushed the doors open.

The Never-Ending Men.

They entered a study where a black-wood writing-desk was set below the deep sills of two shuttered and bolted windows. The desk's drawers had been removed and leant against its left side. There were small objects sheltered under these but the objects had been carelessly placed. To the right of the writing desk and in the right corner was a set of three rickety shelves that had a few books in them. A small and open black-wood trunk with wide languages written on it had been overturned in the centre of the floor where it had spilled some black-silk slippers, some old grey shirts, hats and other items across the black-wood floor.

The sprite shone his starry lamp about.

"After deciding about the carpet I searched all of the eighth floor cupboards and set things together, just as those that searched for Esferini put like with like in the rooms about the stairs half a heaven ago. They were seeking to find objects that might be entrapments, that might send a person away and that unusual guests might have brought in ages before. There are many such things here, many things that are more powerful than they should be. This floor had become a repository for them."

Farva Mop passed through the study whilst following the sprite and it was next the bedroom that received their light. A bed was draped in grey, much as her own was, and a wardrobe had its doors open but it was empty. The dressing-rooms and the extra bed-chambers and bathrooms were all as she expected, just as if Mr Grolle had not even entered them.

When they returned to the study she saw the sprite approach the desk and then he motioned that they should both sit on the dusty floor before it. Under the removed and slanted drawers was sat a party of dolls of various sizes, each having been served a pretence of tea in tiny cups from a lidless teapot. As Farva Mop looked then the dolls appeared to watch her with their jewelled eyes, while they in their turn seemed shambled in their baggy cloaks that seemed hurriedly made.

The sprite then continued with his report.

"I spent most of today in this room," the sprite said thoughtfully.

Farva Mop looked around at the few things.

"But there is nothing here," she remarked.

The sprite did not speak. Instead he picked up a pencil that lay on the floor before the desk and he pointed it around as he was speaking.

"These dolls belonged to a child of the house named Carua Lasanti who could slip through the bars on the stairs when she was very young. Here she met Esferini, long after the adults had given up looking for her, and then she and Esferini became friends."

Then the sprite sat back.

"Esferini is not a ghost," the sprite said, "she is a sorceress, although she is not a real one."

Farva Mop started at this.

"But Esferini is very much like a sorceress," Farva Mop declared, for she rather felt she cared for Esferini very much. Then she shrugged her shoulders, "Even though she sticks candles and people to ceilings."

Then as she watched the sprite raised the pencil and pointed it.

"Esferini is a character - from that book," he said.

The sprite had turned and was facing the corner and its three shelved bookcase where on its middle shelf there were some tall thin books. The volume the sprite was pointing at was shaken and darkened. It had a title printed down the spine in thick silver letters and the title read:

Stories For Any Age.

Farva Mop raised her lamp and went forward to take it out.

"You cannot touch it," the sprite said, causing Farva Mop to immediately draw back, after which the sprite was pointing that pencil again.

144

"A comoglin hides in that book," he said, "and since there was not room enough for both of them Esferini was forced to leave. Books are crowded places," he said.

Farva Mop smiled briefly at the sprite, who seemed not to care whether he made any sense or not.

Then the sprite continued even more confidently.

"I believe that the comoglin in Esferini's book was previously in *Nails and Screws of Uncertain Lengths*, which is there," and he pointed at a rather dreary looking book amongst others on the bottom shelf.

"That was Ogral Grolle's own book, because he marked his name in it. It was a book he brought from his boat but while it was here a comoglin entered it."

He paused.

"When Mr Grolle opened that book they met. The shock of meeting caused Mr Grolle to immediately exit the house. However the comoglin was much disturbed too, since they are shy creatures. The comoglin left Mr Grolle's book and entered that one," and he pointed to *Stories For Any Age*.

"Esferini's book," Farva Mop whispered.

"Exactly," the sprite said with much importance but which was quickly changed to one of impatience.

"It is a tale for children about a sorceress who lives above The Great Cold and who one suppertime warns the heavens of a sinking ship, but she is not once believed by the residents of the houses above her. Her own boat is very small one, and the stricken ship, called The Anriassa Serain, is very large. However Esferini is able to use her boat even so, and saves the passengers by sticking them to every part of it."

The sprite then appeared unsatisfied with the story.

"Then the extra passengers which she could not find a place for were stuck to each other in long chains. Esferini is good at fixing one thing to another," he said.

Then the sprite's starry eyes sharpened.

"The comoglin in that book is very interesting," he said, "I saw him when he could not see me. He is not as unreasonable as the others and I believe you might manage to talk him. "

145

"Alright," said Farva Mop, who could see no harm in reading a book.

The sprite then took *Stories For Any Age* from its place on the shelf and he set it ready before Farva Mop.

Then before matters could proceed he made a little speech.

"I have examined all of these books without being detected. I found another comoglin in *An Inventory Of Stinking, Unpleasant And Disagreeable Plants*," the sprite said.

He then folded his arms.

"You see now we are dealing with imposters, false-lights and jack-in-the-cupboards, but they are also, as I have said, the rarest of things and we must respect them for that."

Then next he came to speak in a grave manner.

"When you meet this comoglin it should afterwards move to another book on this floor, and not all of them are as safe as these, but that is the perilous risk we take."

Farva Mop peered at that middle shelf and began reading the titles out loud.

"A History Of Secret Stairs.

*

Jonja And The Dexicular Lamp.

*

Doorknobs In Heavens Seven Hundred Down To Six Hundred (Excluding The Six Hundred And Fifteenth).

*

Thumper-Snails And Other Noisy Midnight Beasts.

*

Who To Know And Who Not To Know In Sock-Making.

*

The lower and higher shelves contained books that were too peculiar to consider, such as *Nails and Screws of Uncertain Length,* which the sprite had already mentioned, and then *Invisible Hats and How to See Them.*

Then there were books on the history of small items, these being histories of breadcrumb dishes, thimbles, belt-buckles and other such things, which resembled those items that the sprite had removed from the panel -cupboards.

Then finally, when she was invited to by the sprite to do so, she picked up *Stories For Any Age* and set it lightly in her lap.

First there was a page of contents where five stories were listed:

Then turning to the first story she saw a large black and white printed picture on a thick white page. The lower half of the picture showed what must have been The Great Cold, with its grey ruins and wrecks, and in the upper half were many unhappy stars staring down. Then finally, and between these two, was shown Esferini's boat.

Beneath the picture and printed in an old fashioned style were some words that read:

"One day, when Esferini's boat was drifting above The Great Cold."

The boat was a rather shallow one that had a hut on the deck for a cabin and had a short mast for the stars. Esferini was shown standing on a box at the prow but as Farva Mop looked she saw it was not Esferini at all, not in the slightest, for instead there was a most extraordinary little man.

The man was shown to be short and plump and instead of trousers he was wearing two fingers of a woollen glove. His boots were thimbles packed with rags and for a shirt he had a silk pouch cut at the corners. His black bushy hair was gathered together and held above by a knot of string and aside from these he had a large black moustache that was like an upturned crescent.

The man's face seemed very proud, for he looked out across The Great Cold as if he owned it.

As Farva Mop watched then those tiny drawn eyes blinked and that chest swelled up like he was about to explode.

"GO AWAY!" the little man shouted so loudly that the book shook and a great boom of sound was sent about the room.

Farva Mop nearly let go of the book and only just managed to stop herself from leaping away.

Instead she cringed and sighed and then finally spoke in a gasping way.

"What – a noise!" gasped Farva Mop, "what a bad-tempered comoglin!"

"WHO IS A COMOGLIN?" the comoglin shouted so loudly that Farva Mop could see the comoglin's mouth wide open.

"Why, you are," Farva Mop said, who had turned her face away from the noise of his voice.

"THERE ARE NO SUCH THINGS AS COMOGLINS," the comoglin shouted back.

Then once again he pushed out his chest to shout.

"I DO NOT KNOW ANY, I HAVE NEVER KNOWN ANY, I DO NOT WANT TO KNOW ANY AND I HAVE NEVER BEEN ONE!" the comoglin said in his tremendous way.

The comoglin next walked unsteadily in his thimbles across the deck towards the cabin and he gave her an offended look as he opened the door.

"Wait!" Farva Mop called out, "I want you to help someone."

"I DO NOT HELP ANYONE!" the comoglin screamed back.

"But you do!" Farva Mop insisted, "in this story; you rescue the passengers of a ship."

The comoglin made an unpleasant face.

"THEY HAVE NOT WANTED TO BE RESCUED BY ME – NOT EVEN ONCE!" the comoglin bellowed.

"I am very sorry to hear that," said Farva Mop, knowing he was in a book where he was not wanted.

The comoglin then stared long and hard at her and then his manner changed.

He left the doorway of the cabin and shuffled about on the deck and finally he leaned forward and seemed ready to confide in her.

"I was much happier as a picture of a circular nail," he said calmly, "they are hard to use and hard to make. I was very complicated."

Farva Mop nodded, because to her a circular nail did seemed very complicated indeed.

"Why do you hide in a book?" she asked.

The comoglin puffed up his chest again and Farva Mop in turned her head.

"I AM NOT HIDING!" the comoglin shouted. "I AM A WORKING MAN," and he stood up straight and began to count on his fingers. "I HAVE BEEN EVERYTHING I HAVE. TABLES, TALL-BUCKETS, SHOE-LACES, DOUBLE AND TRIPLE PUDDLES!"

"But you must have been someone before you were in books," Farva Mop said, interrupting him.

"I do not remember where I came from," the comoglin said quietly.

At this Farva Mop dropped her shoulders.

"Neither do I," Farva Mop whispered.

The two of them watched each other then the comoglin walked unsteadily back towards the cabin door whereupon Farva Mop spoke again.

"Does this mean Esferini is coming back?" Farva Mop asked hurriedly.

"HOW WOULD I KNOW," the comoglin screamed, "SHE WENT OFF IN A LIFEBOAT TO WHO KNOWS WHERE," he said, "I JUST DO THE WORK!"

He then pulled the cabin door open wide and paused in the doorway before walking through it.

"STORYBOOKS!" the comoglin complained and then he was gone.

Then as Farva Mop watched she saw a little shape gradually appearing on the deck. It was a spin of smoke that became a girl, a girl with thin fingers and long trailing black hair who wore a black dress that curled too. The girl grew taller and then glanced about, like a brooding spectre of ink, then after this she peered out of the book at Farva Mop. Then a slender smile caught on that face –

those black and lightless eyes fixed on hers with a moment of recognition and then they were still.

Then outside in the corridor on the eighth floor thousands of candles fell. The noise seemed to come from the farthest end of the corridor and sweep past the stair-head and towards their rooms like a thundering wave.

Farva Mop let go of the book and pressed her hands over her ears whilst turning and saw the candles bouncing and breaking in their doorway behind them. Then just as quickly the noise stopped, save for those candles that were rolling from step to step down those black-wood stairs. The fall of candles had caused the dust on the carpet to be pounded it up and it lingered there after the falls had ended.

The sprite fluttered upwards as she got to her feet.

"Esferini's is a reversing spell," the sprite said. "All that was up shall come down and more besides," he said.

Then his eyes became those sharp little stars.

"I must find out where that comoglin has gone next," he said whilst shining his starry lamp around.

"Understand this," he said next. "Esferini stuck the house to this heaven but now without her spell it must fall," he said.

Then he pointed a starry forefinger at her.

"Go to your boat wearing the clothes that you arrived in, and leave a note for Carua to tell her that Esferini is safe," he said.

Then the sprite fluttered back to the books where he began to handle them carefully in spite of the commotion and became very still and studious. Then seeing her watching him he addressed her loudly.

"You must go!"

A House Falls.

Farva Mop ran out into the dust that nearly blinded her while slipping and skating on the fallen candles. Along the corridor she went in an unsteady fashion and then on reaching the stairhead she hurried down them while candles dropped and rolled beside her. At the middle landing she turned where candles had accumulated and then hurried down the next flight and through the open cageworks.

On the seventh floor she unlocked the door to her rooms and rushed in and in the bedroom she changed back into her ancient grey dress and silk-slippers. When she was ready she left her room and slammed the door shut and next went chasing and skipping down the flights of stairs.

With every skidding turn she came to see the figures of guests that were lowering, their lamps and their mouths opening.

Then when she reached the third floor landing she stopped.

A great thundering rumble began that brought dust falling from the beams above her. It was as if every timber in the house was shifting and creaking and every marble slab had slightly moved.

Then down the stairs she scampered again as a new panic coursed through her.

Down she went, floor by floor, where streams of dust twirled their way, until finally she came to the stair-hall where she landed heavily and slid to the opposing panelled wall and crashed into it. Then spinning around she ran into The Sunning Room and dodged between waiters' and waitresses that were slowly descending from the tapestries above.

The guests were lowering too and while their mouths were opening time and again as if attempting to speak. Chairs that had fallen over were resetting themselves while kettles sucked steam back into their spouts and books that had fallen from desperate hands jumped back up to them.

Farva Mop hurried back to her place at her table where those she knew were also floating down.

Mr Kurigna looked just as fierce, even in sleep, and that angry expression he had was filled with distaste as also his fierce eyes were nearly opening. He came down past the chandelier where he snored a last snore. as if commenting on it. Then when he was nearly in his seat Farva Mop snatched a pencil from one of his pockets and took a napkin from his place and after this leapt along to where Carua was arriving and then on the napkin she wrote in broad letters:

ESFERINI IS SAFE.

Then squeezing the napkin into Carua's hand she turned to make her escape, and then all at once she heard it.

One of the guests away towards the room's centre uttered a flapping, blowing snorting word and then another made some blubbering sound in reply.

At this Farva Mop sprinted as hard as she could towards the doors just as the guests with their eyes tight closed were regaining the use of their mouths. The trolleys that had moved were moving back and while jugs that had spilled were straightening themselves and filling back up.

Through The Sunning Room's doors she ran through the stair-hall and then bolted through the doors to The Shading Rooms. The large lady was lowering while the drips of tea from her teapot were swelling from the puddle and were jumping back up. The lady's hat was straightening too and most worryingly of all her mouth was opening wide that her teeth glinted in it. Those others that were lowering were also turning to speak as their frantic faces began to stare together.

Faster and faster Farva Mop ran and came to that crooked stair and rather bounced down them. The loud booming crash of Farva Mop landing on the entrance hall floor was accompanied by the noise of the brushes and trap-pans chasing around her feet so that she was hopping to dodge the them.

Then just as she was aimed at the great doors she was halted by a voice that came from behind her.

152

She lowered her hood and slowly turned to find Mr Grinsnick attending to his book as he usually did.

Then with sidling steps and much reluctance Farva Mop approached his counter decked with heavy lamps and watched the face that hardly moved and the needle-pen that marked minutely.

All was still in the entrance hall save for the dust that the brushes and trap pans chased about.

Then when she thought Mr Grinsnick would not actually speak then his needle-pen stopped.

"The book says you have...earned your...rooms," he said dryly. "Rooms number...three hundred....and twenty two" he said with his his eyebrow raised slowly as if in surprise.

Mr Grinsnick then watched her with little interest.

"You may return...whenever you wish," Mr Grinsnick said with no tone of congratulation.

Then Mr Grinsnick added some further note to his book.

"Farva Mop," he said. "Occupation...," and he paused, "an ...investigator," he said.

Farva Mop nearly smiled and then waited and then after some time it became clear that Mr Grinsnick had finished.

Farva Mop made a little bow, on account of not knowing what else to do, and then she turned, tripped over a pan-brush, and staggered towards the door and waving away perfumed-fans that were fluttering at her she staggered out through the huge doorway. However she stepped out into that thick grey storm that was whirling outside and was very nearly blown away by it. Pulling the door shut she braced herself against the force of the storm and turned her face from the lightning that across the front square and showed it brilliantly white.

When after many totterings she she reached the quay the boats were being tossed about by the streams of mist that raced between them and when she reached her own little boat the boarding-ramp of her boat it was being raised and plunged and she had to take her best chance to climb up it.

The deck leant steeply as she clung to the deck-rails and as she saw the outlines of the boy whose starry lamp was aiming its pure white beams above her.

Then the mooring-ropes were loosened and the boat pulled away from the quay with the lightning crackling about it and then the boat and rose above.

Next and above the storm there appeared those dull grey stars in a sky that was dismal above them, though she held tight to the rail as the boat turned.

Then when they had risen nearly fifty masts high she saw below them the house was entangled in the tumult. Lightning was sent to its chimneys and to the branches of its tallest trees as if no part might be spared from it.

Then as she watched that great white roof tilted slightly in the direction of the front square while the maids garden was risen up. Then the house went sliding down into an opening dark where some duller stars could be seen glimmering. Then all at once the lamps of the house lit up with an ancient brightness, and then the house was gone.

In the place where the house had floated a great plume of dust appeared that hung hugely in the sky and while the boat was pelted with marble fragments that spun away. A piece of bronze railing twirled by and what looked like branches of the black trees. Things such as hat-racks and boot-brushes and fire-irons came by too, as if loosed from the plume of dust that she could see below them.

The cloud remained, tall and dimming, like a tower amongst the stars until it was lost to black.

Chapter 16.

Tea and Stars.

Some time later Farva Mop was leant upon the deck-rail of her boat. The boat was seen to change course from time to time but always turned back, as if no direction was better than any other. All was peaceful yet cold and vast and beautiful as Farva Mop looked out.

Then after taking a walk about her boat she came back to the mast and found a starry table had been placed there with two starry chairs. A starry teapot of no size had been placed there too and with two starry cups and starry saucers and starry spoons and bowls of starry sugars accompanying them.

Then the sprite came to sit in the furthest chair while she sat in the nearer, just as biscuits appeared too that were star-shaped.

After eating and drinking, though the tea and biscuits had more flavour than substance, Farva Mop sat back and sighed and remembered her general predicament.

"The trouble with The House of Naws is that I don't really understand any of it," she told the sprite.

Then the sprite, whose eyes blurred and then sharpened, explained things to her.

"Esferini was meant to help the passengers of a sinking ship," he said, "but that ship was in a book and she could not return to it. In time she forgot the book and thereafter decided she was a ghost. But characters are much too loved for that and in her confusion she sought the help of the child, Carua, since Esferini was a child too. Carua loved her and understood Esferini but Carua grew up. Then Esferini left all places that were lit and became a secret of the house. She left behind all memories of Carua and forgot everything except her name."

The sprite then sat forward some aspect of his account had finally interested him.

"If Esferini was to remember her story," the sprite continued, "then she must first remember herself. Someone would have to

155

arrive in a little boat; someone who had forgotten themselves also; someone who walked the house and did not know why."

The sprite paused.

"This has everything to do with a man named Mr. Boam," the sprite said firmly. "Mr. Boam's bath exploded and caused, amongst many things, a book to slide from a pile in a room on the eighth floor above. Mr. Boam's complaint was recorded in The Book of Guests, as so many things are."

The sprite then scratched at his head.

"The book that slid in the room above was a story of the earliest age of boats and of a girl and a sprite who became investigators."

Farva Mop slowly closed her eyes and tears swelled in them.

"But that is us," she said.

Then as the boy continued Farva Mop looked out at the heavens that were not her own and could never be.

"It is neither a happy story nor a sad one," the sprite said, "and is complicated, and is titled *That Which Develops To Completion*."

Then Farva Mop composed herself.

"So are we good characters or bad ones?" she asked.

The sprite angled his head as if the question meant nothing to him.

"I am a good sprite but I am not a great one," he said just as he had said before, "and you are a child whose young life has been spent on adventures."

Farva Mop angled her head and felt the solitude of the story yet found it peaceful, given that she and the sprite only had each other.

"So what do we do now?" she asked.

At this the sprite's eyes became blurred with thinking.

"Naws is a private house, only guests may go back," he said.

"Oh," said Farva Mop suddenly, "but I was told at the very end," she said with growing excitement, "that I had earned my rooms as an investigator."

At this the sprite seemed most upset that she knew something that he did not and indeed he seemed most put out by it.

"Though I did not expect it to happen," she said hurriedly to appease him.

Then Farva Mop shrugged her shoulders.

"But then what would we investigate if we went back?" she asked him.

All of a suddenly the table and the teapot disappeared and a large starry door sign appeared instead of it, which might be meant for the door of her rooms. On the door's starry surface there was written every kind of wide-language until there at the very bottom were some narrow words that read:

Miss Farva Mop
& Associate.
Investigators.
All Cases Considered
All Problems Solved.

Then later, after Farva Mop had managed a little sleep in the cabin's dusty bed, she was dressed in a stronger ancient coat and thicker boots and met the sprite on the deck.

Then after she had taken her place before the mirror the mirror lit up and showed all sorts of stars and worlds.

"You must tell it the place where you wish to go," the sprite said.

At this Farva Mop smiled.

"To the house of Miss Aricel Naws," she said to any star that cared to listen.

That previous sky was gone, as swiftly as a child might snatch one that was printed on a drape of cloth. With a great sweep of white light the mast struck up towards the highest heavens and then just as quickly the boat was come down to darkness again.

Then with a loud rumble and shudder the boat hit a white marble chimney that was sparking and pluming before her boat glided slowly over the roof of Naws. Down the boat went, with its mooring ropes unwinding and aimed itself towards the dim-lit crown-lamps of the quay, where the bright-lit boats of the historians were leaving.

Ebetha And The Imps.

The house that Miss Ebetha Cob lived in was halfway between two villages. The village to the north was called Fullmonkton after the hill it sat upon called Monk Top. The village to the South was called Halfmonkton on a small hill called Low Monk. The people of the two villages rarely spoke to each other. However Ebetha Cob received visitors from both places, who in their turn hoped she would declare herself a Fullmonktoner or a Halfmonktoner. Ebetha Cob's cottage was exactly on the border between them. Her living room with its spinning-wheels was in Fullmonkton whilst her kitchen with its long oak table and iron stove was in Halfmonkton. There was even a line carved across the wooden floor at the foot of her narrow stairs that showed where the northern village ended and where the southern village began.

Her father had been the great carpenter, Abernatha Cob, who was from Fullmonkton to the North while her mother, Mavilla Ravilla, had been a craftswoman from Halfmonkton to the South. The Cobs had married in great trouble since at their wedding no one from either village had agreed to turn up. The carpenter had then lost patience with all of them and had built his wooden cottage neither here nor there. His wooden house was given a hull like a ship so that if there was ever such nonsense from the two villages again then he and his wife and little Ebetha could sail away down the wide river Wilden and be free of the lot of them.

The River Wilden was the only river of any note in the tiny county of Midnotwitshire, which is only remembered in our modern times for having been eroded away by the sea. A seaside halt called Moley now looks out upon the unrevealing waters and in the village's museum there is a map showing two hills and a river flowing lazily in the valley between them.

For being so out of sorts in the district Ebetha Cob had never married. She had grown old and the cottage had also not once set sail because by and large the people of both villages had been respectful towards her. Whenever a dispute between the villages was at its worst it had become a custom to 'Meet with the Honest Cob', as they called her, because Ebetha Cob as a rule was not very keen on any of them.

Instead she sold cakes and other foods to both villages when she busied herself as a cook. She also spun and weaved now and then and would even draw and paint sometimes when she was in the mood to. She was also a good carpenter like her father and for this reason the cottage was always kept ship-shape and ready to sail, or as easily as a cottage could.

As for Ebetha Cob's relatives, their two types were never seen together. The 'Northern Cobs' (as Ebetha Cob called them) were her cousin's son, Bramblin Cob, his wife, Militt, and their spoiled daughter, Pompanora, who rarely left their house. It was the Northern Cob's particular delight to show how rich and comfortable they were during their imposing visits. They advised Ebetha Cob to give up her 'silly house' and to instead live with them where she could earn her keep by washing their dishes and cleaning their floors.

Ebetha's cousin and her husband, who lived in Halfmonkton to the south, were very different. They were the 'Southern Ravillas' and they didn't flaunt their money like The Northern Cobs because they didn't have any. They were however very strict.

Hildreth and her husband, Neevil Weently, went in for total silence in their house. An unfortunate grandson named Crive often became their captive for weeks at a time where he would be forced to share the silence with them. The Southern Ravillas were stricter about tidiness even than Ebetha Cob herself. When the Southern Ravillas came to call they would run their fingers around port-holes of the cottage or would see what birds might be nesting in the rigging. Most of all the Southern Ravilla's wanted Ebetha Cob to leave her 'rattle box' of a house with its singing birds and live with them and sit in the dark and say nothing.

Ebetha Cob, however, could live in neither of those places because Ebetha Cob was quite happy where she was.

This story begins one morning when a grey and ragged tramp walked straight up the gang-plank and through the open door of her house and was following the smell of pies.

"I's will have a pie!" he said through a face full of grey whiskers whilst aiming his happy eyes at her that were also grey.

161

"You can have this pin!" Ebetha Cob said and stuck a hat-pin in his bottom.

"Arrgh!" he cried, "would's you put that away!"

"You can also have this poker!" and she drew a hot poker from the coals and chased him with it.

"And this spoon too!" and she threw a wooden spoon with great skill that hit the tramp on his large nose.

"But I's was only wanting a pie!" the tramp cried out.

Then he saw Ebetha readying to throw a wooden bucket.

"No, no," he hooted, "I's don't washes myself in a manner as that."

Ebetha was angry at seeing the tramp's boots scattering dried mud about the floor. She was angry at his sudden appearance, like a spider – although in truth she liked those things because of their being careful creatures.

Ebetha set the bucket down.

"What is your name fool?" she asked loudly.

"I's old Firebright," he said wearily, "Engris Firebright. Tis a long way I's come with's no food and no comfort. No's moneys and no's sleeps either except for them's in hedges."

"And what brings you to these parts?" demanded Ebetha Cob.

"I's has no notion that I's was brung anywhere's," he said, "leastways only by the smell of pies," he said honestly. "Tis a hard road's that follows from the cradle to th' grave when's ther's no comfort on it."

Ebetha Cob was then satisfied that the stranger was no better or worse than a simple man bound on a simple way and so she stayed her hand.

She picked up some laundry tongs and aimed them at him.

"Tell me, Firebright, do you know about plants?" she asked him.

"I's knows the plants of th' fields," he said sincerely.

Ebetha Cob brought him to look out of one of the larger port-holes to the rear of her house that gave a view of the riverbank.

"Provided my riverside is clear of all briars and thorny thickets by this time next week you shall receive a little crossing-boat. It is a small livery boat with oars that is no longer needed on account of

162

the new bridge here, but further downstream a man might earn a good living by it," she said.

"Well's that is in the fullest's way a very kind's thing, Mrs. er - " Mr Firebright whispered.

"Miss Cob," Ebetha Cob replied quickly,

"Miss Cob, aye," said Mr Firebright whilst bowing his head.

He then glanced again towards the river.

"Seeing's as I can't's be sure of my's way on land then I might's as well's take to the waters, eh?"

He then cleared his throat.

"But I's will have's to think on the problem of the garden – 'tis something of a wild spot as I can see f' myself – but I's will tries me best," Mr. Firebright said finally.

Ebetha Cob gave him a firm nod then she went to the door with him and gave the straight south bearing road a long look at and then looked to the north in the same way.

"Tomorrow I shall have visitors," Ebetha Cob told him. "If they should happen to talk to you then you must answer as a gardener would."

Mr. Firebright put a finger to his lips.

"I's will say's nothin' more's than I should," he said reassuringly.

Being thereby employed Mr. Firebright was then shown to a hut that leant sideways beside the river where there was inside, and from times before, a wood stove and a hay-bed. There Mr. Firebright made his home. In time there was a ribbon of smoke trailing gently from the iron chimney and the smell of cabbages boiling in a cooking-pot, which she had also given him.

When Ebetha Cob went to bed that night she had a long and contented sleep and woke in the morning so rested that she was convinced that seamstress-springtime had taken hold of the late winter air and had made a warm and respectable day of it. With a happy smile she tugged apart the little curtains of her bedroom and looked out and was amazed to find the riverbank behind her house was bright with flowers the size of dinner-plates. Mr. Firebright's hut had been straightened and the livery boat was now a river-worthy craft of some merit.

Hurrying to wash and to dress Ebetha Cob made a sudden departure from her house and found she could take a beautiful white stone path to the water's edge.

"I have not been down here for years" Ebetha Cob said loudly on seeing Mr. Firebright helping himself to a breakfast of cold cabbage. Then looking at the work that must have been a month's work even for a young man she prodded at Mr. Firebright with her walking-stick.

"However did you do this?" she demanded.

Mr. Firebright crooked an eyebrow and from a sack that was beside him he removed a carved wooden man that was no taller than the wooden spoon he held and he set the figure down upon the upturned barrel that was his table.

"Tis 'im that did it," Mr. Firebright said rather seriously, "fer he is an imp and also a gardener as yer can's see, Miss Cob."

Ebetha Cob went forward to examine the carving, which showed a man of unusual features carrying a fork and a shovel. The figure quite fascinated Ebetha Cob before she gathered her wits.

"I will not have stolen property hidden here, Mr. Firebright," she said fiercely.

"Stolen!" cried Mr. Firebright who seemed much offended. "I's not a thief of things like this," he said and pointed at the carving, "yer's could not steal him fer yer's can nayer catch him except by creepin' up on him like."

Ebetha Cob turned away.

"You may be mad, Mr. Firebright, but at least you have kept your word and you have earned the boat – you may leave when you wish."

"I's earned no boat here," Mr. Firebright said angrily, "fer I tells you that man there gardened for yer last night –and when 'e was finished I's was lucky's enough and caught 'im up in my sack."

Mr. Firebright made a pained expression.

"If I's had caught him earlier I's might 'ave managed some gardening myself – only's I's has me poorly wayfarer's leg," whereupon Mr. Firebright rubbed at his knee.

Ebetha Cob shrugged her shoulders.

"Then take the boat anyway Mr. Firebright, I have no need of it."

"I's would not without earning it first," Mr. Firebright said proudly. "I's would like some job that I's could do that would be equal to it."

Then he aimed his spoon at Ebetha Cob.

"I's has been done out of my good name by enchantment and I's demands to show that I's a man to be paid as fair and straight as any other."

"Oh, very well, Mr. Firebright," Ebetha Cob said with annoyance, who thought it best to find him some other task and be soon rid of him. "You are accustomed to climbing upon a roof, no doubt?"

"I's am," said Mr. Firebright proudly and putting his bowl of cabbage away for later they ambled alongside Ebetha Cob to the stern of her cottage and to look up at a high cabin that faced towards the road.

"Up there is the attic that should also be a captain's cabin, Mr. Firebright, but I have not been able to use it on account of the rain," then she pointed up where some thatch on the roof had slid away and was nearly falling off.

They would have spent a longer time considering the roof but chance had it that Tyas the baker's boy came along on his cart drawn by his horse Bellmain. The two made for a lazy sight in the thin winter sunshine as they trundled along from the North. As the cart came to a halt then Tyas stood on the seat to gaze across at the hundreds of flowers.

"Mo-rning, Miss Cob," said Tyas, who was surprised to see summer had arrived in March.

Ebetha Cob folded her arms in her usual way.

When Tyas knew that he had annoyed her he leapt down from his cart and followed Miss Cob as he usually did and nodded to Mr. Firebright as he might to anybody.

In her kitchen Ebetha Cob raised a finger at Tyas, who knew when to be quiet.

"Tell your father I made fewer pies yesterday on account of the firewood being low and the flour-man being late."

Ebetha Cob made excuses each morning which Tyas and his father put down to Miss Cob's age and weariness. Ebetha Cob then opened the big cupboard beside the stove but as she did so she and Tyas could see it was filled to near collapsing with pies of every sort. There were pies stowed in every cupboard they tried and even under her old hat there was a pie.

"You h-ave made a lot of p-ies," said Tyas, who knew a full cartload of pies when he saw one.

Ebetha Cob could find nothing to say to this, indeed she was no longer looking at the pies but instead she was giving a sidelong glance at a carving of another imp that was set upon the stove top and which this time was carved to have the appearance of a cook with a rolling-pin.

Then Tyas scratched at his head.

"How did you b-ake so many p-ies, Miss Cob?" Tyas asked and then turned to study Mr. Firebright, who hurriedly took off his cap and spoke.

"To be's fair I's just a gardener," Mr. Firebright said, 'tis gardening I's know's about mostly."

Tyas then rolled his eyes.

"And I've n-never seen a garden like that n-neither," Tyas said as he went out to fetch trays from his cart. He came back whistling and smiling. It was good deal of carrying and stacking before Tyas could rest again.

"My master will be r-right keen to see these pies Miss Cob," Tyas said as he was attending to his horse, but which began behaving rather oddly. The horse was staring fixedly up at the roof of Ebetha Cob's house and seemed fascinated by something. Then next the horse turned to Tyas and it spoke.

"Strange," the horse said loudly.

Ebetha Cob saw that the poor boy was shocked by this, as Ebetha Cob was too, for neither had known a horse to speak before. Tyas then fell backwards and sat down upon the grass verge where he and his horse exchanged the most unusual of glances, though without the horse uttering a word more.

Immediately Ebetha Cob knew what to do.

"If you might fetch some drinking water from the kitchen barrel, Mr Firebright," Ebetha Cob said.

Mr Firebright wandered into the house and returned with a ladle of water that he helped Tyas to drink.

"I's has often's wondered what horses think's about," Mr Firebright said to Tyas calmly. "Near's to say's they's would tell us if they's could," then he nodded towards Tyas' horse, "and's that is one horse that still might."

Tyas stared disbelieving at his horse and said nothing for some moments. Then finally when Tyas was feeling better, Ebetha Cob suggested to him that the horse had sneezed. After this Tyas led the horse along that turned the cart about for their journey home.

When Tyas was safely on his way then Ebetha Cob and Mr. Firebright went to see what the horse had been staring at. Above them they saw that the part of her roof that had been damaged had been beautifully repaired. Then when Ebetha Cob fetched her grandfather's old spyglass she saw what she had half expected to see, for a carving of an imp was sat upon the gable end and was shown holding a mallet and a ladder.

"I's suppose you's never had these here before?" Mr. Firebright asked after he had looked through the spyglass himself.

"I certainly have not!" Ebetha Cob scolded, "And I should wonder why they should appear just as you came, Mr. Firebright – for it is likely you that brought them. You have slept in a glade and you have little people following you wherever you go."

"I's have not so!" Mr. Firebright said and strode about the dust in the road and pointed about him.

"I's had the company of many o' th' wild things – which a wanderin' man is bound to befriend, being friends with no others – but they's not been things that did's fer me as they does fer you. Fer I would be in a palace by now with no need to wander at all."

Then with a new sense of Mr. Firebright began to stare in amazement at what seemed to be a castle being drawn by fine horses along the road towards them.

"Would you look's there – they's is bringin' me's me palace now!" Mr. Firebright shouted – only to be quietened by Ebetha Cob who knew whose castle it was.

"Calm yourself, Mr. Firebright," said Ebetha Cob, "that will be the Northern Cob's who are coming to visit me; they will not speak to a gardener for most times they will not even speak to me. Take to your garden please, though I admit there is little left to do – please find something."

Mr. Firebright did what he could in what seemed a perfect garden and he could be seen carrying a few pebbles around. Meanwhile just as Ebetha Cob had predicted, that carriage carrying both a driver and a footman arrived from the north drawn by a team of white horses decorated with ribbons and bells. The carriage had much drapery in purples and reds and from their masses emerged the face of a most scornful child, and who was Pompanora, who as I have said was not known to leave The Northern Cob's expensive house.

Pompanora was a slight child with red hair and green eyes and in keeping with her spoiled nature, she had every sort of jewellery imaginable weighing her down. She was such a weight of pearls and chains that she was straining to hold steady as the carriage rocked and jolted.

"Who -," said Pompanora, cruelly, " -is that?" asked Pompanora of someone within.

The curtains were touched apart again and a lady's voice spoke almost as meanly.

"That is your Aunt Ebetha, whom you ought to have met before now had you been well enough, blossom," said Millit, who was Pompanora's mother.

Pompanora then looked again and studied Ebetha Cob with particular hatred then she shrank back into the darkness within.

When the carriage finally came to a halt the footman climbed down from his place at the back and opened the little door for Mr. Bramblin Cob to descend rather daintily and who in turn extended a hand to his wife Mrs. Millit Cob who descended next.

Mr. Bramblin Cob was memorable, and indeed unusual, for having black hair upon a very large head but which had very small eyes. It seemed to all who met him that his eyes might belong to somebody else and that he had somehow borrowed them. Mrs Millit Cob was quite striking, being the opposite, since she had enormous green eyes and a very small head ruffled over with red hair. Millit's enormous eyes seemed full of weariness as if she had tried and failed to satisfy the needs of her only child. Then Pompanora had eyes and a head of correct proportion and which had brought her no end of self-importance.

"I am not getting out here, it is a smelly muddy place!" Pompanora could be heard saying to her mother.

Millet's eyes turned massively as she looked from the carriage.

"How clever of you to guess that it is a smelly and muddy riverbank we have come to, my pip," Millit told her, "it is a swamp."

Then Millit turned her huge eyes towards Mr Bramblin Cob.

"Tell her where her Aunt Ebetha lives, Bramblin."

Bramblin turned his giant head where his small eyes seemed lost in it. That head swayed forward as he addressed Pompanora through the nearly closed curtains.

"Your Aunt lives in a swamp," Bramblin said in a satisfied way and took a handkerchief from his sleeve and held it to his nose, "there are plenty of ills in a swamp."

Millit then noticed the rocketing grandeur of Ebetha Cob's garden before seeing Mr. Firebright who was strolling around in it.

Mr Firebright rolled his grey eyes upward as he said what he was supposed to say.

"I's is Miss Cob's gardener," Mr Firebright said loudly and he tipped his cap to Millit but who immediately looked away.

Then a voice came from the carriage.

"Mummy, is that man allowed to speak?" Pompanora asked from her place in the carriage.

Millit made a sorrowful expression at Ebetha Cob.

"We were so worried on account of the Winter, Ebetha. We were worried and concerned, were we not Bramblin?"

Bramblin dabbed his handkerchief about his nose and his tiny eyes blinked.

"We were worried and concerned," Bramblin said.

169

Bramblin then stood in silence, not being as worried and concerned as people thought.

Ebetha Cob folded her arms.

"Would you wish to come into the house for some honey tea?" Ebetha Cob asked reluctantly.

Millit gave the cottage-boat a sniffling look that was not at all favourable.

"Mydes!" Millit Cob called out sharply to the driver who sprang to attention. "Drive Miss Pompanora to nowhere in particular if she does not wish to leave the carriage."

"Very good m'lady," Mydes said, but who was overtaken by events as Pompanora appeared in the carriage doorway and clambered down in a temper, as if she hated being driven around even more.

Bramblin helped Pompanora as best he could, though with his small eyes it was unlikely he could see her. Then without a word more Millit and Bramblin and Pompanora were led up the gang-plank and into the cottage by the coachman who afterwards returned to his place.

The sight of the interior of Ebetha Cob's home caused Millit to quiver with dissatisfaction.

"We have some old things of our own if you should like them, haven't we Bramblin?"

"We have some old things of our own," confirmed Bramblin.

Pompanora tossed her red tresses about as she surveyed the plain furniture and made an unpleasant face.

When her guests were seated at the long dining table in the parlour then Ebetha Cob took the water-jug to the kettle and looked back to see Bramblin, holding a handkerchief to his nose as if he might be in danger of breathing the air in.

When honey tea was finally served then Millit had her giant eyes stare wildly about.

"Oh, Ebetha," Millit finally said as if she had worked up to it, "won't you come away with us? You can bake us our favourite bread if you like – except for Pompanora, who cannot eat the same food twice."

Ebetha Cob set the heavy kettle upon the stove.

Millet continued.

"And of course in the winter this place is lonely and in summer there are only the flies," Millit said witheringly.

"Flies," echoed Bramblin, who pressed his handkerchief more firmly about his lips.

When honey tea was served, and after many speeches by Millit, Ebetha Cob finally joined them at her parlour table that seated twelve.

When Millet complained about the house again then Ebetha Cob sipped her tea and smiled.

"I am perfectly happy as I am and in any season," she said.

At this they all watched Pompanora as she became dissatisfied with her seat and decided to move to another one. As Pompanora moved from seat to seat she found ways to disapprove of each.

"These chairs are so uncomfortable," Pompanora complained loudly while Millit and Bramblin both nodded as if they expected them to be.

Then when Mr. Firebright passed before a porthole window moving a small twig to another part of the garden then Millit and Bramblin and Ebetha Cob watched him go by. However, while they were distracted Pompanora came to sit upon a thirteenth seat she had not noticed was there. Then when she sat angrily down she sank all at once into the wood and disappeared.

Millit put her tea-cup down.

"What an unusual man that Mr. Firebright is," Millit said loudly. "Which village does he come from?"

Ebetha Cob shrugged her shoulders.

Then Millit cast a glance about the table.

"And where is Pompanora?" she asked.

Bramblin turned in his seat and his huge head aimed his small eyes at the place where Pompanora wasn't.

They all sneaked a look under the table but found Pompanora was not there either.

Then Millit looked towards all parts of the parlour.

"She appears to have gone," Millit said.

Bramblin returned to sipping tea and blinking very small blinks.

"She appears to have gone," he repeated.

Millit resettled herself.

"I know she has gone, Bramblin, I was attempting to ascertain: where has she gone?"

They then waited patiently at the table for Pompanora to reappear but when Pompanora did not present herself then Millit went to the foot of the stairs and let out an ear-ripping screech.

"Pompanora you come back down this instant, you don't know if the upstairs is safe!"

After this Millit listened but could hear no one and so she went to the front door and opened it.

"You there – you - gardener," Millit shouted at Mr Firebright who was leaning against a gatepost. "Did my daughter Pompanora leave the house?"

"I's not seen anyone's," Mr Firebright said helpfully. "I's wasn't expecting anyone's comin' out on account's of you's all's only just gone in," Mr Firebright added.

Millit closed the door bad-temperedly with a slam but just as the face of Pompanora seemed to flit across it. A voice then sang out like a little creak from the door and then from the floorboards beneath their feet and then from other wooden parts of the room.

Millit straightened herself and then her large eyes and small face became a picture of annoyance.

"Where are you?"

"I'm in the wood!" came the rather whining reply.

"In the wood?" Millit said.

Then Millet stared at Ebetha Cob.

"But there isn't a wood except for the one that is down the road some way," Millit said angrily.

Bramblin patted his nose with his handkerchief.

"There isn't a wood," he echoed.

"No, no, no!" Pompanora's voice called out as her face sped from one sideboard to another. "Not in a wood."

Then there came a loud knocking from a sideboard, after which an oak bucket danced about.

"In the wood!" Pompanora shouted.

Millit's eyes became enormous and she stared at Bramblin.

"She's in the wood. How did she get in the wood?"

By this time Ebetha Cob went along to Millit and helped her to sit back down.

When all of them were seated again then Pompanora's voice grew louder and a tiny cupboard in a sideboard flew open and Pompanora's unhappy face looked out.

"I was sitting down," Pompanora told her mother, then Pompanora's hand came out of another cupboard and pointed, "in that chair," she said, "when suddenly I fell back," and she made a puzzled expression, "into the wood."

Pompanora next looked at her parents. especially Bramblin, who was simply enjoying his tea.

"What is wrong with them?" Pompanora asked Ebetha Cob miserably.

"They are just a little surprised," Ebetha Cob said. "But if you will just give me a moment I will fetch Mr Firebright who will know what to do."

Ebetha Cob went over to the front door and when she opened it she saw Mr Firebright standing beside a border that had not a flower out of place.

Ebetha Cob narrowed her eyes.

"Mr. Firebright, we appear to have an extra chair," she said.

"I's be alright standing up," said Mr. Firebright said, "I's only to pick up this little twig that I's has just put down and move it again," and he pointed down, "'tis th only's thing to do other than's to eat the cabbage, which I have done to all ends of my stomach already."

Ebetha Cob made a firm face.

"Mr. Firebright, will you please come into the house!"

"I's will," said Mr. Firebright, who came lumbering along and came up the mooring-ramp and in through the cabin door. There he found Bramblin and Millit staring at the wall in a most unusual way. Then Ebetha Cob opened a cupboard in her wide dresser and showed Mr. Firebright Pompanora's face. At the same time a high cupboard that was in the kitchen flew open and Pompanora's foot protruded from it. t

Ebetha Cob prodded Mr. Firebright in the ribs.

"Do something about this," she said.

Mr. Firebright went about the room making an inspection of cupboards. When it appeared that he had seen enough he went over to that thirteenth dining-chair and found a carving of a little woodworker was set on its high back.

Then Pompanora who explained her situation.

"I was choosing a good chair, Mr. Firebright, but there wasn't one and then there was that chair and when I sat in it I arrived here, only," and she frowned, "I feel by bottom is still sitting in it, even if the rest of me isn't."

Mr. Firebright stood in silence then made a speech to anyone who could understand it.

"Well's I should's say that's the chair should be put outside. It should be put where there is no wood, nor timber of any sort; for if it is done that way then's all of her will' be in the chair and none of her can be elsewhere," Mr. Firebright and scratched at his head.

Ebetha Cob came to think.

"There is the river, of course," Ebetha Cob whispered.

This was how Mr. Firebright led a procession comprised of Millit and Bramblin, Ebetha Cob, a puzzled footman, and a driver through the beautiful winter-flowering garden and down to the riverbank. to the riverbank. Then Mr. Firebright took the dining-chair to the water and the chair sank due to the weight of Pompanora's jewellery that was inside it.

Then after a moment up came Pompanora, quite freed from her jewellery and received the applause of Millit and Bramblin and Ebetha Cob. The footman and the driver applauded loudest of all on account of their thinking this was some kind of trick.

Pompanora, now a pillar of shining mud, was led back to the carriage where she silently got into it. The drapes were closed and the horses (that had nothing of importance to say) set off at a canter towards a turning-point to the south. Soon after the carriage returned and swept past where Ebetha Cob and Mr. Firebright stood, Mr Firebright holding a carved figure of a swimming imp that he had picked from the river water.

As the carriage past its driver pointed behind him with great urgency and called out to the two of them.

"I have seen it all now – Darkness himself is coming!" the driver cried out and doubled the canter of the horses to have himself and the other get safely away.

At this Ebetha Cob took a step out into the road and looked to the South where the sound of trundling iron wheels was coming.

"Mr. Firebright," Ebetha Cob said with some concern, "if you would like to lift that twig around a few more times; the Southern Ravillas are coming."

The carriage that rattled along the road from Halfmonkton had a menacing appearance. What had recently come from the North and with The Northern Cobs had been the pomp and idleness, but was next and coming from the South was very different.

All parts of a tall carriage were black, including four solemn black flags that were fitted to the carriage roof. The Southern Ravillas rarely made a journey anywhere and their journey to Ebetha Cob's house was always strange and unusual. Their carriage was not drawn by horses but was instead drawn by their two giant black pigs, because the Ravillas could not afford horses. This had no doubt caused the driver of Bramblin's and Millit's carriage to think that Death himself was approaching. Strangely though, the driver of the black carriage might have been mistaken for Death. The driver was none other than Neevil Weently Ravilla himself, but who was called Neevil Weently mostly.

Neevil Weently was dressed entirely in black. He wore a wide rimmed black hat that gave him a scary appearance. Other than his shadow-like clothes Neevil Weently was tall and thin. Being of great age, but his green eyes were pale and stared out like the last green leaves of a storm-blown winter. His grey hair was grown to rat-tails about his bony white cheeks while his mouth was pressed tight like a line drawn in drying wax.

The black carriage finally came to a halt at Ebetha Cob's garden gate and then the thin and silent Neevil Weently nodded at Ebetha Cob before coming down from from his lofty position. From the back of the carriage he fetched a bucket of water and a bucket of dinner leavings for each of the pigs. Only when the pigs were grunting contentedly did he approach the side door of the carriage and place a black stepping-stool before it. When all was

175

ready he opened the carriage door and a smell of rough soap snapped at all of their noses.

First to appear was a little boy named Crive, whose fear of speaking was so great that he could hardly breathe. He was a kindly black-haired and blue-haired boy with outdoor interests, but whose parents had died and who had been inserted into the Southern Ravilla's house like a key is inserted into a dark lock. There Crive had waited for where life might take him next, but in that strict house nothing did. Crive had a most pained expression on his pale face, for with the Ravillas he had forgotten both laughter and smiles.

Then after Crive had climbed down from the carriage then both Neevil Weently and Crive were stood in terrified poses, for Hildreth Ravilla would be coming out next.

Hildreth Ravilla resembled a great grey-faced bird dressed in a thick black cloak like feathers and a sharp beak-like hat. Her eyes were cast downward, as if to avoid seeing the sun, whilst her long sharp nose was the first spike in an overall jaggedness. As she removed herself from the darkness it was her immediate wish to find more of it and so she nodded firmly in the direction of the house and where Neevil Weently and Crive were pushed to go.

Hildreth carried with her a black walking-stick and as the party move forward toward the gang-plank not a word was spoken and when the visitors were they sat about that long dining table it was as if they awaited a burial.

Ebetha Cob went quietly to the stove to prepare a kettle and a teapot and looked back only to check that no one had spoken. The deathly faces of Hildreth and Neevil Weently seemed to bring a chill to the house, whilst her preparations for tea seemed like a fairground of a thousand merriments in comparison.

The Ravillas had taken to silence like a duck takes to water. Their shadowy lives seemed aimed across the day to arrive safely in the next darkness. It had been a mystery that no one was concerned about because as a result of their secret gloominess few people ever saw them.

When Ebetha Cob finally brought a tray of cups to the table she found the boy Crive leaning towards her with a fixed stare that meant he wanted to whisper.

When Ebetha Cob bent low to listen the voice that came out of Crive was hardly a sound at all.

"May I have a napkin," Crive asked and which caused Ebetha Cob to look across to Neevil Weently and Hildreth incase they wanted napkins too but they slowly shook their heads.

Thus Clive was served with tea and a napkin and Neevil Weently and Hildreth was each served with tea alone and these might be the highlight of their visit, since no matter how Ebetha Cob talked about this or that the Ravillas would not reply and instead merely listened to everything she said.

When enough silence had settled on her poor house Ebetha Cob sat down with the Ravillas to find some conversation in it.

Then Hildreth, sensing that Ebetha Cob might have some pleasant thing to say, directed her beetle-black eyes at

"Be as silent," Hildreth said, "as when the world was made," she growled and raised her cup like her long fingers would spin a web around it. Then Hildreth jabbed Neevil Weently in the ribs who muttered the same words, after which Hildreth completed their little muttering. "Silence is a blessing from the grave," she said before all three sipped their tea together without anything pleasurable having happened.

"Silence," said Hildreth next, "silence for the young and old alike. Silence in the darkness that comes after the foolish daylight," she preached.

Then at that precise moment Hildreth and Neevil Weently stopped. Their faces, which were so stiff and forbidding became even harder, until the two of them seemed made of grey dry wood. Then after waiting for quite some time Ebetha Cob noticed that the two really were made of wood and that she and Crive were the only ones moving.

The change caused Ebetha Cob to spring up from her place at the table, yet even the noise of her chair tumbling did nothing to disturb Hildreth and Neevil Weently, who were as still as statues with Hildreth opening her mouth as if preparing to speak.

Crive meantime had been working hard at the silence and all the doing of nothing that the Ravillas had taught him. His eyes were closed and his arms were folded and it was as if he hardly dared to move incase his shoes should tap on the floor or else his fingers might land lightly on the tabletop.

"Silence is the blessing of the dead," Crive whispered before finally deciding that he was allowed to open his eyes and to drink his tea. At the tumbling of Ebetha Cob's chair he had simply closed his eyes even tighter. Only when there was perfect silence did Crive look about and see those the two unpleasant sculptures were seated beside him.

Then after staring at the two ugly statues Crive glanced at Ebetha Cob.

"Is that a blessing?" Crive asked in his shy way.

"It certainly is," replied Ebetha Cob, who found it such a relief to hear Crive speak.

Then Crive thought for a moment.

"Do you have any biscuits?" Crive asked.

"I am sure I can find you some," Ebetha Cob before hurrying into the kitchen.

Then when they were sat together eating the bsicuits and sipping tea then Ebetha Cob considered the problem at hand.

"I shall talk to Mr. Firebright to see whether we have to throw your grandparents into the river," Ebetha Cob said, without perhaps thinking about what she had said.

Then Ebetha Cob went out of the front door and called for Mr. Firebright and soon enough he came along carrying his twig.

Mr. Firebright was then shown Hildreth and Neevil Weently transformed into nasty-looking wooden figure at the dining table.

"There," Ebetha Cob said firmly then pointed at the two ugly statues, "it seems that no one can visit me who is not meddled with by imps."

Then Ebetha Cob sat down in a dining chair and set her elbows on the table.

"This will be another trip to the river I suppose."

Mr. Firebright shook his head.

"We cannot put's these in th' river, being they's is as old as theye are," Mr. Firebright said. "They's might likely never be th' same after it,"

Then Mr. Firebright tapped his twig on Hildreth's wooden head whilst looking about the room.

"We will's have to find's th' imp that did this and ask his pardon, like," then Mr Firebright pointed up at the lintel-shelf above the door, "and there's he is," Mr Firebright said.

Sure enough as Ebetha Cob looked she saw that upon the high lintel of the cabin door there was a carving of a little man who was shown holding a mallet and a chisel.

Mr. Firebright fetched the carving down and set it before Hildreth and Neevil Weently whose nasty faces seemed to glare at it.

"Now you's put a spell on these that did you no harm, so it's only's right that's you puts things right's for you's done's no real harm so far – not any of' yer." Mr. Firebright said kindly.

Ebetha Cob stood forward of Mr. Firebright to address the little figure.

"What Mr. Firebright is saying is that they may have wished for silence but they did not deserve to receive so much of it," Ebetha Cob explained.

"Yes they did," Crive said, who was arranging the biscuits like the walls of a castle.

"Well I'm sure they didn't," said Ebetha Cob.

Crive looked up from his playing.

"That wasn't me," he s aid, "I was only telling you what he said," then Crive pointed at the carving on the table-top. "It said," said Crive, "yes they did."

Ebetha Cob and Mr. Firebright both turned toward Crive and watched him return to playing with the biscuits.

"Crive?" Ebetha Cob kindly. "Can you hear what the little man is saying?"

"Yes," Crive said plainly, who was next building a tower to each side of his castle's gate.

Then Mr. Firebright and Ebetha Cob organised themselves. Mr. Firebright went to his shed and brought back the carving of the imp he had first caught, then he went high in the attic and out onto the roof to fetch the imp who had repaired it. Ebetha Cob fetched out the swimming imp that had sunk with Pompanora and also the kitchen imp that had been responsible for the pies. When all the carvings were set on the tablet-top before Crive, who was too busy with his castle to notice, then Ebetha Cob and Mr. Firebright drew chairs up close and they had a talk with him.

"Crive, my dear," Ebetha Cob began, "where do you suppose these little came from?"

Crive was busy with his castle because the soft biscuits were defending the castle against the harder ones. Yet he managed to tell the imps' story just as the imps told it to him.

"They are river imps," Crive said, "but they were swallowed by a big fish that was swallowed by a big bird that made a big nest on a big cliff. The bird laid four eggs but the bird knew the imps were in the eggs so she flew down to a forest and buried the eggs in the mud and the mud dried around them so they were trapped. Then a big oak grew in the mud and its big roots got tight hold of the imps and held them for a three hundred years. Then the oak fell after a flood and a carpenter cut up the tree and found the imps and rescued them, a carpenter named Cob."

Ebetha Cob sat back. "My father rescued the imps?" she asked.

"They say so," said Crive, who had noticed how imperilled the soft biscuits at the walls of the biscuit castle had become.

"Then why have they come to me?" Ebetha Cob asked.

Crive paused as if listening.

"The carpenter said he would set the imps free if they performed two tasks," Crive said, who was repairing the castle's southern wall as fast as he could. "First they must be his daughter's toys and second when she was very old they must revisit her."

Then Ebetha Cob watched as the battle of the biscuits became more intense and Crive seemed not to be listening to them at all.

Ebetha Cob scratched at her head and she turned to Mr. Firebright with rather an odd expression on her face.

"Do you know, Mr Firebright, I think that I do in fact remember them," Ebetha Cob said with a rather lost expression upon her face.

"The Little Men of Cob; that is what I used to call them," she whispered.

Then Ebetha Cob seemed to trace some memory about the room.

"For I played with the little figures just here," and she pointed, "just where Crive plays now."

Then she looked toward the stairs.

"And sometimes when I was young I would imagine the little men could jump and run – because my father told me they could. Always alone they would come to my beckoning and I would wander the house with them, for in my memory I see them now."

Mr. Firebright scratched his head.

"Then's maybe's you should release those people there," his meaning Hildreth and Neevil Weently, "before the imps cause too much trouble."

Ebetha Cob stared at Mr. Firebright before nodding fiercely.

"That is the very best idea, Mr. Firebright," Ebetha Cob said and she turned to Crive.

"Crive, my dear," and she watched Crive take no notice of her at first. "What do the little people say I must do to release your guardians?"

"The imps say they must stay as statues for a whole week and not a minute less if any good is to become of them," said Crive.

"Surely not," said Ebetha Cob."

"It is their very best spell," said Crive, "and there will no moving it until its time is done."

"You must play with them," Crive said. "You must play with them, one last time."

Ebetha Cob folded her arms and she glared at the little carved figures.

"And when shall their spells be done with me?" she asked with some annoyance.

"They have only their duty towards you," said Crive, "and that is to play alongside you one last time.

181

"I shall do no such thing!" said Enetha Cob and she gave Mr. Firebright a strong look too for good measure.

"The foolishness of it, and me at my age," she said and then she looked toward the kitchen.

"I have so many things to do that I cannot tell you them all and yet for the sake of peace I should prance about like I had gone mad! No, Mr. Firebright," Ebetha Cob said, "I shall not do that. They must know that I am an old lady now and that I cannot do as they ask."

Crive looked up from his playing.

"They say they will visit you nonetheless, each night for a week" then Crive returned to his castle of biscuits and said no more about it.

The afternoon changed to evening and still Hildreth and Neevil Weently were statues in Ebetha Cob's parlour. Crive grew tired and he was taken to a first floor room where he slept soundly all night. For the sake of cabbage, which it seemed Mr. Firebright did like very much, the tramp returned to his shed and had quite an evening there beside his stove and listening to the river flowing. And it is from him that this entire story was told, for he said he was woken in the night by laughter and he crept from his sacking-bed to see the lamps of the old cottage all lit up.

Then he was worried by what he heard and went at once to find the matter. Then entering the house by way of climbing the hull and going by the great window he found the house lit up by strange lamps in all places. Then he next heard the joy that only big hearts make, for he said the cottage was nearly lifted by it.

"Miss Cob, would's you be there," he had called out, "I's has come in from the garden to know if you's is alright."

Then Mr. Firebright said he climbed to the first floor to see that Crive was sleeping and saw that he was. Then Mr. Firebright said he stole a few steps higher where the hand-rails curve and he said he saw a face there. A face no older than a child's and it was a girl who smiled down at him before running after others who laughed also. Then seeing no harm in any place Mr. Firebright returned to his shed, for he had known magic in the woods that cannot easily be talked about.

Just as the imps had intended, and as Crive had told, there was a week of joyful mights as could not be explained except that a great happiness had entered. And just a surely Crive was free of the silence for a whole week too, and it should be mentioned that he sang much and covered Hildreth and Neevil Weently in many sorts of clothes that caused much laughter too. The great black pigs were taken to be cared for by Mr Firebright, who shared his cabbage. Then when the final morning came then Crive crept down and removed all playful sorts of things and made himself silent. The teapot and the cups, without biscuits, were placed exactly as before and Crive took his place precisely as he had been and so did Ebetha Cob. Then when the sun arched to its low winter place and all shadows pointed near enough to how they had pointed, then the carved imps vanished one by one.

Then a great creaking began as Hildreth and Neevil Weently returned to their shadowy and miserable selves. Their mean eyes looked out upon the room and their crooked mouths and brows returned to sneering.

Then as if they should be worried by the sun that had begun to shine they decided they would go home early to meet the moon as others would the sun. But by all accounts thereafter there was much fuss when they returned, for their two-day cook had reported them missing and the men of the inn had searched the roads. Then some of them had gone to kindly Miss Cob's who had the house by the river, but found only the boy, Crive, and their carriage but who said he could not account for them. So generous was Ebetha Cob, they recounted, that they found she had paid for statues to be made of her darling relations as would a noblemen make statues of his beloved ones. Then after this it was assumed the two had gone too near the water, and such was the sorrow of the village folk for the Ravillas, but who had not uttered a single word to them.

Then on their return the whole village was up and about them, but while the Ravillas had claimed they had hardly been gone an hour. And the mystery thickened with each re-telling until Hildreth and Neevil Weently were speaking each day, and as for Crive he was served with kindness by his guardians and all others in case he remembered more. With the new and ready friendship with the sun

Hildreth Ravilla's face became a real one, with as true as smile as any had.

Then The Northern Cobs that had been so haughty to any slight became honest and giving to the people about, while Pompanora was generous with the best of them.

Then finally there were those times when one of them visited.

"How kind a thing to distribute cakes," was what Millet and Bramblin said on entering.

"As joyful as when the world was newly made," is what Hildreth said happily when she made calls on Ebetha Cob on the sunniest of days. And Ebetha Cob gave biscuits to each without asking, and Ebetha Cob said nothing.

Avelin.

Chapter 1.
A Small Duty.

In November of 1925 I, Lachio Mettini, was dispatched upon the railways by my mother to help her oldest friend renew kinship with her twin sister who had been many years out of knowledge. Pausing upon a journey through soot and smoke I arrived at the home of Mrs Hettie Vernier of Coppleton, she being the lady who was my mother's loyal school-friend and correspondent.

I cannot now recall Mrs Vernier except for her face, which appeared from our first meeting to be stretched always into an expression of utter surprise. Everything I said startled Mrs Vernier and this restricted me to communicating the dullest things I could think of in order to avoid causing her some muscular injury. Mrs Vernier persuaded me that I should take her walker's map showing The Great Northern Moors in case I became lost. Mrs Vernier's hospitality gave me a much needed rest before my journey resumed early the next morning, a journey that took me away from everything I might call familiar and towards something like a wilderness.

Just as my mother's aide, Elma Herring, had explained, there would be nothing but ice and smoke awaiting me at every halt on my journey northward. There would be no advantage in speaking to anyone not paid to give advice since it was likely that other passengers would have the weakest understanding of my destination. Such was the gravity that Elma spoke on my departure that she hardly spoke a word. Whether she knew by some intelligence what lay in store for me I cannot say but it occurred to me later that Elma had some insight into my journey that I could not see for myself and indeed her role came to be that of a confidant, just as she was to my mother, when all had ended.

My stay at Mrs Vernier's had significance besides her high sensitivity. Sometime after dinner and in her study and by means of a large lamp she showed me some papers at a desk and explained some of the circumstances surrounding what she called my 'Expedition.'

Mrs Vernier's face had a most extraordinary baboon-like nervousness as she spoke so that I could hardly listen to her for watching it. However in spite of this she was able to tell me much that my mother had neglected to tell me, albeit whilst sending her glance to every object in the room as if it might attack her.

"I have a twin," Mrs Vernier said whilst giving a sideboard a terrified glance.

"A twin!" I said with interest and which caused Mrs Vernier to leap up.

"I mean," I said more gently, whilst reassuring the lady, "a twin."

Mrs Vernier stared about her.

"We were separated as orphans without rights to each other's lives," she said with passion, "I was not told that my sister existed until your mother discovered her."

Mrs Vernier then leant forward.

"Last year I was able to go to my sister's house, which is in that wild place. But what I found there caused me to doubt my eyes and ears, though I could report none of this to your mother save for the fact that I could never return there. Your mother assured me that she would find means to resolve all misunderstandings between my sister and myself at a better time."

She then looked fraught.

"I had hoped with all my heart that she would forget the matter. Months passed and I was content never to mention my sister again in our correspondence."

Mrs Vernier took some rose water from a china bowl and dabbed the liquid about her neck.

"And now she has sent you, Lachio," she said, "to be my emissary."

I smiled.

"Mrs Vernier," I said warmly, "I am installed in a London college and it is nineteen twenty five. If you are about to tell me that you and your sister are strangers to each other due to your being apart then I am quite aware of such tragedies."

I carried on.

"My mother has often spoken of you in the strictest confidence. My instructions are to dispel any disfavour that your sister has towards you and recognise a bond that can never be broken."

Mrs Vernier made some nervous gesture that suggested she must impart unpleasant news.

"The state of things is odd," she said "– and I say this as one who is armed against the unusual – but my sister, who as I say I have visited once," and Mrs Vernier made a face that took a worrying turn, "has some condition that means she can inhabit things in her sleep."

I set my tea cup down and leant rather too far forward for my companion's nerves, for she immediately retreated.I attempted to calm her.

"You mean she gathers things to her, for instance that she sleepwalks?" I asked.

"Not in the way that you mean," Mrs Vernier said slowly. "Avelin has dreams that makes things move."

I sat back and smiled at Mrs Vernier as I do with any tale that does not run as it should, but Mrs Vernier gave no indication of amusement. Instead she appeared terrified – though that of course was her normal expression.

"But Mrs Vernier," I said haughtily, "I cannot accept that your sister has dreams such as these. Why I have not heard anything like of it."

Then I too glanced about the room.

"Why it would alter the world entirely to have someone who could do this."

"And yet it is so," Mrs Vernier whispered.

I considered the matter for the sake of ending the conversation entirely.

"Then can you not explain this in some other way," I suggested. "Perhaps, though I do not believe in them, this might be the work of a ghost?"

Mrs Vernier shook her head vehemently.

"Then I am afraid I do not follow," I said. "How would you know the changes you say are caused by dreams?"

Mrs Vernier appeared to tremble.

"Bless me that I can help either help you with further information. It was my duty to visit her in her isolation and to renew out kinship. When I found such things as I have described I reported to your mother in the most general way without mentioning what I mention now.

I laughed loudly.

"Mrs Vernier you have obviously been a victim of a pretence — why it is ludicrous that someone could dream in so extraordinary a way."

Mrs Vernier took my outburst with good grace before setting a hand carefully on mine.

"It is only her small staff that know. No one else is privy to it, due to the remoteness of her house. Nor are there regular visitors to it. When I visited High Stoor I was much altered by it," she said. "However I must tell you that my troubles are not just my own and they might be yours too."

She paused.

"For this reason I shall follow after you, on a later train, and stay at an inn that is across the moor. I will be available there should you need me."

I smiled.

"Mrs Vernier you are very kind," I said, "indeed I would welcome a chance to have you nearby so that I might bring a resolution to a family dispute. I shall meet your sister with your best interest in mind," I said.

The two of us were then a picture of awkwardness, for I judged my host to be under some delusion and while she perhaps judged to be inconsiderate.

Then Mrs Vernier seemed relieved that she had briefed me as she had.

Then after this peculiar conversation it was necessary to divert Mrs Vernier from her unusual preoccupation with it. Therefore I told her of my life at Knaidith and of Myda Lowens who had accompanied me on the train.

Myda Lowens, being a reader of extraordinary stamina and concentration had been a silent companion for the whole of the journey. Indeed her studiousness out-ranked most men and her resilience in thought caused most to give way to her. As for the whereabouts of Myda at that exact moment she was resting in a room above, and no doubt still reading.

Then after a cup of tea Mrs Vernier gave a brief history of hers and her late husband's marriage but thereafter she came to broach that peculiar subject again.

"All I can do is protect you with what powers I have," she said, "from anything that might come."

I sat back.

"Mrs Vernier, do you believe there is danger there?" I asked with surprise.

Mrs Vernier stared about her with a look of dread.

"These are things that your mother has deeply inquired of," she said.

I shrugged my shoulders.

"There are many riddles my mother has deeply inquired of Mrs Vernier, because my mother is a philosopher."

Then given that neither of us could comment on philosophy there was a silence between us. Then my mind strayed I should say to the preparations I had undergone at Knaidith College before setting off.

Knaidith College was my temporary home after Mussilini took hold of my native country and caused my mother and my father and I to flee from a university there. Thereafter my father, an historian of maps, joined her in Paris. Being installed there also Mother made quarterly visits to London to provide for me. Mother had made such strides in her brilliant academic career that it enabled her to send me to school in England, after which she had me remain here. England however, has been a cause of constant complaint for me, for I am not suited to this place. I was accused of being over-gentle at boarding school, which caused me much suffering. Then my life's passion emerged that is obscure poetry, which my mother has so strongly disapproved of. Thankfully, and at least, Knaidith College suited my interests very well. Chief amongst my allies was the porter's daughter, the same Myda Owens, who in her own terms had read the library over many

times and would at last be studying there herself the following
October herself. Myda was then a grey-eyed studious young lady.
Her tidy dark brown hair and stolid manner made her a stalwart
ally against Mother, since my mother's plans for me seemed
always to exclude poetry altogether.

When I received my mother's letter stating that she would
arrive in London, she would have me depart forthwith to
Coppleton. My bank account had been profited with a considerable
amount, since I had spent much of my allowance on poetry books,
which had much annoyed her. Also she required me to take a
companion. To say I could not be trusted to navigate the railways
was not directly said but was inferred. A sound and sensible mind
should guide me, was her instruction, and the only mind I knew
that matched the description was that of Myda Owens. Mother had
added a second and equal sum of money to have my companion
assured of his or her place and so I had no qualms about
approaching Myda's parents in this unusual matter.

Mr Lowens, the college postmaster and porter, required full
documentation at the outset of mine and Myda's adventure, for I
did not describe it over well whilst sitting with he and Myda and
Mrs Lowens in their parlour.

"My mother, requires me first of all to visit her childhood
friend in Coppleton in the northlands," I explained as Mr Lowens
listened with a staunch face.

I continued.

"Mrs Vernier, the lady is question, wishes us to vouch for
her sister's well being, something that I cannot very well
accomplish alone, because I am a man," I said.

"Coppleton," Mr Owens had said darkly with hardly a blink.

"Yes," I said, "although the house that we must visit is
considerably further north and more remote."

"Indeed," said Mr Owens sceptically.

I had then fetched out my mother's letter of intent (there
being many pages annotated). On the final page were details of my
companion's fee, which like my own was extraordinarily
generous.

Mr Lowen's expression changed then to one of tremendous shock, for I know now that the said fee was as much as the Lowens' annual household income in those days. My mother, I should say, is one that imposes her will with money.

Mrs Lowens, who had relied on her husband's judgement up until then, found him mute and unresponsive. Then when she read the particulars she too was staring for some moments before she rose and ushered Myda and myself out of the parlour.

Thinking that I had offended her I apologised, which caused Mrs Owens to break into a volley of laughter that she barely controlled.

"So we are permitted to undertake the work at hand?" I asked Mrs Lowens, but who nodded vigorously without comment and we were ushered into the hallway after which Mrs Lowens quickly closed the door.

The next evening on the eve of our departure Myda let me know that she had assumed my trip would be academic and said as much as she helped me pack.

"So Mrs Vernier is a learned lady rather like your mother?" she asked.

"Oh," I said. "Mrs Vernier is no one like that," I said cautiously.

Myda, who as I have explained, was a stalwart supporter of my attempts at independence made a blank expression.

"Then what is it that Mrs Vernier does?" she asked with one of her long grey looks.

I resumed my packing.

"I really cannot think what she does," I said with no enthusiasm whatsoever. "Her reputation is most unusual," I explained.

At this Myda sat down upon my one chair.

"Then what is she usually doing?" she asked next.

I stared about, hoping to find inspiration in the wallpaper.

"She is a lady from Coppleton in Cheshire," I said, "who receives occasional monies from people for whom she serves with her hobbies," I explained prettily.

"And what would those hobbies be?" asked Myda whilst leaning forward to study my face.

"She is a clairvoyant," I said.

I then breathed a heavy sigh.

"Myda," I said with a tone of regret. "I must tell you that Mrs Vernier was responsible for the strangest times my mother ever had. It is perfectly clear to me now that my mother, who has orchestrated this trip like she has orchestrated others, plans to send me out of my mind."

Myda addressed me strictly.

"Why would your mother wish to send you mad?" she asked with the innocence that typified anyone who had not met my mother.

I narrowed my eyes.

"Because," I said with caution, "my mother is a philosopher who has long considered it her duty to send me out of common mind," I explained. "She maintains that I see only the surface of things and that poetry is an excuse for not thinking at all. She would have me give up my Poetry entirely and think as she does."

I quickened in my work.

"She has long used dilemmas of many kinds that have much disturbed me," I said.

Then I glanced towards without hope.

"Were it up to my mother I should be hold up in some dark room barricaded by papers and bottles of ink," I said, meaning to close the subject.

Myda gazed about her at my dusky study where piles of poetry books trapped larger sheets displaying conjectures drawn from them.

"But you are,"she said.

Then closing my travelling-bag I folded my arms and sat down down beside my desk where those copy-books were piled up.

"You see my mother is someone with whom I can neither agree nor disagree, because I do not know what she is talking about."

193

With regard to the events of that later evening the advice of Mrs Vernier had not much further to go. She described the village to which Myda and I should travel and some parts of the lands about it, which were in the main featureless. A map titled *The Great Northern Moor* was given to me, did nothing but disappoint, since it was a representation of an utter bleakness.

Later I retired to a bedroom where the late Mr Naven Vernier seemed present everywhere in photographs and while the subject of spirits and spirituality had a powerful representation in every bookshelf.

In the morning Myda and I were escorted to the railway station by Mrs Vernier herself, for she seemed just as concerned as she had been the night before. Indeed she had packed a travelling-bag herself and intended to catch the very next train after an urgent appointment.

"A Mr Barrit, who is charged to serve you, shall meet you as he previously met me," she explained. "He and his wife and his daughter are the only staff. Mr Barrit shall drive you from the station to the house and he shall be very prompt and courteous I can assure you."

Then Mrs Vernier returned to her earlier concerns as we arrived on the platform, but delayed our stroll so that Myda walked ahead of us.

"If you should wish it in the slightest I shall come with you forthwith and we can face it all together," she said breathlessly.

"Mrs Vernier," said I, "I am visiting your relation, there is no danger in such a thing," I said. "You have provided us with a map and a box of sandwiches. That is help enough I am sure for the small duty Myda and I must perform there. We shall no doubt drink much tea and impress your sister in a most favourable way. There is nothing particularly hazardous in that."

Myda and I then boarded the train, which moved off with me at the window waving towards Mrs Vernier, whose frightened face was distinct amongst a happy crowd that was waving at others.

Our train journey included many changes but at each halt fewer people were boarding or alighting until we arrived in the late afternoon on the wintry and darkening railway platform in the village of Melther. We were met, after a delay, by Mr Barrit, who I shall describe later, and who promptly forecast snow. I had to explain to him that snow was unlikely according to the newspapers and I revealed at the outset my ignorance of the extremes of moorland weather and especially its sudden declines.

With regard to the village itself it was enclosed on three sides by bleak and darkening valley, or dale, the narrowing sides being stacked, as it seemed to me, with close-knit stone terraced cottages. The third side had a railway tunnel that according to my map extended for a considerable distance.

Our train escaped like a mouse's tail into that tunnel and was watched, I would say, by the bright-eyed cats that were those little lamp-lit houses set above us. We then retreated from the smoke and the chill air to one of a row of waiting-rooms that allowed me to read Mrs. Vernier's map by a lantern there. The map gave no indication of a house above the village, in fact it showed no habitation at all. The swathes of shadings and outcrops were peppered only with little farmsteads and then after many miles out where the railway line emerged and proceeded seemingly to nowhere in particular.

Having failed at the map Myda took over and folding and examining it minutely she found High Stoor, which was my aunt's house, at a place where in small letters was printed: *Rack and Stoor Estate*. We then traced a winding lane across Racker Moor, until after a mile or so a drive shown on the left that led straight into another dale that was as narrow and steep-sided as this one. Then tight within the limits there was plotted a house, where the valley sides rose impressively to either side of it.

After returning the map to my travelling-bag I had the most awful feeling that we had been neglected, and that no one had been sent to fetch us. The houses above the other platform were such private dwellings. The noises of cooking for dinners rang about the place just as the cold air made the hour seem later than it should be. In the sky of palest grey there were crows lifting like necklaces of bitter songs and after a time watching them we were visited by a white haired old lady who asked what we might be doing.

"We are waiting," I said politely.

"Wey-erting fer wat?" the lady asked me.

"Oh, I see," I said, realising that in such a village as this no one could keep their business to themselves.

"My name is Lachio Mettini," I said, "and this is Myda Lowens and we are waiting for a driver who is Mr. Barrit from High Stoor," I said.

"Thas made tha-selves polly and pot," was the old lady's brash reply and then she led us to the first shelter in the row where Mr Barrit had been asking the same old lady where we were.

Mr. Barrit was a short stout man who seemed too small for his large black moustache that struck out from his face. His dark brown eyes had such a nervous force in them that I took him for someone who was waiting to be shot.

"Mr Mettini, and Miss," Mr Barrit said with a hurrying glance away. "There is barely enough time," he said.

"Barely enough time for what?" I asked him.

He hurriedly passed a coin to the old lady and then removed from both our hands our travelling-bags.

"Before the snow," Mr Barrit said hurriedly. "We'll catch our deaths," he said, "or the car won't take the hill and we'll be stuck down here for a week."

He then set off with a swaying march carrying our bags. His over tight black suit caused him some hindrance as if he owned only the one.

I then made my remark, as I have already mentioned, about the newspaper's account of the weather, which Mr Barrit seemed neither to hear nor to believe.

The car was a black one and very small and domed I should say the three of us were grateful to manage to get into it. I occupied the front passenger seat where I was forced to closely watch Mr Barrit do what was required to get the car started. It was then a game between gravity and machine and whether the gears could manage the terrifying steepness of the cobbled lane. He drove back out along the dale to where a tight bend allowed us to climb the other way and to ascend above the line of the roofs where more crows were scattered, then to our right began rows of giant black rocks that had done well not to fall on top of us. Then when the engine had perhaps complained enough we came to a level cobbled road that was bereft of houses. Thereafter the cobbles gave way to a rut and gravel surface bordered by high banks of bracken and where all hope of habitation seemed lost from us.

There began then a conversation about the terrain while Mr. Barrit's little car whined and chugged and battled like a fierce dog up further steeps.

"It is terrible here," Mr Barrit said, and he fixed me with a stare before returning his attention to the road.

"The plants stab you, the moor tires you," he continued. "The sky pelts you. The wind blows you down."

Then as if to provide evidence of this the car reached the top of bleak hill where the failing light made for a golden view before us. Beyond I saw pale straw and brown coloured hills with dimmer ones beyond them. Streams had cut deep heathered furrows into the banks that our car whined past and where ewes gazed down upon us with rather noble faces.

Through all this Mr. Barrit talked of the difficulties of the moors and their uncertain paths and sudden fogs and suchlike.

After a time I replied.

"So I take it you drive out often," I said hopefully, "to give change to Mrs Barrit."

This remark caused him to slow the car down.

"Indeed," he said. "My wife and I," and he paused, "try to keep out of the way of things."

I continued.

"And Avelin Stoor is a very private person, I understand," I said.

"Yes. Sir," is all he said.

It then became apparent to me then that Mr Barrit had become rather unnerved by something.

"What do think of the house?" I asked him directly.

My question caused a temporary paralysis and the car was nearly flung into a ditch. Just in time Mr Barrit recovered and the car rather scuttled back and sped on.

Then after taking a few deep breaths and whilst seeing the dusky landscape rear about us like we should be attacked by rocks, I tempered myself.

"I mean," I said faintly. "I was wondering if you find the house suitable?"

Mr Barrit stared forward.

"Suitable for what?" he asked.

"Oh, I don't know," I said, recovering my nerves, "as a place to live peacefully."

Mr Barrit continued to stare forward while his manner suggested some knowledge was pressing upon him.

I felt then that I should change the subject for the sake of our safety and so I mentioned something of our business here.

"Mr. Barrit," I said firmly. "Although we have only just met I must explain that I have not heard of Miss Avelin before, nor corresponded with her. Instead I represent her lost sister, who is Mrs Vernier of Coppleton. They met last year but once again divided, though the cause is as yet unknown to me."

I received no reply and so I continued.

"Myda and myself are here to mend misunderstandings," I explained kindly.

Thereafter the car took us bumping along for a mile at least. Then Mr Barrit had the car slow at two large stone gate-posts to our left and where that drive began that was mossed and shaded by the cliff of a ravine. The cliff rose as we drove along and while out to our left and across flatter ground many dry-stone walls had collapsed to show the marsh and heath where an unfortunate flock of sheep was grazing. Then following the drive the ravine became became a cleft or a gill and where a narrow but strikingly tall house had been built as if to fit it. The house was made menacing by its four towers and the many spiked gables that protruded.To the right side of the house was an ancient barn but which, like the house itself, was surrounded by railings so tall that they gave a strange ferocity to the scene. The chimneys were seemed sharpened to spikes that gave wisps of smoke and while the windows were so narrow that no apparent light escaped them. We halted briefly at some tall iron gates that Mr Barrit unlocked and after this Mr Barrit's car juddered and rattled to a halt with the perimeter of those fortifications.

After mine and Myda's bags were removed Mr Barrit drove the car into the barn, then he returned to lock those gates against the moor. Such an air of protection surrounded us for those railings that were twenty feet tall at least, as if to deter heaven and hell and all else.

Mr Barrit was carrying our bags again, ungainly as before, and he led us up some wide and steep millstone steps to doors that were of a great size also.

"Mr Barrit," I said at my first opportunity. "why should the house be so defended?" I asked.

Mr Barrit glanced about.

"Miss Avelin complains of what she calls choirs of sheep that approach the house at night, sir," he said.

Myda and I then looked back down the dale at the wanton moor that Mr Barrit so disliked. There beyond the railings and through many breaks in the dry stone walls had come the living clouds of the sheep in threes and twos and that studied us like sentinels. Owing to the gathering dusk I could see no further, but then in an instant I became suddenly aware of snow. The snow was falling about us so silently and beautifully that I had failed to see it and I turned to survey the change in the weather like I had somehow altered it myself. The flakes were soon large and flurrying, causing me to think that Mr Barrit had been right in his assessment of it. It became a quickening whitening spinning drift that was soon about us, so that had we remained in Melther we would surely have been marooned there.

Chapter 2.
High Stoor.

To the right of some tall arched double doors there was an alcove overhung by an oil lamp that showed a thick rope for a bell. Behind the rope there was an oak shutter that opened a short way sometime after the bell had sounded mournfully within. Then that shutter slid fully across and a little face looked quickly out. The face gave so swift a glance that I thought myself lucky to have seen it. Then shortly after this the right hand door was unbolted and opened and a thin girl with straw coloured hair and blue eyes viewed us somewhat vacantly.

Then Mr Barrit went forward with the bags and while Myda and I followed him into an entrance hall that had a small door to the right, an arras to the left, a wide straight stair before us and then to the right of the stair an arch where another oil lamp lit a descending service stair. Oil lamps were hung elsewhere and showed a bacchanal mood to the beams and posts about us, for they were carved to resembled vines. The floor depicted vines too. A tall clock ticked as the girl stood by just as calmly and watched Mr Barrit divide our luggage.

"This is my daughter, Kale," said Mr Barrit without looking up.

I endeavoured to talk to Kale but her gaze was sent passed me. Nor did Myda manage to attract the girl's attention, as if the girl had no regard for us.

Then Mr Barrit opened the door to our right and hoisted Myda's travelling bag upon his shoulder and had us follow him into a quaint study furnished with desks and candlesticks. The dark furniture was accompanied by dark rugs that were wide and rich though poorly kept. Beyond tall these a narrow door gave a view to a small cased bedroom with tall thin wardrobes and a washing-table and a mirror.

"These are the old cottage-rooms for you, Miss," Mr Barrit said. "They were preserved in days past for legal persons who might stay overnight, the old Stoors being a legal family themselves."

Myda seemed most approving of that bookish place, there being, I noticed many novels by Sir Walter Scott and some atlases of an old kind and then some general reading that was provincial and which was not familiar to me.

Mr Barrit retreated and made announcements as he went.

"There will be a supper served with breads and soups at around nine, Miss," (the clock had shown the time as ten minutes after eight). We dine in the servants hall, which is down those stairs at the back there; the dining room above us is severely cold."

Then Mr Barrit and Kale and I left Myda to the cottage rooms and Mr Barrit lifted up my travelling-bag and nodded towards Kale

At this I gallantly stepped forward and took the bag myself.

"I could not have you take such weight on my behalf," I said and then I carried my bag towards the stairs, whereupon Mr Barrit touched at my elbow and had me halted.

"If you please, Sir, my daughter will act as your guide about the house. It is mostly disused and has no regular lights in it."

I nodded and turned about and found Kale regarding me as if I hardly mattered. They were bright sky blue eyes that Kale had but they inhabited such a paper white face that it might have been cut from the winter itself. More than this she had so remote a gaze that I could not imagine what she was thinking of. She took down an oil lamp from a low hook on the stair-post.

Then it was indicated by Mr Barrit with a firm nod that I should follow Kale.

I was at first puzzled as to where we should go, then Kale turned the arras, which I should say had a faded embroidery of blossom-laden trees. Behind the arras there was an arch to some narrow steps that went steeply up. Then without looking back Kale went speedily up them.

I called up after her with some puzzlement.

"Should we not use the main stairs?" I asked, for my travelling-bag had some weight to it.

"We should not, Sir," was Kale's faint reply as she flitted upwards. Very soon she had entered upon a balcony where her lamp was showing an elevation above a dim chamber but where I could see hardly anything below.

Then Kale sped along and around the balcony to an arch where another narrow stair ascended. After a passage some steps next went down. Then after a shorter passage I climbed up again."

"But it is surely an unnecessarily complicated route," I said, which caused Kale to pause upon another balcony and to look down into dark.

"The rooms have mice, Sir," Kale said calmly.

I shrugged my shoulders.

"But I am not afraid of mice," I said but found Kale was already along that balcony toward some steps up and was soon resuming her climb. We came upon a narrower passage and I met her light where her lamp was cast across one floor of a library. The library was round and had many balconies below us. I gazed above us and saw the topmost floor above us had a glass dome where I thought moonlight shone through gaps in the snow that was packed upon it. There was lamplight too, though the lamps were dimmed.

We left the library swiftly and I was led into another servants' stair. Thereafter that was arrived as if out through a cupboard into a high corridor that came to discreet stairs to either end. Kale was finally catching her breath though less than I was thinking long and hard while we rested there. The passage, as it turned out, led in a square to four towers with spiral stairs rising to them. We continued walking until we should be back where we started. Then feeling rather at the mercy of my companion, I chanced to think of what Mrs Vernier had said and her persistent fear of this place.

"Kale, do you consider High Stoor to have an unusual presence?" I asked.

"It does Sir," Kale said without hesitation as if I had asked if there was jam in the larder.

"I see," I replied unconvinced. "And you think I might find the cause of it?"

"No, Sir," she replied.

"No?" I asked whimsically.

Kale then turned and gave me a look that suggested some complexity had delayed her reply.

"It is all about us, Sir," she said. "There is no need to find it."

Then Kale unlocked a narrow door and removed a ring of old keys from a front packet.

Then taking my travelling-bag directly into the room I felt suddenly exasperated that out journey had taken so long.

"Why," I asked with some irritation, "did you bring me by such a roundabout way?"

Kale ignored me and saw to a little hearth where a few coals were waiting. She prepared a kindling but let the fire alone without lighting it and next seemed concerned with the rugs, which like the others were hardly worth looking at. She was, I thought, uncommonly resolved to keep her own counsel, which I supposed, in such a wilderness, she ought to be. Indeed she made no effort to answer me at all, even though I inquired of all manner of things.

When she fetched a ewer of water from who knows where from somewhere down the passage she was gone for some time. She returned with the ewer and afterwards fetched towels. During her absences I had looked over a room of no size in which a narrow bed fitted exactly a wall to my right. To my left was the hearth and tiny mantle and a brass guard. Immediately before me were oak shutters that Kale opened when she next returned with soaps. The view was brilliantly set for the day's end where the snow had overswept all tumbledown walls with a kind of innocence. The window was opened slightly for ventilation, though what I felt was something like a sword of coldness cut by my face.

Kale next took two lamps from above the mantle and lit them with a lucifer, so that I should have the comfort of two sources of light, since the firelight might be negligible. She set one on a desk below the window, the desk having a simple wooden chair before it. To the left of the desk stood a bookcase, also tiny, which presented some tiny books.

Kale's silence, which I regarded with growing impatience, led to my finally sighing and pacing.

"You say you cannot tell me why you have led me around and around. Then you do not answer my questions - just as if it is I that is serving you," I said with the impatience that comes with youthful arrogance and with travelling all day.

There was a silence between us that was as complete as the snow's. However, and like she had considered me more worthy by my outburst, she spoke in a whisper.

"Miss Avelin has her own routes through the house, Sir. She has them to herself, and without knowing you properly she would be frightened to come across. That is why she had me to take you by all other ways."

Kale had such a still face, as if no part of wider civilisation had ever encountered it.

Then suddenly she set off around that little room checking that things were as they should be. She drew out hinged boxes from under the bed, which should store my shoes and then beside the hinges of the door there was a recess that was equipped as a wardrobe.

"There is supper now," Kale explained like she was talking to herself. Then dimming the lamp further, which was on the little table beside my bed, she took up her own bright lamp and I was required to follow her again.

There was another extraordinary journey downwards, seemingly by every stair and balcony that could be found. Then when I no longer cared where we went the same arras was touched aside and we were in the entrance hall again. In that place I was required to wait until Myda emerged from the cottage rooms, after Kale had knocked. Myda was dressed in different shades of browns and addressed me quickly.

"What a lovely house," she said.

Chapter 3.
The Supper.

Kale led us both along and we descended that narrow stair to the servants' dining-hall, as Mr Barrit had described it.

The room was one that was narrow and long, and it became at its far end to as a prelude to the architecture of the barn, for a heavy sliding door was slightly ajar and gave some glimpse of it. Before the doors was an untidy area for firewood and coals in buckets, while to the left side of the room there was a recessed window and door, before which there was a deep hearth where a fire that was fuelled up and provided a great heat. Opposite all these was large hatch of the kind that contains a pulley-lift for raising foods from the kitchen to other floors. Set endways to the hatch was a heavy practical table on which plates and cutlery had already been set. Beyond the table and to the right side was stove for kettles with service shelves after it.

At the head of that table, though with his chair turned about so that he could gaze across into the dazzles of the fire was Mr Barrit. Kale dutifully went to sit beside him on th elong side and was facing us. On seeing us Mr Barrit stood quickly up but was ushered by me to sit down, since he looked as tired as I was.

My own chair faced Kale's while Myda sat to my right with a view of the kettle stove but where kettles were ticking and off the heat.

Then Myda and I in unison glanced towards the tall narrow window across the room to our right of us but saw the view blocked by the snow's gathering.

I expected at any moment that Mr Barrit would speak, but he did not. Instead his eyes fixed upon the serving-hatch that had produced sounds of hoisting. Then when some delivery had reached its place Kale hurried over and slid out a long tray with four bowls of food arranged on it.

Mr Barrit then watched me with a most otherworldly expression as if the thought of eating had disquieted him.

Thus to improve his appetite I attempted polite conversation.

"The weather has surrounded us," I said while the bowls of food were passed along.

"I dare say it would be hard to return to Melther and harder to rely on the trains," I said. "Do you expect the snow to melt soon?"

Mr Barrit shook his head.

It occurred to me then that his arrival back at the house had entirely drained the man. His physical appearance, which had previously had a professional air (as drivers have these days), was somehow transformed into a figure more suited to a place of confinement. His face with its quick moustache and alert eyes seemed thrown into mental destitution.

I felt obliged to give the man and his daughter some reassurance.

"Mr Barrit, I feel I must explain what prompted Mrs Vernier to write to Miss Stoor and thereby have Myda and myself received here."

I then turned to Myda.

"Miss Myda Lowens is from Knaidith College in London, where we received instruction from my mother who is Mrs Vernier of Coppleton to find means to reunite the two sisters in friendship at least."

I received my bowl of food but I looked forward.

"Mrs Vernier, I am afraid to say, is very unusual, which I suspect is due to the sad loss of Mr Vernier some years ago. She is given to flights of the imagination."

I picked up my knife and fork but found my meal unrecognisable. It might have been scrambled egg and pie, or something like it, for I could not tell. Then also the meal had small additions which I discovered were shirt buttons, which I avoided. Also something that was like pastry was leathery with very little flavour. I pushed the bowl away whilst noticing that Myda and Mr Barrit had done the same. However Kale, on seeing our meals rejected, set our our bowls beside hers as a sort of a queue and resumed eating and while a dreamy satisfaction settled on her face. Then Kale, after she had finished two bowls, rose and attended to the kettle and poured newly boiled water into a large teapot. Then giving the teapot one stir with a spoon she poured the tea into teacups and delivered cups and saucers and sugar to before returning to her meal.

Myda and I found the tea unusually sticky and sour, so that we both avoided the tea like we had avoided the meal.

Having made no progress with eating or drinking I resolved top talk.

"How, may I ask, did Miss Avelin receive her sister?"

Mr Barrit answered when Kale would not.

"Mrs Vernier's stay was short, Sir," he said.

"How short would that be?" I asked next.

"One night?" he replied.

"One night?" I said as I pushed my teacup and saucer further away and found Kale eagerly receiving it.

Mr Barrit sighed.

"We have very few guests," he said.

Just at that moment three bell rings and then three more and then two cut a sharp sound from some concealed place behind me, and I saw Kale at once stop eating and drinking and listen to it.

Kale then regarded me with such disdain as if I had no rights whatsoever.

"Miss Avelin is ready to receive Mr Mettini before he retires," Kale said.

Then Kale rose and marched along and paused, so that I was required to follow her. I bid Mr Barrit and Myda a hurried goodnight, but whose faces bore the same disillusionment with supper that mine had.

Then resigned to me fate, I followed Kale as before, and who might very likely lead me anywhere.

Chapter 4.
Avelin.

I was taken the long ways upwards and occasionally we passed a window that was not shuttered. From there I could survey the light of a rising moon upon the grey-white distances. The house was so cold that I could barely stand it and even the wavering light of Kale's lamp did not distract me from feeling remote and uncared for. Then after so many complications we arrived on the corridor where my room was situated. We continued past my door and followed the passage to one of the tower staircases and at the top of this Kale approached a pale grey curtain hung before a thick dark door and Kale lightly knocked. Then Kale came to call out in a soothing way.

"Miss Avelin, it is I, Kale, who has brought Mr Mettini of London to see you."

Then the sound of a little bell was heard and Kale entered and then ascended a few steps that allowed u up into a place where Kale's lamp was met by the light of many others.

A conical tower roof was high above us while fitted beneath it were many timber shelves. Stout ladders were fitted to these while hinged brackets were swung out and had oil lamps hung on them.

In the place below and about us was a curved hearth that had a small fire smouldering behind a guard while central in the warm room a round table with ten chairs had been arranged, though mainly for a party of dolls. The dolls watched each other serenely while their places were occupied not by dishes but open books, as for the pretence of reading. Above us also ancient dolls in their brocades and silks were set to lean out and stare down. Then beyond all these of was an arch with a door that was opened inwards and the doorway framed a view of a passage to the next tower room that seemed equipped a kitchen and dining room. Then between the dolls' party and that doorway was set a wide armchair where there say a lady with a most compassionate face. She had beside her a table on wheels that was overspilling with wools and yarns, whilst also there was a brass handbell with a ted handle. As we approached the lady smiled what I would say was the warmest and kindest smile I had ever seen, yet what is more that face was Mrs Vernier's, only happy. More than this I would say it was Mrs Vernier's face as it would be if Mrs Vernier had always been happy. The lady's eyes were twinkling with merriment as she studied my awkward approach, for I was unable to see Miss Stoor without seeing Mrs Vernier first, except that the two were entirely incompatible.

"Miss Stoor," I said, "I am honoured to meet you," I said with little confidence at all. I believe your sister introduced me as little more than a student of poetry, for that is all I am. I have been been sent to discuss the manner of yours and Mrs Vernier's next meeting," I said, "provided it would not inconvenience you."

Then I stood straighter.

"I am here with Miss Myda Lowens, a prospective student, who has guided me thus far, and whom I am sure you meet in good time. London is in such a stir at the moment with political action and forment, and Myda in particular most concerned to understand it," I said.

Miss Stoor nodded and then was most attentive to Kale, whom she smiled at with something more than respect, just as each had in part adopted the other. Miss Stoor had Kale fetch two chairs and Kale was to join us and not have any subservient position.

"I really don't know the wider world," said Miss Stoor kindly whilst smiling.

"Even when Hettie visited I had hardly ever received guests, except for the good ladies from Melther on afternoons in summer, there being many sewers and doll-makers among them."

Then she seemed to gaze with an utter sorrow.

"With Hettie I must had said the wrong thing," said Miss Stoor who looked between Kale and I. "She left so quickly and even left her slippers, which I hope you will return to her."

I nodded.

"Indeed I will, Miss Stoor, and as soon as the snow is passed," I said, "for fortune has brought Mrs Vernier to the inn that is just a few miles from here."

"The Last Light," Miss Stoor said with sudden remembrance.

"My adopted father was a honoured member of the bar and he would us on Christmad afternoon to The Last Light where a feast was set for those that had nothing."

I smiled at Kale upon hearing this but she did not smile back.

Miss Stoor returned her attention to what she was sewing together, which as a doll's embroidered jacket.

At this I looked again at the doll's above us and understood the years of work that had dressed them.

When Miss Stoor returned her attention to us I broached the subject that my mother had been was most eager should be discussed.

"Well you should know that Mrs Vernier is awaiting news of how you might stand between you and she."

"Between us?" said Miss Stoor with surprise. "Why there is love between us," she said, "especially after my adopted parents, the Stoors, have passed from me. Hettie is all I have."

I sat back, feeling nothing but good heartedness from the lady.

"Then when the snow permits you shall meet," I said with great mirth, for it seemed mine and Myda's aims had met with success.

Then feeling that there had to be some explanation for Mrs Vernier's behaviour, I reported my impressions.

"If you would allow me, Miss Stoor, I would say on Mrs Vernier's behalf that she lost her husband some years ago. I noticed a most striking nervousness about her."

"It must be grief, Mr Mettini," said Miss Stoor "for I did all I could to reassure my sister. I also cooked for her here in my towers, owing to the fact that Mrs Barrit cannot cook overly well."

This caused Kale to stiffen.

"Forgive me, my dear," said Miss Stoor to Kale. "I am trying to say that your mother cooks meals that are delightful. It is just that modern people do not eat half so well as you do."

Then Miss Stoor, seemingly aware of my every need, gave voice to me empty stomach.

"Tomorrow I shall make a breakfast for you, Mr Mettini, and for Miss Lowens. My kitchen tower is well stocked for the winter with slated meats and jars of pickles."

I felt suddenly elated.

"Miss Stoor you have blessed me indeed - and Myda too," I said.

I sat back.

"It would honour me if you would visit us both in London. My mother, I am sure."

Miss Stoor smiled warmly again.

"I am afraid I am better here, just as I have always been. But I would have you take some doll's clothes for the poor children that must be in abundance in those places."

"Indeed they are," I said whilst smiling, "your donation would be well received.

Then Kale rose, as if I should be removed, and at this Miss Stoor smiled and nodded.

"Yes, Mr Mettini must be tired."

"I am somewhat weary," I said and I rose too.

We parted well and even though Kale nudged me along I waved back to my host, for I felt her friendliness and hopefulness and I understand our meeting to have been a successful one.

When I was alone in my room, after Kale had left me, I sat at the little desk before the window. The fire that I lit with the lucifers and the kindling had given much heat to so small a chamber. It was a place suited to my reading from a book of poems and enjoying my own company. Beyond the arc of the door and beside the little hearth was a washing-stand with a ceramic bowl and with a shelf for the ewer of water. Soap and towels were there also on a tiny rack and while a small mirror was a good height upon the wall. On that dark bookcase I placed my razor and my comb, then on a hook on the door I hung my dressing-gown and with poems repeating in my mind I caught sight of my lamplit reflection in the window like I was a study in ink.

211

After washing I retired to my bed, which I should mention had heavy starched linens that were fiercely cold. I had retired with another of my favourite books, some verse in Italian, and I made notes on a folded sheet that I moved from page to page.

Then after reading some more I dimmed the lamp and I came to the utter darkness and utter soundlessness that High Stoor has in plenty and eventually I slept.

Chapter 5.
The Upturned Night.

I was awoken very suddenly by the sound of knocking. I raised the light of the lamp at my bedside and then leaving my bed I donned my dressing-gown and slippers and carried the lamp to the door. The knocking continued until I turned the key whereupon the knocking stopped. I opened the door carefully and then leaning forward with the lamp I looked and saw no one. My lamplight was spread across the wide corridor but there was no one in either direction. To my left the passage went dimly passed the head of the stairs on the right and afterwards there was the corner turning left where there were the steps to Avelin's tower, but which was rather too dim to see. To my right was much the same the view towards the next tower and where the corridor turned to the right.

Then like someone was aware of me that knocking began again, but this time from some place on the stairs where I could not see.

"Hello?" I called out with some apprehension. Then on hearing that knocking again I left my door ajar and set off into the cold air and on reaching the staircase I looked down.That straight stair met some wide open double doors and a junction with a passage but where again the dim scene was motionless. Then the knocking came again as if someone was concealed just beyond my sight. Therefore after taking a deep breath I set off down, feeling that I had no other option than to follow. However when I entered the passage there was again no sign of anyone. To the left the grand main staircase with two head-posts and and must descend in turns all the way to the entrance hall where I had first seen it.

Then the knocking came from there and so I crept along.

As I moved my mind was sent back to the particulars of Mrs Vernier, indeed I felt that I was acting on her behalf. For had not Mrs Vernier had some kind of mistreatment in this house or she would not have left it so suddenly. I was finally moved to say this when I again addressed the dark, for a scheme of a kind had come to me that might explain everything.

213

"I am not Mrs Vernier, Kale," I called out. "I am not one to be diverted from my course. I shall remain here and unite the two sister's whether you wish it or not."

Then finding the grand staircase empty I listened, but where the knocking came as a reply, and from someone who was far below on the stair and beyond my lamplight's reach.

Thus I descended more quickly until a mid-landing was there, and where a plain servants' door was discreetly placed. Then from behind that door the knocking came again and so after a pause I opened that door sharply but found a passage there. At the farthest place ahead of me I saw the uppermost balcony of the library, for the moonlight through parts of the the snow-covered dome and also the weak lamplight was there giving some shape to the shelves and books.

"I think I understand now, Kale," I said while peering forward. "I understand now that had Mrs Vernier not learned of Miss Avelin then you and your father would have very likely inherited this place."

I listened but there was no reply.

"Your efforts to frighten all away have not worked, since Mrs Vernier is lodged close by and we shall have an end to this," I said.

I lowered my lamp and strolled forward when a single knock resounded.

Then as I looked I came to see someone once hidden on the balcony was entering my light. It was a small child. Then when I aimed my light I saw it was a doll, much like the ones I had seen before, only it had been set to stand and face me. Then from behind that doll there 'walked' another with an uneven gait and then another behind that. Then soon, though I could not believe what I as staring at, there were thirty or more dolls assembled in the passage ahead of me like a cast of puppets. Then the front line of dolls received from behind them some heavy object that many dolls were carrying, and it was revealed as an army revolver. The dolls struggled to raise the firearm at first, but after many attempts a doll that was looking along the sights and nudging the other dolls to move was taking aim at me.

Without the slightest inclination to see anything more I turned and fled. My breath, previously soundless was now loud and shrieking as I ran without knowing where I ran. Then emerging on the mid-landing of grand staircase again I snatched a glance back around the door-frame and saw the dolls moving the revolver at some speed. Without needing further encouragement I descended that stair with many clumsy leaps and stumbled and recovered many times. The light of my lamp was flashing about and when I reached the next floor I saw a corridor extending to left and right with tall double doors not far in either direction along them.

The clatter of the wooden dolls and the thumping of the revolver's grip as it was dragged step after step was an ominous sound, but fear propelled me. I ran to run to my right but when I reached those doors I found them locked. With a cry of awful despair and terror I ran back the other way and with the briefest glance up the stair I saw the dolls were nearly upon me. It was my unbridled panic that caused me to run so fast and I reached the other doors with a scream of pleading and found the leftward door opened and I leapt through and was swinging the door shut and then searched for anything to bar it. Then finding a plinth for an large urn that I am afraid I broke in my haste, I slid the marble plinth with all my strength until it made those doors immoveable. Then after this I crawled down the corridor a short way and waited.

Remaining frozen with listening I heard the knocking resume and it was like the wooden arms of the dolls were rapping upon panelled walls. I set my lamp aside and pressed my hands over my ears until the knocking stopped and then, open-mouthed and staring I waited.

As if to alert me to another threat I new sound came, but this time from the furthest part of the dark corridor where I was hid. I could see nothing at first and then in time I saw a lamp was uncovered from under black fabric and then the light searched for me. Then it was Kale that came, perhaps drawn to the sound of shattering and she crept steadily nearer but then passed me entirely until she pressed an ear to those doors that had protected me.

I quivered violently.

"Can you even imagine what I have just seen?" I said while my clawed hands stretched to drag through my hair.

Kale returned softly and picked my lamp and had me stand.

"They have never moved in such numbers," Kale said.

Then after seeming to give the extraordinary situation very little thought she dimmed my lamp and hung it on her belt and then half-covered her own.

"They want you out of the house," she said plainly.

"I will go?" I whispered hoarsely.

Kale seemed to listen.

"And there are worse things than the dolls," Kale said next.

"They have a revolver," I said faintly.

Kale regarded me with growing impatience.

"You should not have come here," she said.

I trembled.

"I would not have come here if there were children dressed as dolls intending to shoot me," I said.

"There are no children here, Mr Mettini," Kale said who indicated that I should follow her and this I did.

Then a strange familiarity came to ease my fright, as if following Kale through this confusing house was normal.

Then after a way Kale addressed me again.

"Miss Avelin gets into things in her sleep," she said.

"Gets into things," I replied incredulously.

"Anything at all can serve her dreaming," said Kale. "There is no end to the objects that will move against you."

Then came to give the doors of rooms as we passed them some sidelong glances.

"We are safe so long as we take the balconies and the stairs but avoid the rooms," she said.

"But why me?" I said whilst staring at the doors also.

"Because Avelin's dreams wish you gone," she said.

"Then I will go," I said with sudden resolve.

"Provide me with blankets," I added, "and I will go sleep in the car."

Kale did not answer and we descended a spiralling stair behind a plain door a fit of realisation overcame me.

"What - do you mean the car is not safe either?" I said hopelessly.

"Mother will explain it," said Kale.

"What, the woman who cannot cook?" I replied with further horror.

Kale turned with such fury that I shrank back like a child.

"Mother cooks in the traditional way!" said Kale with considerable venom. "My mother's family are from the high passes, where there are only crofts and no schools but where the food is good. It is always good" she said.

Then Kale's anger ebbed away and that dreamy and rather insular person returned. She spoke hardly at all for the rest of that journey, down narrow staircases and along balconies. Then finally we emerged out at a place that was below the entrance hall and close to the servants; dining hall. Instead of proceeding there however I was beckoned through a strong door that gave entry to a solid set of set of millstone steps. At the bottom of the steps was an arch and a thick oak door that looked as formidable as the main door of the house.

Kale knocked firmly and then she turned to me.

"The night does not upturn very often like this," Kale said."Mother will know what to do."

Chapter 6.

A History of Sleep.

There was a sound of teacups and plates being moved and then after this that thick door was opened and a broad-faced, pink-cheeked and cheery lady of middlesome years was there, but who had in age the same blonde hair and sky blue eyes that Kale had.

I stared carrying all the shock that I had lately suffered and the woman simply smiled a big smile and invited me into a large scullery which had been improved by the addition of three armchairs. The chairs faced to the right where a glorious pair of hearths had a range stove set between them. The two grates fires were low but the two combined with the stove gave such a heat I immediately felt it. To the left side of that formidably built room were many ropes and winches that had hoisted towels up to the smokey warmth above, while after them was a boiling-stove that with copper laundry pans upon them. At the limit of the room another arched door was open to a room where great white bedsheets were dripping and where the mill-stone floor had ruts for the flow of the water. This was altogether so physical a domain that I felt secure in it. Only the presence of the serving hatch in the left wall after the laundry stove, accompanied by a trolley of tea-services gave me pause, but the welcome I received soon smoothed all that.

Mrs Barrit, while she guided me to the nearest armchair, was receiving mouthed silent words from Kale, as if I had become a source of concern.

"Now – you come in, Sir," said Mrs Barrit in a song-like greeting. Her voice had that kind of northern rural dialect that sang along like it was Irish, but with many long pauses that the Irish dialect rarely permits. It was a voice that underplayed all things, so that I could not help but be reassured by it.

"I was about to start a pot of tea when you came knocking," she said, "so we may as well share it," then she smiled at Kale, "and you too Kale, let let us all have the benefit," she said.

I considered the teapot at the table's centre with some fear.

218

"I am not sure that I am well enough disposed to ordinary pleasures," I said. "You see I have had one of the strangest experiences of my life."

"That would be the dolls, most likely," said Mrs Barrit with very little concern.

I stared at her, for I had needed more than Kale to vouch for their existence.

"Mrs Barrit," I said, "what are they?" I asked her.

Mrs Barrit retreated towards the kettles on the far stove.

"They have been a trouble long before our own time," Mr Mettini. "To be sure Fernalls that served here last saw the old Mrs Stoor pass away, after which by her last wishes the Fernalls earned their retirement to Rawgarth, which is near to where that family came from."

Then having no wish to watch a kettle, as no one does, she again seated herself.

"The servants that serve here have always been brought from lonely places, so they would not know the folk hereabouts, so they would not tell others of the predicaments of the house."

She smiled her broad smile.

"It had been the Stoor's way going back many years to treat all residents, whether they sat or served, exactly alike without any being above another, for the reason that they all hid the secret of Avelin."

Then she gave me a steady but unkind look.

"Miss Avelin from the age of eight has had powerful dreams, enough to send bookcases over and doors to open and close and mirrors to shatter. The old Stoors, who were Avelin's adopted parents came to understand that the news stands would make a spectacle of her."

Then seeing that I did not quite understand she smiled again.

"Her dreams can take hold of things and march them along, just as you have seen with the dolls. She has an authority over things that should not have any life in them and gives the the appearance of it."

I cleared my throat.

"So have doctors -?" I began.

Mrs Barrit shook her head.

"No one has ever troubled them with it," she said.

I breathed a long breath.

Mrs Barrit smiled again.

"We are far from the world, Mr Mettini. Here a life has a freedom to be whatever it likes, no matter how odd."

I stared about me before understanding that I had no means to not believe what I was being told.

"Then what does Miss Avelin think of her condition?" I asked.

"Well of course she has no clue whatsoever," Mrs Barrit said kindly. "As a girl she was told she was often sleep-walking and moving her dolls about. She was never once told that her dolls were walking for themselves."

I shivered, even though the room was so warmed through.

"I was nearly shot," I whispered.

"They are a terrible aim," said Mrs Barrit said and she stood to attend the kettle that was steaming.

I spoke louder to secure her attention.

"And was Mrs Vernier threatened too?" I asked.

Mrs Barrit was wearing a fleece mit when she swung the kettle about and poured the hot water into a the teapot after Kale had removed the lid.

"With the Vernier lady it was very different, the dolls loved her," she said, "they stole her from her bed and took her like she was one of their own. They danced her up and down and everywhere."

The kettle was returned and then the teapot lid was rattled on by Kale as Mrs Barrit continued.

"It was all too much for the Vernier lady, who made a such a screaming of it and left us for the night, dragging her travelling-bag after her."

Then Kale spoke to her mother.

"I must go to Miss Lowens and awaken her," Kale said.

Mrs Barrit agreed.

"Yes, bring her here like you did Mr Mettini, for we have a long night ahead of us."

Then after Kale had left Mrs Barrit sat and made a consoling face.

"Miss Avelin's dreaming has never been as hateful as this before," she said; "it is as if you have opened a hornets' nest of murderous intent," she said.

Mrs Barrit then gave the teapot a stir with the long spoon.

"It is very likely that you resemble some hated figure from a book, someone she despised or feared," Mrs Barrit said.

Mrs Barrit added some milk to a teacup and then poured some tea and then passed the cup and saucer to me.

"This is a dangerous house," she said.

I took a sip of the tea and tasted what was surely vinegar and onion skins, and I winced and put the cup down. Then feeling that this was one ordeal too many I lost some of my composure.

"Mrs Barrit," I said louder than I should have, "might I ask you where you learned to cook?"

Mrs Barrit beamed with delight and then immediately out giant tattered book from its place on shelf under the table.

"This book of recipes goes back a long way," she said solemnly as if my outburst had not in the least affected her.

"For in the elder days there was no one even with a bible in the high passes above Gridlegarth but they had this book," she explained before placing her hand firmly on the leather cover. Then with her eyes closing as if in prayer she turned the vellum pages that had boldly written words written in all places over them.

"All that learned to read learned from this bookthis book," she said, "for it was the most precious thing in those days to have a means to rea at all," she said.

"My mother, who was Flessy Garrille," she continued, "made full a use of it and she taught me words," she said. "And so it is with Kale, for I have taught her the reading and the cooking."

221

My heart went out to Mrs Barrit then, for I had never known of such a treasure that was both a source of education and cooking.

"How fascinating," I said, "for you see, Mrs Barrit, books I my life; might I read some of it?"

"You may," Mrs Barrit pronounced with a deep and grand tone and she handed me the volume that I quickly found had a weight that established its importance with me.

I shall remember that book for many years – indeed I might never forget it, for my my eyes settled upon little inaccuracies that became so glaring that I hastened to point one out.

"Mrs Barrit," I said brightly and helpfully, "here it says '*hammer for ten minutes*,' well should that not instead read 'simmer'?

Mrs Barrit came close to look but seemed unimpressed and had a dour face.

"We never had a simmer, whatever that might be," she said, "likes as not we could not afford one of them," she said.

This caused me to stare at her as strangely before I returned to the pages.

"And here," I said with some surprise, "it says to '*bring to the soil*,' but that should not that properly read bring to the boil?" I asked.

Mrs Barrit set her jaw as if she was perturbed.

"Well it was written by people who knew cooking better than either of us," she remarked with some annoyance.

It dawned on me then that I should not examine the book any more, for a realisation was coming fast upon me that did not bear thinking about.

I was next distracted by the sound of footsteps towards the door through which I had entered. Through the doorway came Kale with no particular expression upon her face, and then after her came Myda, whose mood was perhaps sombre, though it was often hard to tell which way her mood was tending.

Mrs Barrit raised the teapot.

"Tea?" she asked.

Looking towards Myda I blinked a long blink and Myda immediately declined.

Then Kale was sent by Mrs Barrit to some other part of the kitchen.

"Find all of the knives and wrap them in linen and put them outside under the trough," said Mrs Barrit, as if this was the usual thing.

Myda, who had sat down beside me gave me a questioning look be leaning towards me.

"I still haven't eaten anything," she whispered, then seeing that I was unable to reply she leant closer.

"It is only a little after ten. Why have we been woken?"

When Mrs Barrit returned with a biscuit for Kale that she dared not eat, then Mrs Barrit told Myda everything she had told me. At the very end she added some critical facts that should concern us all,

"Quite often when there is a rage there will be no end to it until at least nine the next morning," she explained to Myda who had listened without interjection. "But usually it occupies the higher floors and does not overly trouble us," she said.

Then she made a concerned face.

"But this is a so terrible a storm that has been let loose, for it seems all of the dolls and whatever else are set loose, and the menace shall come down to us surely - in search of you, Mr Mettini."

Then she sighed.

"I am afraid that neither the barn nor the old gardening shed shall be far enough on this occasion."

Then she made a sad face.

"Everything in the kitchens shall rise up against us in their efforts to reach you, Sir, and no door shall not unlock in Avelin's pursuit of you."

"What would you have me do?" I asked tremulously.

Mrs Barrit slowly took her seat and set her teacup and saucer away and she had Kale sit too.

"We would have you both take your chances across the snow-bound moor towards the inn," she said.

I started at this.

"But I do not know the way," I said.

Mrs Barrit nodded.

"Mr Barrit could not venture out on account of his chest. It would be your choice to build a fire, provided the fire does not attack you, for the power of Avelin's rage would follow you for miles."

In my appalling situation I came to think of my mother's letter to me and the extraordinary fee she had paid for mine and Myda's services. Although I have been a dutiful son and I have guarded myself from thinking ill of my mother, I understood in that moment that Mother might have known some of the circumstances all along. Deep in my recollections I saw myself with Mother, one summer in times long ago, mentioning a fearsome lady who was hold up in a gigantic house. I had naturally woven the story into my own boyhood imaginings, but now that I was saw that memory in its first form I stared before me. That gigantic house was High Stoor and the lady whose life was bound to it was Avelin.

Then I being subdued by memory, and Mrs Barrit by her need to protect her family, we were a silent party pressed by a most incredible danger, though of course myself most of all.

Then Myda, whose composure had been as impressive as ever, came to speak. She aimed her grey stare at me and her voice remained steady and resolved.

"We must climb the house to Avelin," she said. "We must wake her."

Chapter 7.
The Knowing Dark.

Myda made such quick preparations that neither Kale nor Mrs Barrit could dissuade from following through with her plan. Her return to The Cottage Rooms where I waited outside coincided with the return of Mr Barrit, who reported that the old gun room on the third floor had been unlocked and the firearms and ammunition removed.

"Mr Baritt," said I in a bereft way, "why should there be weapons here at all?"

Mr Barrit, came to shrug his shoulders.

"It was a hunting house as the old Stoors had it, Sir, most often for entertaining parliamentarians and foreign princes. But in recent times, Sir, the guns were the only means to wake the Mistress up. They would be fired outside, Sir, where it was safe, and behind the fences, where the sleep-walking sheep could not attack us."

Having managed to take some of this in I cast Mr Barrit an incredulous smile.

"And the dolls have taken the guns, you say," I said softly.

"All weapons ancient and modern," said Mr Barrit.

I sighed then like it was my last ever utterance.

"Mr Barrit, you and your wife and kale have done everything anyone could ask to contain this. Granted you might inherit a fortune one day, even one divided with Mrs Vernier."

Mr Barrit's calm demeanour persisted.

"The Stoors were the last of their line, Sir. But when Miss Avelin's troubles began when was nine years old, the Stoors cut themselves off from society, Sir. They sold much land to The Racks, the family that aims to own everything in these parts, and then only the ravine was left, and the house. But the wealth that remained from former times is enormous, Sir. Even a portion would keep Kale in riches for the rest of her life."

I came to understand in starts.

"So you feared that if Miss Avelin's state of mind was known then she would lose authority over her Will?" I asked him.

Mr Barrit hung his head and nodded and I nodded too. It was a dilemma that anyone would have found intolerable, perhaps I too would have born Avelin's rage for the sake of it.

Just then Myda emerged from her rooms dressed much as she had been before except that she wore brown flannel walking-trousers instead of a brown skirt and also she was carrying a lit oil lamp in her hand and had a darkened one looped about a shoulder with the strap from her travelling-bag.

"Mr Barrit," she said calmly, "do you think you could draw me a map of the safest way to the attics?"

Mr Barrit paused then nodded.

"There is Kale's map that is already drawn" he suggested.

"Excellent, we shall have that," said Myda, who had effectively taken charge.

When Mr Barrit left I found I had little to say owing to the extraordinary state of things. Then after staring about for some moments I shared my thoughts.

"Myda, you have taken all of this very well," I said.

Myda shrugged her shoulders, just as if nothing could faze her.

Mr Barrit returned promptly carrying a black notebook and showed the pages were scribbled over with a sort of a map.

Mr Barrit retreat from us then.

"We shall remain in the kitchens and bolt the doors, Sir," he said.

I tried to find some optimistic words but I could find none.

Then Myda stepped towards the arras after glancing at the first page of scribbled maps and I followed. After we had entered the staircase I heard Mr Barrit's footsteps fading before the noise of our own climb sounded instead. Occasionally we halted and listened but I heard no sound of the dolls, and so the house and its maze-like complications received us.

Chapter 8.

Listening.

Myda consulted the book of maps at the top of each spiralling stair and when we had first ventured along gloomy balconies. No sound caused us to look about and to my mind I felt like I had imagined all matters, even though the Barrits had done so much to corroborate them. The darkness beneath balconies was each time like some murky pit where the ordinary assemblage of furniture was in the main like any other. Myda in her turns made progress without any hindrance and it was only after reaching a long corridor that we both heard many doors creaking open behind us.

When we turned there was a most curious posse aimed at us that I could not quite see at first. Then as we approached I came to see that we were being followed by pens and pencils.

The rooms behind had sent forth every writing implement and they hopped together like penguins upon the ice flats of the southern pole. So pretty were the pens and pencils together that I was rather charmed by them, having sone a great deal of writing myself.

Then like the mood of the encounter had suddenly changed those tiny things rose up into the air and their sharp points were targeting us like little spears.

Myda grabbed at my hand and was soon tugging me along and we went where we were headed but at a frantic pace. Through a plain service door Myda went and slammed it shut but just as the sounds of impacts rattled like a fierce rain upon the other surface of that door. Then after there was the noise of bouncing pens and pencils that had lost the power of flight and we were returned forthwith to the previous silence that enveloped us.

Myda sent me a cautionary look, as if she then on be careful around anything at all, and indeed our caution was needed. The sudden rising up of things included paintings that flew from walls, carpets that unpinned themselves and rose like snakes, sweeping-brushes that tried to sweep us and pokers that were swung like swords. During the assaults by all these things Myda made some alteration to her route that involved some near door

227

and in some cases she knew what should await us beyond the door of a passage simply by listening closely while she approached it.

We came to climb another spiralling stair Myda placed her lamp a few steps above her and consulted the book and while her free hand made little movements in the air one way and another, and then after replacing the notebook in her pocket we climbed higher.

"We cannot go directly up," she murmured, "we must go down many times."

I knew the peculiarity of the route very well and followed with questioning her. Then as if to alert me to the dangers above I heard those knockings again, though from somewhere high above us.

I cringed as I walked.

"That is the sound those terrible dolls make," I whispered.

Myda stopped and listened.

"They are communicating," Myda said.

"They are communicating," I echoed but with a kind of dread.

Then Myda navigated using her maps and while the knockings continued but while Myda took all ways to avoid them.

We came out from a stairwell onto a balcony where a larger chamber than we had so far seen was in darkness below us.

"The noises have stopped," Myda said as indicated for me to stop.

"Alright," I said while looking to all places where her lamplight was reaching. Then both of us looked down where we saw a large crowd of dolls organised and aiming crossbows at us.

How quickly we moved I cannot say, except that it was nearly not quick enough. I heard the hum of the missiles pass by my ears before the two of us dropped to the floor and while above us the bolts made high pitched cracks as they pierced the ceiling plaster.

Myda pulled at me and had us crawl along the balcony to the next stair but where I feared there might be armed dolls waiting for us. Instead the spiralling stair was clear and Myda got to her feet and had both of us hurried up it. The stair led a passage that went left and right and Myda chose left and we dashed along until we reached some closed double doors and Myda pressed an ear to one of them.

Myda came to look at me in a strange way and then in turn I at her.

Then she spoke with a more pronounced gravity even for her.

"Whatever is behind this door is not a doll," she said.

I made a concerned face.

"Then perhaps it is Mr Barrit," I said hopefully.

"It is not Mr Barrit," Myda said.

Then we both heard from behind us that same hunting-party of dolls hauling the cross-bows behind them. As we listened the dolls were close to the stairhead, as if we should have very little time to run passed them.

In what seemed an instant Myda grabbed the brass handles of those doors and shook them and then turned the left one fully. Then she sprang through the doorway and had me follow and then that door was pushed shut.

Myda took a brown ribbon from her hair and wound it about the door handles tightly and then knotted them twice. Then that door's other side was suddenly pinned by iron bolts and after this I heard the mass of those dolls clatter against it.

After this there came those knockings that sounded somewhere above us and then they stopped.

Then breathing a sigh I llooked for Myda and saw her to my right standing with her lamp raised. Then looking where her lamp's light was aimed I saw arranged ahead was what I can only describe as a herd of wardrobes.

Chapter 9.

From:The Journal of Mrs Hettie Vernier. February, 1924.

What can I tell you of my arrival at The Last Light Inn in the small hours when I beat upon the door and rang the bell? For, God bless me, when a whole contingent of occupants did not open their windows above and rain compassion down upon me!

"I have walked upon the moor - for miles and miles!" I cried out. "I am Mrs Vernier of Coppleton who has become lost. Let me in for I am so cold and exhausted!"

I had with me my little railway-bag. My visit to those parts had been planned as a short one, but that bag, when I had hauled it through the gloom, had gained weight with the dew and I felt it was like a rock that I must drag along.

The inn keeper, who is the kind and dependable Mr Leathen came out from his establishment to take care of me.

"Howev'r 'ave you come by us," Mr Leathen said, "for there is nowt else out 'ere fer miles distant," he told me as he brought me into the front bar and wrapped blankets about my quaking person. Then after Mrs Leathen, who is most kind also, had hurried with a brandy and then like a saint had served me sugary tea.

"Oh," I had moaned when I somewhat recovered, "I was walking out from my sister's," I told them, "who is at High Stoor. I walked into the dusk without remembering it would come so fast and early. Then after that," I said, "well I wandered without hope until your lantern shone from its hilltop to me," and I showed my utter relief to the both of them.

Mrs Leathen had applied such comfort to my quaking soul.

"Then Miss Stoor at that house will receive notice that you are here and you are safe," said Mrs Leathen whilst patting my hand, "and will soon enough be returned to them."

"No!" I had shouted and then rested back. "Do as must for my sister but I will instead pay to stay here," I said whilst I shivered, "for I shall take trains back to Coppleton as soon as I am able. It is my firmest desire, Mr Leathen, nay me firmest wish, to find hearth and home again and be rid of this bleak and dangerous locality."

Something about me made them agree immediately, as if my face transmitted to them the whole of my disquiet. To I was well cared for would be understating it. I was given such charity as heaven itself would give to a wandering soul. I was given a room forthwith and those second and third sugary teas were declared to be free of charge. When I asked for my railway-bag they brought it, then when I said I kept a journal for certain matters they brought in a little desk and a chair and a triple candlestick to see by. Such was the comfort I enjoyed that I was spurred on to write this account immediately. I can tell you that the explanation of how I began on my midnight wanderings was entirely true, and I wish to put things right by He that reads all things.

Further to this small introduction I should explain that I also write this as a basis for an essay, for I have a name in writing, though a modest one. I write as a person of second sight for *The Spiritual Expounder*, a journal of considerable repute in the field, and I write also, and where this first draft shall be preserved, as the founder of *The Coppleton Spiritualist Society*. As for my articles in the said journal I do not write as myself, but under the pen-name Edwardia Loomingbury, by which I am avidly read by sensitive souls in many parts of the country.

I shall not delve too deep into my own past here, except to say that mine was a mission of reunion, for my sister, Avelin and I were cruelly separated by an orphanage in London. Our birth-parents identities, well neither of us can know, for we were foundlings on the steps of Marchenfields Hospital that serves the famous financial district of the great city of London. It was through Marchenfields' administrations that the Lark Family, a family of goldsmiths from Manchester, who paid regular visits to merchant banks. On that day and place of my sudden appearance they heard of me by rumour and adopted me forthwith.

As for Avelin I have learned she was given to a private orphanage. This information I did not glean for myself. Instead my friend, Mrs Mettini, had the information dug out by her many investigators. According to these anonymous agents copies I learned of the discreet visit of the Stoor family, those who in those days were were important in The City. Thereafter Avelin, then unnamed, became Avelin Stoor, and no trace in any ordinary record could have shown what direction my sister was in.

It was Mrs Mettini's diligent work that sent me forth to this wide and wasted land and where Avelin and I rejoiced our reunion only yesterday. We are twins of the first joy, for she resembles me very much in her face and carries some of my calmness and courage. We had such a day of rejoicing that I cannot begin to tell it. However I had reason to regret my arrival when night fell, as I must tell you now.

There is a spirit in that house that I cannot sense or discern in my usual way, just as if I was blind to it. I do swear on all that is true that after dark the furniture of my high room had some strange inclination to move towards me, inch by inch.

First of all I took my copy of *The Spiritualist Expounder* from my bag beside my bed, for there are texts in every issue that allow a person to repel a spirit of dubious intent and send it from the physical sphere. These texts however did not work. Indeed I would say *The Spiritual Expounder* actually encouraged it, adding my shoes to the tally of things that began to dance about my bed.

Then meaning at once to find a different room to sleep in, I dressed before packing my few belongings at a stiff pace but while a wanton pair of my own slippers danced out of my reach. Then when the slippers changed their plans and gave chase I fled with my railway-bag and my coat in hand and I closed the door to my room most firmly behind me.

Then it was that I searched for another bed chamber but little did I know that the phantom again lay in wait, for a party of dolls was leaning against a panelled wall, one after another. Upon seeing me they animated themselves and came to surround me and dance with joy! I could not make my way toward any doorway without them first blocking me and while their dancing became a rhythmical clattering sound. I was unfortunate again when many more dolls appeared, indeed at least twenty of them came forth. With that greater number adding to those that were there I became a part of a celebration, with the dolls hugging about my shins and dancing me along.

I was danced down too many corridors and down too many stairs for me to recall, while objects such as hat-stands joined the celebration as we passed. Throughout my journey with the dolls I swiped at them with my Spiritual Expounder, for what it was worth, but the throng seemed oblivious to my need to be free. Indeed when I waved The Spiritual Expounder many dolls like chorus lines waved back.

I escaped, finally, by charging at the dolls and causing many to topple like skittles. Then when I had forced my way to freedom I ran down any stairs I could but heard my pursuers hopping noisily after me.

How I managed to find my way down to the staff that live and work there I cannot say, but finally I met with Mr Barrit, a responsible man, after calling out for help many times. He took me down a secure kitchen where too soon the dolls were beating upon the door there.

In that place, Mrs Barrit, whom I had not met, but had instead thought about, after drinking her unpleasant tea, gave me information of such an incredible sort that I found it hard to accept it.

The Barrits both informed me that my sister has dreams of such supernatural power that they visit the world we know and take firm possession of it. It transpired that I was harassed but instead loved, nay even adored, by the many objects of the house that would not give up bringing their affection to me.

Meanwhile the beating upon the kitchen door caused such a noise that the Barrits could barely manage to say more.

"If we could step outside for a moment," I told Mr Barrit at the top of my voice.

"That is where I am meaning to go also," said Mr Barrit who screamed back.

Therefore he unbolted another sturdy door and we climbed some stone steps to a cobbled square before a barn. Then Mr Barrit asked me to wait there while he fetched something.

"But will I be safe, Mr Barrit, from the hoards here?" I asked him.

Mr Barrit, forever a steady and persevering man, unlocked the gate in the railings that surround the house and he fetched me an oil lamp from its place at the front door and suggested that I walk a distance onto the heath, for my sister's influence might wane there.

I made up my mind to walk along the drive that was nearly in darkness save for the light the lamp sent ahead of me. I walked into the starry dark and saw no dolls and no objects of any such kind, but after reaching the lane that the drive meets I heard from behind me a sound that filled my heart with pure dread.

A gunshot rang out through the cold night air and then another. The shots caused sheep in their dozens to run in fear, but when they saw me their intentions were changed into something else altogether. The sheep came dancing about me in an Irish fashion and while I made for a forlorn figure amongst them. At the same time my poor mind raced at the thought of poor Mr Barrit and what on Earth he was was shooting at.

Then after a few moments there was another shot and in panic I ran - chased by the dancing sheep, and I ran rightwards along the lane, since that was the way to the village of Melther, but without my knowing precisely the way to it.

Then as the sheep danced faster at my heels I heard a gun shot again. Then suddenly and like the proper instincts of the sheep were returned to them that flock regarded me with their disdainful glances, much as Kale, I should say, who is the Barrits' daughter had regarded me.

Dispersing, those animals removed themselves from my light and became as unseen as before. Then hearing no more gunshots I assumed that my distance from the house was sufficient to protect Mr Barrit from whatever threatened him. In short my absencehad surely saved him.

I meant not to return there.

I set off into the night carrying the lamp and my railway-bag, since I wore my coat, and I walked for a terrible distance but found lamp expired and I was walking with no knowledge of where I was. At one time I thought I heard a voice and I left the lane in search of it, for I assumed that Mr Barrit had driven his car out to search for me and was somewhere across a field. But I arrived knowing that some animal had called out and I made to return to where I knew but found it to be a bog.

Thus I was unable to find a way and through I tried to listen for any such voice that called to me they were the creatures of the night that warned me off. For a time I cannot guess at I sank into mud or was scratched by the thorny shrubs and trees that were like the tigers of that place, until at long last the great lanterns at The Last Light Inn shone brightly from that lonely escarpment were visible above its doors.

Thereafter I made my approach as I have already described and explained such things in the terms that were reasonable for them to hear, since for the sake of my sister they were not the experiences I have here described.

There could be no possible advantage to anyone knowing the particulars of this case, save for the readers of *The Spiritual Expounder Quarterly,* though omit any mention of High Stoor and even the northlands, for I shall site the house in The Forest of Dean, or somewhere quite removed from here. I wish my sister long years and perfect serenity in her remote house, where no unscrupulous journalist can seek to profit from her extraordinary life. No further information can go from me to Mrs Mettini, who has done so much. I shall report that my sister and I cannot be acquainted, as a consequence of too many years apart in different places and with delineations of interests that could not be reconciled, and might never be, in our advancing years.

Chapter 10.

The Domain of Books.

Myda and I watched the wardrobes, which were of many designs, though all were enormous and of the kind that are very hard to move, had anyone attempted to try. Even so they were rocking ever so slightly from side to side in unison and with each landing they had moved forward together a short way. They approached with dull thuds and with all of their iron coat hangers chiming and I stared wildly at such huge things coming to crush us.

However when they were within our arms reach the wardrobes stopped. Their coat-hangers ringing afterwards like thirty or more giant clocks.

Then when Myda stepped forward that entire troupe shook and moved back.

I forced a smile.

"Perhaps they are friendly," I said.

Myda then turned to me.

"I think they are on our side," she said.

Then I too stepped forward.

The wardrobes rocked in an angular way and when they had finished there was a gap in their entire column for us to walk between them, for it seemed that in spite of my apprehension Myda was right.

"Perhaps Avelin also has very good dreams." I ventured.

"Or someone else in the house has learned to move them," she answered before removing the map from her pocket and studying it.

"Who do you suppose that is?" I asked.

Myda paused in her map-reading.

"It must be someone we have not met yet," she conjectured.

"I see," I said, as we passed beside the wardrobes until we were beyond their lines and Myda opened another plain door on the left.

She paused as I approached.

"The main difficulty comes now," she murmured. "In order to avoid the corridors where the dolls are better armed, we will have to cross a part of the library."

"Alright," I said without considering the matter much.

"The library gives access to the whole of the house. It may be where the full menace is concentrated."

After her warning we a spiralling stair and we emerged in one of those passages that gave a view to one of the balconies of the library. I could make out the pale light from above, though it was fainter, that place being many floors below where I had stood before and where the dome was.

Myda and I approached that balcony with trepidation, and I did expect immediate trouble, but as it turned out there was none.

Myda peered above us at the higher balconies where wrought iron filigreed stairs connected each. There were lamps lit below us, though many floors below, so that only Myda's lamp made a view for us.

Myda cautioned me to crouch down whilst she peered out.

"It would be easy to send arrows or bolts at us from those other floors," she said.

However, when we fully emerged from the passage the only presence was that extraordinary collection of books.

They were old casebooks of law on the near shelves along with legal periodicals bound with string. Indexes for long shelves of boxes were set smoothly and also bookends of finely carved kinds There were long benches too with hinges too that could be lowered from the panelled walls, so that the whole effect was one of excruciating time and study.

Finally, being overawed as I looked down and then up to the other balconies I was barely able to speak.

Then as we stepped along there the books became even more precise, with shelves of accounts and administrative affairs, each volume blackened with age, and when we ascended to a higher a floor, which was done carefully owing to the loud steel steps, we came to records of the smallest dealings, just as if the Stoors over the centuries had recorded everything.

"There must have been generations of Stoors," I whispered.

Then I saw Myda was instead considering Kale's book of maps.

"We have to climb up through the library to a place three quarters up," she said before reading the scribbles again, "then I shall take a passage to a stair that will bring me to the vicinity of Avelin's kitchen tower. There I shall beat upon that door with anything I can find."

She elaborated on her plan.

"You continue up the library staircases and engage with the dolls."

I looked about with a frown.

"How should I engage with the dolls?" I asked.

"Present yourself to the dolls with the guns and then run away," she said exactly.

"Right," I said, whilst trying to seem fully agreeable.

"And what if they shoot at me?" I asked with puzzlement.

"They won't," said Myda matter of factly.

"They won't shoot at me?" I asked.

"If they fire the guns they will wake Avelin up and they would not do that," she said.

"But how can you be sure they won't hit me?" I asked.

"Well if they hit you they will only hit you once," Myda said, as if this was an acceptable compromise.

I was in state of mind where I could hardly see the merit of Myda's plan but given that I had no plan of my own I was obliged to go along with it.

I cringed and even fumed a little but when Myda set off marching again and I followed. Meanwhile and from books on shelves behind me came the sound of tearing and when I paused and looked I saw illustrations of untrustworthy looking people had emerged as emerged and were moving in a curling way as only pages could. They were characters with glaring eyes that now glared at me and in their dozens and then in their scores and finally hundreds they were moving in their curling way until they were close behind me.

"Myda?" I said whilst glancing back.

"No - we are sticking to the plan," Myda said firmly.

"Alright," I said and quickened my pace, "but -," I said while the criminal fraternity quickened their curling and hopping procession behind me.

"Be quiet," Myda said.

When we had reached two balconies higher Myda opened a plain door while studying the notebook and then finally turned to me and noticed the hundreds of paper men.

Myda's mouth opened to speak but then closed and while I introduced the gathering.

"Thy seem to be men who were convicted of something extremely worrying," I said.

Then in ways I did not expect the pages folded themselves up like they had paper wings and whirred up into the dark.

"Spies," said Myda with a grimace as we both peered up to try to see where the swarm of pages had roosted. Then all of a sudden the pages were back, for the whole population flew straight through that open doorway and wee gone.

Then Myda gently closed that plain panelled door and turned away from it.

"We cannot go that way now," she said.

Then her face became very glum.

"The books were listening all the time," she whispered, "to everything that we said. We cannot follow through with our plan. The dolls would have ropes or some such thing at the kitchen tower steps. They would be lying in wait for me."

Then she looked up at the balconies above us, where that high snow-covered dome gave such faint light.

"We must take our chances with the crossbows and the pokers and and the bed-poles and paper-knives," she said.

Then without a word more she set off around the balcony to the next flight of steps up, and against my most optimistic thoughts I believed then that all was done for us.

Chapter 11.

The Assembly of Dreams.

Myda had approached the problem of that house with her native common sense, but made such a job of it that I came to think that, instead of Avelin, she was the most extraordinary person of all. I felt incompetent in Myda's presence, even though I was the senior, in college parlance. How I had not found a use for my poetic sense I could not say. It was as if my power to detect the smallest inference was not applicable to guessing the intentions of a blood thirsty army of dolls.

Myda and finally ascended the iron stairs to the penultimate balcony. From there we could see the archway to that fateful passage on the opposing side was visible as its high curve and where no doubt all the crossbows and whatever else awaited us.

"Myda," I whispered while we ascended slowly. "I think this surely my time and not yours," I said. "I must go forward and save you from harm. It is my duty," I added, while I took the lamp from her and overtook her.

"Alright," Myda said calmly.

"I mean," I said next. "I must sacrifice my own safety to secure your own," I said.

"Yes, alright," said Myda, who unhooked her second lamp and raised the wick to its brightest.

"Alright," I said again but in a full chested way, but all the while wondering why my sacrifice had been so readily accepted.

With no courage at all I should say I ascended that final stair with Myda giving me little pushes from behind. As I ascended I fixed my gaze on that arch that was coming more fully into view.

I reached that uppermost platform beneath the dome and saw the dim lamps receive the sweeping light of mine and Myda's, but I saw no danger there. Nor was the passage I had so feared at all threatening either, for though it was dim it was empty.

I glanced above me as if to heaven and cast a smile back at Myda but saw she was entirely surrounded by dolls, each brandishing some weapon of certain lethality. The dolls had followed us up the stairs without our knowing and without a sound, for as I looked down upon that iron stair I saw one doll was laying down to cushion the tread of another. There were scores of dolls, more than my terrified mind had imagined, while time again across the backs of those dolls that were lain down were hauled the cross-bows and pokers and other implements of anger.

It occurred to me then that the dolls had stalked us all this time and our calculations in the library had been quickly relayed to them. They now surrounded Myda with terrible intent and while my retreat towards the passage was also filling. For coming forth as a second danger came extraordinary collections of hats and jackets and dresses and trousers walking as mixtures of women and men. Those strange things came like puppets, with the paper criminals escorting them, while also the pencils and pens were marching also. Then bringing up the rear were the larger dolls like the artillery, shouldering the revolvers and the long barrels of shotguns. Then behind these the dolls with cross-bows made their way to stand before all the others and aim those deadly bolts at me. The clatter of that legion made me step back further and further, until the handrail of the balcony pressed into my back and I could retreat no further.

Along came the crossbows, managed by such happy faces, while their summer fashions sent pearly sparkles from the light of lanterns that other dolls were holding. Then when all parts of their horrible plans were complete the dolls and paper criminals and all other objects stopped and there was silence all about me.

I trembled then glanced towards Myda, but whose expression was rather of impatience than what my own face was sending forth. I tried to mouth some question but she failed to respond to it. Instead her eyes turned again and again towards two doll, some rows behind those that frightened me most, that pressed their wooden hands close to the trigger of a shotgun.

I stared back at Myda and made an expression of incredulity to show that the distance to that weapon was just too far, but Myda repeated her staring with even more force, so that I knew I should take a bolt to the face in my attempt to leap forward as she insisted that I did. I trembled and my eyes rolled and my hands shook.

What happened next cannot be described without first saying that I did not expect it, for a pair woolly slippers to came dancing and stepping upon the heads of the dolls. Then with sudden possession they both bent about the hands of the dolls that covered that shotgun's trigger. A struggled ensued that had the shotgun raised up and then with an ear-shaking explosion both barrels were fired.

The blast of shot went clean through a part of the dome above and parts of a segment of glass down. I curled myself up against the collapse and only after hearing pieces tinkle upon the floor many levels below did I venture to uncurl and stare about.

I had been buried partly by an amount of snow, whilst also large and heavy curved panes of leaden glass were leant upon the balcony rail to either side of me. Then further there were the dolls, their heads and limbs sticking out all ways in the snowy oblivion. Then further towards that passage when I came to stand up and look the animated clothes moved no more, while the criminals were litter of creased sheets. Myda had been freed too, for dolls were piled about where she stood and only those slippers could be heard, lightly tapping and receding. When we looked they hopped down those balcony steps over the collapsed toys, then when they reached the balcony below they danced around and about to towards that next passage there. Their happy sound became less and less until I heard it not.

Then shuffling through the spilled dolls, where pokers and guns and other weapons were unmanaged by anyone we pushed our way along the passage away from that assembling of dreams and while the cold night wind was all that harried us.

We arrived at Avelin's tower stair much as I had earlier, though I came to weep a little. So Myda had me sit down on those narrow steps and as if I would be calmed by her thinking she gave me the benefit of her calculations.

"Avelin aims her unearthly power with hate," Myda said calmly. "But Mrs Vernier's is aimed with love."

I gazed vaguely at Myda.

"Mrs Vernier's?" I said.

Myda nodded.

"Mrs Vernier was not assaulted by Avelin's powers in this house, she was celebrated by her own. Her love caused the dolls to love her, and her slippers to follow her, for love is at the heart of what she believes in."

I frowned.

"But Mrs Vernier is not here," I pointed out.

Myda raised a hand.

"They are twins, but one is more gifted than the other. Mrs Vernier has always been able to make things move, though she attributes them to another realm entirely."

I rubbed at my tired eyes.

"She moved wardrobes and slippers," I proposed, "from over three miles away?"

Myda nodded.

Then from above us there came a gentle voice calling out to us.

"Is there somebody out there?" the voice said with utmost civility.

I stood up quickly and I went close to the tower door and knocked lightly on it.

"Forgive me, Miss Stoor, but it is Mr Mettini. I wondered if you are alright."

"Yes, yes, I am perfectly alright. What seems to be the matter?" Avelin said with some concern.

"Oh, nothing but noises in the house," I said quickly.

"Well there will always be those," replied Avelin. "You remain there until I am ready," she said.

We waited and while we waited there was Kale who came up the stair behind us, and Mr Barrit too.

"I am desperately sorry, Sir," he said painfully, "that the troubles have come to this."

I tried to manage a consoling look when that door was unbolted and soon Miss Avelin was who wearing a bright blue dressing-gown and a golden bed hat.

There were dolls fallen from shelves but Avelin in her devoted way nestled them to their places and then leading us all along we came to that kitchen tower that the lady herself had much spoken of.

In time I had received a cup of tea that was drinkable and a slice of raspberry spong cake that was edible and I saw Myda too consume these like they were the last foods on Earth.

Miss Avelin meanwhile came to inquire of nearly everything.

"Whatever has caused the upset, Mr Barrit," Avelin asked.

"I am afraid a part of the library dome has fallen in due to the snow," he said in his implacable way.

"Oh, how very inconvenient," the lady said.

Mr Barrit nodded.

"I shall put tarpaulin down in the morning, Miss," he said. "And it would be better that you did not visit the place."

Miss Stoor nodded and sipped at her tea before smiling at Myda.

"So lovely to meet you, my dear," she said. "I hope you were not overly disturbed by the noise."

Myda smiled.

"In London there is usually a lot of noise," Myda said.

"I have no doubt," Miss Stoor said.

I can remember nothing much of the conversation thereafter except that it was a normal a conversation about ordinary things as might ever have. Kale and Mr Barrit and Myda and I left the towers and dispersed as we should. I cannot tell you the relief I felt when I entered my room and returned to my bed, but also the discomfort I when Kale woke me at what she considered a normal time. Yet even by that early hour the high parts of the house had been cleared of the debris of 'battle.' Good fortune came also when I was served with the view from available windows that showed that the snow melted sufficiently to allow a journey in the car.

A trip was therefore made in the early afternoon to The Last Light Inn, there being Myda and Miss Stoor and myself, driven by Mr Barrit most assiduously. Then in The Last Light Inn the sisters were settled together in a corner while Mr Barrit and Myda and I had an ale and a sandwich in another place.

"It is hard to believe that I have seen such things as I have," I said with a cautious tone while making sure the landlord and his wife, who were the Leathens, could not hear overhear it.

"We are very accustomed to it. Sir," said Mr Barrit. "There will be no talk," he added, "even if the locals were given to know; the moors are spun with stories already that are barely worth repeating."

"Yes, I see" I said, "and you manage very well as you are, Mr Barrit," I said. "However there is one point on which I am still confused," I said, "why it was that Miss Avelin's dreams took such a dislike to me."

"We do know, Sir, but we felt we could not say," said Mr Barrit, who it seemed had no heart to tell me.

"I must know, Mr Barrit," I said impatiently, "or else I can never consider this matter closed," then I looked at him in a hopeless manner.

Mr Barrit leant forward.

"Miss Avelin has an intense dislike of poetry," he said with much compassion in his face.

Chapter 12.

The Heart of Knaidith.

Myda and I arrived back much chastened by our encounter with Mrs Vernier and her sister. We could hardly mention it for some days and I assumed that Mr and Mrs Lowens were not told anything meaningful because they carried on thanking me for the money. Myda avoided my gaze when I passed by her and it occurred to me that our recent duty had much confused her. The mind and its powers was my mother's subject and not mine, and certainly not Myda's. For a week later Myda's reticence continued however, beyond any explanation I could find, and so I blamed myself for putting put her through far too much and left the matter at that.

I put my new found funds to work ordering rare books of verse, particularly from Cornwall where the poetic tradition in the native tongue had much alluded me. I continued to publish my essays in literary quarterlies but received no firm encouragement back. However there came a day when a letter addressed to me in the post room downstairs had a most unusual postmark on it. The stamp belonged to Switzerland, where the owners of one of the international literary fraternity resided, but on this occasion I was to be disappointed. Instead it turned out to be a letter from Mother.

In order to avoid the needless subtle jibes at poetry I will not include a transcript of the letter. Instead I will tell you indirectly that Mother informed me that Mrs Vernier was indeed a clairvoyant, though no one should necessarily ascribe merit to communicating with the dead any more than voters might consider themselves in touch with politicians. Mother next explained that Hettie Vernier was something, and was for better or worse a regular contributor to the quarterly journal *The Spiritual Expounder*. It was a journal Mother described as "a little known but earnest publication founded by people who were earnest but little known."

The remainder of the letter explained funds that she would forward to my bank, as sizeably attractive as before, provided that Myda was available again. She then outlined a short trip towards a house where a great many clairvoyants were meeting. *The*

Expounder Guild, which might be considered an unusual group, had invited Mrs Vernier, going by the alias Edwardia Loomingbury, to make a speech at a house that was considered the most haunted in Great Britain. None of this, of course, seemed untoward, given Mrs Vernier's interests, until Mother's explained that The Expounder Society had received a blunt message from all those who had agreed to attend that Mrs Vernier would be murdered.

Then later circumstances allowed for a conversation with Myda, when I had failed to receive an important letter from a translator.

"Myda," I said when we were both looking about the canvas and steel mail trolleys that porters have. "I wonder if our visit to the north rather vexed you?" I said.

"Vexed me?" Myda said with a grey stare.

"I mean," I continued, "whether you found the visit over-strange."

"Over-strange?" said Myda.

"Indeed," I said, "for I did find it somewhat strange myself." Myda sighed.

"It was over-strange," she said, "but it is the only over-strange thing that has ever happened to me," she confided.

"Then I remain sorry for such an inconvenience," I told her.

"No - no," said Myda quickly, "I should like to do more," she said.

I stepped back, for I understood then that Myda had not been unhappy in recent weeks but instead bored.

"Well there is another matter at hand," I said.

"There is?" Myda said with nearly a surprised expression.

"Would you consent to visiting the most haunted house in the country?" I asked her.

"I would," said Myda in an instant.

Then it was not a smile she gave, but something along the way to one.

That was the moment when I understood most clearly that I would never find as wise a companion, as discreet a critic, or

247

indeed as boundless a course in life as my devotion to the indomitable Myda Lowens.

As for the case that was mentioned in part, it was written up in a most unusual way by Edwardia Loomingbury in *The Spiritual Expounder*, for those with the determination to find it. For my own part I would strive to share my own recollections here should my recollections thus far be of any use to anyone. Needless to say I should prefer attention was directed to my analysis of poems, and I am much open to that instead, and indeed forever. My address being always: The Post Room Lodgings, Knaidith College, Knaidith Court. London.

Dystopia Heights.

Chapter 1.

For the first part there are steps but also tiredness, a skeleton that wants the opposite of what is done. He looks back down the staircase. There is still a living-room down there where his parents answered the shouting and the surface of that warmth through which his face would come still touched him somehow, made him look down, like a dog would be looking up mirror-eyed where the shoes would be. For a moment there is a slowing and the first part is over.

The fire-door is opened. The staircase sharks back down, takes a plastic-skinned bannister with it which is the way the staircase is every Christmas, promising and promising like it could take you anywhere. Some kind of howling starts up the staircase from a lower floor, louder then so loud that the whole stairwell gapes and the faltering light from a florescent bulb seems stopped then reaching. He gentles the keys in his hand. The children run up to the floor below his and they cry out in meeting someone coming through the fire door.

"Come on! The lift's - Grandma's in the taxi - it's broken - come on!"

His door opens.

There is a greetings card. For a second there are at least a hundred. No, it is an invitation to a church. He peers out of the window to see if there is a church. From this great height there are quite a few. He squints at the card to see which one it is. His lips lick carefully together. His blink is gentle against the bold print.

The letter-box opens.

"Hallo-o?"

His shoe treads a garden pea into the carpet.

"Mrs Nogget!" he exclaims.

She walks past him. The city is growing dark and everlasting. Sunset climbs brilliantly onto the clouds and cars blink over the river's gentle bridge. The sound of the carrier-bag on the hard-top table clatters. The tins and jars, her bunch of teeth smiling.

"Merry Christmas."

He watches her produce a package from her pocket and place it in his hands.

"For goodness sake!" she says, seeming to bounce off the walls and switching the lights on. "And look at this," she says, picking a single Christmas card off the floor and standing it again on the window-sill - reading it aloud with ceremony:

"To Edna."

She looks again and then at an envelope lying on the carpet and then at the bare window-sill, shelves and other surfaces, then resigns to nudge the card with her palms to the best position. Down in the car-park a taxi seems lifted by its spread lights and wide open doors set against the dark surface. Some figures stand cold together and hair blowing.

"Is that what you wanted?" she asked him.

He answered, but she also answered - the lady in the taxi, leaning forward from the back seat and hissing that her daughter should have picked her up and Samantha picked her up every year but this year she knew her place like she was under the ground. Prefer The New Year Love, the driver says. Singing of the bushes in the near distance haunting up thousands of knives and forks or seeming to heave some thing with their branches from one to another and over the fence into the security lights' bright darkness. Darkness hung along the main road, from old buildings in their soft under-lit hoverings or darkness made vast nests out of the various factories' stockyards and amongst these the shaving-brush unwrapped in the reflection, which she was also watching.

"They're all going away for Christmas," she said.

He is in the bathroom placing the shaving-brush on the edge of the sink. She unlocks a door and goes out onto the concrete balcony, pops her head back in. "Don't lock me out this time," her words go off into the air, go empty and big like thrown bed-sheets. Down below the driver has lifted the bonnet and is trying to fix the engine. A father and two boys stand small and some way back.

He sets up the Christmas card which has blown over. "They're all going away this year," he says, "where it's nice and warm."

251

"Well," she says, coming back in and looking at her watch, "let's lock this door."

She locks it and turns back to the carrier-bag on the table.

"There's everything you like," her eyes natter the contents, her fingers raise the cans a fraction and let them go then push some mince pies out of the way to lift out a box containing a broad red candle. "There," she smiles.

"Very useful," he says.

"Don't forget to soften the brush in boiling water," she adds a kiss to his cheek.

He opens the door for her and a voice rails from beyond the fire-door "These bloody stairs!" A draught blows between them. She says she will call on him in the New Year. She says she will have more time then and that she never has any time. He says she must do whatever is best. Her waves her goodbye along the corridor and goes inside and the second part is over.

A lady comes out of the building and walks through the gusting weather, along the muddy tyre-crossed pavements where the padlocked wire gates shiver and clack. She tucks a scarf more securely around her neck, dips her face, as her brisk walk takes her out where the industrial estate's avenues meet a junction with the wide main road. Back at the forecourt a second taxi has drawn up and suitcases have been transferred. The boys run around the taxis and occasionally watch her progress, they lurch forwards to grab each other's arms and go stabbing the air with out-stretched fingers. They look again and the lady is gone. The second driver pulls away with the first driver squashed in the middle of the back seat. One of the boys looks back at the flats which seem almost derelict except for some windows near the very top which are bright and a regular glow of windows on the stairwell between floors. A figure in uniform comes out from an office on the ground floor and gives a short confident wave to the driver and then turns slowly about.

The flat-windows rattle with the wind.

Last Christmas. He looks at the pen in his hand and wonders whether he should choose another. He perseveres. Last Christmas was very quiet. I enjoy the quiet although I know the quiet isn't for everybody. He looks across the sky where the lights of a jet are switching and flicking. Last Christmas the Queen was very informative - he wonders if this was true. He tries to remember what she said. Although I can't remember anything she said. He gives the pen a little shake. I am using the pen you bought me and it is working very well. A sound like pallets blown over in the factory stockyards. The wind pours over the building. I am having a lovely Christmas, he picks a mince-pie from the packet (he shakes the pen and it showers the paper with droplets of black ink). He sits back, nibbling at the mince-pie. He leans forward. Last Christmas the Queen wished that one day we might each own something which actually worked. He continues eating the pie as he walks over to the flat-door. He goes outside and listens to the perfect quiet of the corridor and the falling sort of emptiness there.

He puts his arm up and rests his hand against the door-frame and then bends one knee. That is all? And then his head leans from upright and rests against the door-frame too. He closes his eyes and he appears to be sleeping. So still, he becomes something a cat wouldn't stop for. To be like this. The roughness of the wind against those large cold windows in the rooms behind him. From somewhere the ringing smell of last month's industrial cleaning moves like a constant tide, and from this the insistence that everybody is still here. But listen. The furniture factory isn't loading up its long poster-sided trailers, the 'up-factory' isn't raising hydraulic wails into the night sky (he'd never heard them come down) or any of the dong-ga-dong-ga-dong-ga-dung-ga-dung-ga-dung-ga messages that bounce over the land in the middle of the night. In quiet. To be like this. Never to be like that again. One of his windows gives that same rattle, but now in solo. Far off and barely audible a loud phone bleats on the ground floor in Mr McKraw's office, it switches and trembles down there, almost sailing around for someone to answer it. To be like this. In the corridor the uncertain florescent bulb finally comes on. To be like this, for this is the third part. The door is closed and the shaving brush is fetched from the bathroom and held up in the kitchen and examined.

After softening, knock excess water from

shaving-brush with fingertips. Do not
allow lather to dry. When applying avoid
excessive pressure which can damage the
bristle. Made In Holland. His thumb.
so strong and still and devoted to its purpose; that if his
hands were occupied entirely by thumbs there would have been no
limits and his life could have been hauled from so many little-
finger preoccupations, stood up powerfully like a thumb himself.
He stands there in the kitchen for an absorbed time with his thumb.
He fills the kettle, then fights to put the lid back on which chews
around the rim as usual, scraping that thin edge. He takes a coffee-
mug from the high cupboard and sets it down beside the kettle on
the peeling work-surface of the fridge and stands suddenly
appalled that he has nothing else to do. He goes into the lounge
and switches the television on and turns up the volume until
Francia Zetman and her Christmas guests are rolling back in their
chairs, then switches channels. A chameleon is balancing on a
twig. An opera singer pronounces a huge word. "Not just a bank."
- "I'm in love with Jellyland! Have you been to Jellyland?"

He goes back into the kitchen, tilting his head towards the
music, the window rattles loudly. He opens the window upwards
and outwards to give it a good slam. Tea-towels rise on their hooks
- a calendar on a cupboard-side blows around: October, March -
October, August, February. He stands introduced to a ventilator-
hood on a factory-roof below going around and back, squeaking
and crowing. He leans over the sink to look down.

The kettle is boiling, a stampede of three minutes to get to
the right moment: and then the sudden thought: click: it's now.

The shaving-brush becomes submerged. An arm-ache, like a
meow in his elbow-joint and his lips open slightly and the pale
blue cup is full, and he bends at the knees to put the kettle down.
The wind jumps up from the car-park, that balcony-door judders
then meets an advert which blots it out. The electric-heater in the
lounge tins on, like the peck of a little bird. Suddenly his sniff. A
tea-bag is examining the shaving-brush. He gives them a look of
disappointment and takes the cup to the sink.

He stops.

There is a particular place in his mouth where his tongue can go where the last of his teeth are living. Like the familiar shapes of old toys in the back of a cupboard. His cheeks curve inward and his face looks through and reflects back from the window with the expression of a camel. But also the cars on the slopes of the western estate are searching too, they run like bright rain: to the darker houses, to the annoying-but-have-to-be-visited. Like Mrs Delk. Mrs Delk, he thinks about Mrs Delk. Which flat? (The one where the baby cries.) Ah, his eyes turn carefully towards the western estate, beyond it the regional airport. Her daughter took a flight more than, he waits, more than sixteen years ago. The Great Delk, the children of the flats called her when she played the flute and confused them with books they didn't dare read. So many years so serious and then, the eyebrows on the camel rise slightly, she just won the lottery like that. Like a strong but uninteresting tree, he thinks, that flowered one Saturday evening above every other. The lucky Delk. But also still The Great Delk (wherever that first Delk had gone), for her playing.

The wind is pulling at some young people who are walking along the far main road. The three boys are stopped in front of the boarded up shoe shop and wait for and look back at two girls who are wearing bright and then orange jackets and trying to keep broad-rimmed black hats on their heads. The boys look at the posters stuck on the boarded shop-front and they each step on one foot and then the other and hunch up a little. A large white car stops and the boys get in. The girls walk slowly until they meet the car. The boys get out and the girls get into the car. The boys get into the car and they drive away.

He puts the dripping tea-bag into a bin-lined cardboard box under the window-side work-surface, takes the shaving-brush out of the steel sink and puts it back in the cup. He checks the kettle and then fills it and sets it back and plugs it in and leaves the kitchen. He goes past the television which is singing and opens the door to the box-bedroom and switches the light on. The cream-coloured clock, which had been knocked from the bedside-cabinet onto the floor is still ticking. It is four minutes past eight. The windows shudder in the three rooms and he opens a bureau that is in front of the bedroom window and takes out an old black fountain-pen and some paper. He switches the light off, shuts the door, turns the television down and sits at the plastic wood-printed hard-top table and writes:

GONE FOR MILK FIVE MINUTES PAST EIGHT.

There are eight flats on this floor, "Our doors" and "Their doors." Their doors can be reached by going through the fire-door, over the landing and through the fire-door on the other side. Their doors are theirs and whoever lives there is them and they have their doors. "Our doors" were not the same as "Their doors," or, as it had once been explained to him, all the doors would be the same if they didn't live there.

His flat-door shuts trapping the sheet of paper and he joins the cold of the corridor and turns to his left. Some floors below, and softened, someone walks bang through one fire-door and squeak-bang through another. Mr McKraw is knocking and checking the locks. He listens to McKraw and then carries on down the corridor. Under the florescent strip-light which flickers, past the door on the right where the baby cries, and the next slate-grey door on the right is the one he goes to and finds a key, turns the lock and goes in.

Camphor-cream. The touch of a leaf and smooth of wallpaper as he searches for the light- switch. The curtains are closed and whole darkening and in the feathery light from the corridor a fruit-bowl appears like a carousel of children. Camphor. The light-switch. The light. He goes carefully beside the porcelain figures and into the kitchen. The dry steel sink. There is a note on the fridge.

Remember
to take the white loaf
as well as the milk
Please do not use the toilet.
Mrs Lodgeson.

He opens the fridge, but it's a freezer (full and crackling), then opens the fridge. There is a carton of pasteurised milk in the door-rack and on the middle shelf there is a scrunched remainder of thin-sliced white bread. There is nothing else. He leaves the flat and locks the door, turns and walks quietly into the draught to his own door, unlocks, removes the sheet of paper and goes in. The television has found a horse. Slightly warmer now. The curtains ready to be dragged scraunching and snagging together, the table ready to be wiped clean of ink, the carpet ready to be stamped back flat towards the balcony-door, mince-pie crumbs to be followed. The beginning of the fourth part.

Dear Hilary,

Thank you again for the curtains. As I was saying when we last met, you will be very welcome if you come by.

The lady who has taken your old flat is called Mrs Roales. I haven't met her properly but I was able to tell her, as you requested, that the smell has nothing to do with you. She said she had noticed it but couldn't find where it was coming from. I told her that you had been living there two years and that you had not been able to find an exact spot. She thanked me and also thanks you and said she will try not to worry about it.

The factories will be closing for a full week this Christmas, which is very good, and the new one won't be open before the New Year. I am very pleased to hear that you are enjoying the Home and that you are settling in.

Sincere regards,

Mr Coatham.

In the corridor the fire-door whines open and Mr McKraw begins his routine, a procedure which comes fully to life at Christmas, is ignored for the rest of the winter and reappears for a period during the summer months. That hollow melody of knocks and turned door-handles goes the length of the corridor and then returns. (Dab-dab-tat.)

Suddenly his door is vibrating and the magnolia inter-com telephone receiver slips from its fitting and drops neatly into a vase of water. A giant brown spider in its hole in the bookcase itches forward.

Chapter 2.

The door opens. The draught blows in and in it is McKraw who is leaning forward and wrinkling up his face around his sharp nose.

"Your guest,she came then."

He looks at McKraw.

"Yes," then watches the man's folded up eyes like wallets, "but she had to go." He is nervous about McKraw, the way he moves his head from side to side to find his best ear.

"She had to go…she's very busy."

"A very busy…widow," says McKraw, swaying like he and Coatham are two glasses clinking together.

He cannot say anything to McKraw. His mind wanders. There is the spider, the television and there is McKraw, each having their particular difficulty with letting others go.

McKraw puts a hand on the door which is still only ajar and the pressure on the door makes Coatham's eyes open slightly wider.

"In the New Year she will have more time," Coatham says, wondering just how long McKraw can smile, "-she said she never has any time," and looks at the floor.

McKraw's fist comes out and drills into Coatham's shoulder, "Happy…New…Year Mr Coatham."

He knows McKraw is always like this, but sometimes he wonders if McKraw is mad. Coatham nods and holds the door-handle in a hopeful way but the handle is turned full down by McKraw who has been talking but Coatham hadn't listened.

"All those visitors you've been having, Mr Coatham. There's been a lot of talk…" and McKraw studies Coatham with sharpening eyes.

McKraw is two months older than Coatham. It had been something to talk about when there was nothing else to say and learning this had led to McKraw's painstaking investigation and comparing one life with another.

He leaves McKraw at the doorway and then comes slowly back with the Christmas card and the envelope and gives it to

McKraw and begins to whisper about churches and getting himself lost on Christmas Eve.

McKraw flips the card open and drops his arms.

"Oh - no! This is Deadly Edna's, she was talking all last week about this annual dinner-thing ."

He doesn't look at Coatham. He chews on his top lip and is now muttering.

"My mistake - she's not here as well."

He grits his teeth.

"Ah well…" but cannot hold the card as casually as he would like. He looks beyond Coatham to some kind of vision and takes a slow intake of breath.

" - You might like to go," Coatham is summing up. "I would never go out -" then pauses, "I've never liked those very tiny sausages."

McKraw releases the door and forgets Coatham. The florescent light again pips on, "I know, I'll phone her daughter," he hurries down the corridor, dodging a lady who has come through the fire-door at the far end. The lady passes quite slowly and looks in at Coatham. Coatham stands in the doorway and is turned and is now watching the front legs of the spider rise up and perform a series of slow taps like it is about to conduct an important piece of music. His bottom lip tucks under his top dentures and he listens to the wind waking and whistling. There was never very much to do about the spider. There'd been a chance before it grew so big, yet even then it had that way of running straight through his heart. He had taken to the idea now that he wouldn't disturb it until the spring-time, when the balcony was warm and he could allow it to dangle down from that concrete base to another window and another person's life.

He turns nearly to face the lady but she has continued along the corridor. She puts something through the letter-box of Mrs Lodgeson's flat: a sound like clack-ack-k and then the lady passing again but this time not looking at all - and he, turned from the spider and giving her his full attention... but she has gone. He looks at the wall opposite his door where small dints and scratches in the plaster were made by removed or arriving items, also the scaly-print where a wet football had bounced where few had a habit of looking. (The fire-door. The lady quietly leaving, perhaps McKraw still marching around on a floor below, like two figures of an enormous clock.)

He closes and then locks the door. His hand is aching and the warm air of the flat has been sucked out. He goes into the kitchen, the tea is ready. He opens Mrs Lodgeson's milk and adds a drop, the carton dribbling around and leaving a white puddle. He puts the carton in the fridge then lifts the tea-bag carefully out and nurses it into the bin-lined box. His hands are still cold, the wet cloth is cold too as he dabs up the milk and then supports the cup with the cloth where milk had been ready to drip and then pushes the cloth behind the kitchen tap. He holds the cup and takes a slow sip.

Sometimes Mr McKraw would talk long after he had thought he had gone. Sometimes he would jump and wonder what was happening. Having returned to watching a film or continuing his thoughts in the bath McKraw would speak again. Once he opened the door again a tiny fraction and saw that McKraw was resting a fumble-paged notebook on his fore-arm and was mumbling as he wrote, like people can talk in their sleep. Sometimes he knows when McKraw is on his way, sometimes there is a private and uncertain voice like a bumble-bee searching closer and closer. Often McKraw was not coming to his flat at all but to somebody else's. He drinks some tea. There were many flats to which McKraw paid little visits. He looks into the tea at the dozens of flecks of sour milk floating around and around. He thinks there might be someone even now, talking to McKraw and sharing his tiny office.

He returns to the lounge where the air is sharply cold just above the carpet, but at waist height the air warmed a little by the heater. He sets the cup down on the table-top and goes and steps forwards and backwards and stamping his feet down until the carpet is smoothed back and then bends down to prod the carpet with his fingers until only the edge is curled at the balcony door. He looks out of the window at the city seeming to shrink from the office buildings in the centre towards the year's end, and takes hold of the curtains.

Occasionally they slide quite a way smoothly with the smallest pull, the bright orange and turquoise bars and brown zig-zags of the pattern appearing like butterflies' wings, although not as convincingly as he would like. But most times they snag, the small dark brown wire hooks fasten like the bite of a dog on the bent rail. The music goes out of them. He takes the innermost corners of the curtains and then, at fingertips, begins to ease them close, as if one might not see the other or both might somehow sleep through the whole thing. He sighs for them, but is watching a giant strip of dirty polythene snake around on the road below. The polythene is stained and ripped, is filling and rolling. Now a hunched ballerina scuttling to the cracked mud-tracked right-hand pavement and a stockyard fence which is litter-starred and pushed. The polythene flattens.... flutters. Now taking in air and up in a back somersault now scaring down to the edge of the opposite kerb and a sudden fast crawling, drawn smoothly up, high over the right-hand fence and gone, flight still in the air but invisible. Both curtains stop.

The hooks have clutched together on bends in the rail. He gives them a gentle pull. Stepping back from the window, he catches more of each curtain in his hands and gives the curtains three whip-lash flaps, so that he looks like a man flying, and now steps close. He tries some gentle pulls. The curtains slowly trickle further, the orange, turquoise and brown folds and the last mass of hooks on either side taking the journey. Just within the shadows of the curtains the glass is flooded dark, lights on the hill-sides blown intimate and hanging like tears. He looks out but the windows and their magnolia paint have caught his attention. Their nobbled dribbling. Silent questions of cold night air. He carefully reaches and presses each window-latch more firmly down, his hand stumbling where he is trying to see.

The curtains finally hack together with a number of fierce pulls and scraping squeaks. He smoothes them lightly with his palm. They float gently around with the twirls of air. Last summer his windows were open, late dusk was bringing moths chancing in from the lost pink and purple skies. His chair was cool indoors while tenants on their balconies shouted at cigarette-ends falling from flats above. Behind the Dunga-dunga Eeeka-dunga and pecka-pecka pecka-pecka noises the evening trucks hissed two and fro, the reek of the bone-merchants mixing with the smell of suppers. He listens. The wind catching the ventillator's hood, coming over the corrugated-roofs, piles of scrap wire and kissing chained gates. (A trail of sirens fly for a moment like strange geese.) Suddenly the window-frames startle and shake, the hidden weather knocking and knocking.

He turns from them, takes his tea from the table-top and sits in the armchair and stretches his legs. Holding the cup in his hands he rests his eyes. The inter-com phone receiver fizzes briefly in its vase and makes no further sound.

In the corridor the strip-light again flicks on and off. The floor above has all strip-lights on, but the doors locked and their key-holes empty. The floors below his have no kettles boiling, no cupboards opening and no music playing. At every landing the view down between the hand-rail of all flights below has no hands skipping or flickers in the cage-lamps' regular shine. Outside someone has come out of the building to look up at the high floors and holding a sandwich and gripping his collar. His trousers patter like flags in the gusts of wind. He glares up for a moment and then goes inside.

Coatham lets his elbows rest on the arms of the chair and then lowers his head for a sip of tea. The hours, waiting darkly as moles. The candle waiting for its match. The television like a mad fire. The beginning of the fifth part.

In his armchair, with his eyes resting, he begins to feel hopeful that something might come on the television. He thinks about the newspaper's television-guide which is on the top shelf of the bookcase next to the spider. He presses his lips in a small excitement, there might be.........something. He leans sideways and puts the cup under his chair, then rests his head. He has another think about the television, but sleep, also, on either side of his chair like great canyons. He tries to guess what this especially interesting programme might be, but he is unable to choose between various scattered topics. Amongst these a stray memory of a post-box after terraces on the left side of a leafy minor road curving for a sharp right bend. The high terraces with grey splintered old wood fallen off them in lengths or as countless crumbly pieces amongst brightest dandelions and young spark-thistles. A post-box almost closed by surrounding Elder bushes and providing darkness in the full summer heat. Beside the Elder a red-shale path starting for high meadow and creaky woods. The rain that fell today coming out of the heat and being a noisy rain, but leaving few puddles tonight. The boughs of the silver birch trees, luminous. The calm of big flower-heads in the long quiet, as steady as horses, the back-garden so unfamiliar and murky and still.

A bus moves along the main road. A full bus, juddering after the last stop, the windows steamed up and the glass smeary and streaming with drips. Slightly whirly faces look out and then people standing in the aisles of the upper and lower decks. A bus that nearly a hundred people have crammed onto, nearly smothering the creamy-bulb light - and perhaps, tonight, the perfumes, after-shaves, scents of soaps, talcs, body-lotions and shampoos are a weight in themselves which the bus hauls towards the centre of the city.

McKraw sits upright where he is knelt in his office. His keen eyes snatch a look at the bus and then the cars following afterwards. He straightens his back, scratches his nose then presses a new fuse into the brass clasps inside a three-pin plug and prods the solid pins back into place where they had risen up. He glances at his watch. He fits the lid, takes the small screwdriver out of his mouth and returns the wobbling screw into the body of the plug, then crawls forward. He fiddles and punches the plug into the electric-socket then drags his weight back and blows through his mouth so that his cheeks expand. He scoops up the television magazine from the prickly carpet of the office and he scans rapidly down the programme listings. *Song Night Christmas Special.*

McKraw climbs into his office chair and sucks on one stem of some reading-glasses he has removed from his shirt pocket. He looks out of the square office window. Another bus passes. The full and hot and smelly madness of another bus. Shreds of thin white paper are blowing around the car-park, the same paper which divides the thin razor-edged copper sheets which come to the wire-factory on flat-back wagons.

He smacks his lips and pushes the power-button on the television then checks his watch and looks at the magazine. He waits for the television to warm up and gets to his feet and glances over the desk: through the window-hatch to the foyer where the gale is shuddering and cricking the wire-glass doors. He turns back to the television and pushes the volume slide along. He angles his head slightly and looks through the plastic grill on the top of the television for the tiny orange light. He steps forward and gives the plug a kick. He leans around the television and gives it a casual but loud slap. He tries to push the mains lead in a little further. The weather rises loudly and then stops, like the wind might be hiding in a single tree. McKraw holds the magazine and waits with it. Around him the sound of the weather seems to have widened. He looks at the empty car-park and then the foyer where the crisp-packets are noisily crawling. Something wells up in his face, flowing from the maroon of his uniform and into the garden of tiny blood capillaries in his cheeks. No picture has come, nothing has happened.

Coatham shifts his legs in the cold of the lounge, as if the warmth from the heater which is circulating around his knees might somehow find its way lower, maybe higher and warm his face and his settled hands. He lets the windows shudder along and then listens to the tin clock in his bedroom ticking. The drip of the bathroom-tap also: like the remote and hesitant chipping of stone - so sudden when it comes that his ear passes through, then the silence after and the stitch drawn. He opens one eye: on the dark brown of the carpet beside him there is a garden-pea. A garden-pea, and he closes his eye.

McKraw draws some keys from his jacket-pocket and then a fresh packet of ten cigarettes. He unwraps them, standing by the tall dark green plastic swing-bin which is half full of newspapers, cigarette-ends, ash and Kevin's biscuit-wrappers. (Clifford who "does days" Kevin before him... whoever else, a few more of those

264

young lads who lasted a week or so each). McKraw snaps the cigarette alight and drops the lighter in his pocket and then leaves the office. He locks the maroon door with its tiny wire-glass window. He turns the handle and gives the door a kick to check and then smokes his way to the handle-less "Private" door next to the staff toilet after the lift. The keys jangle and then one to spin the lock and he gives the door a barge with his shoulder and the door clanging as usual into mop-buckets and clackety brooms. He pockets the keys and lumps along in his rubber-soled boots, down a breeze-block corridor lined with the cleaning company's silver jerry-cans of detergent and then that more familiar bottle in a black bucket amongst worn cloths, Dolly Washing-Up Liquid, which he uses himself. The fierce smell of the detergent screws tightly up his nose and the smoke from his cigarette performs for the cage-lights in fading tangles. He pulls on a white spring-lever door and jams it with his heel and the gale blows through and he smokes his cigarette. He descends a steep, bright-lit concrete ramp where the smell of the cleaning agent is quickly welcomed into the welling fruity stench of domestic rubbish.

Sometimes there are teenagers looking in through the X-lever expandable gate at the entrance to the rubbish-bay. When the truck chains up the skip then the wheels crunch over pop-cans squeezed in the diagonals of the gate and then whacked or kicked through. Tonight the rubbish-bay is a cage for the wind, an enclosure for swirling litter and flinching pelts of bits on the cracked concrete floor. He leans on the red hand-rail which follows the ramp and looks down into the large rusted brown and pink-sprayed skip with its upholstery of split or sticky bin-liners piled at one end. Above the skip is the mouth of a four foot diameter stainless steel tube. Next to the lift on every floor is a rubbish hatch, and in spite of any decorum in putting a bin-liner in, (the shooof of the speeding bag), or some who don't let the counterweighted hatch just clang back, the result is the same. The bin-liners wet from some spillage in the tube, some mouldy mishap marking all bags when they arrive like a body punch and send some air around. McKraw whistles the jingle for the Dolly advert and pulls a long boat-hook up from its usual place on the other side of the handrail and leaning against the inner wall and proceeds to roll the bin-liners off their heap in the skip and make the rubbish level. The wooden pole clangs against the metal of the skip and the smell of the rolling and spilling rubbish blows into his face as he grips the cigarette with his lips.

He knocks the end of the boat-hook on the rim of the skip to knock off any remains and puts the boat-hook back. Now he comes down the ramp and across the sharp glass strewn concrete of the bay, into the fresh cold air and checks the padlock on the expandable gate.

Beyond the gate and on the perimeter of the tarmac of the service area is a line of green lamp-posts with dim magnolia beaker-shaped lamps. Under these escaped litter scrapes around. Behind the line of lights the crumbly tarmac ends and the invisible night grass begins, up a steep bank and then a short way to the shrubby fences of the bone-merchants where some razor-whiskered spotlights are shining through.

He returns to the ramp and he jags his boots into the concrete surface to remove any "slips and slimes" and blows the cigarette from his mouth. He rolls his weight slowly on the white door and is back in the breeze-block corridor and the disinfectant and lumping slowly along. Most nights he comes back to foyer to find someone waiting at the hatch. Sometimes someone coming down the steps. He opens the door to the foyer. Tonight there is no one. He locks the service door and goes into the staff toilet to wash his hands. A small pattered plate-mirror has him singing a few lines of a romantic song in a harrrr-ho fashion, and then remembers the television is broken. He dries his hands on a paper-towel picked from a pile on the frosted window's sill next to the broken Hyg-easy towel dispenser. He wets a towel and wipes his face, the television - the trouble with the television and then Song Night - *Song Night Special for Christmas*. He breathes in slowly: for it occurs to him that he might call in on that.that - idiot. A muscle in his jaw twinges.. but not for long. No, not for long (for Song Night).

Chapter 3.

Coatham gets up from his armchair, reaches under for the cup which is still warm and makes his way to the kitchen, sipping the tea again. Globs of milk slip through his lips like soft berries. He slides the cup over the peeled surface of the fridge and opens the doors of the cupboard under the sink and leans forward. A musty smell, where the dripping waste-pipe has puddled the white hard-coated board, rises up to him. A Burgundy and gold canister of spray polish is rusting at the base and has left those rings of rust where ever it has been returned. Two orange dusters have drunk up the water and lie sloppy to the right of the polish. Beside these a selection of cream-cleansers with broody floor-cloths sat on them like wigs. He looks. Two bonus-size boxes of washing powder; one which was for an automatic washer, and so, he has never opened it. The other nearly empty. A bobbin of thick string. He finds the scuffed cream-coloured plastic dust-pan at the back, and its flicky plastic-fibre hand-brush.

Has the weather calmed? He puts the dust-pan and brush beside him and rests a hand on them. No, the weather is merely under itself. He closes the cupboard doors which clack shut after a short way and he gets to his feet. The kitchen reflected in the glass is only patches. On the high and dissolved land above the western estate the freckle-lit roads are flying. The weather coming back like harsh dry wishes in the car-park below. That bus on the main road, with the cars inching.

The wind comes back at the windows. A box for forty eight packets of Tartan Aire shortcake, now empty, in the gap under the work-surface for a washing-machine he doesn't have. In the shade from the window by day and half hidden at night. A black bin-liner rolled over the sides and then wet and dry tea-bags, two empty cans of luncheon meat, and now the dark brown fluff gliding. His fingers adding the fluff out of the bristles of the hand-brush and then waving it free. Sometimes the bristles coming out and then they too fall and the tread of the bristles on his palm. The beginning of the sixth part.

He goes into the lounge and begins flicking the pastry crumbs into the dust-pan. The smaller crumbs merely dither and then go under the straight edge of the dust-pan, which is slightly arched. He goes back for them, pressing the straight edge down so that the edge is true. Mince-pie crumbs. Then one of the garden peas coming in from the faint shadow of the table. He sweeps away as the carpet gives up its fluff, then standing and wandering the carpet, kneeling again for another moment. And the fluff. The fluff coming from anywhere he chooses. He sets the dust-pan and brush aside and goes into the bathroom. He comes back with a rust-spotted orange carpet sweeper which is slavering with fluff and proceeds to squeak the carpet-sweeper backwards and forwards with a steady increase of speed.

McKraw thinks. The deliberate quiet of the steps above him. He looks to the main doors where they are still and the strips of white paper just following themselves in limps and twirls. He wuffles loudly, and begins to climb.

His rubber-soled boots squeal on the scuffed and clay-smeared cloudy grey surface of the steps. He pays his hand up the plastic covered hand-rail while the grip of his boots are the certain and undeniable stop. His hand touches along and then the hand-rail's sudden turn for the next steep. He glances in his knowing at chocolate wrappers fanning themselves in the tugging flaffs of the cold drawn air, the furthest of a pair of plain square magnolia-framed windows at the next half-landing reflecting the next flight. He belches and puts his free hand to his chest in a formal manner. (There were places where people came slightly to bits and on these steps people did. He didn't, and he was in charge.) McKraw lets the thought go and there are just his boots squeaking and his hand patting along. Flattened cigarette ends. Matchsticks, that ran away with the children who were too young to be smoking. A fire-hose, the red paint of the reel scratched over with zig-zaggy names. He stops,

finds the cigarettes in his jacket-pocket, mouths a cigarette and shelters the lighter in his hands like he might hold his thoughts. (He is only balancing. He draws on the cigarette. He is only pausing.)

The wind is in from the North tonight. The evergreens amongst the shrubs are itching like big bears, or spanking like midwives from which the wind cries. One of McKraw's thrown cigarette-stubs runs in the car-park, toddles rapidly until speed blurs it.

McKraw is climbing and the aches have begun in his calves. His wuffly cough and then an emergency grabbing glance at his watch where Song Night seems carried impressively by silver hands. He trudges around the hand-rail at another landing and his boots are heavy. He aims some swear words around but declines to say them. He thinks. He tries to man-handle an expression of joy and a happy greeting. He rehearses some Surprised-To-See-You and then thinks better of it. These that worked with everybody else like the sudden appearance of an important day... but not with him. He blows the cigarette smoke and returns to his squeaking tread and his hand passing up the rail while some ash drops from his cigarette like a soft hat.

On the cloudy grey linoleum of the seventh floor a slimy trail from some dragged bin-liner arcs around to the rubbish hatch. McKraw puffs himself slightly and waits. The fire-doors on both sides of the landing are tight closed. Strip-lights through the reinforced glass, the light so creamy like it is barely trying... only the corridor on the left has a strip-light flickering. A narrow landing with the two fire-doors halfway along and the third wall dominated by the magnificence of the lift. The fire-hoses, extinguishers, and to the right of the lift's silver doors is the dark grey steel of the rubbish-hatch.

McKraw pinches the filter of the cigarette. He goes to the rubbish-hatch, pulls the hatch forwards and down and smears the cigarette around on the hatch's inner side, and then lets both go. He steps back slightly from the noise, the zooming echo with no other noises to accompany it, and from this McKraw walks officially with greater and firmer strides, through the fire-door which bangs, past the door on the right which is Lodgeson - Lodgeson - Mrs., the door on the left where the young mother lives (under the strip-light which flickers), and fifty three. He takes a glance diagonally to the door of the flat which is empty.

McKraw wavers for a moment. He might not knock on the door. A fluster comes over him and his eyes dart away, the lines he had fixed together wouldn't step forward... and it is Christmas Eve, and best leave that man to his sawing. McKraw narrows his eyes slightly. The plain magnolia door. That tight and aggravating, piercing sound.... a kind of metalwork.

McKraw wavers for a moment. He might knock not on the door. A fluster comes over him and his eyes dart away, the lines he had fixed together wouldn't step forward... and it was Christmas Eve, and best leave that man to his sawing. McKraw narrows his eyes slightly. The plain magnolia door. That tight and aggravating, piercing sound... a kind of metalwork.

McKraw knocks. He knocks a light knock, a knock for the old ladies and those who have children who will huddle around the door and stare at him. A gentle knock he has to brace himself to do and which makes his face redden.

Coatham stops sweeping the box-bedroom carpet and looks back into the lounge. He keeps his face still and then opens his eyes wider to listen. There had been a noise. He listens.

The wind is hoofing and rolling, big and small. From behind the closed door of the bathroom: the ceiling extractor-fan and its vent to the outside - and sometimes the air being drawn and making the dust-plastered propeller whir. The daddling of the window-frames, although the wind is falling. He listens.

McKraw stands outside the flat-door. He chews his mouth around and listens. The squeaky sound from behind the door has stopped. The rise of weather, far off, from the direction of the staircase and the touch of cold air at his ankles and around his face. He sniffs and waits. The almost sweaty appearance of the magnolia gloss on the door and the light from the faulty florescent bulb (in buzzes and odd "zuvs") flooding and chattering across it. His eyes harden with impatience and he looks back down the corridor to the red and wire-glass fire-door. His jaw chews and juts out. Usually there are tenants walking miserably around for the next flight of steps, but tonight there is no one. McKraw wakes slightly and looks back at 53: the black plastic numbers finger-printed with paint from when they had been screwed back on.

Coatham manoeuvres the carpet-sweeper around and drives it over the rough and smooth of the bedroom carpet, the blue and bronze flowers fighting like buzz-saws. Crumbs spin out as the jamming brush-rollers skid or grind, the pressure of his attempts rubbing up the tufts and sending the vibration through the pole-handle and into the grip of his hands. Some dark brown fluff from the other carpet makes a big appearance, more crumbs and then the "Hoo-eek" singing after them as the sweeper is pressed forward.

McKraw knocks louder on the door. The letter-box is lifting and ringing - and he steps back. His heaping, whipping cough and loud wuffling. He stops. He straightens his maroon tie and creased white collar. "Paradise - the hupper lupper der der d"

McKraw listens.

The key turns.

McKraw brushes at his maroon jacket.

The door opens.

The ink-dabbed face appears.

McKraw loosens his knees and bends slightly to show he's not on official business. He raises his eye-brows and opens his eyes wider to make them sparkle and then his Christmas- smile so that Coatham will relax with him.

"It's me."

Coatham looks out and the colder air from the corridor flaps through the lounge and joins the draughts from behind the lounge curtains, making them inflate slightly. McKraw's face is thrust forward and an odd smile is wiped off it when he smooths his hand over his mouth.

"Still in then."

Coatham opens the door wider and tries to think of something to say.

"I would never out." He looks at the print the football has left on the facing wall. The strip-light flums but remains on. Coatham looks down at the swirly grey vinyl floor-covering, the corridor cleaned late in the month but the extra comings and goings of Christmas have added fresh difficulties, shoe-prints and other technical matters.

McKraw is staring at Coatham.

"It's alright," McKraw raises a thick hand, "nothing official."

There was nothing official this Christmas. McKraw had thought about this when the last taxi was leaving and the smell from the sewage works was stretched thin and almost unnoticed in the harsh weather. The big darkness above and the cigarette in his freezing hand and his practised wave to the occupants as the taxi drove away - meaning suddenly nothing.

Coatham opens the door a little wider to be pleasant.

McKraw sees Coatham standing with an old carpet-sweeper. Behind Coatham a dining-table, the brownish surface cluttered at one end by Coatham's shopping. Magnolia walls and glossed balcony-door, the weather loud, some horrible curtains.

McKraw sulks into his thoughts. He chews some spit around in his mouth and then looks out at the carpet-sweeper. He swallows the spit and then throws out his hand and points.

"Does that work?"

McKraw comes forward. "That."

Coatham steps away.

McKraw rubs his nose expertly and takes the sweeper. He sets it down on the hard vinyl of the corridor and gives it a push. The squeak.

McKraw looks at Coatham. "This isn't very good."

Coatham waits.

McKraw sniffs and stands very still. "You haven't emptied it."

The two of them look at each other.

Coatham remembers the nights he has spent standing here. Last Autumn when the lift was repaired and McKraw travelled up and down at night to stop tenants from dropping litter. Sometimes in the evening McKraw would come to show him wrappers and cans, holding them tight so that the cans creaked. And Coatham obliging and talking about litter but McKraw annoyed and talking about something else. Coatham then talking about something else, but McKraw then talking about litter - and somehow behind this Mrs Ledgeson's face, her make-up like an explosion and her eyes owning everything. "McKraw?...Who?"

272

McKraw is possessed again by his official capacity. He carries the sweeper past Coatham and clomps across the lounge and into the kitchen. He checks that a rubbish-box under the work-surface isn't full and then draws it out carefully and pulls the white catch on the sweeper. He wuufles at the sweeper and pulls the base-plates fully open and lets two compressed specky wigs of fluff fall into the box below. He gives the sweeper a strangling shake and then with a thumb and forefinger he pincers at the brush-rollers to remove the fluff. His nails scratch on the rust and then he grips the base-plates shut and clomps back into the lounge where the television stops him like a shot through the head.

Coatham yawns and closes the door. He turns around and makes an effort to take an interest in the carpet. He concentrates. "I've never enjoyed this carpet."

McKraw glances from the television and at Coatham in an ecstatic way. "Hmmm?"

Coatham looks at the carpet where the beginnings of fluff are in most places the awakening of a brown mist. Most times the fibres of its felt-like dark brown surface are spun along by the scuff of a shoe or the pad of a slipper into gathering worms. (The changing and unpredictable moods of the carpet.) Coatham continues. "I come from the bath in bare feet, and as I walk." He thinks. He points in a general direction.

McKraw puts his hand to his chin. It was Hum For Money. Hum For Money was the rival show on the other channel which started five minutes earlier than Song Night, although everybody turned over. The windows rattle. He looks at Coatham who is making some speech and striding around and pointing. There was still Victor Delmondo - who sang in the second half. Victor Delmondo was a millionaire. Women fainted. McKraw becomes aware that he will never be Victor Delmondo.

Coatham looks at the carpet in a grave . " I have to be very careful." He looks at McKraw who is scratching his chin.

McKraw begins to move. A slow movement that disconnects his hand from his chin. His other hand has found the pole of the carpet-sweeper leaning against the kitchen door-frame and he lets go of it. He walks forward in a contented stroll, past the dining-table and chairs on his left and the armchair on his right and presses a channel button on the television and slides the volume along and strolls back to a dining-chair and sits down. The final and fluttering note of a lady in a red dress hangs like a drop of water. The applause opens and McKraw is gone.

Coatham looks at the lounge and raises his eye-brows slightly. The noise of the television in the room and the solid figure of McKraw is like the sudden appearance of a different day. McKraw turns in the chair , which makes a sound like a snap, and points a finger.

"No one sings Seashore Of Your Life like this man."

Coatham looks at the television where there is a gentleman with a wig and a drinker's nose. Coatham looks and sees that it is the man who also judges the beauty contests, but can't remember his name.

McKraw turns back, makes a kind of growl then folds his arms. He knew of course that Coatham wouldn't understand Song Night. He pushes his lips out like he is tasting wine. The coloured spots of light at the back of the stage have begun to sway, one way and then the other. McKraw taps his pocket and takes out a beige and brass coloured tobacco-tin and lifts the lid. He sets the lid aside as an ashtray and ignores the tin which contains a small red box of matches and a blue packet of cigarette-papers. He finds his cigarettes and his green plastic lighter. He fumbles around and lights a cigarette and remembers the television in his office. A part of him wanders there, fetching out the long box of florescent bulbs and the bright red Easy-Ladders which clang uncontrollably on the hard steps. A part of him is in the rubbish-bay, yes, a part of him was always there - where somehow everyone in the flats finally met. And Clifford appears. McKraw's eye-brows tighten on the thought of Clifford. The ready-sharpened pencils he leaves everywhere behind him. In Summer, Clifford walking home off shift along the muddy and clay-spoiled and uneven pavement and office-workers opening windows to wave to him.

The applause again, the presenter hurrying from the back of the stage, being very aware of his own wig, and the lights behind going dim. Coatham watches. His eyes just now following some

274

trail. An unimportant glance back across the floor and the wood-effect table-top to the shallow rectangular shiny brass-coloured of "Sea Friend" Tuna. The white and ivy-green label and the top of the can embossed with "Sea Friend" but interrupted by a turn key and a blob of glue. He thinks about the box-bedroom and the violently-flowered carpet there half-swept. The box-bedroom having its own particular mood, and at night like sleeping in a keyhole or the private place of the tin-clock and its jig-jigger jig-jigger accompaniment of the factories difficult sounds.

McKraw is somehow fattening in front of the television.

Coatham fetches the carpet-sweeper from the kitchen doorway and carries it along towards the box-bedroom. The brief face-full of warmth which the heater is extending to remote parts. His standing in the box-bedroom while McKraw takes a failing interest, and Coatham wandering there and finally out of sight.

McKraw looks back at the television.

The mother placing the massive gravy, and the children wondering how long they have to peel their eyes back, now the father staring over his newspaper. The mother again. The father. The music. The end.

McKraw is over another advert. The winding of his innards, like his innards are trying to learn them while the rest of his body is trying to forget.

McKraw pinches at the bridge of his nose and closes his eyes then relaxes and draws on the cigarette and turns his attention to the lid of the tobacco-tin and taps. He didn't like adverts. Adverts were nocturnal, they followed him remorselessly in the dead hours when he was sat in his office. (He looks back at the television...his innards begin. He looks at the tin-lid.) He taps the cigarette. It had always been difficult - but he preferred nights. The five o'clock change and then slowly towards nine. The film, or the documentary. The slip of hours and it would be suddenly twelve. Downhill after that, down to three. Then home. Home and leaving the vacant short-shift behind him, the shift they hadn't filled since Clifford changed. McKraw smokes the cigarette and hears the unbearable pause before they allow Song Night back on.

275

Coatham draws his finger along the magnolia-glossed window-sill. The silk of dust. It's gentle stubble on the pale paint and the finer dust revealed only by touching. He rests the carpet-sweeper against the window-sill.

Coatham looks through his shadow and through the glass. In the car-park below the strips of white paper have gone. (He thinks. Gone dancing over the dark grass to the right of the building, where in Summer the footballs climb from duffing stomachy up-kicks and pipes of shouts.) The weather oophs. The twin handles on the window with their r-shaped plates which once entered slots and squeezed the window tight no longer do so. There has been too much paint and for the hinges there have been too many loosenings. The dig-dog sounds as the frame moves. The agreeing dig-dogs from the windows of the other rooms. Here at the window the oophs, the dig-dogs and the fanning cold air. The city through the window is mostly sparkling. From the lounge "Tip-toe Through The Tulips" is being devoutly sung, and McKraw's deep hooting chant following also and now booming out.

On the main road the traffic has come to a halt. The headlights of each car shining fiercely on the car in front like pieces of daytime. (McKraw sings.) The wind returns careless but leaves the window half-done. He watches the cars which are nudging forward. That closed down and boarded-up shoe shop where some shreds of older posters flap, the dark windows of the floors above and then the attic with a tiny window perfectly forgotten. Plumbing Supplies next door, which he has sometimes looked in. Its window with pastel-shade toilets in formation, old sun-bleached leaflets gone strange and crisp and piles of dead insects in the window-bottom. The plumbing supplies in that row of unused premises and those other window-panes hairy with cobwebs and the doors padlocked. The cars are beginning to move, their squatting somehow as they set off, fleeting and belonging elsewhere like a strip of film.

McKraw closes his mouth. He breathes in through his nose and stares gravely at the singer who is receiving his applause. McKraw leans and prods about with the cigarette in the tin lid, which was still burning. He looks for Coatham and then rubs the underside of his nose. He wants to call out that Song Night is on - but Coatham knew that Song Night was on. He juts his jaw out as the presenter strolls out and is clapping gently as the man dressed as a tulip shuffles off stage. McKraw stretches his arm and looks at his watch. Song Night would be followed by the news and weather, but he sometimes changed channels, having read the papers which Clifford always bought and then left precisely re-folded on a clear desk. McKraw stares at the television then sneaks a glance at that small bedroom. He chews his dentures and then sucks them back into place. A draught from the windows is touching at the skin above the line of his sock like a flippering slice of ham. The windows occasionally shaken by the wind. (The presenter is extending his arm to the next guest.) Where was Coatham?

Coatham claws his hand and runs his nails into the groove and then levers the polished flap of the bureau away from its cabinet. The bureau squeezed between the foot of the bed and the right corner of the facing wall. The flap opening with a bird-whistly slide of rods and lowering, its side edge just clearing the magnolia window-sill. (From behind him the noise of McKraw and the television singing together.) To his right the window rattling. The mellow honey-acorn-brown bureau open with its double H of pale rough shavy ply-wood the bright colour of swede. A fostered scent of camphor. A moment. He looks around for the odd-legged mink corduroy kitchen-stool. He draws it under the window and around the carpet-sweeper from the other corner. He sits down in the position the kitchen-stool has decided and he rubs his eyes.

A paper-bag.

A paper-bag gone grey and glassy from the doughnut inside left too long. He moves the paper-bag out and feels around in a wide black lidless tin with Turner's The Hay Wain repeated on the side and the tin pushed almost under a shelf. He feels what he is searching for, guarded by drawing-pins which skate around his fingers. He pulls the tin out whilst looking at old coffee-jars containing press-seal polythene bags containing nothing. McKraw mutters. A startling noise...but now just the rainy sound of applause and McKraw has stopped.

Coatham removes something from the tin and picks up the doughnut and closes the bureau. He gives the box-bedroom window a glance and now looks around. The bed with its thin ribbed peach bed-cover. A tiny teak-effect headboard peeping above the lump of the hidden pillows. The magnolia wall. The cream tin clock on the teak-effect surfaced bedside cabinet, a shelf beneath for the press-wrapped packet of biscuit-coloured sponge ear-plugs (one pair remaining of three) and the cabinet's white cupboard door, its handle like a hard caramel bun.

McKraw takes out another cigarette. He looks at the television. The windows rattle.

For a while now he has been listening for Coatham, like a portion of his right ear has remained in the cold of the room - even during the most vital songs. He has sometimes narrowed his eyes and looked at the bedroom door, but Coatham wasn't there.

He flicks the green lighter and lights the cigarette. He raises his eye-brows and looks down his nose at the presenter who is laughing and checking camera positions. McKraw looking precisely with raised eye-brows, as when he is wanting the most careful thing to happen. As when, in the early hours, he is coaxing the sticky-sharp point of a needle to appear again and again through the hole of a button. That long and beckoning pause after the drunks come back at twelve, when the factories have changed to melody and doors are silent, the simple ways, when a button can have great power in the world.

Coatham wanders out of the box-bedroom carrying the paper bag. He steps along to the kitchen and past McKraw who gives him a grave look.

Coatham stops at the kitchen door, and then goes in. He drops the bag and doughnut into the rubbish-box where he notices the compressed pads of fluff and grittings from the sweeper. He turns the cold tap which sucks suddenly with a release of air and then chugs in bangs and letting water out as a by-product of this which splashes back up from the stainless-steel sink as touches of droplets.

McKraw leans forward thoughtfully towards the television and ignores the noise. He smokes his cigarette and the noise stops. His body softens back and he chomps with his dentures as the presenter hands the stage over to the next singer.

McKraw can hear Coatham scratting around in the kitchen. McKraw takes no interest. McKraw can hear Coatham coming back into the lounge and pulling a dining chair around. He hears him slowly sit down and then pull himself forward under the other leaf. McKraw breathes in through his nose and squashes his lips together and watches the television.

Victor Delmondo is acknowledging the applause and taking a silver model pistol from the holster at his hip and is pretending to fire it into the air. He is blowing his cheeks out under the shade of his ten gallon hat and is adjusting his brown riveted leather-trousers and gallops on the spot in his pointed boots. The audience continues to applaud. Victor Delmondo is raising his arms and the audience begins to settle.

McKraw presses his lips together into a kind of a smile and then hears Coatham pushing the moving the carrier forward and tapping about behind him. McKraw tilts his head and speaks.

"Victor Delmon-do is a millionaire." He turns and sees Coatham dealing out playing-cards for a game of patience. McKraw emphasises the point and closes his eyes. "Women have fainted." McKraw looks at Coatham who is dealing the cards.

Coatham holds the next card and looks at the television as McKraw turns back.

Coatham watches the singer who dramatically takes off his hat and twirls it away. Coatham looks at the man who has a full head of his own grey hair and a large nose and rather scrunched eyes. Coatham lets the face impress upon him. Victor Delmondo has a face like McKraw's. Coatham looks thoughtfully at the halibut. The grey halibut on a rose pink background. On the back of every card there is the halibut. On the card box itself it is there, only on the downward side. On the upper side the words, Marvel's Games. Series 18. Fishes Of Home Waters. No.4 The Halibut.

He studies.

He remembers.

279

A five-bar gate in the rain. The rain-drops glittering on the underside of the top bar, where they hesitate to fall, like the old cracked wood is teaching them. Three's and two's. He sits in the beech-shade, on a bank of roots, beech-mast, damp and dry leaves piling down into floppy packed garlic growing out of the air. The steep rain-draughty bank overhanging a tiny and mossed wall with skeleton-ferns and then the edge of the black-mud path below - locked like a spine with uncovered sandy stone where the long rain crashes, frying up the puddles.

Beyond the gate the clumpy uphill meadow is silvery dark. The white-flowering hawthorn where birds are also sheltering. Every bird in the one song. The giant cloud black, but at the crown of the hill the final edge of it behind the rooks' nests in the deads of trees, where the sky is milk.

Chapter 4.

The windows rattle.

A two.

He studies. A black two.

The two of clubs, but the game is stuck.

The windows second rattle.

The wind's heeeesh…and floof! He listens. The wind's usual balancing - and far off now the swarm of whistles amongst the factories, or from further. (That other noise, but he ignores it.) The two of clubs, and this card slightly worn and rough on his finger and thumb tips and he can see at the bottom left corner: the little crease hinge and the corner's furry edges. The useful cards are under the halibuts. The television is switched off. McKraw snores.

He looks at McKraw who has his left cheek settled on his left upper arm. The left fore-arm leans against the top of his head and the left hand limp in the air above his right ear. His upper body is squashed over the tin-lid ashtray and the wipe-top of the drop-leaf dining-table. The table adds a creak to the snore. The table warps a little with McKraw's weight. McKraw stirs. A snore is chewed and chomped then McKraw breathes out. That particular snore is gone and McKraw now has a quiet maroon uniform which is free of snores. Coatham listens for the terrible voice of the snore. It has worn a deep groove. It is sawing the night in half. The wind returns. The windows rattle. The tread of the frames, the dig-dog noise of the bedroom window. The snore returns.

Coatham gets up from the table and takes his cup into the kitchen. The cold air from the windows wipes around him. In the lounge the tin heater clinks on. A drawing pin imbedded in the sole of Coatham's right shoe taps on the hard vinyl floor covering. He stops and twirls slowly and looks at the floor.

It is a difficult floor because the vinyl was never cut properly to fit and there are swells in it. A swell at the front of the sink where the beige and white freckle-patterned vinyl never treads down. This swell has a replying swell from the white base-strip of the lower double kitchen cupboard on the opposite side. These two swells might have met, but for the electric cooker which sits between them. In the end, he long ago decided, there was nothing wrong with the little swells. Every flat, he had been reliably told by Mrs Lodgeson - except hers, suffered from "bad trades"; and Mrs Lodgeson had visited all the "better apartments" to point this out. His was not visited. He looks at the vinyl. In fact, the "better apartments" were something of a mystery. No other tenant had seen here was like Mrs Lodgeson.

McKraw snores. The sound nawps and in amongst it there is a deep bubbling.

He is concerned about the snore but McKraw is less worrying like this, the strange word coming out of him again and again. McKraw is sleeping and no longer singing or walking about. The wind is at the windows but the "Dung-ga Dung-ga" factory is closed. He puts sugar in his cup and pours water into the kettle to a low measure. He sets the kettle working on the wood-look work surface on top of the fridge and finds a tea-bag. He brings Mrs Lodgeson's milk from the fridge and closes the rubbery door. The fridge makes the little tinkle sound it likes to make. The wind "oofs" outside but the kitchen windows merely nudge. Chilling night air spills into the air that is merely cold. The snore rises. The beginning of the sixth part.

Outside the wind shakes the wire-fencing of the factories' stockyards. A single dark and oily puddle persists under some chained and padlocked double tubular-steel and wire gates. The gates test and snash back. The down-set padlocked bolt-rod simply stirs the water, the concrete surfacing having cratered from the tyres of wagons when they crackle and pivot. The gates swing and shock in their chains and the puddle's ripples tear up the shine from the security lights, while the ripples and the black surface are also biased by the force of the air. A thick knot from a blue nylon rope and a purposeless cube of black rubber, both handfuls, have been left on the cracked pavement where a streetlight gives them long tails. The industrial estate is empty. The main road flashes along with pulses of cars, they are unwrapped sudden and shiny.....and the road is empty. There is a knock on the door.

Coatham waits ready with a tea-spoon and listens. He stands at the fridge where the kettle is fetching its far off sound. He looks at the flat-door.

There is a "tap-tap-tap."

He carries the tea-spoon and leaves the kitchen and goes to the flat-door and worries about who is there. He looks at the carpet and thinks. There is no one expected. He turns the flaked brass-look, curved scroll-edged door-handle and opens the door for a slight gap and looks out. Someone is waiting, but the figure is withdrawn to the wall (as someone might wait for a police photograph). The figure is a small elderly man with thin greying strands of hair greased back over a bald head. He has black bar-topped glasses and, by this, rather aquarium eyes which watch Coatham quite endlessly. The elderly man's face and forehead have lines and wrinkles caused by a denture-smile so magnificent that it overpowers his other features. The man continues to smile. It is Mr Trevis.

Coatham gazes at Mr Trevis.

Mr Trevis' smile broadens: "Home sweet home!" The voice is round and boomy, but the pale eyes remain bright-lit in the glasses and stare and blink softly.

Coatham wonders what he means.

Mr Trevis face reddens with amusement. "Safe and sound!"

Coatham raises his eyebrows slightly.

Mr Trevis smiles. "Quiet night in."

Coatham thinks about this.

Behind Coatham the croaking bubbling snore begins.

Mr Trevis puts a forefinger to his smiling lips. "She's asleep is she?"

Coatham thinks about Mr Trevis. Mr Trevis called occasionally, usually in the summer. Mr Trevis had unusual capacities. Coatham wonders what to say.

Mr Trevis steps forward. He is dressed in an oversize brownish tweedy jacket, baggy tweedy trousers and polished but creased black shoes. His nose looks second-hand also but in fact it is real and rather purple in colour. Mr Trevis comes close to the gap of the door and smiles into the room. Coatham waits then stands back and opens the door and Mr Trevis wipes his shoes in a kind of shuffle and enters.

McKraw snores and Mr Trevis makes a little o-shape with his face. The smile returns and Mr Trevis makes a slight nodding bow, "Mr McKraw - good gracious."

Coatham stands at the open door while Mr Trevis draws the dining-chair away from the playing cards and he sits with his elbow on the table's corner and facing the kitchen where the kettle rumbles and clicks off. Coatham closes the door and wanders into the kitchen to find another cup and looks back to see if Mr Trevis is still there. Mr Trevis is smiling.

Mr Trevis lived on the first floor and had no use for the lift and had a dishwasher, washing machine, full cocktail bar, several vacuum cleaners, kettles, bathrobes, 'Power Body' bar-bells, The History Of Hollywood video set, video-recorder, television, Madame D' Paris' Spring Knicker Collection, four steam-irons and three months' supply of quilted toilet tissue.

Coatham wonders when he had last seen Mr Trevis.

Mr Trevis had last visited in the early spring. The chemical works behind the flats had released something poisonous into the drains and a squad dressed in masks and suits had visited all nearby buildings and explained there was nothing to worry about. McKraw had knocked on doors or pinned the chemical plant's Medium Level Spillage notices to them and Mr Trevis had called in at flats here and there and had come to Coatham's and delivered the caution with a beaming smile. The toxic alert team had later observed there was no better man to announce that nothing was wrong. His face later shone out from the local newspaper under the headline "Factory Workers In Chemical Scare." But Mr Trevis had also been "Mr Bingo Wins Holiday To Mauritius" and "Shopper Is Millionth Customer!" (Coatham has found a second cup and is lifting the tea-bag from one to the other. He gazes at the tea-bag and the dried up summer cupboard-beetles which spin around in the spare cup. He looks at Mr Trevis and Mr Trevis smiles back.) Mr Trevis was set apart for unusual prominence.

Coatham slides the beetle-cup aside and gives the other cup some of the milk from Mrs Lodgeson's fridge. He spoons out some of the floating sour flecks and takes the cup of tea and the spoon and a saucer of blue wrapped sugar-lumps to Mr Trevis who receives them with delight.

"Just the ticket!" Mr Trevis' smile and submarine eyes shine about.

Coatham tries to think of something to say.

Mr Trevis brightens. "Good cup of tea, good company."

McKraw snores.

Coatham tries to think of something to say.

Mr Trevis drinks some tea. "And there's many not so lucky," the words charge Mr Trevis up. "There's many with nowhere to go - and should be down - the Bingo, Mr Coatham." Mr Trevis stares at Coatham but is apparently unable to see him. Mr Trevis produces a glittering smile. "I wasn't fond of Bingo." Mr Trevis stares. "I wasn't fond of product-competitions…not quizzes of any sort."

Coatham remembers that Mr Trevis carries a strange light. Mrs Lodgeson had commented one day when he had returned with her shopping. Mr Trevis had won another iron and she was distracted from checking the list and drawn to the subject of Mr Trevis. "There are people who carry …a strange light, Mr Coatham." She had looked at him over her shopping-list spectacles - as if nothing more should be said about it, and nothing was.

"Blimey, I said," Mr Trevis is staring but remains smiling, "blimey!"

Coatham's attention is gradually wandering. Were there packet soups in the carrier-bag on the table? He looks at the table. There might be. There might have been packet soups or there might have been a tin. Then there was the harvest festival box which was pushed to the back of the bottom cupboard, amongst the pans. He thinks about the harvest festival box.

Harvest festival boxes arrived in a dark month of rain. Harvest festival boxes were often delivered to McKraw's office and thereafter some bargaining began amongst older tenants so that one box contained only prunes. Coatham had been fortunate this year, but not successful. His was a box containing foods which families had not found the strength to eat, but not so strikingly unpleasant that he can remember what these are. Coatham's forefinger settles on his chin as he considers this.

"-Won the food-mixer from a packet o' peanuts."

Coatham takes the carpet-sweeper, that is leaning against the frame of the kitchen door, and carries it slowly along the short way to the bathroom. He presses the exterior light- switch and the difficult buzzing droning sound of the ceiling-fan begins. Coatham goes into the bathroom and lets the door swing towards closed as he dances the carpet-sweeper into the gap between the sink and the magnolia wall. Mr Trevis' voice booms behind him.

"But Bingo has been right champion Mr Coatham. Birds of a feather!"

McKraw wakes up. His face rises and he turns awkwardly and looks in horror at Mr Trevis.

Mr Trevis is smiling.

McKraw turns back and massages the skin on the bridge of his nose. Trevis was here. McKraw's shoulders tense up and he hunches forward and he smoothes his hands down his face. His eyes, usually hidden by thick lids, appear and stare and then the folds of his face return and give his eyes their usual occasional glint. McKraw breathes in wearily and straightens the jacket of his maroon uniform and finds two curled and squashed cigarette-ends dangling on the left side. He picks them off with his big hands and drops them into the tobacco tin lid which had pressed its small amount of ash into his jacket sleeve. He strikes at the sleeve with his right hand and looks under the table where his cigarettes and green plastic lighter have fallen. He blows slightly as he reaches down and growls as he draws himself back up again. He looks at his watch: nearly ten past ten.

It was a difficult situation. McKraw pulls at the thin brown socks which have travelled a little from his ankles and to just below the tops of his heavy boots. He pulls each sock in turn and waggles the foot about and both socks recover a small way. There was the urgent matter of the late movie: 11.15 pm The Attic. Starring Rosie Meadows. (Repeat.) McKraw allows his upper dentures to slide in his mouth. He could forget about the late film and go downstairs and spend the late shift sitting in his office. He could manage, though he had never tried this at Christmas. Still, there was a first time for everything. McKraw's upper dentures go aslant in his mouth. The building is near empty and tomorrow would be Christmas Morning. There would be no late drinkers at eleven thirty, no pizza-cars delivering at twelve. This year nearly every tenant had signed out for the duration…but he would manage. He thinks about the late film which finished about ten past twelve. Not a long wait then until three - and the end of it. Clifford would take over. Clifford with his long list of advanced hobbies. Clifford who spent the early hours reading technical magazines and soldering circuit-boards. The thought makes McKraw shrink somehow, and he remembers The Attic. (Repeat.)

If he just sat here then Coatham wouldn't bother him. Coatham would carry on doing - well what did Coatham do? This question is too difficult and McKraw's lips push out, his upper dentures being thoroughly displaced. No, it was Trevis…Trevis. McKraw's upper dentures slip back into position. He would have to get rid of Trevis.

McKraw takes a cigarette out of the packet. He had seen Cyril Brandman act tough in the early movies. The late night apartment in down-town Chicago, the smoky room, the fedora with the brim drawn down at the front, the cigarette, the girl filing her nails at an open window with a crooked blind, the red light from the "Larry's Bar " sign switching on and off. The hoods have arrived and block the door. McKraw turns.

McKraw lights the cigarette. "Still here are you?"

Mr Trevis shines. He cottles the empty cup around on the saucer between the sugar-lump wrappers and indicates with a raised hand that he is thinking of where to start.

Coatham wipes at the bathroom sink with the ropey cloth. The slop of it on the clear plastic handle of the cold tap and the tap is running and wavers a stem of water around under the florescent light. The extractor-fan is droning, whining and murmuring…so that a moment can get gnawed up in it, and when he is in the bath? When he is in the bath he is starting over and over, like the fan extracts everything: the business of being there at all. The wind blows through the shaft again. The usual zoo-zoh, zoo-zoh - slowing deeply, until the fan recovers.

He wrings out the cloth a little. He takes half a step back and the heel of his left shoe collides with the bathroom door. The door dithers but remains nearly closed. He looks at the narrow windowless magnolia bathroom. The grey-plastic mop-bucket with its peeling sticker. "Super Home" in pale blue letters on white, and the mop itself which is a bundle of grey foamy loops and a handle of grey tubular plastic - but is telescopic. Coatham remembers that he must lift the dripping mop higher and higher and at an awkward angle to get it back into the bucket. that the telescopic inner handle slides too easily and drops the mop-head suddenly and unexpectedly into the bucket and splashes in every direction. The mop set had been given to him as a present, or at least as a kind thought, by an animated red-faced lady who was trying to get it into the rubbish chute. Coatham gives the tiny white bathroom sink a last wipe. The bath is also peppered with black bits.

The black bits came from the extractor-fan when the fan (and the light) was switched off and when the weather was windy. He looks up at the extractor-fan's magnolia-painted casing and the quickening and slowing movement, sometimes stalling enough to see the cream, dirt encrusted, hard plastic propeller. There was something in the shaft, something that crumbled into light black porous grit - but he didn't know what it was.

Miss Holweizen, who lived on the floor above said it was the "Making of da liding unschticked." Coatham had nodded that this was probably true. If the liding was old or the wrong liding had been used...then that was the problem with it.

He turns the cold bath-tap and the choking sound of the water competes with the noise of the fan while the water pools and inches around the plug-hole where a magnolia gloss boot-print had been scratched at but remained clear. He wets the cloth and helps the assorted fragments of grit to score along the far rim of the bath - gently where the magnolia coated tiles above the bath are loose - and the larger fragments of grit skate down into the bath and join those already there. He continues to wipe. The cloth is crunchy with fragments. He wipes inside the bath and the grit fragments cut along like lost teeth, the grit piling and bobbing slightly where they cannot get down the plug-hole. He pinches these out with his fingers and drops them into the toilet.

Still, the bathroom was a secure place when McKraw came. Those times when McKraw would wait outside the door - then he himself could stand in the bathroom. From the corridor the noise of the fan could be heard slightly. When he was genuinely having a bath then McKraw, on those unusual occasions, would stand outside just the same. But he knew that McKraw would abandon his "stand" when the extractor-fan was on. The small maroon official clip-file which McKraw carried about would mark his leaving with a sharp snap and McKraw would set off down the corridor. Sometimes there would be a short conversation a passing tenant and McKraw would make his wuffling noise and then remark that he was "[mumble] busy [mumble]" or something of this sort. Coatham's shoes are crunching pieces of grit on the bathroom's freckle-pattern vinyl floor-covering. The fan struggles against a whistle of night air.

McKraw's attention drifts to the wind's nudging at the windows. The loose frames galloping somehow - and had never noticed them before. (For a moment he hears Mr Trevis, his speech on the Merry-Go-Round Bingo Club has been going along.) And had Coatham mentioned the windows? McKraw stares into the strange eyes of Mr Trevis. Yes, Coatham had been given the BW/15 complaint form. McKraw remembers this because every tenant had requested a BW/15. An average had been calculated at the city estates office and the result (McKraw had phoned them and explained that his responsibilities required him to be informed) was that an average of .75 of a window and .13 of a door had some notable difficulty in each flat. McKraw had in turn informed those tenants who were interested that their complaints must have reached a high level to warrant such research. McKraw took an interest in the city estates office. He enjoyed their accuracy. He enjoyed the certainty that, however things might look, a matter could be measured. A matter could be presented to him on sturdy and slightly ribbed paper with a crest on the top, just the way he liked it.

"Baked bean competition?" I said to her. no no There is a tremendous weight in Mr Trevis' pause. His normally unmoving eyes turn down a little,

"It was as if the double breakfast toaster was waiting for me Mr McKraw!"

McKraw ignores Mr Trevis. He listens to the loud burring hum of the fan in the bathroom, which is rather soothing. McKraw thinks, no one can annoy Trevis. Trevis was here for the evening in the same way that Trevis could come to the wire-glass sliding window in the wall of his office. On those occasions McKraw would immediately pick up the old cream-coloured telephone, which had long since been disconnected, and he would make humming replies to nobody. At those times the two of them were somehow equally displaced, somehow distant, but for Trevis vagueness was natural and sometimes Trevis could out-wait the phantom call and McKraw would be forced to hand over another parcel and listen to what Trevis had to say. Not that any of this mattered. After the rush of BW/15's from new tenants and then the lack of response from the landlord there would be few tenants calling at the window.

These days when there was a repair to report they preferred Clifford.

McKraw's hooded eye-lids and slightly squashed mouth are motionless. It had a lot to do with the fact that Clifford could mend things. Clifford could mend things in his pencilly way and sometimes didn't give out BW/15's at all. Clifford even received birthday cards.

McKraw sighs. The smiling face of Trevis is like some weird moon. McKraw finds another cigarette.

Coatham picks up the shaving-brush and the small lemon-coloured plastic beaker (containing three blue disposable safety razors and a dark green toothbrush) and herds them with both hands on the back of the sink so they don't topple. He stops: he is inside the zoo-zah-zoo-zah noise of the extractor-fan. The full noise in the bathroom and making the bathroom small like it's the casing for some difficult machine which can never stop … he pauses, or else some dream a bee might have. And inside the

290

noise? Inside the noise there is occasionally the voice of Mr Trevis - he is talking about, about Bingo - but indistinctly, as if the extractor-fan and Mr Trevis have joined. And beyond these…yes, beyond these the realisation that he has been in the bathroom for quite some time.

McKraw stares at the wall of the lounge. The streaky magnolia gloss paint over a previous pale blue and recording the slanted strokes of a wide brush. The strokes of magnolia never catching up to the vertical and he follows the struggle to the corner where a single and strong stroke marks a fresh beginning on the right wall. From this corner and drawn out on a very short flex is the standard city estates magnolia thermostatically-controlled electric heater, and then Coatham's low single shelf teak-effect bookcase.

McKraw's attention floats along : the dusty bookcase top, the dried pea on the carpet the magnificence of the television (switched off).

Mr Trevis aims a finger at the air above him, "and I suppose it was not to be. Not to be, Mr McKraw, since I only won another set of his and hers towels."

Mr Trevis's expression is reduced to a mere normal smile, and his eyes register some earthly sorrow.

McKraw turns suddenly on port-able tele-vison. A kind of joy opens his eyes and his clenched dentures appear in a terrible grin. The force of this makes Mr Trevis blink.

McKraw wipes a palm across his mouth. He makes his wuffly cough.

Coatham crunches around on the porous grit and takes a last look at the bathroom. The small pale green bucket on the floor, between the white plastic clothes' horse and the sink, and on the rim is the cloth and inside is the tall and broad bottle of Dazzle Hand-Washing Liquid. Dazzle - or new automatic formula Deep Down Dazzle (the advert where the neighbour is shamed for doubting Dazzle). Coatham looks at the Dazzle. He needed some more dazzle. Coatham still sees the sunny day in the luxury house and hears the music rising over the roofs. He leaves the bathroom and switches the light and the extractor-fan off. He sees McKraw is awake but also clapping his hands with delight at Mr Trevis' words, almost before Mr Trevis has said them. They both smile vastly at Coatham.

There is a knock on the door.

Coatham stands and looks at the door.

The small horror of it.

He looks also at McKraw, then at Mr Trevis who is smiling.

The beginning of the seventh part.

Chapter 5.

He opens his door. The draught of air. The lady who is blowing her nose, but also his need to simply walk out. His foot could step and off he could go. He looks at the corridor and its magnolia ceiling. He thinks: that it could be anywhere, anywhere at all.

"Mr Coffam," She glares, "I shouldn't be calling like this but I cudda sap stup -" her face makes little jumps and she dabs at her eyes with another tissue she has drawn from her sleeve. "They don't want me Mr Coffam," she sniffs and recovers with a quivering intake of breath. "My own daughter though."

She holds the tissue to her mouth and winces.

"My onl...y daugh..."

Coatham gazes down at the cloudy grey linoleum. He nods slowly.

She watches him carefully.

He looks sideways slightly and to the right where the fire-door is loudly ticking closed.

She makes a kind of growl.

"I knew you would understand."

Coatham steps back and opens the door wide.

She holds the tissue to her nose and enters and her tearful eyes snatch a glance at Mr Trevis who is smiling and McKraw, whose face seems wide with horror.

There is a silence.

The windows rattle. The fire-door's ticking stops. Coatham carefully closes the door and looks at the carpet.

The lady sits down in the armchair to the right of McKraw and the television. Her weight settling into the foam-filled seat cushion and her bottom within biting-range of the steel springs as the cushion collapses at one side through the row of spring-ended rubber belts.

Coatham sets off and wanders into the kitchen. He takes the full cup of tea in which the dried beetles are floating and pours the cup's contents into the sink. The cold tap lurches on and has those sneezing effects as the water bangs through, and now the water is steady. (He lets the water deepen gently in the plain dark blue cup and then empties it.) There are no voices from the lounge. He sets the cup next to the kettle and lifts the shiny metal lid, which is still warm, and sees the water inside is too shallow. He takes the kettle to the sink and the tap sneezes into it and the water pours until the kettle has a certain weight and he turns the tap off and carries the kettle to the top of the fridge and crottles the lid's thin edge around until the lid drops. He pushes the thick plastic connector-plug into the tight socket in the kettle and lifts the kettle to its place and slides the tea-bag jar along.

The tea-bag jar is large and has brown-tinted glass and a brass-look metal turn-top. The label on the side has black and gold stripes overlapped by a white panel in the shape of a chef's hat. On the panel: Barkers' Foods in black copper-plate script. Beneath this a silhouette of a short but branching tree and beneath this: stuffed prunes, and beneath this: New! He gives the top its sudden popping turn and sees inside the tea-bags squashed together like cushions. His fingers nip at a tea-bag and he lifts it out. The windows rattle. The heesh! and the strike of the wind and, somewhere behind, the ventilator-hood on the factory roof skreeking as it is forced about. The kitchen curtains move gently. The draught of air.

Mr Trevis stares at Coatham and at the brown jar. Barker's Foods. Barkers...mainly fruits, some pickles. Hardly mentioned in Competition Quarterly, not even in the back issues. He lets time go by. He thinks about nothing...he stares at the lounge curtains. The thick bars of orange and turquoise, the brown squiggly scribbled lines. He stares. He thinks about nothing. He can't look at the curtains anymore. He stares at the white tea-cup, on its saucer, with a few blue sugar-wrappers. Probably Mr Sweet's standard sugar-lump, the economy quality. He thinks about nothing. Sold at Quicko's and perhaps Pocket-Save...although Quicko's stock the voucher-pack...to send off for Mr Sweet's sugar-tongs. He stares. He looks at Coatham, but Coatham has moved out of sight.

It had been a fair Christmas. The Merry-Go-Round Bingo Club's Pensioner's Christmas Luncheon. The pudding rather tough. The custard cold. He stares. The potatoes soggy. He thinks about nothing. The cutlery dirty. The hard sprouts. But Mrs Ansleigh had kissed him. Her moustache. He stares.

If it had been different he would not have sat between Mr Garstall, who belched and Desmond (he cannot rightly recall his name) who was the top winner the previous night, but was over-proud. His eyes flick softly to the carrier-bag and some displaced items of shopping.

They were mostly happy - the people at the luncheon. The sprouts were consumed, and the icy custard found its way into them. But was he happy? (Now then, he shouldn't be thinking like that.) He stares. Well, he would be happy if he won clothes. He never won clothes. How did he win at all? He didn't know that, but he never won clothes.

"Never you mind, Mr Trevis," Miss Kellin had said to him. Miss Kellin, the finely mannered lady with the pure white hair and sparkly blue eyes, who lived two flats along, and had been slamming her door in huge movements to get it to shut. Miss Kellin had told him he should take some of his prizes to the Round Again Shop and find himself a nice jacket and trousers while he was there. He stares. He looks at the High Health Orange Juice (add water to taste) 'Now With Vitamin C!'

Orange? Why yes, he had had an orange this morning. He smiles. The Satsuma sort. Wasn't it lovely to have a Satsuma orange at Christmas. Didn't they peel so easily! Weren't they delicious, the tangy moment of a Satsuma orange - the scent too. The pile of afterwards-peelings in the palm, a kind of leather. A bouncy jig-saw. He smiles. An orange this morning. Mr Trevis' thoughts widen to cinema-scope. *The Teddy Fruits Ltd 'Marvin The Melon' (flavour T6) Pre-Store Competition (Prize Draw fall-back and Secondary Prizes.).* [Competition Quarterly's Style Tips: Last year's winning slogan: "I'm no slouch - I'm a strongberry!"].

A bump.

Mr Trevis stares. His shoe is kicked.

Mr Trevis moves his foot.

The shoe is kicked again.

McKraw keeps his upper body still and indicates with his thumb in small hooking movements in the direction of the television that is switched off. He tries some squashing winks with his left eye but Trevis is not able to understand him then suddenly Trevis appears to.

McKraw watches as Mr Trevis leans slightly over and smiles at the lady in the chair, who does not notice him.

Mr Trevis smiles broader still.

"Here we are then!"

The lady raises her face from her tissue. She looks at Mr Trevis in a keen but tearful way.

"Yes, here we are Mr - Mr Trellop," she pauses after the name, then looks at McKraw who has his back to her and has his shoulders hunched up, "and you…Mr McCrock."

She lightly blows her nose.

McKraw turns in his creaky chair and looks at the lady, then turns a little way back and quickly clears his throat but when Edna glares at him he says nothing.

Mr Trevis remains smiling at Edna who has returned to her tissue. She retrieves the other tissue from her right sleeve.

"Dare say I'm better here than where I have just come from." She looks at the fluffy trails that have scuffed across the dark brown carpet. Her dark brown eyes glare. "Never thought my daughter would," she sighs and dabs with a tissue "turn me away…" she falters slightly, "at Christmas."

McKraw broods on the thought.

Mr Trevis is still smiling.

"Happy families!"

Coatham turns the oatmeal-coloured kitchen curtain. At the end of the magnolia window-sill, above the kitchen work surface beside the fridge, where he must flick the rough curtain-fold aside and quickly feel about behind it (where the air is draughty and cold) he can feel the sugar-lump box. He pushes his hand through what must be the carton's top-flaps and can hear the sugar-lumps as they scrumble. He can feel them like smooth tight-wrapped dice. He manages a handful and draws back and his hand is cold. He lets the blue-wrapped sugar-lumps fall onto the white saucer and returns the saucer to its place next to the freshly made tea. He carries both out of the kitchen and into the lounge.

No one is speaking.

He wanders around the back of the armchair where Mrs Hykely is sitting. He bends and settles the cup and the saucer amongst the fluff on the dark brown carpet where tiniest pale crumbs become visible and have patterns like fireworks.

Mrs Hykely looks over the arm of the chair and whispers.

"Thank you Mr -Coop..ham." She blows her nose lightly. She looks at Coatham who straightens up. She makes a kind of biting movement with her teeth, but is actually whispering again.

"It's been a bit of a shock."

Coatham looks at Mrs Hykely.

Tonight Mrs Hykely is dressed for Christmas. She is wearing a strong-shouldered burgundy-coloured trouser-suit and a fresh red carnation in the left lapel. As usual she has the black eyebrows which have been drawn on, but high above where her eyebrows should be and her lipstick is a bright red. Behind these she is a pensioner and lives two floors above him. From a distance (when he had seen her on dry days and walking between the factories' wagons and towards the flats) she had a kind face and a concern for the rubbish, which the factories left at their gate-sides in dented wheeled-bins. Late summer and autumn she could be seen weeding and trimming a small plot of ground, and in the spring there would be crocuses amongst the discarded metal next to the gate to the bone merchants. From a distance Mrs Hykely was persistent and able to lift rusty oil drums all by herself and drag a hoe through intricacies of tangled wire. These qualities earned her the respect of all those who watched from their balconies on those Sunday afternoons. As if to test her goodness she had been given rather a difficult temper and such a forceful stare that it could strike like an axe. He watches Mrs Hikely in the armchair. She is waving him closer to whisper.

He thinks. He bows slightly.

She grabs his shoulder and pulls him towards the glare and the eyebrows.

"I don't blame my daughter really..." the bright lips reveal the biting teeth, "...it's him."

He watches the teeth. She is whispering. The sound of the words. She is wearing a clip-on earring, an arrangement of coral (like lentils) around a gilt rose. Her hair scratches at his face. She lets him go and he slowly straightens.

He continues to gaze at her teeth, but she simply nods the affirmative nod - that the truth has been told.

He wonders about this. The windows rattle. The high scrowing and whistling gusts. The low draught comes from the lounge curtains. He wonders if there might be a tea-cup left for himself. Was there one in the bedside cabinet? A chipped cup he sometimes used for flu-relief powders.

Mrs Hykely unclips her shiny black handbag and from the clickiting and papery sounds she produces an oval silver compact.

Coatham turns, then pauses, then goes into the box-bedroom. He looks at the bedroom carpet, the blue and then bronze shapes like flowers - but too large a pattern for the small room, and sees how the carpet is only half swept. There are still crumbs and invading drifts of fluff from the other room. He wonders about the carpet and hears McKraw's wuffly cough from the lounge: "Let's have the TELEVISION on shall we!" (Then the click of the compact.) "I'd much prefer you didn't Mr - McClack, if you don't mind."

Chapter 6.

Down in the foyer the wind releases the main wire-glass doors. The half-inch gap closing and the litter which has been tinkling or scratching along (in front of the maroon staff-toilet-door marked "Private" , or else here and there) must stall. An empty plastic bottle, which bounced down a high flight of grey cloudy vinyl steps some minutes ago, has made no further descent. On a high landing it makes those slow teetering rockings towards a landing-wall when the draughts draw together, but is mostly still. On this landing (as with some others) the dark grey steel rubbish-hatch does not properly close. The counterweight which should swing the hatch up (like a bottom lip) is not faulty in most cases, but instead the "lip" has been fitted with spots of chewing-gum which have hardened into stony warts, and on certain landings the warts built upon like tusks so that a hatch gapes. On this landing the rubbish-hatch simply has warts, but from this an extra draught comes, and the varying sound too: and might be all the hatches (and their various apertures) or else the sound from the rubbish-bay itself, but changed by the distance.

On this floor the fire-doors on either side of the landing show the florescent strip-lights of the corridors beyond through their wire-glass windows. Through the right hand fire-door (from the direction of the stairs) a piece of faint-lined writing-paper flaps on the first magnolia-painted door. The flapping message reads:

Gone to number fifty three. (Mr Coop-ham.)
- Edna Hykely

Edna Hykely rests her hands on her shiny black handbag. Her mouth is slightly open and she breathes in and leans forward to speak but is unable to do so. She settles herself again. There are occasions to interrupt the man at the table, who is talking to her, but she has not yet found her chance. He is talking about Bingo. She bides her time.

Coatham moves the odd-legged mink-coloured corduroy kitchen-stool. The bureau's flap is closed. The bedroom window rattles, is nudged...noddled. From the city-scaped bedroom window, a draught of air. The boomy babbling voice of Mr Trevis, then the wind's returning in tumbles and tearings. He turns. The other side of the bedroom where the rusty orange carpet-sweeper has already "hoo-eeked" some of the stray crumbs and fluff away.

That dark splatter-shaped stain where the spill-proof Medi-Sure medicine glass had spilt - a little way beyond it: the bedside cabinet.

Coatham looks again at the bedside-cabinet. The air in the box-bedroom is cold. The draught from the window chilling the back of his neck.

He listens (He wonders if they have gone.)

He hears McKraw. That 'shurrrrp' sound as he breaths in over his top dentures after chewing them.

Behind him the window rattles. The wind crinking the glass. The thudding gallop of the other windows. Between these, the after-noise from the empty factories' stockyards. He turns (and sees himself) and through the window's reflection - the flash of cars beneath the blunt dark of the shut shops on the far side of the main road. In the lower distance the winter pallet-stacks have ribbons of sheet- polythene streaming, tangled and wrestling - winking in the security lights.

He listens.

"Never sent me a card though; she'd written his name inside, but it wasn't from him." (Mrs Hykely.)

"Oh deary me," (Mr Trevis.)

"And what is more…." (Mrs Hykely.)

Coatham looks at the bedside-cabinet.

Mr Habadan had brought him the cabinet - and how long ago was that? (He couldn't remember).

Mr Habadan was a retired salesman who had sometimes painted walls for Mr Reynolds, who was the first caretaker (before McKraw came). Mr Reynolds said that Mr Habadan could paint walls if he liked, because Mr Habadan was happy to help. Mr Habadan then lived on the top floor and sometimes the smell from the sewage works was overpowered by the smell of gloss and emulsion and this was Mr Habadan who had a flat-door wedged open and would nod at anybody who passed by. Mrs Lodgeson said she would never let Mr Habadan paint in her flat again after he had sung in it. Mrs Lodgeson had angled her face towards him so that the point was very clear. He thought that if Mr Habadan had sung in Mrs Lodgeson's flat then it wasn't deliberate.

Mr Habadan had been a very tall thin man and quiet-voiced. He would speak slowly in a whisper through thin lips and with a straight face whilst looking down upon people with steady grey eyes. He didn't wear overalls but wore an old paint-spattered slate grey suit with flat paint-dotted black shoes. Mr Reynolds would let Mr Habadan have the keys to any flat which became vacant and this was how Mr Habadan would find things.

He remembered that early one morning in the early autumn he had answered his door and it was Mr Habadan who was there and stooping a little so he could fit in the door-frame and was holding the bedside-cabinet under one arm and his other hand was palm-upward and gesturing at it. Mr Habadan's grey eyes had looked gently down and he had begun a steady whispery speech.

"A fine self-assembled bedside cabinet. Some ordinary wear at the base... Teak-effect with white door." Mr Habadan's grey eyes were steady, his face serious and his thin lips moving only slightly. "Ideal for any bedroom. Should match fitments, as a suite." Mr Habadan looked directly and sternly. "Looking for a good home."

He had looked at Mr Habadan and at the bedside cabinet. Behind him the donga-donga-donga-dunggadunggadunga noise from one of the factories was beating (and having beaten all night).

Mr Habadan began again. "A nice piece. The wardrobe of this set has been taken unfortunately...this is the only bedside-cabinet at this time."

He remembered now that he had never said yes - but also that he had never said no. The bedside-cabinet had been placed in his hands at a point when he had agreed that it had a cream-coloured door-knob that was replaceable and convenient to clean, for its being round, resistant to inks and oils and quickly wiped with soap and water.

Mr Habadan had given him a firm nod. The quiet voice saying something, but not loud enough to be heard, and then he'd

taken a couple of lanky strides down the corridor and looked back
- that firm grey stare.

That is how the bedside-cabinet had come here.

He looks at the bedside-cabinet.

When ever he opens the door of the cabinet he has to
remember that the magnetic door-catch is very strong. When he
opens the door of the cabinet he has to hold the cabinet down like
he is pulling a tooth, or else the chip-board cabinet can topple and
scratch about on the fluffy carpet. He never tried to open the
bedside-cabinet when he was in bed. A white, onion-shaped
bedside-lamp with a plain misshapen frilly magnolia shade has
rolled on the top surface and now rests on its side. The bedside-
cabinet is skewed to face his left. The smooth white door is open.
In his hand he holds a spare coffee-mug he wanted, red with the
picture of a naked man into which the handle, shaped like a naked
woman, appears to neatly fit. 'Sex Commando' reads in fiery
letters around the base. Mr Habadan had described it as 'recent
edition novelty-ware'. He stands with the coffee-mug and listens
to the windows rattling. The coiling sound and the wind
booooofing. He goes back to the door to the lounge and stands
where the strike of Mrs Hykely's voice is suddenly sharper. He
holds the coffee-mug and looks across the room and wonders if he
should have coffee or tea.

"Not that she would listen to me," Mrs Hykely's bright red
lipstick crashes into McKraw's sneaked glance, "he was always
going to be a weak little man."

McKraw sniffs. From over his shoulder he hears Mr Trevis
piping along - "Yes indeed!"

McKraw chews at his dentures and looks hopefully over the
rim of his cup, but there is nothing in it. He hears Edna reciting a
list of failings. He stares fixedly at the television which is switched
off. He slumps a little so that both his belly and the flesh under his
chin squash out.

The windows rattle behind Mrs Hykely's voice. The pause.
The second rattle that doesn't come. The warmth from the electric-
heater blown off course by a cold draught and towards the
bookcase where the spider lives.

McKraw sighs, rests his elbows on his knees - so that he squashes out in other places too - and feels his office keys swing forward in the right-hand outside pocket of his maroon jacket. His keys: all together on a large hand-sized ring and otherwise kept on a brass-coloured hook screwed into a cupboard's side in his office. The keys which, at the beginning of a shift, he would throw noisily down onto his desk-top where they would spread out like a coat of arms. They prove that he is charge of the thirty ninth tallest building in the middle fringe of the city. McKraw's upper dentures slide forward. That is why he couldn't remember the uses for all the keys and, also, he would add a key from time to time. It was always important to have more keys than Clifford.

Mr Trevis smiles broadly at Mrs Hykely who is continuing her list.

Mrs Hykely looks briefly back at him as she speaks, at Mr Trevis' eyes looming in the lenses of his glasses.

"Anyway," she feels for the tissue up her sleeve, "what can be done Mr Mc-Cock?" Mrs Hykely looks down at the carpet with its newly emerging fluff, "My daughter loves him."

The room goes quiet, except for the rattling, as Mrs Hykely studies. Her hands rest on her hand-bag and her face so still but so animated by her clothes and make-up that all the time she appears to move. Coatham stands in the doorway to the bedroom. He holds the Sex Commando coffee-cup, he looks at the carpet also (as Mrs Hykely is doing) and at the same spot. The windows rattle. McKraw stares at the television. Mr Trevis beams at Mrs Hykely, but Mrs Hykely doesn't look back. The windows rattle loudly. The rattle continues. The wind drumming on the glass.

Chapter 7.

At the back of the flats, and along the downward-hooking grey section-steel fencing that decides the separation between the rubbish that occupants of the flats have left and the rubbish that factories have agreed to remove, there is indeterminate land.

Tonight that landscape is dark and its shrubby silhouette is crackle-lit by the piercing security lights of the chemical plant and which cause the first of many 'glades' of soaring red-painted pipes (which rise from the ground) to seem to hover in the air. At those pipes' second or third heavy-bolted 'joinings' the light from below fails to illuminate them and the pipes rise higher into the unclear framework which supports them. Within this framework there are other smaller white lights trained on triangular signs or steel cases, and above these the pipes bend to horizontal in unison and head south-east. In the daytime one can see further, to gantries and pipes fascinated with each other and forming the high process units (with adjoining bulk cylinders) and are like blocks of flats themselves. Tonight the nearest of these is simply a brilliant tableaux and giving no sense of scale or distance; only trails of fumes show any habitation, although tonight the silvery chimneys' fumes are cut from the tops by the violent weather.

The tea-bag is in the Sex Commando cup. The tea-spoon is there also. The hard wood-effect surface of the fridge-top is peeling, revealing the hardened glue-swirls on the rough dirty chip-board panel beneath with its white and brown bread crumbs, nestled down the edge; the smallest ones running a little to the vibration of the kettle and the fridge. The kettle clicks off, its 'vrooooo' having been taken over by the tumbly rumbly water - and now quiet. And now Mrs Hykely and Mr Trevis battling to speak over each other to talk about different things.

The kettle is heavy. The water. The brief glass of it when it is most pouring and the steam. (McKraw interrupts the other two and sounds like 'Budbag-biddlybiddly-dib'.) The tea-bag big in the slowly staining water and the tea-spoon he shovels it with, and the light clink sound at the rim and the woody note from the base.

His lifting the tea-bag a small way and then dunking it back in - and again.

He takes the tea-bag, steaming and somehow exhausted on its spoon, and turns towards the work surface. He bends slowly and lets the tea-bag drop onto the two larger mounds of blue carpet-fluff which the carpet sweeper had made. He straightens and drops the tea-spoon in the thick bottomed glass that is on the fridge-top and which holds another spoon. He opens the fridge. [The plastic kiss-sound of the fridge-door.) (The ba-dum sound of the fridge also and its trickly-whistle.) (Mrs Lodgeson's milk.)

Mr Trevis presses his right forefinger on the table-top, "I never eat fried vegetables -"

Mrs Hykely's hand-drawn cosmetic eye-brows appear to move upward, "And that's the last time the lift worked Mr Mc-Clot -"

"- Informed me at my office they were awaiting," McKraw looks down his nose like he is reading, "relevant parts -"

The flecks of milk rising, turning. The bright cheesy bits. The kitchen windows' loud rattling, the lounge windows also - the box-bedroom windows rattling with them. He takes back the spoon and fishes at the sour lumps. He catches a larger chunk, which has come to the surface in the swirling tea and before it sinks again. He takes a step onto one of the higher swells in the kitchen vinyl and leans and turns the spoon over the sink and the sour lump is gone. He feels the draught from behind the oatmeal-coloured kitchen curtains which blow forward, the chill night air coming in and striking the upper side of his right hand as he brings the spoon away from the sink. The distant squawking of the rusty and turning ventilator-hood below the height of his flat and on a factory roof. He looks at the tea with its flock of sour specks. He decides. He puts the spoon tinkling back into its glass. He stares at the wall.

"Temporarily; then it doesn't - work - does it!" Mrs Hykely's bright red lipstick, the teeth biting.

("Sometimes I try some pork that isn't too fatty -" Mr Trevis' finger points to another place on the table-top.)

McKraw continues.

"Then Accounts will pay the money, then I receive a day-sheet, which I put in the Maintenance-Book."

Coatham stands and stares.

The kitchen walls had never been properly painted. There were strange flashes where the magnolia emulsion made for a smooth finish, and then other areas where some magnolia was blue-tinged from the colour underneath. He had often noticed that the kitchen was better in daytime than at night and was better in summer than in the wintertime. In a bad season or at a bad hour there was a noticeable effect like the kitchen walls were raining.

When Mr Habadan had re-painted the kitchens walls he said that the paint the estates company had provided was "Very economical, providing a moderate mood for the home environment, thin in application and subtle over all," and then, "easy to rinse from brushes and available in many sizes of metal-look tins." Coatham had, soon after, thought that the walls would improve when the paint was dry, and then discovered that it actually was.

Coatham stands and looks at the wall. He sips his tea, the sour lumps jostling towards his mouth.

At the main road a small dark blue car turns into the industrial-estate, its headlights shining for an instant at some shaking wire-fencing and through them to the blue-dyed pallets in short stacks. The car slows to let a long strip of clear plastic-sheeting rise and coil its way off the road and then the car continues across mud-fanned entrances to stockyards, over loose white hard-core from stretches of pavement where the tarmac has inexplicably finished, and now past the many outlines of factories where the security lights dazzle and the car pulls in near the main door of the flats and stops. The passenger-door opens suddenly and hits a lamp-standard with an audible 'clump'. The door closes. The car drives forward a short way and stops in front of the main doors. A dark figure steps quickly out of the passenger-side and slams the car-door and sets off walking and guarding themselves from the harsh weather. The driver, a taller figure, climbs out and locks the car and hurries around to the passenger-side but is motioned at by the first figure. The second figure approaches the

306

first and points back at the car with one flaying arm and holds their head with the other. The first figure points at the second figure - again and again - until the second figure throws their arms down by their sides and then they both go in.

At the far main road cars and taxis flash by in both directions. In one direction the cars slow down. The cars queue from the left, and in the direction of the city, they nudge forward and then slowly they are moving again; a last car comes slowly to the queue - while the queue loosens - and now all cars go forward. Some cars flash by in the other direction and then the main road is empty.

From many cold floors below, the dundly topperty sound of two pairs of shoes is coming. The difficult voices and the slow and unwavering sound of the shoes are dividing each other, so that, and at this high landing, they are a jig-saw with only its less useful bits. Another floor, and they are disagreeing clocks of foot pats and slaps on the steps hard vinyl, and heavier too, as the steps tire them. On this landing a draught comes from the rubbish-hatch, studded open by the hardened plobs of chewing-gum, and in the window on the sub-landing, where the steps turn for this floor, the lonely apparatus of the steps and the thin magnolia-painted steel banister-supports and girders (and grey, plastic-coated, coin-scratched banister rail, and cage-lamps above the fire-doors) are presented as a bright florescent wash in the pane's reflection. That window, and all hidden lower windows bluther with the force of the cold night air. The fire-doors on this landing chill with the dancing of draughts while some floors above that empty plastic bottle rolls a little in crescent. The voices and shoes have come a floor higher. Some of the 'jig-saw' fits for a brief moment with a woman's voice, "How the bloody 'ell would I know!" A reply is chopped up with patting shoes. Those shoes are louder now but slower, even on the sub-landings the tread of them is clomping with recovery. The voices louder, and also loud sighs, and also slaps of palms on the bannister-rail, and the noisy weather hurrying at the windows. The freezing draughts. The voices, now and then, rasping slightly.

Coatham drinks, avoiding a chip in the rim of the coffee-mug. The kitchen windows rattle. He turns and drinks and sees Mr Trevis smiling broadly at him. He wonders about Mr Trevis, and drinks again. He feels the lumps of sour milk go under his top lip. Mr Trevis is still smiling and also his eyes that are unblinking and large in his glasses. There is no one talking in the lounge now. When Coatham sets the coffee-mug down on the wood-effect surface of the fridge he hears the chairs creak as those in the lounge listen… in case it should mean something. Coatham stands in the kitchen.

A man's highly polished black shoe comes firmly on the landing and then the second shoe is drawn weakly up and joins it. A lady's white shoe with many delicate straps and a tiny white silk-petal rose on a broad band (some pink nail-varnished toes) stamps onto the landing - and now the following shoe - later than the man's. Some hands grasp the cold banister-rail that turns for the next floor, and then breathing. Breathing, and then the shoes weak stomping and toward to the right hand fire-door, and a hand hauls it open - the door's squeaky creak, the quickening of cold draughts.

Mr Trevis is now ready to touch the table-top in a new place and explain to Mr McKraw and Mrs Hykely the many difficulties of Bingo. His forefinger hovers, but it doesn't come down. The quiet of the room He looks at Mr Coatham again, who is in the kitchen and drinking from a bright red cup on which might be written 'sex command'. Mr Trevis' finger waits. He smiles at Mrs Hykely who is not looking, and then at Mr McKraw who has his back to him. His finger stops.

Mr Trevis knew that most of the effort of the Merry-Go-Round Bingo Club was about securing by invitation one of the four places at the Christmas Luncheon's Dinner-table No1 where the manager sits. It was Mrs De Vaulier, who had been invited first and who had arrived, yet again, in the same hat. Mrs De Vaulier who must struggle down to the shop to buy the same lucky mints, must walk painfully in the same lucky shoes and sit in the same lucky seat and immediately leave the building if any game begins with the number 75. Mrs De Vaulier whose luck was locked in battle with Miss Cullins, who carried three horse-shoes in her hand-bag, and also the Metherson Brothers who had a quarter of a cup of salt between them. This year Mr Trevis had not been so lucky. He stares. But was it so very important? Was he actually lucky? He never tried to win; he hardly tried at all… He stares. The prompt for the 'Good Evening Sir' [trademark] gentleman's thin wool-look sock Economy Range Competition reads across his thoughts. "I like'Good Evening Sir's thin economy socks because…"

An ear is placed to the door of number fifty three. A large ear that listens. Eyes turn. A mouth whispers. A man's voice. "Can't be fifty three - must be eighty three. I told you it was eighty three."

Other eyes look down. A mouth whispers back. A woman's voice. "It looks like a five - I know it's a five Malcolm, I'm not walking up more steps!"

The ear squashes closer. The mouth waits. "There's nobody in."

Those same eyes look down again. "She must have been here, with Mr Coopham."

The ear listens. The ear hears McKraw's 'Shurrrping' breath over his upper dentures.

The mouth tenses. "Wait a minute - there's a dog."

McKraw makes his wuffly cough.

The ear pulls away from the door. The first eyes stare at the other eyes. "There's a man and a dog in there."

The other eyes look hopelessly at the ceiling. "Alright then Malcolm, how can we ask him about Mother?"

The first eyes stare down the corridor. The fingers of a hand rub them.

Coatham wipes the fridge-top with a ropey cloth. Some spilled milk and a little water is patted out of sight, and replaced with a slither of onion. He wipes. The onion is exchanged for a spray of tea-leaves - the tea-leaves for the onion again. There is a light rapping knock at the door.

The lounge is quiet.

McKraw is looking around.

Mr Trevis is smiling broadly at Mrs Hykely.

Mrs Hykely who is patting at her hair.

Coatham stands at the door to the kitchen. A thin towel is in his hands and he is rubbing old tea-leaves from them. He looks back at the greying ropey cloth which sits next to the kettle. A moment to think.

The knock comes again.

The beginning of the eighth part.

Chapter 8.

Coatham goes to the door and unlocks it.

He opens the door a short way.

A short middle-aged woman is standing there. She looks at him and then is blinking down at the doorway where there is a small view of the carpet in case there is a dog.

Coatham looks down and then backs away a little.

He looks at her.

The woman looks at Coatham's face which is stained with splashes of black ink.

Coatham now sees a rather short dark-haired man side-step into view.

The woman has light brown hair tied back tight over a round reddened face and very jittery bright green eyes. She has pink-red lip-stick and small ears. The man who has very thick ears has some product to keep his thin black hair flat to his scalp and is wearing a strong dark blue suit, a black bow-tie and has firm staring blackish eyes which seem to be open extraordinarily wide.

"I'm so sorry," the woman says and looks at the door-number.

Coatham nods and prepares to close the door.

"Mr Coop-ham is it?"

Coatham stops, and feels a terrible worry pass across his face.

He nods.

The woman fills with happiness.

"I'm Loretta and this is Malcolm." (Malcolm's eyes stare in a rather wild fashion.)

"Is my mother here - Edna Hykely?"

Loretta looks past Coatham and her nervous green eyes harden and she makes a lunging inspection around the magnolia door-frame, her finely strapped white silk-rose decorated shoe arrives in Coatham's field of vision. The soft-wide perfume. The pink lip-stick. The tap of the diamond ring on the magnolia gloss.

Loretta's chin is jutted out and aimed.

"Mutha."

The moment.

The windows rattle.

Mrs Hykely's heaving recognition "L-orotta."

Coatham opens the door wide and the draught from the windows is icy against his cheek.

Loretta checks her tiny polished black handbag and adjusts its thin strap at the shoulder of her black rain-proof bulgy foam-panelled knee-length coat. The snagging grace of an ankle-length dark blue silk dress as she steps into the flat. Pink varnished toe-nails. Her sparkling green smile at Mr Trevis who is smiling back..

Malcolm's over-wide eyes grow wider and he dips his head around the door-frame.

Mrs Hykely's smacked lips. "- M-udcock."

Malcolm wiggles his fingers at Mrs Hykely in a tinkly wave, "Whatever."

McKraw watches the two of them.

Mr Trevis smiles at the turquoise-banded lounge curtains. The curtains swaying into the room with the cold air. Coatham closes the flat-door and the curtains deflate.

The tin-heater clinks on.

A momentary silence. The windows rattle. The wind coiling back and whistling away.

Coatham turns from the door.

Loretta shakes her head slowly at Coatham, "It's an awful night…"

Coatham wonders about the flat-door.

A chair creaks loudly. McKraw has got to his feet. He lightly shakes the jacket of his maroon suit and puts a rubber boot forward - and also his large strong hand. He smiles and raises one eyebrow like Victor Delmondo,

"Glad to meet you Lorotta," McKraw then leans to see Malcolm, " - Mudcock."

McKraw's eyes are hidden again by the heavy lids.

"I'm McKraw - I work here, I'm in charge," he says but a Delmondo tone.

Mr Trevis gets to his feet now.

Coatham looks at the flat-door again.

Mr Trevis' voice, but Mrs Hykely's voice interrupting him and introducing him as Mr Trowel. (The handshakes with Mr Trowel). The drip of the bathroom-tap, its far off stone-like note. The sudden loudness of the wind at the windows that rattle across every room.

Coatham goes into the kitchen and picks up the sodden ropey cloth from the top of the sink (that leaves a tiny slither of fried onion there) and holds the cloth under the coughing and spitting cold-tap.

He squeezes the cloth and the droning run of the water onto the stainless steel.

He looks at the curtains and their slight movement.

He hears Mr Trevis talking to Mudcock. He can Lorotta speaking low and perhaps hurried words to Mrs Hykely. He can hear Mrs Hykely's strong voice coming down in that whispered but hammering way.

"Only if he-says he is...sorry."

The word 'Bingo' coming innocently into the room like a stray feather.

Coatham watches the cream-slubbed oatmeal coloured kitchen curtains move. They sway that touch every now and then with the strengthening of the draught. The curtains resettle. The many detours of the wind amongst the factories' empty places.

Behind him the struggling voices of the lounge cover each other, knock each other out, or talk on, undaunted. The windows rattle. The draught from the curtains feels like it cuts into the bones in his fingers.

The windows rattle.

He had stood here five months ago. It was a weekend which some tenants, who talked about weather later claimed was a whole month of full sunshine - while others extended it to five weeks, because there were those weeks leading up to the heat and when there had been a few bright days.

The foyer was the place where these things were explained, by those who had heard the weather forecast but had had some extra insight: into the workings of the sky, the destinations of clouds, and everything. Chief amongst these was McKraw, since

313

he had the time to observe the subtle changes and make careful assessments of the balance of things and how things might tend. McKraw had long ago explained that he was at one with the weather, and had to be, in his job.

He had stood here five months ago and in the early evening and McKraw was on the sunny balcony of Coatham's flat and was shouting to a tenant on a balcony below that the hot weather would be with them for another fourteen days and that the clouds were 'too low for rain'. He had also bellowed this as a reminder to Mr and Mrs Backley, who were new tenants, and were the elderly couple who both had trouble with their feet, and were stepping with extra care along the rubble pavements and between the bone-wagons and were smiling and waving back. Coatham had stared at the couple in their thin white cotton clothes and then towards the East side of the city which was put out of the sun by low black purplish cloud.

McKraw had been checking the balcony-door, which wouldn't shut, and as the first rain came he said he would fill out a BW/15. However, since Mr Habadan was coming to look at the bathroom fan, (which wouldn't turn off) then the door might go on the same day-sheet as an extra. Mr Habadan would be reporting to McKraw later that evening but Mr Habadan wouldn't have the authority to alter the day-sheet until there was a BW/15, which was procedure, and after which the BW/15 could be removed from Maintenance Pending, and then cancelled.

McKraw had then become interested in the rain, that was torrential and nodded that it was 'just a shower'.

Soon after McKraw had left the thunder began. Coatham had then stood by his balcony door which wouldn't shut and watched the roar of the rain on the balcony's concrete surfaces. The air was whistly and the sunshine gone and in the peculiar light he could just make out, beyond the bone-wagons, the Backley's sharing one small umbrella as the lightning flashed and the thunder tore and crumpled and moved great boulders of sound. The warm air was drawn out of the flat like a flow of silk and the 'thick air' replaced it and only the wavering drone of the bathroom fan replied to the storm, and had to, since it had been whirring and droning for three days.

Malcolm is sitting at the drop-leaf table where the playing-cards are spread in front of him and there is also the carrier-bag and some removed items of shopping. He is facing McKraw, but McKraw has his back to him and is hunched forward and McKraw is rubbing his eyes with his fingers in a slow manner. Diagonally to Malcolm's right is Loretta, who is squatted down on one knee and a little to the right of the armchair and so partially obscuring Malcolm's view of Mrs Hykely, although her eyes fasten on him whenever he looks. He knows that the elderly gentleman, Mr Coopham, is behind and to his right and is in the kitchen and is probably busy. To his left and talking to him is Mr Trowel and who is drawing invisible drawings on the table-top with the forefinger of his right hand and, when he had last listened, was explaining the seating arrangements of a Christmas meal he had had.

Malcolm had managed to interrupt some time ago but Mr Trowel had mistaken his comment for a question about bingo and had simply continued. Malcolm runs a hand over his greased-back black hair and pats the soles of his shoes on the fluffy blue carpet to a remembered happy tune.

Mr Trevis' mind moves like a crane and his finger rubs out Mr Hardford, Mr Hardford's tiny round bald head, small eyes and choking tie disappearing and then Mr Hardford lifted by that finger like a featherless budgie and put on the opposite side of the table - and Miss Mounton put where Mr Hardford had been sitting. The finger pauses. He is aware that Mudcock is speaking again.

Malcolm moves his over-wide dark brown eyes in the direction of Mr Trevis, and his eyes open even wider, "- and you'll no doubt have had " Malcolm puts out his left hand in a brief way, "Cowes' Lemonade this Christmas, Mr Trowel."

Mr Trevis smiles brilliantly at Malcolm.

Malcolm smiles back at Mr Trevis, "It just so happens, though I don't often tell people this, that I'm a member of the team who designed the bottle-top."

Mr Trevis' finger hovers over Sidney Pitworth, then withdraws. Mr Trevis speaks: "Cowes' - gracious me. Cowes' - yes - yes - Cowes'."

Malcolm's eyes widen even more but also he shakes his head. "Third Team had waited months for something to come along - First Team designed the bottle, Second Team were too busy with the inflatable herd for the promotion." Malcolm finally blinks. "It all happened so quickly the whole idea- the Bubble-Gum Top," Malcolm opens his hands, "it came to me one morning."

McKraw turns a little in his seat and gives Malcolm a long puffy-eyed stare. "So…it was you."

Malcolm trains his staring eyes at McKraw.

"Yes - yes, it was."

Mr Trevis smiles at Malcolm,

"By Jove! Cow's 6L39 series sweet-topped."

Malcolm puts his hand to his forehead in delight,

"Mr Trowel - you know."

Mr Trevis stares hypnotically at Malcolm,

"Lemon flavoured yellow, Gleach Chemicals Ltd. Foods Division."

Malcolm puts his left hand to his mouth.

"Yes-yes, there was that - but the market already has a lemonade with lemons in it."

McKraw breathes in through his hairy nostrils and rubs his eyes again. He yawns, the yawn lifting half of him up as his belly pushes out. There was Cowes' Bubble-Gum everywhere in the building and there was something unusual in it which helped it fix anything to anything else. McKraw breathes in a big breath and makes a loud snorting sound. That man, Mudcock, was responsible for it all. McKraw lets his dentures slip forward and he makes a slurping breath to suck them back in. McKraw enjoyed finding out who was responsible for things. He enjoyed carrying a single crisp packet daintily after the tenant who had dropped it and following them up the steps and along the appropriate corridor and be with that tenant just as they were opening their door and presenting them with their litter. He enjoyed asking them questions such as

316

how many people did they think used the foyer? Then he would fold his arms if the tenant didn't answer. And what if all those people who used the foyer dropped a crisp packet? We wouldn't be able to get into the building would we? McKraw thinks about the many shrinking tenants on lonely corridors. He thinks about those infuriating people who never dropped litter, not even a bus-ticket, not even accidentally. He thinks about Coatham. He thinks about Trevis. There was little to do about Trevis. Trevis belonged here - talking about - about nothing.

At least there was this lady, Lorotta. McKraw looks across with a slow turn of his head but finds Edna Hykely staring straight at him. He slowly returns his head and rests his elbows on his knees and runs his fingers down his face. Anyway, Lorotta was working on Edna. Lorotta and Mudcock were going to take Edna away and then there would only be Trevis and Trevis had a portable television - Trevis had many portable televisions - and it would simply be a matter of taking one away. Taking one little television away until Clifford was here and then tell Clifford to repair the old one. McKraw chews his dentures. He could easily turn around now and ask Trevis for his television. He could turn around right now and do it. He could turn around, but he can't. He can't because everyone here would say that McKraw was no longer McKraw. People might afterwards start calling in at his office and asking if he was alright, just like they did for Mr Belcher. He was McKraw: he would carry on. He will have a working television tonight, he will sit down comfortably in his office tonight, he will watch the strange clammy early hours' programmes tonight - just like everyone else did.

Loretta looks around, so that both she and her mother are staring at Malcolm, then Loretta turns back. "He's not like that, Mother."

Mrs Hykely is still staring at Malcolm and who is pretending to talk to Mr Trevis. "He's - not right L-aracka," Mrs Hykely breathes in through her teeth and her pencilled eyebrows are kinked by her expression. "He won't stop talking about bottle-tops."

Loretta puts a hand on her mother's, "He's knows a lot about bottle-tops, it's not every man finds what he should be doing."

Mrs Hykely allows her sharper teeth to slide together and then the bright red lipstick becoming a single alarm of red and the lips press together very hard. Then:

"Why didn't you marry D-ullward?"

"Edward, Mother, Edward," Loretta removes her hand and makes a little sigh. "I couldn't marry a self-employed anglers'maggot-farmer - I thought I could," Loretta looks down at the blue carpet where shoes and slippers have rolled the fluff into those trailing worms, "but I couldn't. It was the buzzing mostly - and the special species he kept in his cellar." Loretta's eyes grow larger and she studies the carpet-worms. "The ones from the cellar would escape and there'd always be one on his kitchen window - always at least one giant black one." Loretta's green eyes fix on the carpet-worms. She looks at her mother again but her mouth has dropped open slightly "- and then when you met him you called him Dunghead."

Mrs Hykely bares her sharp teeth, "I couldn't have - he misheard me - I couldn't have." Mrs Hykely rests a hand on Loretta's shoulder, "I never forget a name."

At the back of the building and where the waste land is a burial ground for bricks, and where, in the drier seasons, nettle-banks and thistles sway and sharpen, the high grass and rotten stems are being violently combed. The last rain added to soggy places where the mass of the vegetation was undermined by near-permanent pools, although the smells do not come from these. At the limit of the waste ground there is a line of leafless winter shrubs and then another against the chemical plant's tall wire fence. Between these rows of shrubs the ground dips sharply like a ditch and where there is mud trodden up and slid into furrows by the shoes of children. A stream there carries many foams and industrial slimes which give the mud its orange colour and gives the stream its near-formaldehyde reek. Around the flats there are many smells with which the stream must compete. The bone-merchants, after its recent addition of a low building at the chemical plant's fence, offers the stink of rotting flesh and acidic vapours. Immediately beyond (to the East) are the sewage pans where there is that rather spiralling smell of excrement. The outlying process-units of the chemical plant, and which seem like brilliant but nonsensical ships on nights like these, seem to float towards the fence from the North, and for sixth months of the year, in accordance with their licence, can smother the other smells with sulphurous discharges and those smells which accompany the fine peach-coloured powders which settle on parked cars in the mornings between four and seven. There are other smells too, although these are from the West and beyond the playing-fields, and are most often simply an excess. An excess of detergent from Spring Joy Ltd's cleanser-bottling plant or the fish-innards which are simmered, compressed in jelly, and extruded in the pet foods factory. Tonight the silhouetted branches of the shrubs are gnashed and shocked by the wind and the unseen liquids of the stream gabble and splash. The back of the flats rise lightless and the only obvious movement is at a top flat where a faulty lock on a balcony-door left the door diddling and nudging and finally swung open into that lounge some hours ago. The door bangs, though muffled by the wind's noise, and for the keen ear there is the occasional sound of things falling and during those hours also the sight of paperwork swished and chased onto the balcony and to its new life.

Coatham remembers.

Today clouds of thistle-down had floated over the fields and gardens. Over dry-stone shambled walls the feathery seeds had puffed and caught in webs like scores for songs. Thistle-down clung to his mother's soapy bed-sheets pegged like wrinkled skins in the sun and breeze. Thistle-down like snow from the high fields and the holly dells. On the rugged sandstone path behind their terrace the down was tumbling and snagged onto grass like spawn. The land that had tides after all. The land that was meadow and field and wood and moor again after the rain-clouds had darkened it. After the battering rain. After the terrible storms.

Today he had taken Mrs Caircy's dog out on its chain, being the day without chimney-smoke and Mrs Caircy in the garden with

319

her rugs said he should take him: 'Fu'ther thant fleas c'n foller 'im.'

Mrs Caircy's dog guarding the toilet day and night and being in there in the worst weather and sometimes at night its chain chinkling across the flat stone, and its rarely barking.

He had looked back from the ridge which the root-tied muddy sandstone path cuts over and could see after the roofs of the terrace to where the shabby elder lane bends to the right and then down. He could see where the bend is tightest and on the left where the bushes are grown together is the start of the pale track leading eventually to Slaithes' Farm. He had climbed a tree there once and away from the geese that were loose and raising their necks at him and doing their nipping dance and there seemed no place at all to get down. That way to Slaithes', that way to the armies of cabbages in Radford's fields and where the caterpillars are an army too and make the leaves stink.

After the bend the lane going steeply down, but the very tops of the Lasser Terrace rising over, though before them the trvellers' camp and their tin stables and funny shack house (but all hidden away by the beech trees in summer, so that only their smoke is there). The Lasser Terrace sleepy these days and nothing told of them. Then the lane going down to the dale-bottom and the mill-school. Then, somehow clearer, the other side of the dale rising up green, brown, yellow and purple and where the houses are blacked out at night and the valley black also and the stars dancing. Netherholm, far to the left, and like a spill of grey parcels in its steep ravine and its roofs as close as lice. Then the moors. The sky, ravelled up over them, greys and whites, after the arch of the wisp and blue. Pudes Hill, highest of the blacktops and searching for murky weather, and they call 'the cradle.'

Chapter 9.

On the rear side of the flats hat top flat's balcony-door blows inwards and over-wide so that a fine crack in the door-frame deepens and the screws in the hinges move. The door swings to return and the crack in the door-frame tightens again, and the assorted screws seem to nestle back in. The lounge ceiling's light-bulb and shade dances to the rough air, the dark lounge showing no obvious damage except for many sheets of paper turned or slipped from a teak-look sideboard, disordered newspapers, a standard-lamp knocked over by a drying-frame of clothes which toppled. The wind blows. The wind scooping and sending things around. The door straining the hinges and loosening the screws - one of the ill-fitting tiny brass ones that was held in with a hopeful dab of glue moves freely now. The wind blows.

"I suppose so," Mr Trevis has stopped listening to Malcolm. "I suppose so," the canter of Mr Trevis' mind allowing him to hop over the matter of bottle-tops themselves as an individual part - though he knew the production codes for the popular designs just as everyone did.

"I suppose so," though he never completely ignored anyone. Only the other week Mr Townsley had explained that someone had left a half-eaten cheese and salad sandwich on his bed when he was not in. He tries to remember Mr Townsley but a stray caption runs through his mind. (Stop running, stop hiding, stop scratching, with Anus-Ease.)

"I suppose so,"

Malcolm sighs. He had given Mr Trowel enough clues. The other man should have made the connection, the man in the uniform -even though he was turned around.

Malcolm gives the drop-leaf tabletop a giant stare. None of it mattered really - except that it did, it really did. He couldn't even sit in his lounge at home without it mattering. Alright, well it was a kind of reward for the bubble-gum top.No other designers in Third Team thought radically enough. That is why he was in First Team now. That's why he was in on the Cowes Sales Promotion.

That's why he was in the television advert as the fifth cowherd from the left. That's why it mattered

Malcolm looks at Mr Trowel. Malcolm knew it mattered, because now he he was famous.

"That was then, Mother. That was a previous life with Edward. It now seems a long time ago.

Loretta thinks about Northlock Lane. She sees the semi-detached house with its badly scratched pale blue back door open. Tall prickly rolls of aluminium gauze stand against the disused pebbly concrete coal-bunker, its top stacked with large gauze cages and with third-hand angling equipment. The back garden's lawn grown high with thick grass, docks and woody plants while ruts through it trampled down as paths to the fly-sheds.

A '*tszzzzzz*' sound… always in the house somewhere and always the reminder that these were not invading flies (and in winter they couldn't be) but these flies were theirs. They were their flies.

Sometimes she watched them for hours. Then Mr Hoft would arrive standing with Edward amongst the weeds and their both examining jam-jars filled with a constant undulation of maggots. Mr Hoft smiling sat the lines of hatching sheds and pupation cages and crawling trays. Edward smiling modestly at the sheds himself. Edward who was no longer a library assistant (but had retained an interest in types) and had taken to his interest in types of maggots with surprising ease. He did not hesitate to draw her attention to something which had previously seemed like a large brooch on the wallpaper during dinner.

"Eldritch was a nice boy," Mrs Hykely removes the crumpled tissue from her sleeve and dabs at her nose. "He looked so proud in the newspaper with his jams."

"Yes mother, and not jams" Loretta sees her mother glaring at Malcolm. "but Malcolm is actually on television at the moment, which is quite an achievement."

"M-arvin - dressed as a cow -" Mrs Hykely frowns at Malcolm.

"Not a cow Mother. Malcolm is a farmer or something. The director said he has wonderful eyes."

Mrs Hykely continues to glare at Malcolm, but Malcolm isn't looking. Malcolm is turned slightly and looking towards the kitchen.

Loretta turns and looks at Malcolm also. She then turns slightly the other way but finds she can't see enough of the kitchen. She turns back again and waves a hand at McKraw, "Mr - erm."

McKraw lifts his face out of his hands and looks at Mrs Hykely.

Loretta smiles.

"Mr McCrass - what does Mr Coopham do?"

McKraw stares at Loretta. He turns heavily in the wooden seat which makes a splintery creak. Behind him Mr Trevis continues to talk about brands of pickled cabbage. McKraw stares in the direction of the kitchen, his right hand waves in no particular way

"He.........er," McCraw says but who finally shakes his head.

Loretta looks at her mother, but Mrs Hykely pretends to be examining her hand-bag.

Loretta looks at the two of them and also looks at the carpet.

The windows rattle. The draught carrying past Loretta and Mrs Hykely and towards the tin-heater which clinks on and coincides with the drip of the bathroom tap.

Mr Trevis' finger hit's the table.

"But I never eat cabbage on a Wednesday - oh dear me no - never on a Wednesday."

Coatham thinks.

He watches the oatmeal coloured slub-cotton kitchen curtains move after the last rattle.

It may be that he hadn't bought the kitchen curtains after all, but, also, neither had they been given to him. It may be that they were hung there when he had first moved in, and so looking at them now was like finding one pair of shoes in the bottom of the wardrobe that were never yours. Someone else had stood here. Someone else had drawn these curtains apart in the morning and pulled them together at night. (Then left to this window when the rest of the rooms were cold and empty.) And no doubt when that person owned them they were (just as now) curtains that autumn wasps get caught in, being a snaggy loose-looped cotton - and, just as now, even the slightest roughness of a fingernail means they cling and pull and he has to prise the cotton free. And perhaps, just as now, there were those long threads of fine cotton which make one curtain dance unexpectedly, when he moved the plastic washing-up brush, but always the right curtain and not the left. And even now, he looks, there is that nearly unnoticeable thread - wound around the cold tap from when it had last been turned.

At the back of the building and at that top floor flat the lounge light comes on. The lounge bulb and dark blue shade swaying with the rush of night air through the room and into the florescent-lit corridor. A soft brown-leather shoe with a spot of dried magnolia on the toe steps towards the clothes' drying-frame and lifts it smoothly up. The white plastic-coated wire drying-frame with its assortment of damp socks is carried towards the balcony-door. A hand steadying the door. A forearm pressing hard to re-align the sliding hinges. The drying-frame set to the handle to keep the door shut and the door now only juddering. A moment. A hand reaching over a coffee-stained dark pink sofa, its upholstery fabric made sharp and gnatty from other liquids having been spilled, and the hand opening a cracked smoked-glass door of a hi-fi cabinet and pressing a silver-grey button which enables a record to play - but the record repeating a single 'shee-ornee' 'shee-ornee' 'shee-ornee' sound, but the figure not noticing and walking calmly into the kitchen where there is the immediate noise of a pan planging onto the floor and cutlery dinkling. (The figure coming back.) The shoes treading over to the intercom phone handset which is lifted by the left hand and the right hand's forefinger pressing a key on which there is already a magnolia fingerprint. The mouth waits. The mouth receives a blue cocktail cigarette and a silver lighter clicks politely. The left hand puts the lighter into the outside pocket of a navy blue suit's jacket pocket. A navy blue bow-tie is adjusted. The receiver nestled on a shoulder and under a cheek showing some grey stubble. The left hand returning to the pocket and searching for something. The record continuing to 'shee-ornee' 'shee-ornee' and the left hand finding a slim mobile-phone and setting it for a call and then passing the mobile to the right hand which holds both receivers. The cigarette held in the steady lips which whisper.

"Where are you?" (There is an inaudible gluffy reply.)

"I see."

The figure turns casually and looks to a place next to the hi-fi.

(The whisper)

"Your television? Broken - I see."

The figure waits. The left hand reaches and spreads old mail across the surface of the sideboard where earlier a pile of BW/15's and blank day-sheets have spilled and blown around the carpet,

"Mine too -" the figure turns slowly around,"I dropped a frozen turkey on it."

McKraw leans hunched forward with his black vinyl-bound radio-phone. His guffling voice guarded by the palms of his hands. He waits. He gives the radio-phone a shake and listens again. He breathes through his nose and shoves the radio-phone back into his jacket's right inside pocket and shifts his rubber-boots forward and then sits back into the monologue from Mr Trevis. He chews his dentures around until they push a little way out of his mouth and then he sucks them back in…Habadan was back.

Malcolm narrows his eyes a fraction at McKraw. He looks briefly at Trevis who is talking about his groceries then back at McKraw. Malcolm tries to think… McCrass? Wasn't the janitor McCrass? McCrass - that was the janitor. That was the man he had met last year on the evening of Edna's birthday and who had walked up to him and asked him if he had enough bluebottles . He had told McCrass that he didn't know and then McCrass had said 'Still got plenty have you.' He had expected McCrass to laugh but he didn't and instead McCrass was ready to compete with him on his knowledge of the subject. When Edna's door had opened and Loretta had said her mother would allow him to enter now he had then looked down the corridor at McCrass who had walked through one set of fire-doors and was standing and staring at the others while the fire-door behind inched shut. He'd asked Edna if she had any problems with flies and she told him E-arwig used to come and take them away. He had later asked Loretta if 'Earwig' might be her old flame Edward but Loretta simply reminded him that Edward worked in a library. Malcolm stares at McCrass and tries to decide if McCrass looks like an entomologist. Malcolm puts his elbows on the table and watches McCrass' ears move up and down as McCrass chews something. Malcolm's eyes drop and he stares at the table-top just as Mr Trevis' finger arrives in front of him.

"To be an honoured guest at Furlow's Pickles -" Mr Trevis' finger rises and points, "and - Ha Ha! - the factory's only over there!"

Malcolm looks at the bar-pattern of the brown, orange and turquoise lounge curtains.

Loretta and Mrs Hykely look at Mr Trevis' face, which is full of joy.

Coatham remembers.

The loose rattles of magpies' calls from the branches of tall maples. The wet and draining bank to his right hedged with nightshade and from above it, steeply, the dark and sun-dappled mossy bank coming down mushy smelling and noisy with the hidden birds. High up there was the ruined terrace called Styers, though most of the stone taken and the rest swallowed by ivy and the wood. That path of sunk cobbles crossed by trickle-water from the wet bank, and on his left the high piled-dry stone wall blackened by chimney smoke. Today the claw and clink of Mrs Caircy's dog huffing and chugging him along like a train amongst the alarmed birds and the matted shaggy brown dog sniffing in the flowers and blowing them out again as they came out of the trees.

There were hedges on the left and right growing high over the path, and the grass stalky and long and bushing, where tiny straw moths bustled and ticked about. There were still midges from the last trees and in the lower woods to come the crows rose and fell amongst the branches. The land to the right was Hinch's Meadow, going up to the Dells and above them again the high fields. The land to the left was Wyatt ground, wounded by little shafts, down which children were sent to cut lead - and all a long time ago and the holes no better than jagged slots and with grass weaving over them.

Below the woods the path had dried after the rain. On the other side of the dale and far along was Haden Heath, where Melston's little streets fasten all dirty around the railway and the factories, and after there the line to Radworth, and along the canal with its scoured water.

Today the crows were noisy in their green castles and the church land bobbing with buttercups, clover and daisies and the summer heavy there and not sparing a breath of cool. He'd sat there on the chapel's steps and from sideways through a slat fence the orphans were teasing towards the dog with their eyes and fingers. Their city-faces quick or thin or sullen and watching the dog that stood or else lolled and scratched. Their far voices tugging too on their funny accents and the girls in green and the boys in brown dropping grass seed onto the sunk-angled paves and where the grass was already tight there.

All the lights go out.

"Arrrrrrrrr-hrrrrr!"

In the dark the continuous flow of Mrs Hykely's voice stops.

"Mother!" Loretta pushes at her mother's shoulder, "Stop it Mother, we only have to open the curtains and then we'll talk to Mr McCrass."

"Who!?" Edna's voice aims around for someone.

Loretta looks up and across from her squatted position and at the dark lounge curtains which are being man-handled by Malcolm and McKraw, except that the curtains won't draw open. They flap in beautiful waves of faint city-light and some kind of metal is holding them back and makes high-pitched squeaks. Loretta sees the dim outline of her mother in soft-edged outline and who remains looking forward in the armchair and her make-up is somehow different and making her face indescribable.

"My side- my side- my side Mudcock," McKraw saying, but talking from his stomach which is something he learned from Removals Teams when directing them up and down the steps when the lift was again broken.

McKraw sees Malcolm's wide staring eyes as the gaps in the curtains appear and he hears the wire curtain-hooks somehow jamming together and his having to shake the right-hand curtain and trying to find a manner that looks professional. Professional - the word coming into his mind and giving him great satisfaction.

"What is M-adcow doing?" Edna Hykely remains staring ahead.

Loretta stays crouched down next to the armchair and looks at her mother's face.

"He knows what he's doing Mother, he's a designer." Loretta swivels some way whilst holding on to the arm of her mother's chair. "Are you alright Mr Trowel?" and sees Mr Trevis' unmoving glasses flicker and the unchanging gleam of his dentures.

Malcolm sees McKraw giving that right-hand curtain funny shakes that appear to make no difference. Malcolm's large eyes look up towards the curtain rail.

"If I bring a chair I can reach the hooks and I can move the hooks by hand and reduce the leverage."

McKraw stops shaking the curtain.

It was the voice of Clifford. Mudcock was the same as Clifford. McKraw chews on his dentures. Clifford who said things like: 'The stapler won't work without a minimum of one staple in it' and 'The lift won't carry more than ten persons and last month it didn't.'

Malcolm treads stalk-like across the darkened room towards the dining-chair which McKraw had been sitting in.

McKraw watches Malcolm's outline and decides he is watching Clifford. McKraw continuing to watch Malcolm whilst giving the right-hand curtain little tugs.

The night weather climbs again and the wind thudders and shooooools.

The windows rattle. The left-hand lounge curtain which Malcolm has abandoned sways inward with the cold draught.

"Here."

McKraw sees Malcolm setting the creaking seat in front of the curtain.

McKraw chews on his dentures

"That is not very good."

"It is a standard dining-chair Mr McCrass," Malcolm hears McKraw slurping something, "wood has good tensile strength, and the modern designs are - arrrrrrrrrrrgh!"

There is a thundery-thump of Malcolm hitting the floor.

Loretta stands up and looks for Malcolm, "What are you doing now?"

"Ow! ow-ow-ow-ow-ow," Malcolm is blowing and sighing. "Lorra - I've - twisted myself."

Loretta puts her hands on her hips, "You have - twisted yourself?"

"I'm going to take the chair off now - but it can't have been the chair, it must be that sherry I had at Patricia and Donald's."

Loretta moves slowly forward trying to see Malcolm. "At Patricia and Donald's?"

The broken seat of the chair comes free of Malcolm's right leg, he can feel the hot and cold pains in the ankle. He hears McKraw slurping.

Malcolm explains brightly.

"Yes, I told you I would pop in after the supermarket and show them the video of the promotion - remember? I told you."

Loretta looks at the curtains still not drawn.

"And then you had the punch before dinner and then the lagers after it. You're - you're not over the legal driving limit!"

Malcolm feels his ankle. "No no not punch - the fruit juice, the glass of fruit juice that was on the er - the...er....ah."

Loretta waits.

The windows rattle in every room.

Loretta frowns.

"I don't want to believe this."

There is a silence.

Mr Trevis sings.

> "*I don't want to believe*
> *there are plenty more fish in the sea*
> *when you leave me*

"*I don't want to decide*

that you're not the love of my life
when you leave me"

McKraw stops shaking the curtain and listens to Mr Trevis. He looks in the direction of Malcolm and nods his head to the side, "Victor Delmondo sang this."

McKraw sucks air in through his dentures.

"Victor Delmondo's a millionaire; women have fainted."

Mrs Hykely listens. "What a lovely singing voice."

Loretta runs a hand slowly down her face and breathes sharply in and then out.

Mrs Hykely sits forward. "Who is singing?"

Loretta looks down to where her mother is

"It's Mr Trowel mother…Mr Trowel is singing"

McKraw listens to Mr Trevis' singing. McKraw feels suddenly fluent.

"Hear that - Mudcock? No more bluebottles for you if you could write songs like that."

Loretta stiffens

Malcolm stares at the blurred shape of McKraw.

"Mr McCrass -" Malcolm winces as he straightens his ankle, his wide-open eyes staring. "you talked like this once before, but I really don't know anything about bluebottles; maybe I could design a top for one."

Loretta breathes in sharply. "Mr McCrass."

Mr Trevis stops singing.

McKraw slurps his dentures back in and lets the curtain fall back. The room is in darkness again.

Loretta adjusts the strap on her little handbag.

"I'm phoning for a taxi and my husband, my mother and I are going home."

McKraw chews his dentures around again and pulls back the curtain to look at his watch. McKraw sniffs and then stares out at the factory yards and the waving of clear-plastic sheeting. He stares out at the main road where there will no longer be buses. The lonely main road now where lone walkers in the early hours can pass the entrance to the industrial estate and measure the tarmac as they cross - like it's the morning they walk to or a distant country where the night might begin again but with a different outcome. That main road where the morning will surely come and the steel delivery-doors of the factories will jangle open.

Loretta goes into the box-bedroom, sees the odd-legged corduroy-covered stool, in shadow and in front of the bureau, and walks instead in the faint light from the window and sits on the bed which over-flattens due to its weak springs. She takes out her lilac-cased mobile phone and taps into her numbers which makes the screen light up. She goes to the list: Taxi-1 to Taxi-7 and makes a call.

McKraw touches the right curtain aside again and sees the industrial estate's avenue in darkness except for the security lights. The street-lamps of the main road not working either and only the cars' lights running across. He thinks about the taxis on Saturday nights when the students out of parties stare at him like ostriches and are too drunk to speak. Those bleak Saturday nights when he would look down his nose at his dog-eared and creased red note-book with phone numbers scrawled all over in his scored handwriting. He remembers the students staring in through the hatch window, trying to focus on their mobile-phones and staring at the red note-book and making their call. Then behind any main crowd always the local young people wanting to spit on the foyer floor but trying not to. One or two vulnerable youngsters who looked at him and knowing then they had been carried here by some chance and now seeing him as their Uncle or as an instant Granddad. He saw the types every weekend, looking out at the industrial estate and not seeing what he saw over the long hours. McKraw who saw them prance off and then shout back at those still in the foyer or scraping their shoes along the tarmac in the air tinged with the smells.

Coatham draws the left-hand kitchen curtain open and which slides on its plastic C-clasps. He moves on the swells of vinyl on the kitchen floor and to the right and draws the right-hand curtain along now. The curtain carries a bent-pronged fork from its place in the cutlery compartment of the mustard-coloured dish-rack and swings it on a fine cotton thread across to where it spins free and clankles into the dark sink. The washing-up brush also makes a tentative move and some slack of fine thread touching his hand like spider-silk and on its way to the cold tap.

The kitchen windows with less reflection now. The kitchen thrown back and lit dimly like an audience when the main feature begins and the screen crackles with those marks across it and the projector focuses. Cedric Torhill-Merelake sits in a steamy fish-market café in his tailored suit with only an open newspaper for company, and clicks open his gold pocket-watch on its gold Albert chain while the headline reads: "East End Search For Man In Saville Row Suit Continues." The audience staring and looking past Torhill-Merelake to the bulky policeman who rubs a hole in the dirt on the outside of the window and cups his hands and looks in, notes all those sitting in the café and then moves on.

Coatham sees the policeman, standing high over the city and rubbing and then looking. The black and white policeman staring red and green like the lights on the tops of the commercial office-towers and high over the fading policeman's head the switch-winking lights of air-traffic hanging over the western estate and where the unplaced orange streetlights and window-glows shiver with the distance. The weather noisy at the windows. The kitchen dressed in blurry cream colours and the rest full dark, half-dark or blurry again. The noise of the weather. The sound of Mrs Hykely asking a question but the window-frames too loud. McKraw saying "No" loudly, "They're are all booked - no," a pause, "Booked!" McKraw louder. "Booked! Busy! No taxis."

A voice from further now, a strained voice. "Mother, they are pre-booked - we have to phone in an hour."

Loretta sits back on the squashed bed with its sproily springs and watches Malcolm limp into the bedroom. He leans against the door-frame for a moment and makes a half hop on the fluff-wormed swirly carpet to the corduroy-covered stool and sits on it and chooses which of the legs should touch the floor.

Malcolm looks at her with his wide open staring eyes.

"What makes McCrass think I know anything about flies? I mean flies, Loretta."

Loretta puts her mobile phone down on the bed beside her.

"Not flies Malcolm," Loretta whispers, "Diptera; a family of insects with one pair of discernable wings."

Loretta looks at Malcolm sitting in silhouette.

"Excluding social insects, those with four wings or extended parts."

Malcolm moves his wide open eyes towards the ceiling. He pauses.

"You're interested in flies?"

"Malcolm - it was Edward, he sold them."

"What...? in the library...?"

"No." Loretta sighs, "In the fly-sheds, he had millions of them."

"Millions of them?" Malcolm finds his balance on the stool and sits forward and scratches his chin. "You mean people buy flies?"

"No no no," Loretta stares at Malcolm, "well, sometimes Mr Hoft did."

"Flies?"

"Well maggots really - for people who catch fish," Loretta waits.

Malcolm puts his hand to his mouth. He thinks.

"The profit margin must have been enormous."

Loretta stares. "Malcolm, you're not supposed to say that."

The windows rattle.

Loretta continues to stare.

"It was terrible. An awful idea he researched at the library - and it took him over. It took him over completely and he didn't listen to me any more."

Mrs Hykely looks across the room and at Mr T-raffic. She sees his smile is nearly luminous and his glasses reflecting small glints of light. The glasses move a fraction just as a shout comes from the bedroom behind her. ("No Malcolm I don't care - I am not living with flies all over again!")

Mrs Hykely stares at Mr T-rolley. She had always noticed him as a very unusual man. Her late husband was never one to disagree with her but he had disagreed with her on the origins of mankind and stuck to his belief that human beings had developed

333

annoying personalities so that they were unpleasant to eat. He had often mentioned that their neighbour was a 'Survivor' because he picked his nose in public and ate raw onions like other people eat apples. Mrs Hykely now watches Mr T-riple and decides he would not be eaten by any lion on any day of the week. Nothing would eat Mr Mc-Clump and nothing would eat M-illrat; nothing would eat him.

Coatham thinks about leaving the kitchen, but he decides not to because the lights are off. He listens and the rooms are quieter and the only sounds are Lorotta and Mudcock (and Lorotta who has been shouting but has now stopped) and them now both talking, and besides this the squeak bang of the fire-door a moment ago and is now inching itself closed. A sound like shoes, but in long slapping steps. Rather like Mr Habadan's shoes. The slapping shoes. The silence.

Tap-tap.

Tap-tap.

The flat-door opening. The opposing wall of the corridor faintly green from the fire-exit light over the fire-door at the corridor's very end

The steady eyes of Mr Habadan, as he stoops into view, and caught in the light of a big magnolia-spattered torch with a smashed yellow top-light but that bulb staying lit. He dips his head under the door-frame and steps slowly into the lounge and shines the main beam of the torch on Mr Trevis who is turning around and smiling directly into the torchlight like it is a camera. The torch-beam sweeping around to perhaps McKraw and to whom he nods, towards the armchair and then around and now into the kitchen. Mr Habadan looking at Coatham and the torch-beam turned away towards the voices from the bedroom.

Chapter 10.

Beside the playing-fields, where the long and low sheds of the wire-factory extend and block a view of the main road, the wind shakes the wire fences. The fences that school-shoes have kicked and where shoes have stepped onto the unwinds of drooped unravelled holes and stamped them larger. These holes, like some serious and important knitting has lost its shape, have become crude doors into the wire factory's swarf-sparkled heavy-smelling grounds. A burst white and blue football has deflated in a dark puddle - a side-loading diesel fork-truck having run over it, in a pale and nameless hour of cold day hydraulics, when the sky was bleary.

The playing-fields' grassy sigh in the dark. No reference of shape or scale for the abandoned and burned out small car parked in a goal-mouth. Tonight the funny short lamps of the flats' car-park gone out, the street lights on the industrial estate gone out also and the dull cliff of the block of flats' featureless side has no murals of rain on it, or variations at all.

Sometimes in the summer, when the rain is heavier, the children can be seen standing under the sycamores, which the authorities saw back to stricken lollipops, and where the children are dances and with jumpers wrapped round their middles or make full runs along the zoo of the pet-foods' factory's grey-spike fence, where the parked wagons watch them.

Malcolm leans forward on the odd-legged stool and looks with his wide-open eyes into the lounge and with his mouth slightly open.

"Don't stare Malcolm," Loretta's voice coming sharply.

"I'm not - no I'm not, I'm not," Malcolm continues to look. A torch of some kind has been put on the drop-leaf table's top and its beam stays directed into his eyes. "There's someone…in a suit and a bow-tie," Malcolm's mouth drops a little wider. "Must be someone from one of the Executive Flats - maybe it's the owner; they're legally obliged to provide for the tenants remember."

Loretta feels the bed-springs squash down around her and feels wires of some kind which seem to give too much and spread.

"Mother's never mentioned the owner - unless it's Mr B-ackside, I never found out who he was."

"Hmm?" Malcolm looks at Loretta and looks back. "Seems to know McCrass - and Trowel. Bet you he's the owner."

Loretta is no longer sinking. "I don't care who it is Malcolm."

"Shows how business is adopting a human touch - don't you think? This is where design, marketing and management come to life - in a building like this. This is where you see what we're all working towards."

Loretta begins to sink again and she moves along the bed. She can see Malcolm's shadow spread over the bureau and in the reflecting window a part of his greased hair catches the torchlight as he sits back.

Malcolm has stopped looking and now stares into the darkness and sees again Mr Turnihock welcoming him to First Team and who is bent over a computer-projector that won't project.

Malcolm stares into the darkness.

Loretta feels herself sink again, only very slowly.

Mr Trevis rises in his seat to smile at the large multi-handled red vehicle breakdown torch which has "SHOCK-PROO" embossed on its side and the "F" caked with a splatter of dried magnolia.

Mr Habadan moves slowly from the table, having described the torch in detail to Mr Trevis, and turns towards McKraw.

"I've brought these candles," Mr Habadan shows a white carrier-bag, "but I sat on them." Mr Habadan looks back at Mr Trevis in a steady way, "plain white paraffin-wax candles, economy brand, suitable for modest occasions."

McKraw takes the carrier-bag from Mr Habadan and breathes in and squashes his mouth out and looks in the carrier-bag. He takes out a candle which now has three segments.

Mr Habadan stands high over McKraw and he takes a slow step back and reaches down to a magnolia-dotted vinyl shoulder-bag (which might be dark green) and lifts it to his shoulder and looks at Coatham who is standing in the kitchen by the fridge.

Mr Trevis continues to smile at the torch. The torch has a red screw-in handle at the battery-end and a arched red handle at the left side which is facing him. On the top are the remains of an amber dome light which lights his spectacles as two amber eyes. He looks at Mrs Hykely who sits to the right centre of the torch-beam and is looking into her compact's mirror. The centre of the beam goes to the bedroom door where he can see the side of Mudcock's sharply cut dark blue suit. Mr Trevis stares. Would you like to enter a Free Prize Draw that could mean you winning five pairs of Hoick's extra-strong underpants absolutely FREE! (At Mister Retired and other participating stores. Minimum one purchase necessary). Mr Trevis smiling at Mudcock and Mudcock smiling back. Mr Habadan standing in the middle of the floor and staring at the paintwork. Mr Trevis staring at the lounge walls now and seeing how the paint seems to swirl and fade and brighten and flash and dribble, and somehow the torch-light showing this more and more clearly. Mr Trevis seeing Mr McKraw staring too and like they are all at sea somehow or else the lounge is flying.

Coatham notices the lounge walls and how they seem to violently move.

McKraw sniffs at Mr Habadan who has turned slowly towards him.

"Won't be long," McKraw says and his mouth giving more mime than sound, "the electric - never been off for long."

Mrs Hykely sits in the armchair listening for Malcolm.

Malcolm listening for Loretta.

Loretta looking at Malcolm.

"Christmas Eve," Loretta whispers, "never thought I'd be here."

"Yes" Malcolm lets the stool wobble as he sits forward. He looks into the lounge and thinks he can see Mr Trevis smiling at him and he smiles back.

Loretta whispers

"I never knew mother had any friends - it's good seeing friends coming together at Christmas."

"Yes," Malcolm smiles again at Mr Trevis who is still smiling.

"And mother said the people on this floor had a 'thing'.

Malcolm continues to smile at Mr Trevis. "A thing?"

Loretta whispers "A 'thing' - a disagreement."

Malcolm nods, "Oh." He sneaks a glance at Mr Trevis who is still smiling.

"About what?"

Loretta whispers

"I don't know. Mother says Mrs Lodgeson - the lady on this side knows. No one else knows."

Malcolm stares at the carpet. "Why don't they ask her?"

Loretta whispers.

"*I don't know.*"

Malcolm stares at the carpet.

"Mr Coopham will know.

He leans forward.

"This is his party."

Loretta stares at the carpet.

Coatham watches Mr Habadan lower his head under the kitchen door-frame and set a green bottle of wine on the work-surface. Something like a date-pip that was stuck to the bottom of the bottle fires across and into the sink. Mr Habadan takes another bottle from his shoulder-bag and sets it down.

Mr Habadan stares down at Coatham, the grey eyes not visible in the dimness but the face steady.

"Double Save's own brand," Mr Habadan continues to look down. "Easy-open cap and undecorated label. Uncomplicated flavour, ideal for emigration parties and unrepeated events. Low price, low rate of re-fills, low alcohol content, low spillages - also known as 'Accountant's Gratitude'." Mr Habadan stares down. "Buy one get one free."

Mr Habadan takes a stack of plain white plastic cups from his shoulder-bag.

"Disposable-cups, reinforced rim, convenient storage."

Coatham watches as the bottles are opened and the tops roll away onto the floor. He watches, the tart smell of the wine making his eyes close. Mr Habadan strolls out of the kitchen with two cups of wine. He hears McKraw's noise of approval and Mr Trevis' hoot of pleasure. He hears Mr Habadan treading slowly back and sees him duck under the kitchen door-frame again. He hears the wine loip-loib into a single plastic cup and then Mr Habadan treading out of the kitchen and towards Mrs Hykely. Mrs Hykely's suspicious voice, "- Mr H-aversack?" then Mrs Hykely not saying anything and Mr Habadan coming back to the kitchen and under the door-frame and pouring two more measures and staring down at Coatham, who can't think of anything to say.

Mr Habadan leaves the kitchen, Coatham looks out of the window. He moves along the work surface to look to the Western Estate where a distant firework rises and glitters, the tiny red molten shapes flowering into white.

Chapter 11.

A wuffly cough.

A pause.

A snort.

A sigh.

McKraw leans towards his thick hands to urge them into action against the lighter which won't light. He tries again. The black pedal of the green plastic lighter squeezed after the wink of sparks in the candlelight. The chacky strike again. McKraw chewing his dentures and giving the lighter a little shake. His pause. The surprise trigger of his thumb, all of a sudden, like that would do it.

McKraw holds the plastic lighter up towards the candles so he can see through the pale green plastic and hunches up his shoulders. The lighter is empty.

Mrs Lodgeson leans forward in the armchair and slowly bears her teeth.

"Why don't you get us a heater?" Her eyes have a strange shadowy quality, like someone in an audience announcing towards a glowing stage. "A gas heater," her right forefinger pointing. "What are we going to do if we can't stay warm?"

Mr Trevis smiles massively in the candlelight.

"Yes - yes, that'll do it."

The windows rattle.

McKraw sets the lighter down. He squashes forward against the table's edge and fetches the last saucer back and uses the lit candle to light the next. He breathes and chews. He shakes his head until Mrs Hykely has sat back. He takes a glance at his watch. He chews. He lets the wax from the next fraction of candle start to drip and puddle in the saucer. Trevis was right, that would do it. That would do it, but that wouldn't do it in his office and in the foyer, it would be freezing down there now.

Even though his office was double-glazed and Clifford had draught-proofed the office door there was still the window-hatch. He had often felt the draught from there even in calm weather because there were, as Mr Bailing called them, "Bowels of air" in a building like this.

McKraw didn't generally remember what tenants had said because what tenants said wasn't important. Mr Bailing was different because Mr Bailing had filled in a BW/15 complaints form and had attached ten extra pages of information in fine handwriting. Mr Bailing had even made drawings of his flat's windows and of his corridor on the first floor and of the staircase and landing and shown how draughts moved and how the smell of Saturday night urine and vomit was served to any direction one might choose to go in.

Mr Bailing's information was of such an order that McKraw had let his chips go cold reading it. Of course, attachments were not permitted with a BW/15 and so he had thrown them away - as a tight ball of chips and "and another thing". Mr Bailing had pointed a steel propelling-pencil at him a few days later, Mr Bailing standing at the hatch-window one evening and McKraw noticing Mr Bailing's neat grey hair and grey woollen cardigan and white shirt and grey tie neatly framed. Mr Bailing had set the door-handle of his flat on the ledge and McKraw had put the door-handle in a large manila envelope and then written on it: 'Habadan'. It might have rained that night but he couldn't remember or what day of the week it had been, or how long before the door-handle was refitted; he didn't remember because he'd had enough to do just making his patrols.

McKraw squashes another candle down. He looks across at Mrs Hykely who is glaring at him so he looks back down. He can hear Mudcock and Lorotta talking quietly in the bedroom. He looks up again and to the right of the lounge window where Habadan has brushed the right-hand curtain aside and is looking out. In the kitchen, though McKraw doesn't turn to look, will be Coatham. McKraw squashes the short candle down hard into the blob of setting wax. On the table-top, to the left of the near saucers and lit and rolled candles, a crescent reflection from Mr Trevis' glasses shines there, wavering a little.

McKraw didn't mind the patrols. The indoor patrols could be made when he felt it necessary and he enjoyed these. He enjoyed climbing to the eighth floor landing and then having a cigarette in one of the empty flats - where there was always an empty flat because of the smells. He enjoyed climbing then to the top and with each floor below make a slow patrol along the two corridors from each landing. He enjoyed knocking on doors to make sure that the property wasn't being damaged and he especially enjoyed knocking on the doors of new tenants.

A new tenant usually moved in during Clifford's shift or during the vacant shift so McKraw had to keep watch on an empty flat after Habadan had finished decorating. There would be a gap of two or three weeks and then one night there they would be and he would knock on the door and make his speech. It was always the same speech (there'd never been a need to change it) and he enjoyed seeing the tenant's face stare in wonder at the BW/15's and that, especially, is what made the job worthwhile, that's what made his job important.

McKraw chews on his dentures.

The outdoor patrols were not so enjoyable. He was supposed to make patrols of the car-park and of the perimeter fence at the beginning of his shift and twice in the early hours at his own choosing. He was also required to make an extra patrol if there were any unusual sounds outside. In the warmer months he didn't dislike a walk. In the winters it was different.

In the winters he took an interest in the weather. He would read the weather-forecast in the newspaper and planned his patrols to miss that showery morning or those icy temperatures before dawn. He'd also adjust his patrols so that he wouldn't miss television programmes of interest. Also he wouldn't patrol the whole of the car-park because he could see some of the car-park from the window. Also he didn't need to patrol the ground at the back all the way to the stream because people from the chemical plant had told him he didn't need to worry about the stream. As for patrolling following unusual sounds, the factories made lots of unusual sounds - very loud ones and for all of the night too. If there were ever any other unusual sounds then he would need to be instructed which sounds were more unusual than others. As a precaution he had explained this in a BW/15 which he had filled in himself and sent to City Estates, and nothing more was heard of it.

McKraw squashes the last and shortest candle into its saucer of wax as at the same time his belly squashes against the table's edge, the two squashing similarly. He had already decided he would patrol late tonight, perhaps in the early morning, perhaps indoors only and not outdoors...if he could find a lighter. He stares into space, thinking, his sharp nose aiming at the bookcase and then moving slowly along to the right.

Mrs Hykely watches McKraw's nose turning, his folded up eyes coming to stare at her. She glares at him but this time he seems unconcerned. She continues to frown at him. She didn't like daydreamers.

Her late husband didn't like daydreamers either. When either of them seemed lost in thought then the other would have to shout "Found asleep!" If she caught her late husband daydreaming he would often say he was trying to think about something and she would then ask him what he had been thinking about and he would then say it didn't matter and she would say it did matter. He would then hurriedly find something he might have been thinking about, but she knew he had been thinking about nothing and so she would ask him what he had thought about whatever it was. He would then say that he hadn't decided. She would then say that she would help him decide and eventually a whole plan had been decided about something he hadn't been thinking about at all. She'd found that the interrogation process was long and sometimes painstaking and involved the demolition of thoughts he said he was thinking about but admitted he wasn't. She licks her teeth. Now, and of course, he was thinking about nothing because he was dead. It was a biological certainty that he could no longer think. L-owacka knew this too. She and her late husband had told her from an early age that daydreaming was bad because animals that daydream get eaten.

McKraw lights a cigarette in a candle-flame and puffs at it. His eyes move around behind their thick hooded lids. He feels the cold draught from the windows. He was better here than sat down in his office with no electric, no heating and no lighter. Even

343

though Trevis had turned up it didn't matter, and Edna - and those other two... it didn't matter, they'd all go sooner or later. When the electric came back on...well he'd stay here and catch some of the late film and fill up with news. He puffs at the cigarette. Coatham wouldn't care - and even if Coatham did...weren't there the master-keys? (but he would never do that). He chews on his dentures. He would never disturb empty flats, no professional would ever do that, no matter what was on television. There was Pallant. Pallant had been security at the bone merchants a few years ago, everybody knew of him, everyone who passed would see his mo-ped parked in the yard after 9 pm and knew he was there. McKraw sniffs. Pallant left his snap-box on the MD's desk. It was soon over and done with as these things are; Pallant's mo-ped no longer there and a waste-skip put there regularly instead. A sorry business.

McKraw nods slowly at his thoughts.

McKraw nodding and finding he is looking vacantly into the eyes of Mrs Hykely, who has her arms tightly folded.

"What about a gas-heater!" Mrs Hykely unmoving and glaring.

Loretta appears, looking around the doorway of the box-bedroom.

"What about what Mother?

Mrs Hykely turns a little. "Mc-Crab's going to fetch a gas heater."

Loretta smiles at McKraw.

"Oh, that would be nice," Loretta looks quickly at Habadan who has turned from the lounge window, "it's freezing."

Loretta waits.

McKraw makes a wuffly cough and straightens his maroon tie. He looks at Habadan.

McKraw breathes slowly in through his hairy nostrils.

"Where is there one?"

The windows rattle from the kitchen to the bedroom. Habadan lets go of the right lounge curtain and lets it fall back into the play of the draughts. He turns and his grey eyes fix on McKraw.

"Officially," Habadan looks at Loretta and then back at McKraw, "they're against regulations...gas canisters...industrial and domestic, we confiscate them," he looks at McKraw.

McKraw nods and makes an official and approving noise and puts his hand to his chin as he'd seen professors do in films.

Loretta smiles. "Yes. How many have you confiscated?"

Habadan gives her a long steady look. "One."

Loretta looks at her watch. "One...ok. Where is it?

"Where is what?" Malcolm appears behind Loretta, his eyes stare wildly at Habadan.

"The gas-heater - the cylinder heater thing," Loretta looks over her shoulder but cannot see Malcolm.

Malcolm blinks. "Good idea - but we're leaving soon."

Loretta twitches. "Not for us Malcolm - for Mr Coopham."

McKraw's chewing stops. "Who's Malcolm?"

Loretta nods her head backwards for McKraw, "He is."

McKraw looks at Malcolm and shifts his rubber boots, "Who's Mudcock?"

Loretta sighs. "Mr McCrass," she smiles and turns back to Habadan.

"Mr...er - where is the gas heater?"

Habadan watches the paintwork for a moment.

"The bad flat, 96."

"Oh dear!" Mr Trevis smiles broadly in the direction of no one in particular.

McKraw moves in his seat.

Loretta watches Habadan.

Habadan takes a bent cigarette out of a packet in an inside pocket of his jacket and walks calmly over to the table and lifts a saucer and candle and lights the cigarette. He puts the saucer back which nudges a plastic cup of wine and which splashes up and onto the table. Habadan straightens and stares down at McKraw.

"Safest place to put it. The only empty flat that hasn't been vandalised."

The windows rattle.

Loretta draws the collar of her coat under her chin.

"Well Malcolm will help you carry it - won't you Malcolm."

Malcolm finds his First Team voice and narrows his eyes a little.

"I dare say the electricity will be back on before too long, there's really no need to worry."

Loretta stiffens.

"No Malcolm." She waits. "If there's a serious fault, if there's no electricity in the morning then it's Mr Coopham who will worry - it'will be Christmas."

Malcolm takes a step backward into the box bedroom, his eyes widening again. He snatches a look out of the box bedroom window in case there's a taxi but there obviously isn't one.

Loretta puts her hands together and smiles at McKraw. "So?"

McKraw chews and watches the table-top candles moving with the draughts.

She looks at Habadan who walks smoothly back to the lounge curtains, smoking.

She looks towards the kitchen, but Coatham is not in view.

She looks at Mr Trevis who is smiling broadly at her.

She smiles back as well as she can.

"Mr Trowel, would you like to fetch a gas heater from flat 96?"

Mr Trevis' eyes shine behind his candlelit glasses.

"Oh dear me no. Oh no no," his face fills with joy, "it's haunted."

Loretta laughs.

Behind her Malcolm delivers a corporate interjection. "Completely irrational."

Loretta looks around the room but no one is looking at her except Mr Trevis.

She looks at her mother who is looking at herself in the mirror of her compact and applying some more lipstick. "...Only edible things walk the Earth."

"Exactly Mother." Loretta folds her arms and waits.

McKraw puts his elbows on the table and lets his face rest on his palms. His eyes disappear altogether.

Coatham stares at the dim shiny kettle on the fridge's hard wood-effect work surface. The stainless steel kettle which has no warmth to it. The kitchen colder for the draughts from the kitchen window which nip at the candle-flame. The candle on its saucer on the cooker behind him, and which sends his shadow over the shiny kettle, the fridge and hugely up the wall. The kettle with its lid which never fitted as easily as it should. The kettle that in the mornings, if he remembered to look, had made a little puddle in the night. The kettle which normally showed his and the kitchen's reflection in the steel, so that he looked like a present freshly opened from cheap magnolia paper.

Tonight he is a silhouette and the kettle's curved surface mainly dark, except at the curving extremes where the ceiling and walls and cupboard-fronts and the window-panes too are candlelit and dithering.

Across the dark playing fields the pet foods factory's bulged diamond wire fencing is mostly invisible. Winding along it, and seen more clearly in the brief and low-angled winter daylight, is the paused raspberry-bind's advance, turned to rust itself now. There are dried wild annuals too: Hedge Mustard, which clowned all summer like a contraption of wheel spokes; Parsleys that have become the webs they kept; Willow-Herbs now antennas. These share the bushy perimeter with a living brightness of lager cans and dirty long-flown plastic carrier-bags which have puddled down against the wire. Some of these flinch or shake in the wind and are seen clearest where the sharp emergency lights, between those citadels of piled rusty drums, cut a view. All these, ordinarily, occupy the domain of that throaty smell when the pans are boiling and the drums of offal are opened and hoisted. Tonight the smell is subdued - by the weather, the holiday, and by the fumes of the sewage works and chemical plant together, which are ruling the air.

At the flats the main wire-glass doors inch inward when the wind whistles and spins. The cold air drawn into McKraw's office through the wire-glass hatch-window which Malcolm, on arriving, had left a fraction open. The air, that carries those smells only lightly, gives a slight sway to the chrome-chained pull-switch on Clifford's technical lamp.

"Why did you open the door - you have blown the candles out!" Mrs Hykely shouts at Malcolm.

Malcolm stands stiffly in the flat doorway and is clenching his fists.

"We are going to fetch the heater - you wanted the heater - we're going to fetch it."

Loretta finds her way across the lounge.

"That is very good Malcolm. You and Mr, err. You both go and fetch the gas heater."

Mrs Hykely tries to see Malcolm.

"M-illclott has put all the candles out!"

Loretta looks back at the armchair.

"There's a candle in the bedroom Mother. We can light the others with that one."

Loretta turns back to the doorway.

"Malcolm, if you can close the door we can light the candles again - there's an awful draught."

Malcolm pulls the flat-door closed and the rising draughts stop . He shakes his head and looks up at Habadan, who is already in the corridor.

Malcolm nods towards the flat.

"Families eh - not good for business."

Habadan switches his torch on.

The torch-beam sweeps around, under Malcolm's staring eyes and towards the fire-door where the green exit light is glowing. Habadan walks along the corridor with a slow stride and pushes the ring of keys which McKraw had given to him around his outside left jacket pocket but misses and the keys smash loudly onto the floor. Habadan bends slowly and picks them up.

"So," Malcolm waits and looks the other way down the corridor to where the green light can't reach and he can see nothing, "off we go then." He turns back. He sees Habadan is now shining the torch-beam on the next flat-door on the right and appears to be examining the paint. Malcolm side-steps, he looks past Habadan and down the corridor at the green-lit walls, the fire-door with that lit green sign above, and a second green light shining on the landing beyond it. Malcolm blinks. "Time to visit the spooks."

Habadan nods slowly and moves along. At the fire-door Habadan stops and points the torch-beam up to the ceiling and looks down at Malcolm in his fixed way.

"No one has lived in the even-flats on the top floor for twenty years. No one inquires about them. No one looks around them. No one talks about them. No one goes there at night." Habadan continues to look at Malcolm. "Six flats, commercially unsound. Useful for storage of paint, ladders and general tools." Habadan opens the fire-door, dips his head under the door-frame and goes out onto the landing. On the wall next to that fire-door and above the steps going down that next green exit light is shining. Beyond and above them, at the mid-landing, there is a square window which partially reflects a green glow from the next floor.

Habadan sets off up the steps. He looks back at Malcolm.

The wind whistles faintly in the foyer below.

Malcolm stares back at Habadan and his large eyes seem to flip up to look at the steps above them. "So we'll bring the heater down how many floors?"

Habadan stands casually. "Three -"

"Three - that's fine; and the heater is how large?" Malcolm levels one palm above the landing floor whilst looking quickly at Habadan.

Habadan calmly watches Malcolm.

"I can't remember."

Malcolm nods.

"And it's approximate weight is..."

Habadan is unmoving.

"I don't know."

Chapter 12.

The flame of the re-lit and replaced candle wavers on the hard wood-effect surface of the drop-leaf table. The flame, leaning away from draughts from the windows, reveals again the wine which Habadan had spilled, the crumbs of mince-pie pastry, smears of ink, then herded together tins and packets from the drooping carrier-bag that is beside the dealt game of patience which McKraw has his elbows on.

Mrs Hyklely sighs heavily.

"Sending M-adclam to fetch the heater is a mistake,"

Loretta moves the two candles and saucers along towards the spider.

"It doesn't matter Mother. Let's all get on shall we."

Loretta presses her lips together as she did at home when Malcolm said something annoying. She fetches the blown-out candle down from the top of the television. She turns again and looks at Mr Trevis who is smiling proudly at one of the newly lit candles.

"You don't complain, do you Mr Trowel. You're a treasure - a real treasure."

Mr Trevis smiles back at her in his extraordinary way.

She notices how Mr Trowel smiles at Mr McCrass but Mr McCrass does not have the manners to smile back.

She goes back into the box-bedroom and to the lit candle on the little bedside cabinet and sits on the rapidly sinking bed. She snaps a dead candle from its wax setting in its saucer and then stops.

The poor man. She looks towards the box-bedroom doorway in case she might have said this out loud...but no one is speaking in the lounge. The poor man - poor Mr Trowel. Poor Mr Trowel who probably knows all about candles. Mr Trowel who probably hasn't a penny to spare and more than likely lives in one of these little flats and stirs processed peas every evening.

Poor Mr Trowel. What did he know about lower middle management lifestyles, holidays in middle-band luxury apartments in medium range tropical destinations? She lets the dead candle rest on its saucer and watches that lit flame move and flutter. It was hard for Malcolm and herself, she had to admit it was - it was hard persuading Malcolm's new colleagues that she too was interested in bottles. 'Oh...' she'd had to say, 'is that how long bottles have been in mass-production?' Then steering the conversation to Malcolm who then made a little presentation using those incidental bottles he had deliberately put there two hours before.

Loretta rests her forefingers on her temples and gently rubs them. It was odd how all the men she'd known had become fanatics. Fanatics - was that the right word? - or was the right word...'mad'? She stares at the candle. Daddy wasn't mad: he hid from Mother; he hid in garden-sheds, in greenhouses, he hid in the toilet.

Then there was Edward.

When she first met Edward he had been working in the branch library for about ten years and was mild and learned and appreciative of most things. She would have said that no one was less fanatical than Edward. He was never like that - he told her he stared out of the window at work, he waited for people to walk down that concrete ramp from the concrete-surfaced forecourt with the dwarf conifers. She'd walk down that ramp herself and he would be there: sensitive, immediately observant, eager to see her. What was fanatical about that? Even Uncle Dennis liked Edward - and Uncle Dennis could instantly hate anybody. But Daddy envied Edward, Daddy ill in bed and nursed all day by Mother. When Mother buried Daddy and when the other library assistant was laid off then something changed.

Nobody believed her of course. Everyone at the Home Economy Class had told her to simply make more rags. Make more rags, the teacher had told her, save up for that rainy day and a penny from your pocket will make a pretty pot-full. But nobody there understood. None of them were there in the back-garden in their household rubber-gloves helping him to build the fly-sheds. And Edward needed lots of rags, he had her making rags all day.

Loretta stops rubbing at her temples and lets her hands fall to her sides. And Malcolm didn't know anything about bottles when she first met him. One day she had just finished gathering the fly pupas and sliding them in their baking-tray into one of the gauze cages when she picked up her mobile phone from the top of one of the crawling-bins and phoned him. Phoned Malcolm, some man who had been promoting Hurke's Home Delivered Frozen Meals in the supermarket just the previous day.

Mother didn't like Malcolm from the start, and Uncle Dennis hated him. Mother called him a staring-eyed shriek and Mother and herself didn't talk for a while. When Malcolm started promoting Cowes' Lemonade it was she who paid for the tickets to The Artificial Foodstuffs Conference and it was she who walked him around until he ended up in the design tent. Design Team Four had men just like Malcolm and it was she who persuaded them to enrol him on their internal training scheme. They wanted to train her at first; they said they'd rarely met anyone as committed to bottles, especially that Mr Turnihock, who was from another team and who was suave but with spit wetted around his mouth and told her bottles were his life.

That's how it started. Now that Malcolm was 'majoring' in bottle-tops they had cupboards of them...and in just the way that Edward had come to have sheds full of flies.

Loretta picks up the dead candle and lights it from the one on the bedside cabinet. What was she doing wrong? Why should both men turn out the same? Why couldn't they just be happy - even if they were desperately needy like Mr Trowel...poor Mr Trowel.

Chapter 13.

Habadan stops on the mid-landing between floors nine and ten. He waits for Malcolm who is climbing and talking.

"In design," Malcolm continues and stares large-eyed at the sticky and urinated steps in front of him, "...there is only the future."

Malcolm reaches the mid-landing and waves his hand gracefully at the cityscape through the square window as Mr Turnihock would have done, "there's no going back to, erm-" then Malcolm struggles, but Malcolm can't remember what Mr Turnihock had said.

Habadan slowly nods and begins on the final flight.

Malcolm follows, studying and trying to mend the quotation.

Habadan reaches the tenth floor landing pulls the fire-door open and dips his head under the frame and Malcolm follows.

Habadan unlocks a flat-door on the right. He waits for Malcolm...and goes in.

Malcolm pushes the door open wider and watches as Habadan points the torch around.

"You are right," Malcolm says, listening to the increased noise of the wind and keeping his eyes wide, "...commercially unsound."

Habadan shines the torch back at Malcolm.

"This isn't 96. This is my flat," Habadan says, "I'm looking for a lighter for the candles."

Habadan turns away from Malcolm.

"I dropped the last one down the toilet."

Malcolm makes a hurried cough and then watches the slow sweep of that torchlight across streaky-emulsioned walls and towards the far left corner and through a doorway into the kitchen.

Habadan enters.

There is the sound of pans falling onto the floor.

Malcolm waits.

Habadan comes out of the kitchen and puts a lighter into an outside jacket pocket with his free hand.

The torch's beam searches around again; across a dining-chair propped against a balcony-door which nudges with the wind.

Malcolm steps backwards as Habadan comes out of the flat and into the corridor.

Habadan hands the torch to Malcolm.

"Hold the torch."

Malcolm shines the torch around and onto the flat-door as Habadan gives it repeated slams.

The key finally turns.

Malcolm leads the way down the corridor with the torch. He pushes the fire-door open and holds it for Habadan who walks slowly and is taking another cigarette from his inside jacket pocket. He puts the cigarette in the side of his mouth while his other hand draws out an emulsion-stained blue clear-plastic disposable lighter and McKraw's large ring of keys. He lights the cigarette and then points keys and lighter together at the other fire-door.

Malcolm blinks and directs the torch-beam at that fire-door and sees there is no green light from it's other side. There is the reflection of the two of them in the reinforced wire-glass, some graffiti in black spray paint across the fire-door's top red panel, and there is darkness. The graffiti reads "Cool" and then below it, where there is less space, "Ghoul."

Loretta looks at the candle now lit on the top of the television. She takes the dining-chair which Malcolm has broken to the right of the window and sets it at the kitchen and lounge's dividing wall. She looks around at the occupants of the lounge who are not speaking and she walks business-like into the box-bedroom. Finding her mobile-phone in her handbag she presses her lips together as she taps into the taxi numbers. She watches the screen. She holds the phone to her ear. She listens. She hears the 'engaged message' after the first number connects. She angles her head. She watches the screen. She blinks rapidly. She listens after the second number connects. Engaged.

She takes the handbag over her shoulder and takes the odd-legged mink-coloured corduroy stool too and goes into the lounge. She sets the stool on the far side of the armchair so that she can block her mother's view of McKraw and she sits down. She sees her mother suck on her teeth and turn her attention to the television which isn't working and to the candle on top which flutters in the draughts.

"Well," Loretta smiles at her mother, at McKraw and at Mr Trevis, "how are we all doing?"

The wind whistles away.

The top floor landing similar to the others except for the counterweighted rubbish- hatch, kept open by a lilac and brown vinyl pouffe which had been squeezed into the chute until it was stuck. The pouffe having moved a short way down with the help of cooking-oil which had been poured over it and afterwards that empty clear plastic oil-bottle left tidily under the hatch and heading a queue of full bin-liners all the way to the lift.

Habadan carefully stubs out his cigarette on the nearly horizontal hatch-lid and looks to his right at Malcolm who is staring at his reflection in the fire-door and letting the torch shine onto the floor.

Malcolm now looks at Habadan.

Habadan angles his head and aims his steady look at him.

Malcolm brings the torch up, takes hold of the fire-door's handle and pulls.

The fire-door opens with the sound of releasing unset bubble-gum and a slight sigh from the door-lever. Malcolm now shines the torch along that corridor. He looks to his left at Habadan, his eyes larger than usual.

"It's fine - I mean it's ok - I mean it's really interesting." Malcolm steps forward and the fire-door sighs shut behind him.

Habadan strolls to the fire-door, lowers his head and opens the fire-door a short way. He sees Malcolm aiming the torch at the first doorway on the left. Malcolm looks back at him in his staring manner.

"Look, all of the flat-doors are open," Malcolm says, blinking.as they step into a lounge.

Coatham looks out of the kitchen window.

The candle on the cooker-top, which almost blew out with the recent commotion, is re-lit and steadier now. The draught from the windows simply knocking the flame about, just as that draught also worries him, makes him feel like a solitary thing; like a single thought in the morass of the power-cut. He looks out across the industrial estate's now entangled boundaries, where one half-lit rusty drum might easily belong to another...or those flaring cars along the main road's cold and windy darkness might all belong to the same street.

Habadan stands at a flat's open door. He is stooped to look under the door-frame and is watching Malcolm directing the torch across closed lilac flannel lounge curtains and towards a kitchen where the thick dark blue curtains are edged by lights from the chemical plant. In the swing of torchlight also is a lounge carpet with purple and dark blue stripes whilst strewn over it are old magnolia paint-tubs and cans and other rubbish, while the walls are fine and smooth and painted a pastel grey.

Malcolm takes hold of the left hand lounge curtain and stands ready to pull it firmly; that lilac curtain draws back easily and lets shafts of light from the chemical plant stream in.

Malcolm looks at Habadan. "Of course," he shines the torch at the ceiling, "I could fit these flats out for you with modern economy self-assembly - transportation costs simply speak for themselves -" he angles his face and winks, "- and I should know about shipment-to-unit ratios and with modern immediate obsolescence , well - you can get it all dirt-cheap!"

Malcolm now draws the right-hand curtain smoothly across.

"What did you call these flats - 'commercially unsound'?" Malcolm laughs and puts a forefinger to his chin, "I think we can call that" Malcolm finds a deeper voice "superstition." Malcolm tries to narrow his eyes and makes a cabaret-like step across the carpet and between the paint-tubs, "Let's just remember what they say," he stares into space, "...there are no ghosts in design, only mules," Malcolm tries to remember the Turnihock quote, "- only muses."

Habadan nods slowly.

Malcolm slowly turns to profile. He stands in the light of the chemical plant, the dazzling lights of one of the main units making for a general milky glow. The noise of the weather increases

356

beside him but the strong firm-fitting lounge window muffles the sound.

"Take me for instance," Malcolm's eyes are giant and staring, "I'm a designer." Malcolm points the torch at the lounge window and steps back to the curtains. He takes hold of the right-hand curtain, "You give these old design rails one shock beyond their tolerance," he pulls hard on the curtain but nothing happens. "That's their tolerance - ok, so lets go beyond it - let's see what they designed into these rails twenty years ago..." he wraps his arms around the right-hand curtain and swings on it and his voice becomes strained. "Do you hear that - do hear the fitment creaking!" Malcolm lowers himself and looks at Habadan who is framed in the doorway in faint factory light.

Malcolm leaves the window and steps along in a Turnihock fashion, the two of them strangely waltzing between painting debris and into the kitchen where he shines the torch around.

"Really, unless you've been trained, you can't see how things have improved."

Malcolm waits for a reply.

Habadan peers at the lightless corridor ahead of him and starts a stroll further along it.

Malcolm tugs at a wooden handle on a cupboard-door but it doesn't come loose.

"And that's an interesting question isn't it - what is design?"

Malcolm listens.

He can hear the sound of Habadan's shoes patting in the corridor as he walks, now the boofing and splashing sound of a weighty plastic bottle being kicked along. A steady pouring sound now followed by Habadan's slow but heavy tread across something folded and flappy. Now the patting of Habadan's shoes at an easy pace. The click of a cigarette-lighter. The clang and clashing sound of steel step-ladders falling over.

Loretta is slumped a little and is staring at the dark blue lounge carpet.

She stares at that place where the candle-cast shadow of the table's edge wavers, where she has set her shoes like at the edge of a body of water and where there is a large crumb. She'd thought that she might pick the crumb up but that would mean touching what looks like a small amount of filling which is attached to it and she can't see what this filling is. Of course, if this was her home she wouldn't hesitate and she would pick the crumb from the floor and take it straight away to the bin. She stares at the crumb. It was just that in someone else's home it was all so different; it was different because in most cases she didn't know how long a heavy crumb had been there.

Loretta bites her lip and studies the crumb and moves her left shoe and feels the still sticky bubble-gum on the sole of the shoe snatching at the carpet. She can feel a large amount of some kind of fluff move also. She presses her lips together and forgets about the crumb and about her shoe and looks informally about and tries to gaze pleasantly to her right and into the corner of the lounge to the left of the bookshelf - but where the emulsion seems to move in streaks and trails and so she is forced to look down again - she sees the crumb. She looks up again. She looks at Mr Trevis who is smiling at her.

She smiles kindly back and places her hands on her lap.

"And have you anything you would like to talk about, Mr Trowel?"

Chapter 14.

Malcolm finds his way down the corridor and shines the torch around. Ahead of him is a small puddle of bleach and then that large bleach-bottle with the emulsion hand-print which has fallen over. The bleach has seeped under a folded heap of beige floor vinyl over which Habadan's bleach shoe-prints glisten and beyond the vinyl are some steel step-ladders lying open across the corridor. At the very end of the corridor and on the right-hand side a flat-door is open and a cigarette-lighter flashes and flickers.

Habadan stands in the dark lounge. There is again a removed sound of the weather but from a bathroom away to his right, and where the door must be open, there is a slight whirring of the extractor-fan from the drawing of the wind.

Habadan lights the cigarette-lighter again just as behind him the torchlight comes and he turns to see Malcolm in the shine-back from the white-glossed door of flat 96 and where in the widening gap between door and frame Malcolm's eyes appear wild and staring.

Habadan gives a single slow nod to Malcolm and then turns back.

Before them both are some long sage-green velvet curtains which are drawn closed at a lounge window where Habadan's torch-cast shadow is flying like a flag and also stooping menacingly across the ceiling. The shadow suddenly shrinks as Habadan strolls forward and a rolled and upended and leaning remnant of brown carpet finally falls from the edge of a trestle; it lands heavily on a long magnolia emulsion-spattered plank which catapults a quarter-full and open can of magnolia gloss into the air and which sprays beautifully in the torchlight. Malcolm turns the torch to the right: to the magnolia gloss running alarmingly down silver-green wallpaper on the exterior of the bathroom wall. Then moving the torch again: to the dramatic last pour of the dinted gloss-can as it rolls in an arc across a deeply varnished dining table, but which has already been spoiled by wild saw-cuts at its right edge. Malcolm adjusts the torch skilfully to catch Habadan's expression, but sees Habadan still strolling and towards the open box-bedroom door on the left-hand side of the lounge, where he clicks his cigarette-lighter.

Malcolm turns the torch and stares at the runny paint splash again. He stares at Habadan. He narrows his eyes a little and finds his way around piles of unwashed emulsion paint-rollers and bent screw-drivers and stops next to Habadan and he aims the torch.

Ahead of them in the doorway of the box-bedroom is a small free-standing pale blue enamelled gas-heater with caster-wheels and with a stainless steel D-handle on the top. The mesh and the ceramic tiles at the front are bent and then cracked and above these is a simple printed picture of a desert palm-tree with leaves which spell out: 'Sun-Warm' and then: 'Deluxe'.

They stare at the gas-heater and they stare at each other until Habadan slowly nods. He reaches down and takes the torch from Malcolm and steps slowly forward and dips his head under the bedroom door-frame. Habadan wheels the gas-heater into the lounge; it trundles off-course on its squeaking casters and he squats beside it and opens a panel at the back He stares inside and nods and slowly gets to his feet. He points the torch at places here and there in the lounge then he hands the torch to Malcolm who shines it back at him.

Habadan stares down at Malcolm in his fixed way

"Standard domestic gas-canister...might be in the kitchen."

Malcolm stares across the lounge and moves in the direction of the kitchen and on the way passes a large snapped pasting-table with carpet-tape unwound over it as twists and knots. When he reaches the kitchen doorway he stops and hunches a little and stares at the door which is ajar. He adjusts his tie, blinks and steps onto the smooth black and white chequered vinyl.

Habadan lights his cigarette-lighter. He kicks at a wide gloss-hardened paint-brush which is stuck to the carpet. Malcolm comes back to the kitchen doorway.

"Hmm?"

Habadan stands casually in the light from the torch and puts the lighter back in his pocket.

"Standard domestic gas-canister -" Habadan says calmly but Malcolm stops him.

"No, after that."

Habadan stares at Malcolm.

Malcolm thinks and then goes back into the kitchen. There is the sound of cupboards and cardboard boxes opening. There is a pause.

"Would I like a cup of tea?" Malcolm laughs. "What -in a power-cut?"

Habadan steps to the green velvet lounge curtains and turns the far edge of the left curtain aside and looks out.

Malcolm shouts from the kitchen.

"Mr -er...it's not here. Maybe it's in the bathroom."

Malcolm appears and the torch light strikes across the dining table. He points the torch into the bathroom and looks at Habadan in a sudden way.

"Happy? - of course I'm happy."

Malcolm studies for a moment and then lets the torch swing limply by his side.

"Well, just between you and me," Malcolm whispers,." I was dead against chasing after her mother."

He juts out his jaw.

"I made it very clear when I put the film back on; I said this time we were all going to sit quietly and enjoy it."

Malcolm scratches his head and his eyes recover their normal staring largeness.

"But would she sit quietly? No she wouldn't. I even gave her the T.V. guide and I said: '*You read that - there they are: all the actors and actresses names - there they are; you don't need to tell us who they are!*'

Malcolm stares at the carpet.

"It was only when that didn't work that I fetched the Pro-Talk flip-chart and easel and wrote the full cast out with a thick marker," he sighs, "extra-bold.

Malcolm's eyebrows arch together in a kind of distress.

"I didn't know what else to do," he sighs louder, "I mean, whoever heard of two people called 'C-rabface' and 'D-rabtit' singing a duet?" Malcolm looks at Habadan and quickly shakes his head, "No - I mean, thank you, but I don't want a sweetie,"

Malcolm stares at Habadan.

Malcolm shrugs his shoulders,

"Anyway that's why she left." Malcolm makes a painful expression. "If only she had drunk that spiked drink instead of me - as she was supposed to - then she would be asleep now and I wouldn't be here."

Malcolm shines the torch into the bathroom and steps inside. He finds the gas canister in the bath and shouts back at Habadan.

"Frightened of you? Why should I be frightened of you?"

Mr Trevis runs his finger along the table-top.

"Mr Doll - goodness me no, Mr Doll wins if it rains in the morning - Mr Henford wins if it rains in the afternoon -"

Loretta is speaking over him and is nearly shouting.

"But if Mr Henford wins if it rains in the afternoon and Mr Doll wins if it rains in the afternoon,"

Loretta raises her voice still louder.

"And Mr - whoever he is - wins if it rains at night," Loretta's face then reddens with anguish, "then why, if it rains, does anybody else bother going!"

Mr Trevis' finger moves along and he smiles brilliantly at Loretta. His eyes move joyfully behind his spectacles.

"That's Bingo!"

Loretta starts shouting but Mr Trevis ignores her.

Coatham steps to the fridge and his left shoe sinks into one of the vinyl's swells. He looks out of the kitchen window and towards the city but hears the noise in the lounge getting louder. He can hear the lady's high screaming words which seem to bounce off the ceiling, but her voice also divided by the kitchen window's rattles - then those other windows playing out in the lounge and in the bedroom. The cold draught coming now and stalling the candle on the cooker. He turns from the window and sees the candle on the drop-leaf table in the lounge fluttering too, but because the lady is leaning forward and bringing her hands down hard on it and making the saucer jump. He sees the contents of the carrier- bag move with the impacts and sees also McKraw sitting with his elbows propped on the table and his eyelids just visible where his hands rest on his face; those eyes narrow, perhaps closed, as the commotion continues. His face bobbing a little as his mouth chews.

Habadan turns the torch towards Malcolm.

Malcolm is holding something up. It is the gas-canister.

He slowly nods.

Malcolm smiles uncomfortably.

"You nearly worried me with those stories. I don't believe in ghosts."

Habadan nods slowly.

Malcolm stares into space.

"Though remember that rumour can also be profit from your reputation."

Malcolm pauses dramatically then rests his fingers on the edge of the dining-table where a run of gloss paint has dripped onto the carpet. He sets the torch on the dining-table to shine at the gloss-spattered wall and relaxes in the half-light like it was the First Team Projector Presentation Room. Amongst the dinted cans and the piles of ruined brushes the rest of First Team sit and are smiling at him.

"But what is reputation?" Malcolm waits until Habadan nods, which Habadan does.

"Reputation, after all," Malcolm continues, "is a wandering baboon with our name on it."

Habadan slowly nods.

Malcolm shakes his head "- Balloon - a wandering balloon."

Malcolm lowers his voice.

"Fame sends us where it will," he says.

For Malcolm the members of First Team begin applauding.

Habadan slowly nods and now stoops slowly. He feels for the gas-heater's handle and then moves it squeaking along and next lifts it over piles of rubbish.

Malcolm stands in the applause of First Team and picks up the torch from the dining-table and steps gracefully after Habadan and out through the door of flat 96.

He answers the voice with a Turnihock flourish of his free hand.

"No - I'm not selling paint - I've never sold paint."

Loretta and Mrs Hykely glare at Mr Trevis. The room is quiet except for the rattling of the windows from the wind. Mr Trevis smiles broadly back at them. Mrs Hykely and her daughter both have their arms folded and are sat very upright. McKraw remains staring at the table and says nothing.

In the kitchen Coatham looks back into the lounge at the drop-leaf table but can only see Mr Trevis and McKraw. He turns back to the kitchen window and rests his right hand on the work-top and puts his fingertips into a puddle of wine which Habadan had made. Without looking he moves his fingertips to another place on the work-top where there is another puddle. He moves his hand to the front edge of the work-surface but where he can feel the wine forming drips. He removes his hand, and glances down at the barely visible puddle of wine in the dip between two swells of vinyl, where there is also a packed wormy length of fluff from the carpet sweeper when McKraw had emptied it. The fluff stretching dimly in the candlelight from the cardboard-box with the bin-liner wrapped over it - and to his trouser-leg where it has snagged on the fabric below the knee. He steps nearer to the box and raises his right leg a small way to allow the length of fluff to come loose and hang over the plastic edge but the fluff remains. He takes a step away from the box and the worm of fluff unwinds and lengthens and brings another fluff-worm with it which the first is carrying on its back. He waits. He watches the fluff-worms while his right hand at his side feels the damp patch at his right jacket pocket where he had leant against the work-surface's edge. He now reaches down and pinches the fluff free of his trousers and feels the fluff cling to the wine on his fingers; some fraction of the fluff coming free as he sends the fluff-worms back into the box, his fingers now coarse with hairs, fragments of biscuit and anonymous flakes. He stops. He takes the hand to the stainless-steel sink and to the brick of hard white soap on the draining-board and the flakes bite into the soap, some of the fluff-hairs stretching around it. His shadow cast diagonally to the left away from the cooker, the wet soap and the flakes and the hairs revolving in shadow and light.

Chapter 15.

Habadan lets the gas-heater down every two vinyl covered steps at a time; the loud rattling clunk as he does this. The clinky adjustment of the gas heater's patch-cracked chrome D-handle as it drops in its brackets. The front of the gas-heater with its dinted criss-crossing thin chrome bars dint a little more when the gas heater swings slowly each time to hit the higher step before landing - the furthest castors knocking and turning. The pause, clink, chring - rattle-clunk, pause...clink, chring - rattle-clunk...pause. Habadan's right shoulder lowered and now the bracing of his arm, then his two slow steps down then the swing of the gas-heater. His other hand running down the scratched plastic-coated rail. Crisp-packets and chocolate-wrappers nudge towards a sudden uncertain fall between the steps towards some other floor, but the slow engine of Habadan's descent continuing while above him Malcolm's speech also continues, and to which Habadan nods.

Malcolm shakes his head.

"It's terrible really," Malcolm points the torch around and carries the bright blue gas-canister under his right arm and descends rather gracefully, "everyone on first team has watched me on television except me."

Malcolm's eyes open wider as they reach the landing and he stares out at the distant speckled lights of the city.

"I don't mind of course - I mean professional actors take things in their stride."

Malcolm strokes his chin and pauses on the steps.

"I expect I'll be offered more work," he watches Habadan setting the gas-heater on the landing below and reaching into his jacket pocket for a cigarette.

"That's what happens when you are on television - you get noticed, you get talked about, an agent gets in touch...a film role,"

Malcolm's eyes enlarge and he stares at Habadan who slowly nods. Malcolm moves the torch beam like a floodlight to the gas-heater, the front chrome bars now bent inward.

"Funny how talent gets to the top."

Loretta yawns and she turns to her mother.

"It won't be long now.

,   McKraw's hands move up his face to cover his eyes and his thick fingers push up the sides of his nose.

Mrs Hykely gives her daughter a sharp look.

Loretta looks sharply back.

"Well he is, you can't argue with that; he's qualified is Malcolm - and he's been promoted."

Mrs Hykely licks her teeth and leans slowly forward to whisper.

"B-ubblehead was a better man."

Loretta leans closer so that the two are face to face.

"I'm not going to talk about Edward all over again, Mother, I'm fed up, I'm freezing and Edward isn't bringing us a heater - Malcolm is. Malcolm is bringing us a heater and I, for one, am very grateful for it."

Malcolm strolls elegantly along the landing of the next floor as Habadan lifts the gas-heater in stages down the next flight of steps.

"Expect I'll get fan-mail; everybody gets it."

They reach the next mid-landing together and Habadan lets go of the gas-heater. He stands straight and looks down at Malcolm in his steady way.

Malcolm raises a hand at Habadan.

"IThe director loved me eyes."

Habadan looks above him and takes a cigarette from his inside pocket and pats around for the lighter. He finds the lighter and stares down at Malcolm.

"Sometimes she follows people."

Malcolm blinks. "Who does?"

Habadan looks up and Malcolm looks too. They both listen.

They both hear the wind searching in the foyer far below. From the landing below them the moaning tunes of weather from the skip-dock which plays up through the rubbish-chutes. Those mixtures of sounds which might be windows rattling on every floor combined with the noise from the factory yards.

Malcolm continues to stare up at the green shine on the floor above and now at the concrete underside of the stair above with its uniform magnolia paint.

"Who follows people?"

Habadan slowly looks down at Malcolm.

"Unknown invisible presence. One fixed origin in flat ninety six. Numerous accounts of 'followings' and confused communications. Some moved or thrown objects; mainly plastic items from cut-price shops; easily transportable economical wares in a limited choice of colours."

Habadan stares at Malcolm who is staring back at him.

Mrs Hykely stares at Loretta and brings her face close to her daughter's and whispers.

"W-oodbug had a 'proper job' in the library."

Loretta shakes her head and whispers back.

"Actually Mother, Edward gave up his job in the library."

Mrs Hykely shakes her head now.

"He didn't."

Loretta turns her face but remains staring hard at her mother.

"Yes he did."

Mrs Hykely shakes her head again.

"He would have told me if he had left the library."

Loretta hunches her shoulders and bares her teeth too.

"He left the library Mother, I should know - because he went to work...well...in the garden."

Mrs Hykely bears her teeth now.

"That was just a hobby with his jams."

Loretta straightens a little and her shoulders fall.

"Well, we can't talk about it now."

Mrs Hykely rests a hand firmly on the worn upholstered arm of the chair.

"I could have helped, L-arragga, you were only going through a bad patch."

Loretta slowly sits upright.

"It doesn't matter, I'm with Malcolm now."

Mrs Hykely glares.

"M-adbin who only talks about bottles.

Loretta raises a hand.

"I'm not listening to you Mother."

Loretta turns away.

She looks at McKraw who is slowly massaging around his eyes. She looks at the candle on its saucer on the drop-leaf table. She watches the flame sway wildly from the draughts. She feels the cold air and she rubs her hands together and opens her handbag and finds her mobile-phone.

She finds the first taxi number and makes a call.

She stares at McKraw who is still massaging his eyes. She sees he is chewing on a sweet or something. She suddenly smiles warmly at the wall.

"Oh - hello. Hello - I'would like a taxi as soon as possible please." Loretta listens and is still smiling and now at McKraw who cannot see her. She bites her bottom lip and then smiles again.

"No I haven't booked. Well you see I would have booked but my partner's had a little too much to drink and -" Loretta sits straighter.

"Yes I am everyone says that."

She listens and then looks at her watch and stiffens.

"Not before then?"

She looks at her mother who is glaring at Mr Trevis and who in turn is smiling back at her. Loretta puts a hand to her forehead. Loretta holds the phone for a moment after the call is finished. She sighs. She moves her left shoe and the pad of carpet-fluff moves too which is stuck to the bubble-gum on the sole.

The windows rattle.

She closes her eyes and listens to the wind tearing and shoofing and to the windows rattling, only less violently. She hears the fire-door at the end of the corridor whine open. She hears Malcolm's voice but accompanied by a squeaking trundling and rattling. The fire-door's creak-bang.

Loretta opens her handbag and takes out her mobile-phone and retreats into the box-bedroom away from the draughts. She sits down on the sproiling spring-twang of the bed and next to the bedside cabinet and stares at the phone.

Chapter 16.

The flat-door opens. The rise of the draughts in the dark lounge where all the candles go out.   Coatham turning in the kitchen to look and seeing Malcolm's eyes in the torch-light and then the giant figure of Habadan leading a small heater which seems to have its front grill punched in. The gas-heater with a bias to its wheeling and makes a detour towards the back of McKraw's chair then Habadan casually lifting the gas-heater to a place between the dining-chairs and the kitchen doorway. Malcolm pointing the torch around and seeing Loretta coming to the bedroom door and sees her in silhouette and talking on her phone, and he holds the gas-canister up in a triumphant way.

"We've got it!"

Malcolm holds his expression and the gas-canister and is pointing the torch at Loretta who has put her hand up to shield her face from the light. She turns away from the bedroom doorway and into the light from the remaining lit candle on the bedside cabinet and bows her head a little to speak into her mobile phone.

"You're coming now? - No, that's wonderful." Loretta pauses and covers the mobile phone and turns back to the doorway and looks into the lounge where Malcolm is now crouching behind the gas-heater and is about to fit the gas-canister. "Malcolm!"

Malcolm's eyes spring up and he moves the torch so that it briefly shines towards Mr Trevis and now shines at Loretta who shields her face.

"Malcolm - which flat are we in!"

She sees Malcolm's eyes fix on her through the blur and brightness.

"Fifty - er - fifty three."

Loretta turns her back on Malcolm and bows her head again.

"Fifty three...that's right." She pauses and then slowly stops the phone and puts it back in her bag. She turns around towards the near darkness of the lounge, the silhouette of the gas-heater is lit from behind by the torch and on the outer wall of the bathroom and on the ceiling Malcolm's shadow is enormous. Malcolm looks up and his face is lit from below. He smiles menacingly.

"A taxi?" Malcolm smiles more menacingly. He sees Loretta standing still in the doorway of the box-bedroom and lit faintly by candlelight from the left side..

"No Malcolm," she clips shut her handbag. "Edward's coming."

Malcolm smiles more broadly. "Really - I mean - well, you could have phoned Patricia and Donald."

Loretta puts her hands on her hips.

"What do you mean Malcolm?"

Malcolm raises his shoulders and looks nervously about and sees Mr Trevis's spectacles shining in the peculiar light.

"Nothing...Well," Malcolm scratches his head, "I mean - well you could have phoned anybody."

Loretta stares at Malcolm.

"Do you think I want anybody to know I spent Christmas Eve like this?" She continues to stare at Malcolm who stares back at her. "If anybody asks Malcolm we spent Christmas Eve at home, just you, me and Mother and we watched a film. Do you understand?"

She waits.

Malcolm scratches his head and turns the torch away from Loretta. He looks painfully at Mr Trevis who is now smiling broadly back at him.

"I don't know: you could have phoned Rupert and Angelina?"

Loretta shakes her head.

"Rupert met Turnihock at Horace and Bimbi's party."

Malcolm stops scratching his head.

"Oh - yes." Malcolm frowns a little. "What about, er -"

"What about - nobody Malcolm, I'm not interested. I phoned Edward because he is sober, he has got a car, he is free and he doesn't know anybody important."

Malcolm tilts his head and his eyes roll downwards to look at the workings of the gas-heater.

"I just thought he'd be busy with his - well with his -"

"He probably is, Malcolm,"

Loretta stares at Mr Trevis who is smiling at her.

She goes to fetch the candle from the bedside cabinet to re-light some of the other candles.

Mrs Hykely smacks her lips together.

"B-edbug isn't at the library any more, he stays at home and makes his jams."

"Not jams Mother," Loretta calls from the bedroom.

"JAMS!" Mr Trevis says loudly.

"Anyway," Loretta says as she comes quickly into the lounge carrying the candle in its saucer and picks up the unlit candle and saucer from the top of the television and angles it towards the other until it lights.

"It doesn't matter so long as we all get home."

She puts the candle and saucer back on the top of the television and walks around the armchair to the bookshelf.

"And Edward will be here soon because he's only got to check on the - well the jams."

Loretta steps carefully across the room, the Cowes' bubble-gum on the sole of her left shoe has collected a larger pad of fluff which flaps a little as she walks.

"We have to be ready to receive Cindy and Horatio tomorrow and have a normal Christmas. Oh and also there will be Uncle Dennis."

Malcolm makes a nearly imperceptible sigh and slowly stands and flips open the magnolia enamelled metal flap on the top of the heater under which there is a black knob with a grooved outer surface. A white arrow pointing from the middle of the knob can be aligned with white markings reading clockwise: OFF. IGN. LOW. MEDIUM. HIGH. SUPERHEAT.

"Here we go,"

Malcolm looks across at Habadan who is leaning against the flat's doorframe and is slowly nodding. Malcolm presses the knob down and turns it to IGN.

The knob makes a sprung chime. There is a small fluvv sound.

Loretta pauses at the drop-leaf table and looks across at the gas-heater. Mrs Hykely leans forward in the armchair and watches the gas-heater too, her drawn-on eyebrows tightening. Mr Trevis

371

smiles at the gas heater. Habadan has a cigarette in his mouth and searches in an outer jacket-pocket for a cigarette-lighter and nods to McKraw who is now searching for his cigarettes. Malcolm rests both his hands on the top surface of the gas-heater and stares down at the bent front grill of the gas-heater. Just in front of the cracked ceramic plates there is now a weevling blue pilot-light.

Malcolm takes hold of the black plastic knob again. He turns it. The knob turns a short way, very nearly to LOW and stops. He turns the knob back to OFF and presses down. There is again the sprung chime as he turns the knob to IGN when there is the fluvv sound. There is that straining sound of the knob being turned almost to LOW.

There is the turn to OFF. There is the sprung chime and the fluvv. There is the straining turn.

Everyone in the lounge leans listens.

There is the off. There is the sprung chime. Fluvv. The straining turn. There is the OFF.

Loretta takes the saucer and candle from the top of the drop-leaf table and brings it carefully to the lit candle which she has brought from the box-bedroom.

There is the sprung chime and the fluvv.

She lights the candles.

She slides a newly lit candle and saucer back onto the surface of the drop-leaf table to a place just in front of Mr Trevis - the candle lights his smiling face, his eyes are motionless.

Loretta steps around the odd-legged mink corduroy stool to the bookshelf where two unlit candles are waiting.

There is the sprung chime and the fluvv.

"Hmm," Malcolm pushes himself up from the gas-heater and looks around the lounge. He sees McKraw has lit a cigarette and is handing the lighter back to Habadan who is standing and smoking.

"It's a perfectly good design," Malcolm says, his large eyes move to look down at the gas-heater.

McKraw props his face up with his left hand and allows his right hand a poetic grace which taps the cigarette at the tobacco-tin ashtray. He lifts and turns his face and lets his cheek squash onto his palm so that he is looking around at the gas-heater while his hooded eyes move with a quick blink. He sees the gas-heater with only its tiny blue pilot-light. He lifts his face and turns it back to its previous position and chews on his dentures before returning the cigarette to his mouth.

Nobody in the lounge speaks.

The windows rattle.

Loretta has finished with the candles on the bookshelf and walks around her mother and between the armchair and the odd-legged mink coloured corduroy covered stool and towards the box-bedroom. At the doorway she slows.

"Anyway," she says loudly to anyone and to the looming paintwork on the bedroom wall, "Edward will be here soon." She stares at the magnolia patterns which strike and shift.

"He will know what to do, he is a librarian."

Mrs Hykely turns her head slowly to watch the light from Loretta's candle retreat into the bedroom. She now looks back at Malcolm who is watching her and Malcolm hurriedly scratches his head again.

Mrs Hykely licks her teeth.

Malcolm shakes his head and looks down at the gas-heater. He looks to his right and towards the kitchen and can see Coatham staring out of one of the kitchen windows and while those windows rattle and the gathered oatmeal coloured curtains there touch inward.

Malcolm smiles and steps lightly into the kitchen and onto the vinyl's swells and stands next to Coatham to look out at the city also. Malcolm glancing at the freckled and fierce distance where office-lights and streetlights and far off sprays of estates seem finally to meet.

"It doesn't work," Malcolm raises an eyebrow at Coatham but who doesn't turn to look at him. "The heater I mean," Malcolm nods and hooks his thumb back towards the lounge, "could be a defect in the spring-loaded valve. Might be a child-proof mechanism from years ago I'm not familiar with - there are a number of variables." Malcolm rests his hands on the work surface where the puddles of wine which Habadan had made wet his fingers and he wipes his hands on his trousers.

373

The weather rises. The kitchen windows rattle.

Malcolm finishes wiping his hands dry on his trousers.

"Anyway," Malcolm straightens and stares out of the kitchen window, "a friend's coming to pick us up - one of Loretta's friends; well, a good friend really."

Malcolm's eyes enlarge as he stares out at the city.

"Edward: a very discreet friend."

Malcolm tilts his head towards Coatham.

"You need plenty of those when you're in show-business. He's a librarian - well, he used to be a librarian. He is a farmer now - of a kind."

Malcolm's eyes move largely to watch Coatham's candle-struck reflection in the window. Coatham who does not look back at him or seem to look at anything

"Expect you'll be wanting some peace at the end of the party - just you and Mr McCrass, Mr Trowel and Mr - er."

Malcolm blinks. He returns his gaze to the city and then down at the darkness amongst the factories which the power-cut has made.

"I'll keep a look out for Edward - though, I don't actually know him - I've heard of him."

Malcolm stares out of the window and watches the late traffic on the main road gather for a queue. Malcolm finds himself nodding slowly.

"He's a farmer."

Mr Trevis watches the little blue pilot light of the magnolia enamel gas-heater wavering slightly in the drafts.

The windows rattle.

The lounge curtains touch inward.

Mr Trevis' eyes return to watching the pilot-light.

(Some man was coming who made jams.)

(Jams.)

Mr Trevis' eyes watch the blue pilot-light flame.

Jams. (Fruit-flavoured red, yellow or orange. Preservatives. Emulsifiers).

Mr Trevis watches the little blue pilot light of the magnolia enamel gas-heater.

Homemade jams.

Mr Trevis smiles across at Mrs Hykely who is glaring at him.

There were never any competitions with home-made jams.
Homemade jams.
No one needed help selling homemade jams.
Mr Trevis makes a very slight nod.
It was different with Crawn's.
Crawn's: You know it tastes right!'
'5% extra fruit!'
Crawn's.
Mr Trevis stares at the blue pilot-light flame.
Crawn's.

McKraw taps his cigarette at the rounded rim of the base of the beige and brass coloured tobacco-tin, the tin making a little tinkle-tankle sound due to a slight warp as two corners of the tin knock against the wipe-clean surface of the drop-leaf table. McKraw continues to rest his left cheek on his propping left hand and his lips push out from his loosened dentures to meet the cigarette brought to his mouth by his other hand. He draws in the brief warmth from the otherwise cold room and his eyes make an automatic glance towards the television which is not on. Mrs Hykely is glaring at him. He chews on his dentures and his eyes withdraw under his hooded lids and some smoke blown out of his nostrils makes his thick nose-hairs tremble.

In the middle-depth of his life McKraw was accustomed to power-cuts and all manner of unexpected things. He taps the cigarette. It was his job to notice how things might change - sometimes suddenly - and then immediately take charge. People depended on him, people were secure in the knowledge that he was alert to the tell-tale signs of an impending emergency and that he would effortlessly cope. It was more than procedure: it was his job. He was trained for it.

McKraw pauses with the cigarette and stares.

Sometimes in the early hours a rain could begin, all of a sudden. He would be watching his office television and then gradually he would detect a kind of music, behind the jingle of an advert or else there was some sound he couldn't recognise in a bleary lost news bulletin...and it was rain. Rain out in the car-park and under the streetlights of the industrial estate's avenue; a rain from nowhere in the narrow night, like it was the darkness that was raining. Then sometimes in the rain there were people; most often in the rain before dawn and usually at weekends, when there had been no one for hours and he had learned again every creak of his office-chair and given up trying to understand the wire-bundles of one of Clifford's electrical experiments. Someone would suddenly speak - and there would be a tenant at the window-hatch - usually a young man who was drunk and had walked a mile or two and whilst on this walk had become like a nub of bone, pale and undefined. Some young man who had lost his key or forgotten his flat-number and had come from nowhere like the rain, so that McKraw would find himself staring at both, like the night was breathing.

Chapter 17.

"Of course, you can't go into show-business without ability. Take me for instance." Malcolm smiles at his own reflection. "It all began at Hurke's Home Delivered Frozen Meals." Malcolm stares at his reflection and feels a sudden nostalgic affection for 'Economy Sausage, Processed Potato, Brussels Sprouts with Single Standard Dumpling'.

"And of course design is acting too, my manager, Mr Turnihock says so."

Malcolm stares at himself.

"*Become the bottle*, he told me' *become the bottle and I will fill you with Cowe's Lemonade.*'"

Malcolm stands motionless and watches his reflection.

The windows rattle.

"Anyway," Malcolm angles his face sharply just as Turnihock did, "then I was spotted, noticed...discovered."

Malcolm smiles at himself.

A queue of tiny bright cars on the dark main road drive through the reflection of his head.

Mrs Hykely switches her glance to look for Malcolm, but she cannot see him.

She looks back at the lit candle in its saucer on the top of the television.

The windows rattle. The weather battering along the side of the building and then back to the chingling and blustery distances around the factories. That lull.

The candle's flame wavers from the draughts.

Mrs Hykley licks her teeth.

O-ddblock was coming. He was coming in his car and he was taking them all away. He would go back to his job at the library and T-rolletta would invite that Home Economy Class to her house again. Then B-ogworm would visit her every week, just as he always had.

She stares at the candle's flame struggling against the draughts.

And M-adclap? She sets her teeth together. Her face becomes impenetrable.

Loretta is holding the lit candle and saucer and is staring at the box-bedroom wall at a place above a low and lopsided teak-look headboard. She watches the magnolia emulsion on the wall flinch and change and can hear Malcolm now and then from somewhere who is talking about bottles. Other than this she had heard McKraw chewing when the weather had dropped a little and when the windows weren't rattling.

Loretta's face alters slightly.

Would Edward drive them to his house for an impromptu visit, after all it was Christmas? All trace of her expression disappears. No, he would never do that. She stares at the wall.

And what did Edward look like these days? The expression returns: what if Edward had gone completely mad? She sets the saucer and lit candle down on the top of the bedside cabinet and hears McKraw chewing, the click of her mother's compact and behind these and from the kitchen the word 'Bottle' being said clearly with increasing confidence.

Coatham looks out at the distances, the far and the cold, where the man's reflection raises its hands. The man's eyes big opening wider and the his head angling and now pausing.

"Plastic has so many advantages over glass - I mean, I could reel them off but these days the public have a good grasp of commercial realities."

Coatham watches the icy stretch of darkness below which the man's hands seem to visit sometimes in their gesticulations. Coatham sees man step forward again to the wet edge of the work-surface where he is half removed by Coatham's candle-cast shadow. Coatham sees how the man's reflection is half-illuminated in a portion of the window where a bright reflection of the lounge has appeared and which also contains Mr Trevis' smile.

"I mean, you haven't lived if you've not given a proto-type bottle presentation. The long slide-shows - although, we don't use slides anymore. Ha! No!. We don't even use bottles!

Malcolm pauses.

"Being in the glare of the public gaze is quite another thing. You see fame is a humbling experience."

Coatham looks out at the city, looks beyond the extent of the darkness where the cars on the main road seem to shred its limits. Nearer and beneath and to the right, the tall and corroded straight-sided corrugated metal stock-shed of the wire factory has lost its features, as many of the buildings have done. They have become internal. After parading their wagons or sending figures with dock-sheets striding from one noise to the next, they have lost their purpose. Tonight on the stock-shed's roof that unseen ventilator-hood turns and squeaks and while numerous unseen things knock and clash in a madness of industry, like they should dismantle the world.

A car drives very slowly along the main road towards the junction with the industrial estate's avenue, a car with a long queue of revving cars behind it and which begin to race past as the slower car turns off. The car comes to a lurching halt in the darkness next to the fences of the wire-factory's further buildings, just before the gritty and pitted entrance where the long chained weather-pummelled wire-gates swing and gnash.

Malcolm picks up one of the two near empty wine bottles from the work-surface and pours the two remainders into a plastic cup which he has pulled from a small stack.

"Not that I care now - I mean why should I?" Malcolm's eyes stare down at the cup of unusual smelling wine. "I'm not in Third Team anymore; I've said goodbye to Bulk-Bottle issues." Malcolm tilts his head expertly sideways and towards Coatham who is looking out of the window. "Bulk-Bottle," Malcolm smiles, "that brings back memories." Malcolm's eyes turn hugely to watch himself in one of the kitchen window's reflections. His eyes fix on something and become larger.

"That might be him."

Malcolm points and at the same time he hears the tinkle ring-tone of Loretta's mobile-phone.

Loretta who is sitting on the lumpy bed searches around in her bag for her phone which is plinking and trilling.

"Hello?" She sits upright in a rigid manner. She waits. "Of course they haven't been condemned...no; we're here!" She rests the fingers of her free hand on her forehead. "I know that Edward; there's been a power-cut ." Loretta forces herself up from the bed and follows her wavering shadow to the window and she peers out. "Yes. Yes I can see - is that your car?" She puts a hand to her forehead again. "Well you wait there and I'll send Malcolm to meet you. No: Mother won't be escorted by Malcolm. Who? No; Mr Reynolds isn't here anymore - there's a Mr McCrass...yes, McCrass." She cups the phone, "...but Mother doesn't like him either."

Loretta stares out at the avenue of the industrial estate. She looks away and now comes to the bedroom door and shouts.

"Malcolm! Go down to the main door and meet Edward! Leave the torch - I'm going to Mother's flat!" Loretta aims a stare at Mrs Hykely. "Mother - you stay here - I'm going to fetch your bag from your flat. We're going home."

Malcolm waves a hand back at the kitchen door. "Righty-Ho!" - but continues to look back at the place in the darkness where that car has its headlights on. Malcolm brings the plastic cup nearly to his lips. He holds the cup still as he watches the car set off again and come lurching slowly along the dark avenue towards the flats. The plastic-sheeting is in flight again and the car pitches as one of them swoops into the glare of the headlights.

Malcolm drinks some more wine and rocks the remainder in the plastic cup. He glances at Coatham who is not looking at the car, or at anything. Malcolm leans forward over the wet work-top and just as the car trundles close to the building and out of sight. He draws away from the work-top and the jacket of his suit is wet and he pats at the fabric and glances at Coatham.

"Of course...Edward will ask why we're here," Malcolm stops patting his jacket and shrugs his shoulders and stares, "and it'll be - all my fault - " Malcolm makes a large mouthing whisper, "- not her mother's." Malcolm's eyes enlarge a little. "I mean if-fair's-fair I shouldn't even have driven here to fetch her - after nearly a pint of punch." He watches the vague outline of one of the strips of plastic-sheeting continuing to lift and scuttle about. "Then there's how she got here: she phoned for a taxi and one turned up straight away," he puts his hand out towards his reflection in a pleading way and lets his hand fall to his side. He stares into his wine and also rocks his head from side to side. "I only wanted to watch a film and watch the television. What's wrong with watching the television? After all I was on the television, what better reason is there for watching television than that?"

Chapter 18.

One of the plate glass doors of the main entrance swings inwards. The door returning and reaching the piston-lever's damping point and returns slower but the wind also hampering it and making it gasp open a short way. A figure has entered the foyer and steps over to the window hatch and waits. The litter makes some final chase before settling back to occasional movements. The wind strengthens, the weaker of the two main doors is blown open a short way and the night is whistling.

Loretta stands at the bedroom window. She had kept meaning to go into the lounge but she had stayed. She had watched the car's headlights approach and had thought they might precede the mad eyes of Edward - if Edward was now indeed mad. She presses the nail of the forefinger of her left hand onto one of the large dollops of dried splattered gloss on the windowsill and her nail bends.

She remembered now that it had never been her intention to suddenly leave Edward, it had simply turned out that way. She had come out of the fly-sheds one morning and she had phoned that man and asked if he could deliver one of Hurke's Home-Delivered Frozen 'things' later that afternoon when she was visiting her parents' house. The man had said he could deliver three for the price of two so long as the two were the reconstituted dumpling, or however he'd described them. From then on Loretta had ordered Hurke's twice a week and Mother fed them to Daddy. Looking back it was an unusual time because it seemed to her that at around 3pm on Tuesdays and Thursdays she was young again; opening the door of her parents' house as if she was a girl and talking crazily to Malcolm as he brought in the latest order. She often ordered lots of whichever 'trial meal' Malcolm told her wasn't selling in order to improve his commission. Malcolm never noticed that the meals which other households were reluctant to eat were coming to their house. Of course Mother didn't like Malcolm but Mother said she wouldn't come between father and daughter. Eight months later when she told Daddy that she was leaving Edward and was moving in with Malcolm and that Malcolm was now a trainee designer, and wouldn't be delivering Hurke's meals anymore then Daddy had gazed at her with tears in his eyes and had been unable to speak.

As for Edward, she left him the house much as it was; she had never slept well in it. She had only properly maintained the house when she had followed the clip-files of instructions drafted and endorsed by The Home Economy Class. For years after the class was abolished she had done what anyone else would have done in the circumstances and tried to understand the flies. She never once called in to see Edward after she left. She assumed he would be in the garden. Edward was in the garden, but when she couldn't assume what the garden looked like these days then she remembered him in the library. That branch library hadn't changed because she had happened to visit when she and Malcolm had been passing and it was the library's late night. It was a new library assistant who had watched them with great eagerness as they came from the little car-park and past the same potted-conifers and down the concrete ramp. There were even some dried flies brushed into a corner of a pine window-pit which Loretta had known the Latin names for; this had prompted her to tell Malcolm that her previous boyfriend's name was Edward and he had been the library assistant in this library but that he had left. She had told him Mother didn't know that he'd left and that Mother had tried writing to Edward but had perhaps written the wrong name on the envelope. Malcolm had agreed that they needn't tell Mother. Then standing there in the library she somehow had felt the complications of Edward finally leaving her and she was facing the future, arm in arm with Malcolm who was talking about bottles.

Loretta takes a deep breath and leaves the bedroom and meets Malcolm at the kitchen door. Loretta opens and checks her handbag in a brittle manner.

"I'm going to fetch Mother's travel-bag from her flat; I've got my key." She looks at Malcolm who crouches a little. "Be nice to Edward - and talk about normal things."

Loretta checks her handbag again and then snaps it shut. As she and Malcolm pass the gas-heater she picks up the magnolia-splattered plastic multi-light torch.

Habadan casually stands aside.

Loretta shines the torch around and at him.

"I'm just fetching my mother's bag."

Habadan nods. He opens the flat-door for her and the lounge candles blow out. Habadan closes the door after her.

The windows rattle.

Malcolm follows Loretta down the corridor, Loretta flashing the torch around ahead of them. When they go through the squeak-bang fire-door Malcolm stands in the green light of the exit-sign as Loretta goes on across the landing and goes through the squeak-bang fire-door on the other side. Malcolm turns nodding and muttering and goes to the stairwell and descends slowly. A chocolate-wrapper twirls down between the plastic-coated handrails from one of the landings above him and skates to a halt on the steps below. He sees his green reflection as he passes the little square window on the mid-landing.

Towards the end of the industrial estate's avenue and on the left and opposite the wire factory's first winding facility the new shiny-roofed factory-unit is poised for its new year opening. This unit has some two storey offices further along the main road with a view of the traffic lights at the multi-flow junction and where those on foot, (who are not related to anyone working at City Planning), must run screaming with their push-chairs when the split-second light-changes allow.

Those air-conditioned, air-filtrated and sound-proofed offices attracted much attention from the tenants of the flats when it seemed likely that first Delphi Health Spars and then Babyland Cash and Carry Warehouse might move there, but this interest then waning when Cralkstroka Heavy Plant Repair and Panel Beaters acquired the lease. A giant florescent plastic sign, which has been attached by steel ribbon to the shaking litter-strewn rubble-warped wire fencing reads: 'Bladdock's Interior and Exterior Commercial Fitters: A finishing touch to the environment.' The vacant factory's extensive reinforced concrete yard still offers rising displays of tangled red and white hazard-strip. The hazard-strip ensnared forever like the concrete-hugged shrubs which are flash-lit and leafless.

Loretta steps out of Mrs Hykely's flat with a small tan-coloured vinyl travel-bag. The bag is compact with broad-belts, though these belts have been pierced crudely owing to their not having buckle-holes in the right place. She looks down at the travel-bag in the torchlight, reflecting off the dribble-glossed magnolia door which she has just locked. She stares down at the bag.

This travel-bag had been their present to her mother after she and Malcolm had moved in together - Malcolm having carefully put Loretta's choice back on the shop's stand and told her it was not quite right. Malcolm had then checked several other travel-bags for their weight and had given a short speech about 'ease of opening' and 'robustness versus cubic capacity'. He had picked out this particular travel-bag which he had then painstakingly described to her and to some other shoppers who had stopped and listened. Malcolm's travel-bag speech had been the first occasion when she had fully appreciated how attuned Malcolm was to the modern world. He had also made an enthusiastic speech about some new out-swinging automatic-doors which were scaring people backwards and also a luxury pay-to-use toilet booth marooned in the centre of a wide paved area which would attract the full and rapt attention of the whole precinct if anyone tried to use it.

Loretta tears down the note which her mother had taped to the flat-door some hours before and lifts the heavy travel-bag and steps sideways to avoid its hard plastic base hitting her shin and whilst also pointing the torch around with her other hand. She reaches the squeak-bang fire-door and pushes it open and passes quickly onto the cold landing. She walks somewhat sideways to avoid the bag and across the landing to the other fire-door and knocks the torch about the handle as she gets a grip of it and pulls the fire-door open; the cold draughts from the landing meet the cold draughts from the corridor as she hurries through. The fire-door bangs shut behind her after some steady shifts and she strides forward towards the strip-light which flickers. The bag's base manages to 'bite' her so she slows down and straightens her arm to send the travel-bag away but with its overlong handles the travel-bag begins to swing so that her steps are unequal. She finds herself trying to walk at an angle but the bag begins to swing again. She reaches the door of number fifty three and holds the bag whilst trapping it against the door-frame with her right thigh and hooks the torch handle with her left thumb and grabs the flat's door-handle with the fingers of the same hand and turns it and pushes. The bag drops quickly and at the same time she straightens to save her left knee-cap from the travel-bag's hard base. A row of candles on the wipe-top table which McKraw has been energetically lighting blow out and she points the torch past him and at the armchair where her mother is sat up with the expression she reserved only for Edward, for she is smiling.

Malcolm comes down the last flight of steps in a happy manner and looks for Edward. By the window-hatch there is someone silhouetted against the dim landscape of the car-park and Malcolm waves in a hopeful way.

"Ha-ha! - Edward - glad you could make it," Malcolm makes the Turnihock walk and extends his hand at the third beat.

Malcolm's hand is taken by a smaller hand but which shakes firmly. The man is shorter than Malcolm with cropped neatly combed hair and Malcolm can see he is wearing a well-cut suit, white shirt and narrow tie. Not much else is visible on account of the dark.

The wind blows at the main doors, causing one door to gasp inward and which sends litter around in a crawling way.

Malcolm rolls his eyes and smiles.

"Won't be long. They're just - I mean they're just - you know, getting ready."

A little whisper comes back from Edward which Malcolm has to lean forward to hear.

Malcolm tilts his head.

"I'm sorry - can't hear for the - you know, for the weather."

The whisper comes again.

"I have a torch in the car."

Malcolm opens his eyes wider and waves his hand about.

"No need. They won't be long." Malcolm nods vigorously but can't stop nodding.

"There was just a little -" Malcolm straightens, "ha-ha! Just a little problem. "

"Well," Malcolm looks back at the steps. "My fault really."
Malcolm cringes.

"Had too much to drink. Shouldn't, er, shouldn't - shouldn't drive." Malcolm leans forward in case Edward says something but Edward doesn't. Malcolm looks back at the steps. "Won't be long."

Loretta and Mrs Hykely wave goodbye excitedly to the silhouettes of McKraw, who is unmoving, Mr Trevis, who is leaning and perhaps smiling and Coatham who is still in the kitchen, before handing the lit magnolia paint-spattered multi-handled torch to Habadan who nods slowly and closes the door.

Loretta sets off down the corridor at a clipping pace before the travel-bag causes her to suddenly circle somehow around it. She waits for Mrs Hykely.

"Now then," Loretta says carefully, "what's this about Malcolm having to apologise?"

They stroll along and Mrs Hykely stares unblinkingly at the green exit sign ahead of them

"M-adclap doesn't want me in the house."
Loretta sighs.

"Mother. We invited you for Christmas. We will always invite you for Christmas." Loretta pushes the fire-door open. "Why shouldn't we want you for Christmas?"

They both hear the noise of the weather coming eerily up the rubbish chute. They approach the steps and Mrs Hykely sniffs.

"He never talks to me, not like B-edbug did."

"You know that's not true, Mother," Loretta drags the travel-bag behind her and which slides and drops one step at a time.

"You may not accept this Mother, but Malcolm is a kind and understanding person - and he likes Uncle Dennis. He relates to all kinds of people all of the time in his job - he's a very good communicator."

Malcolm tilts his head.

"I tried to knock her out with a punch - a cocktail I mean not a -" Malcolm shrugs his shoulders.

"You see there was the film. The three of us were watching a film but she kept doing what she does with names - only they weren't names -" he sighs, "they weren't even words." Malcolm cringes a little. "She knows she is doing it, Loretta says she doesn't but she does. Loretta says no one could fake a condition like that for sixty eight years, but do you want to know something: there's a pattern to it." Malcolm leans forward to listen to Edward's response in his accustomed way.

"Uncontrollable issue of subconscious composites."

Malcolm smoothes his hand back across his greased back hair.

"I mean, I know it's some kind of problem - I mean - ha ha! Not that I usually take any notice," Malcolm adds gravely, "- I mean normally I don't have time, what with -" Malcolm stares at Edward and blinks. "Subconscious what?"

Loretta gives the travel-bag a sideways kick along a mid-landing towards the next flight of steps down.

"It's when you get mixed up with words Mother, that's all it is -"

Mrs Hykely puts a hand on Loretta's arm and stops her. Mrs Hykely licks her teeth in an expert way.

"I've never had trouble with words, L-owutter, that's what M-adloop says to hurt me. H-eadrot always listened to me; he never said anything against me." Mrs Hykely pauses and gives Loretta's arm a squeeze. "Why don't we get the old days back."

Loretta leads her mother forward and they descend the steps again, Loretta dragging the travel-bag behind her, its hard plastic base striking the reinforced concrete. Loretta makes a forced smile. "If I could go back Mother I would go back to when I was little and when you and me and Daddy would go to the Caravan at Slembeach. It would be sunny all day and we'd have a field to ourselves so that no one could attack Daddy." Loretta makes a forced smile again and leads her mother along. "They were lovely times Mother - but I don't think we can ever get them back." They descend and Loretta hauls the travel bag which clatters on the steps behind and above her. "Just like I can't go back to Edward,

Mother, because I live with Malcolm. Nobody's perfect, Mother, just like we're not perfect; we are all just ordinary people."

Malcolm's silhouetted figure nods at Edward's. "And you say I have - I mean you think I have denied my er -" Malcolm leans to listen to Edward whisper.

"Possession of your expressive function for deferred self-promised self-actualisation, yes I do."

Malcolm's eyes roll slightly.

"And I want -"

"To project the consumption and expression which you cannot accept for yourself onto others. Thus your career in foodstuffs reinforces a displacement of your bodily functions onto extra-personal totems which appease your body."

Malcolm leans in as Edward whispers.

"Of course there is evidence from brain-chemistry which under-pins such motivations - specifically but not exclusively derived from generative studies of fruit flies."

Malcolm stares in a fixed way at Edward's silhouette.

"Well I've always been interested in fruit - I mean I sold more Hurke's gooseberry-coloured frozen artificial mousses than anyone else in suburban sector two."

Edward's head moves and whispers.

"Which you resented later."

Malcolm looks out at the dark car park and nods and blinks.

"Yes - well of course. I mean, nobody in the other sectors could get customers to eat the gooseberry things; I only sold so many because Loretta fed them to her dad."

Edward nods almost imperceptibly.

"You mustn't reproach yourself; it is tacitly accepted that the easiest way to dispose of bulk-stocks of non-toxic chemicals is to get people to eat them."

Malcolm shrugs his shoulders at Edward.

"I mean - I deserve some credit - even the managers at Hurke's wouldn't eat the gooseberry things."

Chapter 19.

McKraw slides the lit candles across the table and glances over at the armchair where Habadan is now sitting, all elbows and knees, and who is re-positioning the lit candle on top of the television; a manoeuvre which hardly requires Habadan to reach at all. McKraw sniffs and chews his dentures around at Habadan who is casually looking back at him. McKraw makes a short wuffly cough and nods sideways towards the door.

"Strange people - those types. Thought I'd keep an eye on them," McKraw exercises his shoulders in his uniform in a slow fashion and looks at Mr Trevis who is smiling back at him, "Especially in a power-cut; can't have people like that wandering about."

Habadan nods and now McKraw nods too, mostly to himself.

Four figures leave through the main doors of the flats and the two women guard themselves with their arms against the ferocity of the weather. A shorter man walks rather daintily and silently over to an old brown car which is parked aslant and some way from the taxi which was abandoned some hours earlier. This man methodically unlocks the driver's side and then opens a door in turn for each of his passengers and who squat and squeeze into the small car which has some fine wide white-meshed cages clearly visible through the glass of the back window. When all passengers are secure the man goes to the driver's side of the car and climbs in. After more procedures the car's engine is finally revved and the headlights are turned on. The car lurches backwards a few yards before revving loudly and juddering forwards to make a wide turn which is prevented by Malcolm and Loretta'a car which is parked ahead of them. The car stops and the handbrake is applied. The car revs and then the car reverses again and stops. The car now revs loudly and jolts and lurches forward and around the turn and towards the avenue.

High above them a red and white carrier-bag sails over the factory-roofs. A carrier-bag with a full breath of air and riding the caprices like the night itself must be priced and charged to somebody; the dilemma of apparent unending 'free of charge' somehow flying with it, like a bemused spirit. The carrier-bag rising higher than the flats into the icy night, like it has acquired that something no citizen can buy and no litter can show when all is over.

"Malcolm? It's Edward's car - leave him alone."

"Alright - I mean - I didn't say anything."

"I shall soon be signalling right."

"That's perfectly alright Edward, isn't it Malcolm."

"Hmm...? Yes - I mean - excellent."

"I am signalling right."

"Oh no! Malcolm - what was that!"

"What?"

"Don't what me Malcolm, open a window and shoo it out!"

"Shoo what out?"

"The 'Diptera Calliphora' - you see it there. There on the side window - get rid of it!"

"What is M-uckdog doing?"

"It's alright Mother, Malcolm's opening the window.

"I am proceeding West."

Coatham watches the car indicate and lurch and turn right along the main road. The carrier-bag too is diminishing in size, and which he has to look steadily to find again against the city lights until it cannot be seen at all.

Tonight the wire-factory's yard is cut-lit by emergency lights. These lights do nothing to show the great performances of plastic sheeting or the stirred litter (tossed over or pushed through the wire fences by adolescents and children). Instead those lights find cigarette-ends and countless unnameable small parts and fragments, fitted into the concrete's cracks and craters and fissures, which no longer require names. Here the wind mixes the low smells from the sewage works, the bone merchants and the chemical plant into new blends whilst clanking, rattling and flapping things seem to populate the darkness. Added to and removed from these are the occasional lights and noises of vehicles passing on the main road, even at this late hour. They are bright 'canisters' of healthy but private air brought in from the suburbs, reflected by the window of McKraw's dark office as the view's only significant light. Amongst the empty crisp-packets and pop-cans on the windowsill where the traffic is shown queuing again is the television's remote control which has been discarded. On the facing wall a medium-sized photograph of an egg-faced man, signed Mr. M.S. Nerle, can be seen smiling through the Perspex of the pine-look plastic frame.

It was Clifford who had telephoned City Estates one day and suggested that a 'Hardship Fund' could be established by adding some small change to the rent. These monies would in annual totals provide basic equipment for any community-minded tenants who might wish to decorate the flats of pensioners or tenants disadvantaged by illness or convalescence. The proposal was warmly received by City Estates who had promptly sent a letter back stating that a surcharge would be levied on the fund to cover their administering of the scheme (so that its administration was thorough and comprehensive) and that also decorating would be limited to economy emulsion and gloss paint (since administrative costs might rise) and that, additionally, only one tenant and not many would perform this role, since that person would be a key-holder to the room or rooms the paint was to be stored in. Further to this, works undertaken by the fund could not henceforth be entered on BW/15 Complaint Forms, since such very occasional decorating would be considered a 'charitable act'. City Estates then, with immediate effect, gave Mr McKraw, the senior warden at the flats, responsibility for the day-to-day running of the scheme (but which might, unavoidably, lead to additional administrative costs).

As a result Clifford returned to his electronics and McKraw gave the role of decorator to Habadan (because McKraw liked to be in charge of people taller than himself). City Estates thereafter cancelled decorating contracts to firms where it was likely Habadan would decorate instead, with the result that in the months that followed professional decorators were rarely seen and then not seen at all.

As a token of appreciation City Estates had sent McKraw a signed and framed photograph of the Accounts Director (shortly before his promotion) and this was the photograph which Clifford took down when he was on duty and which McKraw hung up again when he arrived for his shift. Sometimes tenants included descriptions and sometimes photographs of Habadan's decorating in B/W15 Complaint Forms (forms which were therefore invalid) and Clifford would retrieve them from the litter-bin and mail them to local politicians - such people rarely advised more than the customer asking for their money back and in one case commented that the decorating looked "Very nice."

Habadan's handiwork was generally very well received by those he had never decorated for. When in time he decorated for some of these too it was suggested that he shouldn't decorate quite so much. Those who would 'Never let him in' were apt to be criticised for being mean-spirited by those who hadn't so much...let Habadan in...as not let Habadan in yet. On all floors however a keen interest was shown by retired, unwell and recovering tenants in Habadan's work.

McKraw takes a deep nostril breath and watches the reflection of Habadan in the armchair in the dark screen of the television. It had not been Habadan's right to sit in the armchair since it was he, McKraw, who was the senior of the two of them. McKraw chews and watches the television and at Habadan who makes the armchair seem more comfortable than it perhaps was.

McKraw chews. He watches the television.

McKraw disliked programmes on the television which showed people who were slumped in chairs. This was not because he too was usually slumped in his chair in his office, but because he regarded himself as an athletic person - just as every uniformed person was. People in uniforms chased suspects through crowds in detective series (and more often than not shot them). People in uniforms could run and climb too and make clear and flawless decisions at lightning speed. They were often young with toned physiques which showed through their white shirts as they guarded themselves with their jackets when running into burning houses. Sometimes McKraw's own face became grafted onto the character's in a subtle way: when characters might stop and stare; when they ate their meals; when they hung up their coat or answered their telephones. Sometimes in mid-winter during early

393

hours' broadcasts of international sporting-events from the other side of the world then McKraw's face would appear amongst other faces as runners warmed up in uniform track-suits. It seemed natural for McKraw's face to be there, more natural. it seemed, than the spectators' faces smiling and applauding in the summer heat. After all, the competitors carried a seriousness like he did; they wore uniforms like he did. Without such people the world would stop: the world would stop. When he would happen to glance away from the television and towards the window and see the desolate late night view of the industrial estate he would see his own face reflected back, along with Mr. M.S. Nerle's photograph,as if McCraw's face was a photograph too, still and resolute, commemorating all that they had done.

Printed in Great Britain
by Amazon

36812695R00218